Praise for

"*The Keeper's Calling* is .... r read."
—Morgan

"Once I started *The Keepers Calling,* I couldn't stop. I literally finished the book in one day—something I don't do usually . . . I loved it! So excited for *The Keeper's Quest!*" —Mikela

"I would give the book an A. When I finished it, I thought to myself, "I want a counter!" This book is a wonderful read for anyone who is looking for a fun adventure." —Alex

"*The Keeper's Calling* is full of action, angst, and romance as Chase Harper travels through the centuries on his quest of duty and love. Readers will enjoy traveling along with Chase as he forges relationships not bound by time." —Sheila

"I couldn't put it down once I started reading, and I'm looking forward to the next book." —Jeni

"*The Keeper's Calling* was a great read. I . . . couldn't put it down! I can't wait for the sequel!" —Shelby

"I can't believe what a creative, well-written story! I loved the characters!" —Amy

"It was exciting, creative, and different from anything else I have read. It was sad and cute. I just loved it!" —JaneLovesBook's

"*The Keeper's Calling* is a fun and adventurous read! With great characters, interesting plot twists, clean romance angle, and wonderful character development, it's a book young and old can enjoy." —Connie Sokol, author of *Motherhood Matters* and *Caribbean Crossroads*

"This book was such a joy to read and left me wanting more. The time-travel idea isn't new, but the author created such an interesting concept and it works splendidly! *The Keeper's Calling* wasn't just a good read, it was a GREAT read." —Jenn

"Time travel, romance, magic, adventure—this book has a little of something for everyone." —Laura

"This book was awesome! . . . It's a time-travel, romance, adventure, and fantasy novel. . . . Couldn't put it down, read it in less than twelve hours." —Jenny

"This was an amazingly well-written and created story. . . . It was an interesting experience to read a romance that is solely from the point of view of the guy, but it made for a wonderfully adventurous story that still had great romantic elements." —Clean Romance Reviews

"Beware, you'll be hooked. Excellent young-adult read." —Stephanie

"I loved this book! It seriously has it all: action, adventure, romance, and a bit from the future as well as the past. I highly recommend this book to everyone!" —Stacy

"I love a book that I can get right into and don't want to put it down until I am finished." —Kim

"I look forward to the second book in The Keeper's Saga, since this one had surprises on almost every page!" —Sarah Beggs, author of *Pathway to Sunset* and *In Deep Waters*

"WOW! I really enjoyed this book! I cannot wait for the sequel!" —Amanda

"What a great book!!! I can't wait for the second book in the series. Loved how the story built over time and was not predictable at all." —Caroline

K^{the}eeper's Quest

HAPPY READING!

Kelly
♡

THE KEEPER'S SAGA: BOOK TWO

the
Keeper's
Quest

Kelly Nelson

WALNUT SPRINGS PRESS

Walnut Springs Press, LLC
110 South 800 West
Brigham City, Utah 84302
http://walnutspringspress.blogspot.com

Text copyright © 2013 by Kelly Nelson
Cover design copyright © 2013 by Walnut Springs Press
Interior design copyright © 2013 by Walnut Springs Press

ISBN: 978-1-59992-876-0

This is a work of fiction. The characters, names, incidents, and dialogue are products of the author's
imagination and are not to be construed as real, and any resemblance to real people and events is not
intentional.

The Keeper's Saga

The Keeper's Calling
The Keeper's Quest

For my sister Sandra,
who sparked the idea for this book when she told me
The Keeper's Calling just begged for a sequel.

Acknowledgements

First, thank you to my husband and children for their love and encouragement. I wouldn't be where I am today without them. Thank you to Linda, Amy, and Garry at Walnut Springs Press for their continued support of my writing career as well as their friendship. Thank you to Georgia and Barry at Brigham Distributing. A special thanks to all the Costco managers who opened their doors and welcomed me into their stores for book signings. Thank you to Jessica Nelson, Tyler Nelson, Dave Morse, Wade Ellis, and John Morin for helping me check various facts in The Keeper's Saga. I'm also grateful for my family and friends who read the early manuscripts and offered valuable feedback. Thank you to Tracy Anderson of Tracy Anderson Photography and to Jennifer Payne, for designing the graphic of the counter featured on the back cover. Finally, thank you to all who have joined me in following Chase and Ellie's journey. Without you this book wouldn't be possible. But most importantly, I am grateful for a loving Heavenly Father who hears and answers my prayers.

ONE
Home Sweet Home

A sweet melody floated up the stairs as I opened my bedroom door. Ellie was playing the piano. I smiled as I turned on my phone. It was Saturday, December 31—New Year's Eve.

I slid my other hand to my counter, which resembled an oval-shaped pocket watch. With my thumb, I traced the shield etched in the gold casing, then pressed the latch to trigger the opening mechanism. A blue light emanated from the tiny glass replica of the earth that lay inside the counter. Below the globe were three buttons—Return, Shuffle, Go—and the date dials. The power to harness time lay in the palm of my hand, and with it came a tremendous responsibility. My life was irreversibly connected to my counter. As its Keeper, I alone could access its power. If someone else wanted it, they had to kill me. Apparently, there were plenty who wanted a shot at me—Lord Arbon being enemy number one—but fortunately, not many of them frequented my world.

I sat on the edge of my bed and reflected on the strange detour my life had taken. Discovering the magical counter last summer had taken me to Ellie Williams in 1863. I smiled at the flashback. Seeing her for the first time had left me speechless, and not much had changed since then.

Knowing of the counter from her grandfather, Ellie had helped me escape the past. She returned with me to the present, pretending to be an orphan with no home, and my parents had agreed to take her in. My twin sister Jessica coached Ellie on the art of living in the modern world, and I don't think anyone suspected she was a transplant from another century. Other than Jessica and Ellie, none of my family and friends knew I had the counter. They would never have imagined I could time travel.

Ellie had left following my fight with the vaqueros. Enduring the months of her absence had been the hardest thing I'd ever done. Eventually, I went looking for her. A few days before Christmas, I found her dying of pneumonia in 1863 and brought her back with me. I prayed I would never have to live without her again.

I listened to the next three songs before the urge to see her overpowered me. Throwing on a T-shirt, I headed for the bathroom. After an unsuccessful attempt at taming my blonde hair, I hid it beneath a baseball cap.

Chase Harper—somewhat athletic at six foot one but nothing extraordinary—that was me, until I clicked the button on the counter for the first time. Then everything changed. The magic of a counter transfers to its Keeper. I held the Protector's counter. The original Protector had supposedly been a great warrior. My speed, strength, and agility had increased since assuming the responsibilities of Keeper. As Garrick, a fellow Keeper, put it, it's a nice perk if you don't mind living such a complicated existence.

Ellie was still at the piano when I walked into the living room. She smiled. "Good morning, Chase."

"Morning, Ellie." I put my hand on her shoulder. "How do you feel today?"

She gave my hand a squeeze. "Better. Every day I feel stronger. It's truly a miracle I'm well. That's twice you've saved my life."

"You're welcome, but I did it for selfish reasons. I was a mess without you. Even my coach and my dad were stressing out. It was bad. Promise me you won't ever leave me again."

Ellie cast me a disbelieving smile. "Was it really that dreadful?"

"Absolutely."

"Well then, I promise not to ever leave you."

"Good," I said. "I plan to hold you to that."

I decided to make French toast, and as I stood flipping it on the griddle, Jessica came into the kitchen.

"There's a New Year's Eve party tonight at Adam and Amanda's," she said. "Are you going?"

Adam and Amanda were our cousins. Amanda was a freshman, and Adam was a senior. Not only was Adam my cousin, he was also my best friend. I couldn't remember a time when we hadn't hung out.

Ellie had come home from the hospital six days before, and I'd pampered her until I'm sure she felt smothered. I didn't want her out in the cold, reminded her to take her antibiotics, and suggested she take a nap if she even cracked a yawn. But other than an occasional fit of coughing, she seemed healthy.

I smiled and handed her a plate of French toast. "What do you think, Ellie? Do you feel like partying it up?"

"Yes," she said emphatically. "I thought you'd never ask. I was beginning to think you intended to hold me prisoner in your house forever."

"That settles it. We're going," I said.

Jessica slid two pieces of French toast onto her plate. "I'm picking up Ryan at eight. Do you want to come with us? Dad said I could drive his new car."

Our parents had shocked us when they came home from Christmas shopping with a brand-new black BMW for my dad, Joe, a professor of accounting and information systems at Portland State University. My mom, Jennifer, worked as a nurse at the local hospital. They had never been the type to buy new cars, let alone a BMW. My guess was that Dad's recent birthday—his forty-seventh—had thrown him into a midlife crisis. He probably figured time was running out.

Worried that Ellie might get tired and overdo it, I said, "I'll drive the truck, in case we need to come home earlier than you."

When I left the house with her that evening, my parents eyed me curiously. Although I'd liked her for a long time, I'd kept it hidden until I brought her home from 1863 the second time. Before that, the only person who knew how I really felt, other than Ellie herself, was Jessica. My parents had always assumed Ellie was merely my sister's friend. I'm sure letting it out in the open wasn't the wisest move on my part, but I couldn't keep it secret any longer.

I opened the door for Ellie and offered her my hand as she stepped into the truck. She looked beautiful tonight, as always. Her hair was the color of honey and full of natural curl. Her green eyes sparkled with excitement when I stuck the key in the ignition and winked at her.

"It's powerfully good to be back," she said with a smile, "and I am looking forward to seeing everyone again. I didn't realize how much I'd miss them until I left."

The diesel engine in our farm truck roared to life amid the drizzle of a Northwest winter's night. As I drove away from my family's house in Hillsboro, Oregon, I noticed my dad at the window, watching us.

Fifteen minutes later, Ellie and I parked on Adam's street and walked hand in hand toward his house. When we passed

Randy's red Jeep I raised my eyebrows, wondering how the night would go, and glanced at Ellie. She nodded in the direction of his Jeep.

"Is that one Randy's?"

"Yeah," I said, leaving it at that. Last fall, Randy had thought of Ellie as his girlfriend. I didn't think she had a crush on him or anything, but hopefully seeing him again wouldn't change her mind.

Teenagers were packed in Adam's house like a can of sardines, and we squeezed through the kitchen. Bowls of popcorn, chips and salsa, and M&M's covered the counter. Most of Adam's football buddies sat on the couches watching the bowl game. Among them was Randy, quarterback and student body president of Hilhi—the nickname for Hillsboro High School.

When Ellie saw her friends, I stuffed my hands in my pockets and hung back. All the girls seemed excited to see her again. I'd say Jessica was Ellie's closest friend, but with Ellie's warm personality, she'd made quite a few in the two months she'd been at Hilhi.

Lauren gave her a hug and said, "Are you back for good? I've missed you."

I was so busy watching Ellie, I didn't notice Randy until he put his arm around her. He looked like he had a missile lock on her lips and was about to kiss her. *How'd he get over here so fast?* Like a match to gasoline, jealousy flared inside me. Gritting my teeth, I managed to keep my temper and my tongue in check.

"Ells, you're back! Why didn't you call me?" Randy said.

Thankfully, Ellie turned her head and gave him a quick hug, leaving him only a second to brush his lips across her cheek. "Hello, Randy, it's good to see you," she said as she stepped away.

He moved closer to her. "Why don't I take you home tonight after the party? I want to hear all about your trip to Boston."

I could have interrupted; but I chose to wait and see what Ellie's reply would be. "Thank you, but no," she said. "I have a ride home. I'm here with Chase." She moved to my side and slipped her arm under my elbow.

That was all the invitation I needed. Leaning forward, I smiled and slapped Randy on the shoulder. "Don't worry, man. I'll see that she gets home safely."

The look on his face tempted me to stay and gloat, but I walked away with Ellie. She furrowed her brow and glanced up at me.

"Perhaps I was too blunt," she said. "He'll certainly think me rude. Do you think I hurt his feelings?"

I lowered my head. "He'll get over it, don't worry. Actually, it would do him good to eat a little humble pie."

"Chase, I can't believe you'd say that."

I chuckled. "Hey, it's the truth. I thought you did great. I've wanted to be rid of Randy for a long time."

She giggled, tipping her head into my chest as we walked. "Have you now?"

We sat on the couch next to Adam and Rachel, who passed me a bowl piled high with caramel corn. I leaned over to Ellie. "Open your mouth," I said, picking out a particularly delicious-looking piece. I set it on her tongue, then touched her lips with my fingertip.

"Yum. That's good."

As friends came and went throughout the night, Ellie told and retold the story we had concocted to explain her two-month absence. Meanwhile, Aunt Marianne and Uncle Steve kept close tabs on the party. I may have been paranoid, but it seemed like they were particularly interested in watching me, and I had a sneaking suspicion my dad put them up to it.

The countdown in Times Square blared from Adam's flat-screen TV. Everyone paused to ring in the New Year. To heck with being spied on. As soon as the ball dropped, I kissed Ellie and whispered, "Happy New Year."

"Happy New Year to you, Chase."

The party was still in full swing when we left. I let go of Ellie's hand before we walked inside my house, but if Aunt Marianne and Uncle Steve had their eyes on me at the stroke of midnight, it was already too late. Mom and Dad were still awake, and I talked with them for a few minutes before going upstairs.

Glancing over my shoulder, I waited for Ellie in the hall. When she was about to walk into her room, I put my arm out to block the doorway. Looking surprised, she met my gaze. I brushed her curls away from her cheek and stepped closer. "Thanks for tonight." Before she could reply, I kissed her.

I hadn't finished the kiss when she pulled back, sliding her fingertips down the outline of my jaw. "Thank you, Chase. I had a wonderful time. Good night."

She ducked under my arm into her room, smiling as she shut her door and left me standing in the hall.

I exhaled. "Wow."

TWO
The Bills

After the first hospital bill came, I faithfully checked the mailbox, hoping to intercept the others before my parents saw. That was one conversation I hoped to avoid. Although I needed to get working on the money to pay those bills, I didn't relish the thought of leaving Ellie.

Since she didn't have medical insurance, I planned to return to 1817 and dig the Erie Canal with Garrick. The gold half eagles and silver dollars the canal paymaster dropped into my palm after a fortnight of labor would be worth a substantial sum when I took them to a coin dealer in 2012. A little work in the trenches of the past should earn me enough to pay off her debts. Saturday would be the perfect day to start. My parents would be at Jessica's swim meet in Washington, giving me the ideal opportunity to disappear.

Christmas vacation ended, school started, and they let Ellie resume her schedule. Thankfully, I hadn't destroyed the fake ID I got from Uncle Roy. Mrs. Peterson in the school office smiled as we handed over the birth certificate and Social Security card.

Freaking out after Ellie left, I'd decided to wrestle this year instead of playing basketball. Maybe I was looking for an excuse to beat the snot out of somebody. I would never forget the night I wrestled Travis DeMarco. We had wrestled together in the youth program, but I'd never beaten him. Things had changed since then. After six weeks of hard physical labor in 1817, I was bigger and stronger than ever. Plus, I had a chip on my shoulder over losing Ellie. Our wrestling match had quickly deteriorated into a bout of boxing, resulting in a double disqualification.

Lately, however, things were different. Knowing Ellie waited for me in the library, or sat reading in the gym, made it easier to concentrate, and I had no desire to lose my temper. By the end of the week, my wrestling coach seemed to relax a notch.

When I woke up Saturday morning, I put on my Erie Canal clothes and Wellington boots and went to find Ellie. A smile brightened her face at the sight of me.

"You look nice," she said. "Pray tell, what is the occasion?"

"I'm going to work."

"With the other Keeper?"

I pulled two bowls from the cupboard and handed one to Ellie. "Yup."

"I wish you didn't have to. I know I'm the cause of it and I'm sorry."

"Ellie, I want to do this," I said, pouring milk over her Cheerios. "I won't be gone long, I promise. Plus, I'm excited to see Garrick again. He's like the brother I never had."

"You'll come back for me, and you will be careful, won't you?"

I smiled at her and sat down. "Always. Will you wait for me in my room?"

Ellie took her place across the table from me. "If you'd like me to."

When we finished, I dumped our bowls in the sink and took one last look at the modern conveniences of a kitchen. I led her by the hand to my room.

"Wait here, please." I placed my hands on her shoulders and lowered her onto the edge of my bed. I pulled the counter out of my pocket and glanced at my clock—11:37 AM. "See you in a minute or two."

I set the counter for Rome, New York, October 1, 1817—the day after I'd left Garrick to return home last Thanksgiving. I would tell Rose Adams, the owner of the boardinghouse, that I'd changed my mind and decided to delay going west. I figured my bed was still available.

A Keeper's destination is strongly influenced by his or her thoughts. Once I set the approximate location on the globe, I could place myself exactly where and when I wanted by simply envisioning it. I imagined the room I'd shared with Garrick, at the pre-dawn hour. My thumb hovered over the Shuffle button. I glanced at Ellie, then leaned down to kiss her goodbye. "I'll miss you," I said, then pushed the button and disappeared.

I would always be hunted by Master Archidus' enemies—Lord Arbon's Sniffers. Shuffling sent me to five random dates and places en route to my final destination, each stop lasting anywhere from one to five minutes, making it more difficult for my enemies to track me.

I shuffled through a beach in Thailand, the mountains of Eastern Europe, and the Alaskan tundra, before appearing in Chicago in 1968 in an alley of what looked like the ghettos. A group of men stood huddled around a fire burning in a rusty barrel. I doubted anyone noticed me appear, but it didn't take long before one of them looked in my direction. By the lift of his eyebrows and the smirk on his face, I guessed he must be wondering where I'd come from and why a white boy was dumb enough to be in their alley. I was definitely on the wrong side of town.

I pocketed my counter and turned to leave, hoping not to attract any more attention than I already had. But one of the men yelled, "Get 'im, boys!"

Hearing that, I took off at a dead run. I exited the alley, my boots sliding across the slick concrete as I turned the corner, the angry mob hot on my heels. I got my feet under me again and continued running. My sight blurred and the air shimmered around me. My next shuffle zone was imminent and I skidded to a stop.

I reappeared in northern Mexico, face to face with a towering cactus. Before I could congratulate myself for not running into it, a sharp, stinging sensation shot through the back of my leg. The counter had dropped me in the middle of a cluster of smaller cactus plants. I was bent over picking cactus needles out of my pant leg when I shuffled to my final destination.

I could hear Garrick's deep breathing in the darkness. Although living in 1817, he had been born in 1944. He'd never shared the details of why he'd left his time, but he'd been away for nearly six years. Having spent that time in the past, he hadn't aged. He had been twenty-four when he left, and by all physical appearances he still was.

I tiptoed to my bed and lay down, waiting for the roosters to sound the wake-up call. Thoughts of Ellie filled my mind as I stared at the dark ceiling. At the first cock-a-doodle-doo, Garrick sat up and looked across the room at my bed. "Who the— Harper? I thought you left."

I rolled onto my side and sat up. "I did, but now I'm back."

"Why are you back so soon? How long were you gone, anyway?"

"I went home for Thanksgiving, and when I left this morning it was the first week of January 2012."

Garrick pulled his shirt over his head and shoved his feet into his boots. "I'm glad you're back, but that doesn't explain why. I wouldn't have pegged you as the running-through-time type."

"Remember the girl I was with the night you came and helped me?"

"The pretty one in the red dress? I thought she left you."

"Her name's Ellie, and I got her back. I found her in Boston in 1863, dying of pneumonia. Three days in the hospital and some antibiotics cured her, but now I've got a load of medical bills. I figured I'd work on the canal and convert my pay into gold coins. When I take them back to 2012, I should be able to sell them for a nice profit and pay the bills."

Garrick stared at me, his eyes wide. "Are you saying you took that girl from her home in 1863 to the future with you?"

"Yeah, why?"

"I thought that was forbidden," Garrick said. "Hasn't Archidus done anything to you for taking her out of her time? He made it pretty clear to me I wasn't to ever take anyone with me when I used the counter."

"When he summoned me, Ellie had already left 1863 and was living in 2011. Archidus wasn't too happy about it, that's for sure. He left me in agony with a splitting migraine. I guess he decided to let it slide, because he said something like 'I see I'll have to overlook it in the future as well.' I think he liked Ellie's grandfather, who had the counter before me. In fact, Ellie expected to be the next Keeper and was the one who showed me how to use it. I haven't heard from Archidus since, so hopefully I'm okay."

"That's lucky for you."

I nodded. "I guess so."

"Was she happy about that?"

"Yeah." I thought back to the letter she had written in 1863, pleading for me to come back for her. "She was definitely happy about it."

Garrick smiled at me and stood. "Well, that's good. I'm glad it worked out."

I stood and picked up my hat. "Thanks. Should we go dig some dirt?"

He motioned toward the door. "After you, little brother."

The next three weeks passed in a blur of dirt, tree stumps, and sweat. The mild weather held out, and we were able to work almost every day. On Saturday, Garrick seemed anxious and preoccupied, like he had something to tell me but didn't know how to start. Finally, he said, "Hey, Harper. I was fixing to ask Rose on a picnic tomorrow, but . . . well, it would sure be nice if it was just the two of us. I thought maybe you could watch Davy."

I chuckled. "Sure. I always wondered if you had a thing for Rose."

Garrick scowled back at me. "I don't have a thing for Rose," he said testily. "It's just a picnic."

"You can't keep your eyes off her."

"Mind your own business, Harper."

"You don't have to get defensive with me."

"I'm not being defensive."

I shrugged my shoulders. "Whatever."

Later that day, Garrick meticulously scrubbed his clothes, spent twice as long as he should have in the bath, and then labored over shaving with a straight razor in front of a cracked mirror. When he wasn't looking I muttered under my breath, "Yeah right, it's just a picnic."

Sunday afternoon found Davy and me hunting for something to do. Garrick and Rose had left hours before with a rented horse and buggy.

"Hey, Davy, you want to learn how to play soccer?" I said.

The five-year-old scrunched his eyebrows and stared at me. "What's soccer?"

"It's a game. We need a ball, though," I said. "Come on. Let's go see what we can find."

I searched through the shed behind the boardinghouse and spied a pile of burlap sacks. After stuffing a few bags into the smallest of the sacks, I arranged them into a spherical shape and tied off the end with a piece of twine. I tossed the ball to Davy. "Here's our soccer ball."

Carrying an armful of logs, I found a flat piece of grass. "This is your goal." I arranged two logs ten feet apart. "You'll try to kick the ball past me and between these logs, okay?"

"Yes sir, Mr. Harper."

I walked in the opposite direction and set up the other goal. "Davy, bring the ball to the middle." Once the burlap ball was centered in our makeshift field, I said, "You go first. Start kicking the ball toward your goal, but remember, you can't touch it with your hands."

Davy swung his foot wildly, missing the ball. He tried again and it wobbled across the grass. I moved lightly on the balls of my feet as I let him work his way down the field. Occasionally, I intercepted the ball and kicked it behind him, smiling each time he raced down the field with his little arms chugging back and forth. I let him get past me and score the first goal.

Davy jumped up and down. "I did it. I won!"

"Hang on. Not so fast, little man." I retrieved the ball and centered it for the next kickoff. "Now it's my turn to kick off. You try to stop me from getting a goal."

At a pace Davy could match, I dribbled down the field. He ferociously battled to take the ball from me, but my competitiveness won out and I couldn't resist scoring. "Yes!" I yelled, pumping my arm and starting a victory dance. "We're tied up, Davy! One-one."

He darted after the ball as it rolled down the incline behind my goal. While I gloried in my score against a five-year-old, I heard a woman's voice behind me. "Mr. Harper?"

I spun around to see Anna Van Dousen walking in my direction. I stuffed my hands in my pockets. "Anna, how are you?"

"I'm fine, thank you. Seems you're enjoying yourself. What is this?" She waved at our field.

"I was teaching Davy to play soccer. I'm babysitting him."

"Pardon me?" She shook her head. "Babysitting? Soccer? My English is not so good. Please, explain?" Anna was a Danish immigrant, and her father had tried to get us together the last time I was in town.

I looked away from her and scratched my head. "Um—" I doubted soccer was a part of *anyone's* vocabulary in 1817. "What I meant to say was, I'm watching Davy while Rose and Garrick are on a picnic. I'm teaching him a game I used to play with my dad, when I was a kid. But that's enough about me. How's your family? Did your mom have her baby yet?"

"Yah, she had a baby girl, Ingrid, three days past. You should come by. Perhaps tonight? Bring Davy and come for supper at six o'clock. My father would be happy to see you again. He's still fixing to change your mind and wants you to work for him. Pa is a kind man. Trust me, you'd like him."

I began wondering if her dad had put her up to this visit, or if she had put her dad up to offering me that job. "I'm sure he's great to work with, but it's not for me."

"Next week then. I'll tell my pa you'll be to supper next Sunday. And you're welcome to bring your brother, as well. My little brothers are begging to play with him again. I'll see you soon, yah?"

Thoughts of Ellie flashed through my mind as Anna walked away. I couldn't sit through another supper with her pa trying to push his daughter on me. "Wait," I said. She spun around, an eager expression on her face as she walked back to me. "Anna, I'm sorry, but I can't come to supper again. I'm not going to be in town much longer and then I'll most likely be gone for good."

"My pa says you might not go west. A lot of men dream of going west, but many never leave. Shouldn't you enjoy all that Rome, New York, has to offer while you are here?"

This girl just won't take no for an answer, I thought. *Time to play the girlfriend card.* "The truth is, I have a girlfriend and I wouldn't feel good about going to dinner at your house again." Motioning toward Davy, I said, "I'd better get back to the game."

Anna placed her hand on my arm. "What do you mean, girlfriend?"

I racked my brain for the best way to explain it 1800s style. "I guess I'm her beau and she's waiting for me."

"Where is this girl?"

I ran my fingers through my hair. *The far-distant future.* "Uh . . . well." I knew Lewis and Clark had probably barely discovered Oregon, so the full truth wouldn't work. "She's from Boston, Massachusetts."

"How long have you known her?" Anna looked forlorn.

I stepped back. "I don't remember exactly—maybe four or five months."

Anna smiled and moved closer. "Why that's not long at all. You can still come to supper. She can't expect you not to eat."

I pulled my arm away from her caressing hands. "Anna, she doesn't expect me not to eat, but she has every right to expect me not to eat with another girl. Look, I'm serious about her. She means the world to me, so I won't jeopardize my relationship over dinner. Really, I'd better go." I jogged away, saying, "It's your kickoff, Davy."

Glancing over my shoulder at Anna, who had turned to leave, I noticed dark clouds gathering in the northeast. Within minutes, the wind picked up and the temperature dropped. Davy scored another goal and then I called the game. "You won, Davy. Two to one. Let's put everything away and get inside before this storm hits."

We had just put the wood back when lightning raked the prematurely dark sky, followed by a boom of thunder. A wall of hail hit the street in the distance, advancing toward us as the wind whipped into an icy fury.

"Come on, Davy." I grabbed his hand and we sprinted, as fast as his little legs would go, into the kitchen of the boardinghouse. No sooner had I secured the door than hail battered the roof like a herd of thundering horses.

Jumping up and down, Davy pointed out the window. "Look, Mr. Harper!"

I walked to where he stood. The hail bounced off the ground like thousands of tiny Ping-Pong balls. The dirt soon disappeared beneath a blanket of white ice. We watched the unlucky few who were caught in the weather clutch their hats and scurry to find shelter. Tied to hitching posts up and down the street, horses paced the length of their ropes. The animals stamped their feet and lowered their heads as the icy pellets beat their backs.

Davy tugged on my sleeve. "Where's my ma?"

"Don't worry. Garrick will take care of her. I bet they'll find shelter and wait out the storm." We watched as the hail turned into sleet and the thunder rumbled away to the west. What remained of the fading daylight surrendered to the blackness of an early night. Thick storm clouds blanketed the sky, blocking any trace of the moon or stars. It would be pitch black before long.

"I'm hungry," Davy said.

My stomach grumbled. "Me too. What do you want to eat?"

The house was quiet. I guessed most of the boarders were at the tavern, and with weather like this we wouldn't see them for a while. I looked around the kitchen, feeling like a foreigner. *Where are the corn dogs and frozen pizzas when I need them*? I looked at the hearth, its coals neatly banked in the corner. Three iron hooks, from which pots could be hung, were securely fastened to the frame of the large fireplace.

"Can you cook me an egg?" Davy asked.

"Sure, I can make scrambled eggs. But where are the eggs?"

The little boy puffed out his chest. "They're in the cellar— where else? I gathered a whole passel of 'em from the henhouse this morning."

"Okay, I'll follow you." We dashed through the rain to the cellar. Feeling my way along the door, I found the latch and pulled it open. The wind threatened to yank the door from my grasp. "We forgot to bring a candle," I said, looking into the black hole.

"They're at the bottom of the stairs. I can find 'em," Davy said, feeling his way onto the cellar steps. I followed him to get out of the rain. "How many eggs should I get?" he soon asked.

"You found them?"

"Can I have three?"

"That's a lot of eggs for a guy your size. Why don't you get six and we'll share them?" I heard the eggshells bumping into each other. "Do you need help? What are you doing down there?"

"I'm feeling for the biggest ones."

"Davy, come on. Just grab the first six you touch. I'm going to starve to death up here waiting for you."

"I'm coming, Mr. Harper." The little boy scurried up the steep steps and bolted into the rain as soon as I opened the door.

"Where are the eggs, buddy?" I called from the cellar.

"Right here—safe in my shirt," Davy yelled as he ran for the kitchen door.

"Slow down so you don't slip and fall on 'em." The wind whipped away my warning, and I doubted Davy heard it. I closed the door and secured the latch before racing after him.

Once in the kitchen, I shook the rain off my head. I added kindling to the coals and started a fire. Davy pulled the eggs from his shirt one at a time and set them gently on the table. Once I had the fire going, I looked at him and said, "Now what?"

He pointed an accusing finger in my direction. "I thought you said you knew how to cook eggs."

"I do. I just don't know where everything is. Why don't you tell me how your ma makes her eggs? Then I'll try to make them like she does."

"Yes sir." Davy ran across the room. "Ma uses this bowl. She cracks the eggs in there and puts the shells in the slop bucket by the door."

I cracked the eggs and picked up a fork. "I bet I know what's next." I vigorously stirred the eggs and added salt and pepper.

"You're doing right fine, Mr. Harper."

"Now, what does she cook it in?" I eyed the assortment of cast-iron pans hanging from the ceiling.

Davy ran to stand beneath a pan. "That one."

I pulled the skillet from its hook and carried it to the table. I was about to dump the eggs in when I noticed Davy scowling at me with his hands on his hips.

"What?" I said.

"You forgot the lard. I don't reckon you know how to cook eggs."

I looked at the pan, realizing I wasn't holding a twenty-first-century nonstick pan. After melting a dab of the fat in the bottom of the skillet, I finally got a nod of approval from my miniature supervisor and dumped the eggs into the pan. I set the pan on the grate over the fire. Soon, the mixture sizzled, and I began frantically stirring it off the bottom. It quickly became a losing battle as brown sections of egg peeled up. I broke out in a sweat. *How do I turn down the temperature on a fire?* I grabbed the pan to move it away from the heat. Searing pain tore through my fingers.

"Ouch!" I dropped the pan back onto the grate. "Dang it! That really hurt."

Davy handed me a towel. "Here you go, Harper."

I got the eggs cooked, although they were dotted with flakes of brown. Davy wrinkled up his nose when I set the pan on the table in front of him. "Eat up," I said, handing him a fork.

"Where's my plate?"

"You don't need one. This way, we have less dishes to wash." I sat across from him and shoveled a forkful of steaming eggs into my mouth, then sucked in air to cool them.

"They look kinda burnt."

"Eat 'em anyway," I said between mouthfuls of egg. "They're not that bad."

I slammed down a couple more oversized bites. Davy must have realized that if he didn't start eating soon, the eggs would be gone. At first he picked at them but was soon chewing with gusto.

I slid the pan closer to him. "Here, buddy. You finish them off."

With his mouth full, he mumbled, "You're right, Mr. Harper. The eggs taste mighty fine. They just look ugly."

The front door banged open, and I heard footsteps coming toward the kitchen. Garrick burst into the room with his arm wrapped around Rose. Both of them were drenched and shivering. Like a drill sergeant, he let the orders fly. "Harper, stoke up the fire. Davy, get your mother a quilt." Then, turning to Rose, he gently said, "Why don't you change into something dry?"

I loaded the fireplace with logs, while Garrick steered Rose toward her room. While she changed, he stripped off his soaked shirt, hung his hat from the back of a chair, and started drying himself in front of the fire. "Davy, can you run get me a clean shirt from my room? Harper, can you take the horse and buggy back to Samuel at the livery? They're out front. I didn't want to keep Rose out in the weather any longer than I had to."

"Sure thing." Before I left the kitchen, I glanced over my shoulder at Garrick. A shiver shook his shoulders, and he glanced at Rose's closed door with a furrowed brow.

Unfortunately, I didn't own a coat in 1817. The utter darkness of night enveloped me as I dashed through the downpour to the buggy and gathered up the reins. Sparse candlelight emanating from windows outlined the road. The horse tossed its head as it trotted down the street. I let the animal find his way as we entered the livery yard, counting on him seeing better than I could. He took himself all the way into the barn before stopping. Only the tail end of the buggy jutted out into the driving rain. I ran up to the house and knocked.

"Mr. Harper, what can I do for you?" Samuel looked surprised to see me on his doorstep.

"I brought back the buggy and horse Garrick borrowed."

Samuel pulled on his coat. "Oh, good. Is everybody all right?"

"They're just wet and a little cold is all."

A cheery smile lit his face. "This nor'easter is a fast-moving one. Sure caught a lot of folks unawares this afternoon."

"You're right about that."

I followed Samuel, who hunched over his lantern to protect it from the rain. The warm glow filled the barn as we entered, and a chorus of neighs greeted us. No doubt the horses were hoping for another serving of grain.

Noticing the wet horse's quivering flanks, I said, "Sorry about the horse getting so cold and wet."

Samuel began unhooking the traces of the buggy. "He'll be fine. Get a rug from the rack and we'll dry him off." He pointed to a stack of woolen blankets.

Samuel led the horse to an empty stall, then set an armful of hay and a bucket of oats in front of him. "The first storm of winter can be the hardest on a horse. Their winter coats aren't in yet—catches 'em off guard." He took the rug I held out. After he gave the horse a good rubdown, steam rose from the animal's back, and he had stopped shivering.

"Sorry again about bringing everything back so wet," I said.

Samuel hung the rug on a hook to dry. "No harm done. It can't be helped sometimes."

"I appreciate your understanding. I'd better head home."

"Take one of those dry rugs to keep you warm on the walk back. You can return it the next time you're passing by," Samuel said.

"Thanks. I think I'll take you up on that." I picked up a clean rug that still smelled faintly of horses. Holding it over my head and shoulders, I stepped into the rain and zigzagged down the road, avoiding as many puddles as possible. In spite of my efforts, my boots were caked with mud by the time I got to the boarding house, and the rain had soaked through the rug.

After leaving my boots at the door, I walked into the kitchen and found Rose seated in front of the fireplace, with Davy on her lap and a thick quilt over her shoulders. Garrick stood behind her, brushing her long, dark hair. Rose's brown eyes twinkled as she listened to her son. Her cheeks were flushed, whether from the heat radiating out of the fireplace or Garrick brushing her hair, I didn't know. I pulled up a chair and sat down. It took only a moment to realize Davy was telling his mother about my lack of culinary skills.

"Thank you for watching Davy, Mr. Harper," Rose said.

"You're welcome. We had fun, didn't we, Davy?"

The kid giggled. "Yes sir."

Garrick told us about his picnic with Rose. The hail had caught them by surprise, and they'd taken cover under a large oak tree. As it got dark, with no sign of the storm letting up, they had braved the downpour to come home.

Davy fell asleep on his mother's lap while we talked. When Rose started to stand, Garrick pulled the little boy into his arms and carried him to his bed.

Garrick, Rose, and I watched the flames dancing in the fireplace and listened to the rain drumming against the windowpane, until Rose excused herself to go to bed. Garrick banked the coals, and we went to our room. As soon as the door closed, he turned to me, grinning. "Harper, I think I'm in love with Rose."

"With all of our time-travel baggage, do you really think that's a good idea?"

"No. But I can't help myself. I've tried to avoid her, but it never works."

I sat on the edge of my bed. "Maybe you should leave for a while. Let things cool down."

Garrick shook his head. "I can't leave her now, not with winter coming on. She's bound to need wood split, and somebody ought to do some hunting to bring in meat for the winter. I'm sure it'll be fine."

"You be careful. Whatever you do, don't break her heart."

He threw back his blankets and climbed into bed. "Don't worry. I won't."

I frowned. "I hope not."

THREE
Nightmare

That night, I plunged into a familiar nightmare. Shrouded in darkness and drenched with rain, I ran through a forest. Lightning lit the night sky, and random shadows splintered the trail ahead of me. I was searching for Ellie. She had been taken, and an overwhelming urge to protect her consumed me. At the crack of thunder, I stopped and rested my hands on my knees, breathing heavily. I thought I was alone until something crashed into my back, sending me sprawling face first onto the muddy trail.

I jumped up, struggling to free myself from what I soon realized was the itchy, woolen blanket off my bed. I woke wet with sweat, standing in the room I shared with Garrick. I took a deep breath, trying to calm my racing heart.

"Quiet, Harper. People are sleeping," Garrick mumbled.

I tossed the blanket back onto my bed. He had turned over and was already snoring. I walked to the window and scratched a peephole in the frost. Snow fell softly from the heavens, dusting everything with white.

Why am I still having these dreams? I wondered. After I got Ellie back from Boston, I expected the nightmares would stop. Obviously that wasn't the case, and this dream had been even worse. The anxiousness I'd felt over Ellie hadn't left when I woke up, and the urge to see her was crushing me like a vice grip as I paced the floor. I had to know she was safe. I grabbed the counter from under my pillow and pushed Shuffle, then Return.

It wasn't until I appeared in my first shuffle zone that I realized I'd left without my shirt and shoes. My muddy boots were still by the door, and my shirt was hanging on a chair by the fire. I found myself standing in lush grass, dotted with boulders, near a gurgling mountain stream. It must have been a spring fly hatch, because large rainbow trout were jumping up to swallow the insects hovering above the surface. *If I just had a fly rod.* As I analyzed where I'd cast, I shimmered to my next shuffle zone.

The counter put me on a gravel road, in the middle of nowhere, with the sun beating down. The baked ground burned my feet, and I shifted my weight from one foot to the other on the sharp rocks. "Ah . . . ouch! Come on already."

Next, I appeared on a beach. Although I stood in hot sand, at least it was soft. The surf broke nearby, and I ran toward the water, not stopping until the waves splashed up to my knees. I smiled at the cool water and soft sand beneath my burning feet.

My next shuffle put me in a busy Midwestern town during the 1940s. Immediately, I drew curious stares from everyone in the vicinity.

"Excuse me," I mumbled as I pushed through the crowd of people, looking for a safe place to disappear. No doubt everyone wondered why I was barefoot, shirtless, and wet from the knees down. Time was running out. I would soon vanish into thin air. I dashed into a store and ducked behind a clothes rack before the woman behind the counter glanced up. "Can I help you? Is anyone there?" she called as I disappeared.

My last shuffle zone pained me as much as the hot gravel, but at the opposite end of the thermometer. I appeared in an old-time Western town at twilight in the dead of winter. I stood in the middle of the street in six inches of icy snow. The wind blew past me, stirring up clouds of drifting snow. On one side of the street was a saloon, and on the other was a general mercantile with a covered porch. My feet stung as I walked across the icy road toward the store. The bitter cold left me shivering by the time I got there. A Closed sign hung on the locked door. Crossing my arms, I rubbed my shoulders.

A gruff voice from across the street caught my attention. "Boy, you crazy? What you doin' out here half naked?"

I spun around to see a man leaving the saloon, sporting the silver star of a sheriff's badge. He headed straight toward me, his rifle swinging loosely at his side. I knew I'd be gone before he crossed the street. Without saying a word I vaulted over the side railing of the porch and ran behind the building.

"Wait, I ain't gonna hurt ya none," the sheriff yelled. "Come back here, boy. You need help."

The snowy landscape started to shimmer around me and I slid to a stop, waiting. The snow gave way to warm, dry carpet beneath my feet. I blinked my eyes, trying to figure out if I was in my bedroom, if Ellie was where I'd left her. Sometimes I feared the counter would fail me—drop me in some obscure time and place and then quit working. I considered it a small miracle every time it took me home.

My eyes cleared and there sat Ellie, exactly as I'd left her. Sighing, I pulled her into my arms, smothering her with kisses. "Oh, Ellie. I missed you so much. Are you okay? I was so worried about you. It feels like forever since I've seen you."

She caressed my shivering shoulders and looked into my eyes, her brow furrowing. "Darling, whatever are you carrying on about? Of course I'm fine. You left me only a minute ago. But what happened to you? The way you're shivering, you're apt to catch a cold. And where is your shirt? And your boots?"

I chuckled and buried my face in her sweet-smelling hair. "Darling? I think I like the sound of that." I cupped her face in my hands, soaking in every detail of it. I started to kiss her again, but she put her hands on her hips and wiggled away from me.

"Chase, you're making me powerful mad. Now tell me why you're carrying on so."

Although Ellie's speech had for the most part conformed to modern standards, I found her lapses into 1860s vocabulary entertaining. I let go of her and flopped down on my bed with a sigh. Grinning, I patted the spot next to me. "Come here and I'll tell you."

She sat down next to me as I pulled my covers up to my chin. "I had a bad dream," I said.

"Are you teasing me?"

"No, I'm serious. I dreamed you were lost in the woods. I had to see you for myself or I never would have been able to get back to sleep."

She smiled. "You shouldn't let a dream worry you. I have no intention of ever leaving, or of getting lost in some woods."

Her reassurance made me feel a little better, although in my nightmare she hadn't wandered off and gotten herself lost. I kept that detail to myself.

"How long were you gone?" she asked.

"A little over three weeks. It was snowing when I left. I still need to go back for my pay, though I have a feeling we won't be doing any more digging."

I told her about my time in the canal, babysitting Davy, the storm, Garrick falling for Rose, and Anna's persistence.

Ellie laughed at my egg-cooking exploits. "I wish I could have seen that."

"Maybe we can build a campfire this summer and I can duplicate the disaster for you."

She smiled. "I'd like that. But what if I help with the cooking part so the end result tastes better?"

"Hey, my eggs might not have won a beauty contest, but they tasted good."

"Then let me clarify," she said. "I'll help you cook them so they *look* more edible."

I chuckled. "Okay, it's a date." Warm and comfortable, it didn't take long for me to fall asleep.

The sound of the garage door opening woke me. I remembered I wasn't alone when Ellie closed her book and jumped off the edge of my bed. I couldn't resist teasing her as she walked away. "Thanks for sleeping with me."

She whirled around, a look of shock on her face. When I laughed, she shook her head and said, "Chase Harper, watch your tongue! I was not sleeping."

My stomach grumbled, and as much as I loved Rose's cooking, nothing beat a big bowl of Honey Nut Cheerios. Plus, I wasn't ready to leave Ellie yet. I'd wait until tonight before going back to Garrick. I changed my clothes, showered and shaved, then went down to the kitchen.

"Hi, Chase," my dad said. "What have you been up to?"

"Not much." I pulled out the milk and cold cereal.

"Did you just wake up?"

"I took a nap."

"Have you cleaned the stalls yet?" my mom asked.

"Um . . . " I turned my back to my parents, pouring the milk on my cereal as I struggled to remember back to three weeks ago when I'd left. I didn't think I'd done the stalls. "No, I guess I still need to do that."

My dad frowned in my direction. "After wasting your whole day, you'd better get on it."

"Sure, Dad," I mumbled, wondering why he was so grumpy.

I finished my bowl of cereal, then left to do the chores. Ellie came running out behind me in the new coat and hat I'd given her for Christmas. "Wait, Chase. I'll help you."

I turned. "You don't have to. It's cold out here and I don't want you getting sick again."

Holding her head high, she marched past me. "I'm not a fragile little thing you need to keep locked away."

I shook my head and smiled. "All right then. You can help."

As we cleaned a stall together, I asked, "Will you come to my room tonight and wait for me, while I go back and finish my week with Garrick?"

"I suppose I can, if you want me to."

"It's easier to leave when I know you're there waiting for me."

She smiled. "I'll be there then."

That night my family watched a movie. I sat by Ellie, but under my parents' scrutiny I kept my arms folded. No hand-holding for me. The magic of movies still astonished her, and by her expression I could tell she loved this one. I probably watched her as much as I watched the show.

In my room that night, I layered my thermals beneath the Erie Canal pants and put on my Under Armour shirt. I wasn't about to go back barefooted, so I put on wool socks and my cowboy boots. After dressing, I opened my door and climbed into bed.

While I waited for Ellie, my mom walked in. Luckily my clothing was hidden beneath the covers. She sat on the edge of my bed, like she had when I was little, and brushed the hair off my forehead. "Chase, your dad and I have noticed you seem to really like Ellie."

"Mom, it's no big deal."

"If this is a boyfriend-girlfriend thing, we can't have you two living in the same house."

"She's just a good friend, Mom. I'm keeping it cool. There's nothing going on between us that you need to worry about."

"We'll see, but please use good judgment and be careful. I love you." My mother kissed me on the forehead.

As she walked out and turned off the hall light, I frowned, knowing I hadn't heard the end of that.

A few minutes later, Ellie tiptoed into my room. "Chase?" she whispered.

"Yeah, I'm right here." I tossed my covers aside, then got up and closed the door behind her.

"Thanks, Ellie," I said, pulling the counter out of my pocket. "I'll hurry back." I kissed her goodbye before I pushed Shuffle.

As I shimmered away, I heard her whisper, "Goodbye, Chase."

I went through five easy shuffle zones with mild temperatures, disappointed that there was no hot gravel or snow-packed ground to cover on this trip—now that I was prepared. I began to wonder if my counter had a twisted sense of humor. During the last shuffle—a warm day on the Great Plains—I glanced down at it. "You're real funny, you know that? But I don't appreciate your tricks. Not one little bit." I snapped the counter closed as

I shimmered into my room at the boardinghouse. Garrick was snoring as I took off my boots and extra layers, then climbed into bed.

The next morning we walked through six inches of snow to the canal site. Big, fluffy flakes were falling as everyone gathered to listen to the boss. "Attention, men. As you can see, we won't be working today or in the foreseeable future. For all we know, this may not clear up 'til spring. You'll be able to collect your pay after five today, at the office in town."

Thomas Macaulay put his arms around Garrick and me. "You lads comin' to Tyke's tonight? It's me farewell party. When the rooster crows, I'll be on me way to New York City."

"Sure thing, Thomas," Garrick said. "Wouldn't miss it for the world. How about you, Harper? You coming?"

I'd refused every other invitation from Garrick or Thomas, but this was Thomas's farewell. For all I knew, I'd never see him again. There couldn't be any harm in delaying my trip home for a few hours. "Sure," I said, "I'll be there."

FOUR
The Hunt

Garrick opened the door to Rose's boardinghouse. "Since we've got a free day, do you want to go hunting?"

I followed him through the house. "What are we hunting?"

He pulled two rifles off their hooks and handed me one. "Whitetail deer. Rose said she'd be much obliged if we brought in some venison to get her through the winter. With all the mouths she has to feed, a couple of deer would be a welcome sight around here."

Toting a muzzle-loader rifle, with a pouch of lead balls and a powder horn hooked on my belt, I followed Garrick into woods. "Do you realize I have no clue how to load this rifle?"

He stopped in his tracks. "You don't?"

"I think you put some powder in and then the ball, but you'd better show me or I might end up blowing my head off."

Garrick held the rifle with the barrel pointed up. "Watch closely. You uncork your powder horn, like this, and pour the powder into the measure." He pulled the top off with his teeth and measured out the gunpowder. "Then dump it down the barrel. Turn the rifle, lock side down, and tap it. That settles the powder. Next, get a patch and a ball out of your pouch. Lay the patch on the barrel opening and set the ball on top of it. Once you get the ball started, use your ramrod to drive it down the barrel and seat it on top of the powder charge. When you're ready to fire, cock it back like this, and remember to aim a little high. These lead balls drop faster than the bullets you're probably used to. You got all that?"

"I think so," I said.

"Good, let's go hunt."

We hiked another hour before Garrick stopped, raising his hand to point. "We'll split up here. You angle west, then circle back around through that there draw, while I go east. Meet back here an hour before sunset."

Before I could reply, he hiked off to the east, leaving me isolated in the backwoods of New York. I had inherited the avid-outdoorsman gene from my dad, but this wasn't the type of hunting I was used to—no two-way radio communication, no binoculars, and no high-powered rifle and scope. I figured if I saw a deer, I'd be lucky to even load this gun before the animal ran off.

The freshly fallen snow muffled my footsteps, and before long I came across three deer, feeding on the brush at the edge of a clearing. I hid behind a tree, mentally reviewing the steps Garrick had shown me. I measured and dumped in the powder. Then I laid the patch and ball on top of the barrel. When I unfastened the metal ramrod, it clanged against the rifle. "Dang it," I mouthed.

Peering around the tree, I saw two of the deer bounding into the woods. The third paused at the tree line, ears pricked forward and nostrils flared. I seated the ball firmly on the powder and dropped the ramrod in the snow, then cocked the rifle. I raised it to my shoulder and moved from behind the tree. The lone deer lowered his head to eat. I sighted down the barrel, aiming for behind the shoulder. The deer took a step toward the trees. Fearing it would run off, I pulled the trigger. The bullet went between the deer's legs. I had rushed the shot, forgetting to aim high.

The animal disappeared into the forest, and I bent to retrieve the ramrod. Before I could attach it to the rifle, a vision flashed in my mind as if I was dreaming. I found myself in an old-fashioned house, peering into the living room at a family of three as the radio played classical music in the background. The father had his nose buried in a newspaper, the mother sat sewing a button on a shirt, and a young teenage boy wandered around the room, looking completely bored. A loud knock sounded at their door. The man glanced at his wife and asked her something in German. She shook her head. He set aside the paper and stood.

As soon as he opened the door, two men in long, black trench coats with Nazi swastika armbands barged into the house. They beat the man. Then, one of the Nazis forced him to his knees, holding a gun to the back of his head. The teenager attacked the other Nazi, who was walking toward the woman. The man barely broke stride as he backhanded the youth, sending him sprawling across the floor. The mother screamed and tried to run to her son, but the Nazi intercepted her. Everyone was yelling in German. The second Nazi ripped the woman's shirt, exposing a gold chain around her neck. The Nazi yanked on it. The last thing I saw before returning to my own reality was the devilish grin on his face as his hand wrapped around her counter.

I woke to the flash of counter coordinates and a rush of adrenaline. Suddenly, it hit me. I was a pawn in someone's game of chess and I'd just been moved. Master Archidus required my services. I was a Keeper—the Protector, to be specific. I hadn't wanted this, but I wouldn't shun my duties, either. The other Keeper's life wasn't the only one at stake.

The urge I felt to go protect the woman and her family overpowered every other emotion. I fastened the ramrod to my rifle, then set my counter for Germany, November 6, 1938. With my heart racing, I took a deep breath and pressed Shuffle, then Go. The counter was kind, and I didn't run into problems during my shuffles.

Garrick had arrived first and stood near the window, alternating between arguing with the man and glancing at the street. "Sir, you need to take your family and leave," he said. "The Nazis are coming. It's not safe for you in Germany anymore."

In halting English the man replied, "No, no, you must be mistaken. Who are you and how did you get in here?"

"I'm a friend, sent to warn you. Trust me. Your wife is Jewish, right?"

"Her mother was Jewish, but her father was German."

The woman put her hand on the man's arm. "Fredrick, he is a friend. We must listen to him. Come, let us go."

Cursing under his breath, Garrick let the curtain fall as he stepped away from the window. "Too late, they're here."

Fredrick peered out the window. "Gestapo? But what could they want from us?"

I walked into the living room, turning my rifle so I could use it as a club. "What took you so long?" Garrick growled.

I positioned myself next to the doorknob. "Gosh, Garrick, they haven't even knocked yet. What's got your feathers ruffled?"

As he pressed his back to the wall by the door hinges, he said, "I had a plan, you know. Avoid the confrontation by getting them out of here early."

In my loudest whisper I said, "Then next time let me in on the plan in advance. I'm not telepathic, you know."

Garrick scowled and motioned for the family to leave the room. The Gestapo's knock vibrated the door. I undid the lock and twisted the knob. As expected, the two Nazis burst into the house. I clubbed the one closest to me across the chest and his pistol dropped to the floor. He lunged for me, but I sidestepped him and then slammed the butt of my rifle into the back of his head, knocking him out cold. Glancing up from the fallen form of the Nazi, I stood face to face with the other German, his devilish glare focused on me as he pulled a pistol from inside his coat and took aim at my heart. At the sound of gunfire I glanced down, clutching my chest and anticipating pain. I was relieved to feel nothing as the Nazi crumpled to the ground in front of me.

I smiled at Garrick, who lowered his rifle. "Good shot," I said.

He stooped to retrieve the Nazi's fallen gun, then looked it over. "Luger pistol—these are nice. Harper, shut the door before somebody sees us."

I dragged the dead man over to the unconscious one. As I stepped toward the door, a hand clamped onto my ankle. I gasped and stumbled forward, yanking my foot free as a gunshot rang out behind me. Wheeling around, I saw the pistol in Garrick's hand aimed at the other Nazi. I watched in horror as a stain of blood spread across the floor from beneath the man I'd thought was unconscious. "What did you do that for?"

Garrick pointed at the gun in the man's hand. "Looked like he was fixin' to shoot you in the back."

"Yeah, but—"

"There are no buts, Harper," Garrick said loudly. "You were happy when I shot the first one."

"The first one was a lot closer to killing me. Couldn't you have kicked the gun out of his hand or something, so we could have tied him up and left him? I thought he was out cold."

Garrick rolled the first dead man onto his side and yanked his coat down his arm. "He wasn't out cold if he grabbed his gun and was raising it to fire. This is World War II. I can guarantee he was about to kill you. Now help me take their jackets off."

Stunned, I just stared at Garrick.

Fredrick rushed into the room with a look of terror on his face. "What have you done?"

"If you don't leave Germany now," Garrick said insistently, "I can promise you, your wife and son will soon find themselves dying in a Jewish concentration camp. And you, sir, will either be forced to stand by and watch, or will die trying to stop the inevitable. Now, please leave."

"They wouldn't do that," Fredrick argued. "I was a soldier for the Fatherland. I fought in the Great War. Surely, that will count for something. I can protect my family. You are mistaken, Herr Garrick."

I finally found my voice. "Sir, he's not mistaken. Hitler will stop at nothing to destroy the Jews. It won't matter who you are or what you did in the past. If there is even a drop of Jewish blood in your family, they will be condemned. Hitler is mad."

Fredrick shook his head. "How can you know this?"

His wife, carrying a small bag and pulling her son along behind her, handed him his coat. "Trust me, Fredrick, they know. I will explain later, but we must leave before it is too late for us. We will go to my sister's home in the country. From there we can travel into Poland. Do you remember Gertrude, my cousin in Warsaw? We will stay with her and start a new life. Think about Hans—we can't risk our son's safety. We've heard the rumors about Rabbi Lentz. You can't deny we've suspected something isn't right. Please, Fredrick, let's go quickly."

He sighed and took the coat from her hand. "Yes, you must be right. Let me gather a few things."

Reluctantly, I helped Garrick take the coats off the Nazis as the family quickly packed. "Danka," the woman said before closing the door behind her. We watched them load their things into their car and drive away.

My stomach knotted at the coppery smell of blood and the sickening sight of death. I brought my fist to my mouth. "Now what?"

"If we get these bodies out of here and clean up the mess, maybe we can buy the family some time."

I nodded as Garrick handed me a hat and one of the Nazi trench coats. "Put these on and then turn off the lights. We'll hide the bodies in their car." Like a robot, I did as he said.

Behind the curtain of a dark night, we executed our cover-up. As we stuffed both bodies in the trunk, I glanced nervously at the surrounding houses. More than once I shoved my hand in my pocket, wrapping my fingers around my counter for reassurance. I imagined a Sniffer stepping out of the shadows and running a sword through my back, or a swarm of Nazi soldiers descending on us, and the counter was my ticket out of there.

"What do you know about her—the Keeper we just helped?" I asked Garrick as we scrubbed the floor with rags we found in the kitchen.

"Her name is Ruth, and she got the counter from her mother, Helga. Her counter is Perception. Did you notice how she didn't question us? And how quickly she persuaded her husband to follow her?"

"Yeah."

"Because of her counter she has amazing perception— the ability to discern others' thoughts and feelings. Once, I visited with her mother Helga about the power of perception. She talked of knowing some things before they happened, of discerning the truth in someone's words, and of changing the perceptions of others by her thoughts and actions. She claimed she could keep a perfect secret, because she was able to persuade everyone to see things as she wanted them to be seen."

"Interesting." I stood up to survey our work.

Looking around, Garrick said, "We're done here."

He pocketed one of the Nazi pistols and handed me the other one. I stowed it in the pocket of the trench coat, where I found two extra ammo clips. We picked up our rifles and cowboy hats and hid them under our jackets. I tossed the rags in the garbage can on our way out, then locked the door behind us. The dead men's black car had two small swastika flags flying near the front bumper. We climbed into the car, and Garrick took the wheel and pulled away from Ruth's house.

We drove through the quiet streets of the German town. After brooding in silence for a few miles, Garrick glanced over at me. "Harper, look, I'm sorry I snapped at you back there. It's the Nazis—they make me nervous. My dad joined the army after Pearl Harbor and fought his way across Europe until a German machine gun took his legs right out from underneath him." Garrick paused as he stared at the street in front of him. "He spent months in an overcrowded hospital in London, trying to get well enough to travel. He was lucky he didn't lose his legs, but after that he walked with crutches. I was born the year after he came home from the war. When I was little, I used to wish he could play ball with me like the other dads did with their kids."

I studied Garrick's profile in the shifting light from the street lamps. "I'm sorry. I had no idea."

"Crap, look at that," Garrick muttered, pressing on the brake pedal.

I glanced up. Ahead of us loomed a Nazi roadblock. "Turn around," I said.

A group of soldiers, warming their hands over a fire barrel, watched our approaching car. Two army Jeeps were parked alongside the road, and two wooden barricades topped with barbed wire blocked anyone from passing. I glanced back at Garrick, who continued driving forward. "What are you doing?"

"We can't turn around now. They've already seen us."

I sat up straighter. "That doesn't mean we keep going. Are you nuts?"

He shrugged his shoulders. "We're in one of their cars, so maybe they'll let us through. But just in case, have your counter ready. Grab onto me and get us out of here if there's trouble."

We pulled the Nazi trench coats tighter around our necks, covering our American clothing. Garrick adjusted his grip on the steering wheel. I wiped the sweat from the palm of my hand and held my counter open in the pocket of the trench coat, with my thumb hovering over the Shuffle button. When we were close enough that the soldier got a look at the car, he motioned for the barricades to be moved and then stood at attention to allow us to pass. The soldier, with his arm raised above his head, cried out, "Heil, Hitler!"

Through the car's open window, Garrick imitated the soldier's action as he drove through the opening between the barricades, yelling back, "Heil, Hitler!" The soldier lowered his arm and stepped toward the car to get a closer look. However, by then we were through their barricade and Garrick laid his foot on the accelerator. I looked back to watch the soldier as we sped away. He stood in the open road staring after us, probably wondering what it was about us that seemed different.

When the roadblock disappeared from my view, I turned around, breathed a sigh of relief, and closed my counter. "That was some 'Heil, Hitler' you gave back there. Have you practiced that?"

"Maybe." Garrick cracked a smile. "I've run into the Nazis before. Once I bailed out Wise Wolf's dad in France, a little later in this war." Wise Wolf was Garrick's nickname for Wisdom's Keeper, Raoul Devereux.

"Do you know where we're going?" I asked.

"No, but I thought we'd drive until we found a good place to ditch the car."

We left the town behind, now passing fields and farmhouses. When we came to a bend in the road near a river, I pointed. "Look. We could drive into that brush near the water. If we cover the car with branches, it could take days for someone to find it."

"Good eye, Harper. Hang on."

Garrick slammed on the brakes, swerved off the road, and bounced down the steep embankment. The car's momentum carried us into the brush until the front bumper banged into the boulders along the river's edge, snapping our heads forward.

"Are you crazy?" I said, laughing.

Garrick grabbed his rifle and hat and opened his door. I cringed as thorns scratched the car's exterior like fingernails on a chalkboard.

"Oh, great," he mumbled. "We're in sticker brush. Whose idea was this, anyway?"

I gritted my teeth and shoved my door open. A mass of prickling thorns met me as I stepped out of the car. I took two steps before remembering my gun and hat. After some painful backtracking, I grabbed them from the back seat. "Garrick, anyone with an ounce of common sense would have stopped and investigated before driving off the road in the dark. I feel like a freakin' pin cushion."

"Quit your whining, little brother. Let's cover this car with branches and then skedaddle back to the land of the free and the home of the brave."

Once we escaped the sticker brush, we looked over the car in the waning moonlight. "I changed my mind on the branches.

That's good enough." Garrick bent to pick a thorn out of his pant leg.

"I agree."

We both got out our counters. "Hey, I heard you shoot before I left. Did you get anything?" Garrick asked.

"No, I forgot to aim high. I shot under the deer's belly."

Garrick slapped me on the shoulder. "Better luck next time. See you back at the rendezvous." With that, he disappeared.

I took one last look around, hoping this would be my only encounter with Hitler's Germany, and pressed Shuffle, then Return.

After the shuffle zones I reappeared in 1817, standing in my snowy footprints deep in the forest. I closed my eyes and leaned against the tree. Looking at things in the most brutal light, I had been an accessory to two homicides. On the other hand, we had saved a couple of innocent lives and protected Archidus' counter from the Nazis. And after all, we were talking World War II.

I was thankful Garrick had shot the Nazi who had his gun aimed at my heart. If he wouldn't have, I'd be stone dead right now. But the second one bothered me. It didn't seem right to gun someone down if there was another option. I would have bet Garrick could've stopped the guy from shooting me, but then again, was the gamble worth my life? Plus, if Garrick hadn't killed him, he would have reported Ruth and her family's departure, and the Nazis would've been after them in a heartbeat. I shook my head. What was done was done, but the memory of it left me feeling numb. I didn't know how long I stood there, just thinking.

It wasn't until I heard movement on the other side of the clearing that I pulled myself back to reality. Leaning around the tree trunk, I gasped. The biggest whitetail deer I'd ever seen pawed at the snow. It had points and stickers coming off in all directions. Granted, being from Oregon I had never come across any whitetails, but I had watched my share of whitetail deer-hunting shows on cable TV and knew this was a trophy. I pulled out the powder horn and silently cursed the muzzle-loading process. When the gun was ready, I dropped the ramrod in the snow and seated the rifle against my shoulder. I took a deep breath and moved from behind the tree.

The big buck rubbed his antlers against an evergreen on the edge of the clearing. I eyed down the barrel, taking aim where I had on the previous deer, then raised the rifle to compensate for the drop in the ball at that distance. I exhaled and gently squeezed the trigger. The buck lunged forward and then crumpled onto the soft snow. All thoughts of Germany fled my mind in the adrenaline rush of the hunt.

While I was cleaning the deer, I heard two shots echo through the hills. Drenched with sweat, I labored to drag the buck out of the woods. It was a heavy-bodied deer with massive antlers. Every twenty feet or so, I stopped to catch my breath before continuing. Retracing my steps, I returned to the rendezvous point. Exhausted, I sat down on the deer's back to wait for Garrick. An hour later, he emerged from the forest with a small doe slung over his shoulders and blood soaking the collar of his shirt.

"What's that puny little thing?" I called out, lifting the head of my buck.

Garrick let his deer fall to the ground. "No way, Harper! That is the biggest whitetail I've ever seen." He analyzed the antlers and counted all the points, while I stood there smiling.

FIVE
The Tavern

On the hike back, Garrick hounded me for a play-by-play of the hunt. As we dressed the deer and hung them in Rose's cellar, Davy followed our every move, asking a nonstop stream of questions. Garrick never seemed to grow tired of telling the hunting stories, and he obviously enjoyed the attention from his little friend.

I'd never seen a woman happier than Rose at the result of a man's hunting expedition. Watching her reaction, I realized that once the snow arrived, the only food you had was what you brought in from the hunt or what you had harvested and stored in your cellar. For a widow like Rose, getting two deer was a windfall of good fortune for the long winter ahead.

Garrick and I warmed some water and cleaned up in our room before hurrying into town to collect our pay. With a pocket full of coins each, we set out for the tavern. The place reeked of sweat and whiskey, and wisps of cigar smoke floated toward the ceiling. Because of the snow, the canal diggers had sat around the tavern all day, and most of them looked drunk.

Garrick and I worked our way through the crowd of men, some talking and laughing, some playing cards. We found Thomas's table and pulled up a couple of chairs. Garrick ordered a shot of whiskey. I declined despite the peer pressure from Thomas and the other men at the table. I had no desire to start on something that could become an addiction I'd have to deal with the rest of my life. Some of the guys wouldn't let it go, and one even filled his shot glass and slid it in front of me. I slid it back.

"Don't be a coward, kid. It ain't gonna hurt ya none."

Garrick slammed his fist on the table. "Boys, drop it. My brother's too young to drink. Our ma wouldn't let me hear the end of it if I let her little boy take up drinking."

Thomas nodded his head as he took another swig. "So right, so right. Easy to forget he's still a lad."

My face flushed, but there was nothing to do except play the part of the kid brother. As the night wore on, I saw that in the last two hundred years, men hadn't changed all that much. Garrick told about our deer hunt, embellishing each detail. His glorious account of my trophy whitetail sparked a round of hunting stories from every man at the table, each attempting to outdo the rest. The weapons and the voices were different, but the stories were a mirror image of the ones I'd heard my dad and his brothers tell.

Amid the racket and laughter, I noticed something brewing across the room. A slightly built Irishman with curly red hair and an easygoing smile was winning big at the card table. The unfortunate part of this scene was whom he was beating. I recognized the man who had attacked Garrick the first night I'd come to 1817. I had since learned his name—Billy Larson. Two of the men he hung with were his brothers, Paul and Johnny. Billy picked up the cards and said, "Another round?"

The Irishman shook his head and slid his winnings into his hat. "Sorry, but I best be on my way, lads. Sure been a pleasure." Turning his back on the bullies, he walked toward the door.

A sour look crossed Billy's face. He drained the whiskey from his glass and motioned for his brothers to follow him. I felt compelled to protect the innocent Irishman, who was about to get his butt kicked. I looked at Garrick, who also watched the three men follow the Irishman out of the tavern. Garrick and I exchanged a glance, then stood in unison.

"Well, boys, it's been a long day," he said, shaking Thomas's hand. "Good luck to you. Hopefully, I'll see you in the trenches come spring."

I backed away from the table. "See you later, Thomas. Have a good trip."

Once Garrick and I stepped outside the chaos of the tavern, I asked quietly, "Where did they go?" The overlapping footsteps in the snow made it impossible to track the four men.

Suddenly, the sound of a commotion floated on the night air. We ran toward the noise. As we darted into the alley between the silversmith's shop and the livery, Garrick yelled, "Hey, Billy, why don't you pick on somebody your own size?"

I slid to a stop next to Garrick. The three brothers, caught in the act of assault and robbery, stared back at us. They tossed the bloody-nosed Irishman into the snow and turned their full attention on us.

Billy looked smug as he chuckled. "Like you?"

"Yeah, like me." Garrick encouraged him with the flick of his fingers.

Billy laughed as he rolled up his sleeves. "Well, now, I've been hopin' to get my hands on you and your brother. It's mighty nice of you to drop in—unarmed."

Garrick must have been itching for a good fight, because he didn't bat an eye at our lack of weapons or the fact that we were outnumbered. Glancing around, I saw a pitchfork next to the livery barn, half buried in the snow. Before I could move to grab it, Garrick and Billy launched themselves at each other like caged pit bulls. The other two brothers rushed me. I ran for the pitchfork, but one of them tackled me into the snow before I could reach it. I scrambled to my feet and lunged for Johnny, driving him to the ground and hitting him in the stomach. I should have kept an eye on the other guy, because he caught me off guard with a swift kick to my face, sending me flying off his brother. As I tried to clear my ringing head, I saw that the pitchfork now lay within my reach. I got to my feet and yanked it out of the snow.

I whipped the makeshift weapon in front of me and smiled as Paul ran into it. The sharp metal tines pierced his thigh. He screamed in agony and jerked his leg back. When I pulled on the pitchfork, he grabbed it, starting a tug of war. I refused to let go of the splintered handle, knowing if I did, Paul would run the tines through me next.

Johnny glared at me as he climbed to his feet and started in my direction. In that instant I caught a glimpse of Garrick and Billy. By the light of the moon reflecting off the snow, I saw blood covering Billy's face. Barely a trickle oozed from Garrick's nose, and he had a grin as wide as Texas. Billy swung wildly but was no match for Garrick's lithe movements. It seemed like he was toying with Billy when he could've just knocked him out. "Garrick, hurry it up. I could really use a little—"

A fist slammed into my face, interrupting me midsentence. I still refused to let go of the pitchfork handle, preferring to endure the pain of Johnny's fists, rather than risk encountering the other end of the tool. After dodging several of Johnny's blows, I took a couple of slugs in the gut. All the while, Paul kept tugging on the pitchfork. Suddenly, Johnny locked both his hands around my throat in a death grip. I realized this could end badly if something didn't change, and soon. I shoved one hand in my pocket to find my counter. I'd have to take drastic measures if Garrick didn't get his butt over here to help me. My throat burned and I began to feel lightheaded.

In desperation, I kneed Johnny in the groin, hoping he'd loosen his grip on my throat. He didn't. Worried I would pass out, I was on the brink of pressing the Shuffle button, when Garrick punched Johnny in the back, sending him to his knees. After that, it was all over for the three brothers. Garrick was a maniac in a fistfight, and Johnny didn't stand a chance once my "brother" turned his full fury on him. I firmly held my end of the pitchfork. The brother I'd stabbed was losing blood and probably going into shock. His grip weakened and I soon wrenched the pitchfork out of his grasp. All it took after that was a few threatening jabs, and he limped away.

Johnny rolled over in the snow, groaning in pain. Garrick stepped back, wiped his nose with the back of his hand, and said, "Don't let me see you three picking on him again, or we'll come finish what we started."

I leaned the pitchfork against the wall and followed Garrick back to the street. The Irishman, who had stayed to watch the fight, hustled after us. He shoved his hand out in front of him. "Thank ye kindly. I'm Patrick Ackart."

I shook his hand. "Nice to meet you. I'm Chase Harper."

Garrick turned and extended a bloodstained hand toward Patrick, introducing himself.

"That was some fighting," Patrick said with obvious admiration.

"Thanks. I've done a bit of fighting in my day," Garrick said casually.

Once back on the street, we went our separate ways. "What fighting were you talking about?" I asked Garrick.

Raising his fists, he bounced on the balls of his feet. "Boxing." He playfully jabbed the air in front of me. "I boxed for four years during college."

I batted his fists away from my face. "Knock it off."

"I could teach you."

I rubbed the tender spot below my left eye. "Not now."

"Aw, you're no fun."

As we entered our room, Garrick lit a candle. He dunked his hands in the washbasin and began scrubbing his bloody knuckles. I sat on the edge of my bed, gently probing the bruise on my cheek, and opening and closing my jaw. Exhausted from the long day, all I could think about was getting home for a hot shower and my own bed. "I'm heading home tonight," I said.

Garrick turned and looked me over. "You've got a nice shiner below your eye. How are you going to explain that?"

"I'll think of something. I don't want to hang around waiting for it to heal."

"I can't blame you for that. Take your Nazi coat and hat with you. I wouldn't be surprised if Mrs. Perception needs our help again. They've got a long way to go before they're out of Hitler's reach."

"I hope not." I put on the trench coat. The Nazi handgun in the pocket bounced against my thigh as I walked across the room to pick up my two hats and my extra pair of boots. "When do you think they'll start digging the canal again?"

"Depends on the weather, but I'd guess March at the earliest. If you're coming back, wait until mid-April or so."

"Well, Garrick, it's been fun. If we're not summoned for duty sooner, I'll see you in April."

"It's gonna be a long winter without you, little brother."

"You could always jump ahead."

Garrick smiled. "I could, but where's the challenge in that? Besides, I want to stick around in case Rose needs something."

I pulled the counter from my pocket and carefully adjusted the dials to the date and time I'd left home. After giving Garrick a quick salute and a smile, I pressed Shuffle and Go.

SIX
Trouble

After five shuffle zones, I appeared behind Ellie. She was staring at my door. As I tossed my extra clothing on the bed, she turned and whispered, "Someone's coming. Good night." She darted into the hall, almost running into my dad. "Oh, excuse me, Mr. Harper. Good night."

My dad flipped on the light outside my bedroom. "Good night," he said in a tone of voice that left me with no doubt he wasn't happy.

Stunned by my rapidly changing circumstances and on the brink of exhaustion from an extremely long day, I stared at him.

"What are you wearing? Is that a swastika?"

Looking down at myself, I said, "There's a really good explanation." I racked my tired brain, trying to come up with something. I remembered the shiner on my left cheek and turned my head, hoping to keep it in the shadows.

"And this really good explanation would be what?" my dad asked. When I didn't immediately answer, he kept talking. "You're not involved in a gang, are you? Some Aryan Nation group or something?"

"No, Dad! It's nothing like that. It's a costume . . . for a play . . . *The Sound of Music*—that's it. I was having a brain freeze. I couldn't think of the name." In one sentence I'd gone from panic to relief and then to excitement at having found a plausible excuse for standing in my bedroom in a Nazi trench coat.

"I didn't think you did plays."

"I usually don't, but they needed some big guys who fit the German model—you know, blond hair, blue eyes. I don't have to say anything, just march across the stage," I said, finally on a roll.

My dad still wasn't smiling. "Why was Ellie in your room?"

"She has theater. The teacher wanted her to bring the coat home from school and ask me. She was just making sure it fit."

"And this had to be done after ten o'clock in your bedroom?"

"We forgot about it earlier, and she probably didn't want to risk forgetting tomorrow. Her drama teacher needs to know by Monday if I can do it or not." This lie was getting bigger by the second. In an effort to escape further interrogation, I said, "Can I go to bed now? It's been a long day and I'm really tired."

"Long day? Aren't you the same son who told me at dinner that you didn't do much except take a nap?"

I am so busted—so dead. "Well, I'm still tired. Maybe I'm getting sick or something. I don't know. Can we just go to bed?"

"All right, go to bed then," he said, then turned off the hall light and closed my door.

I probably needed to worry about the ramifications of my dad finding Ellie in my room, but I was definitely too tired to think about it at the moment. I stashed all my bizarre clothing in the back of my closet before visiting the bathroom. Sure enough, I had a nice, fat bruise on my cheek and would probably have a black eye to go with it by morning.

Lying in bed, I contemplated how to explain my beat-up

face. I was almost asleep when an idea presented itself. Climbing back out of bed, I set my alarm. To pull it off I needed to be the first one awake.

The sound of my alarm drew a groan from my lips, and the snooze button tempted me like never before. Every muscle in my body filed a strong complaint. Hauling around two dead Nazis and pulling a buck through the forest, not to mention getting into a fistfight behind the livery barn, had left me with a multitude of aches. Yesterday had been brutal.

I dressed slowly and went down to the garage for my boots and coat. The weather was perfect for my plan—gusting wind and driving rain. I fed all the horses and turned them out to their pastures before going back inside. Thankfully, everyone in the house was still asleep. I slammed down a bowl of cereal to quiet my growling stomach and went back to bed. Within seconds, I fell asleep.

Four hours later, I rolled over and looked at my clock. I'd probably slept through Ellie's piano playing. I could hear the girls in the bathroom, so I got up and went downstairs to tell my story, wanting to get it over with.

My mom's eyes widened in surprise when I stepped into the kitchen. "Chase, what happened?" I glanced from my mom to my dad, who scowled back at me.

With as much disdain as I could muster, I said, "Peanut." Peanut is the meanest horse on our property, as well as the one most likely to spook at something.

"And?" Mom asked.

"He head-butted me. He had his nose to the ground when I leaned over to put the halter on. A gust of wind blew some branches down on the roof and he spooked. His head slammed into my face. It hurt like crazy, so I went back to bed." I looked at my parents, hoping they'd buy my story.

"I'm so sorry." My mom walked over to inspect my face. "You should put some ice on that. Nothing's broken, is it?"

I tolerated her scrutiny for a second before turning away. "No, nothing's broken, Mom. It's fine, really." I didn't want her to get too close a look. Being a nurse, she might suspect the bruise had been there longer than I'd led her to believe.

My dad grunted. "Are you sure you didn't try something you shouldn't have and get hit by your girlfriend last night?"

At that my mom's jaw went slack. "Joe! I can't believe you would say such a thing."

Dad shrugged his shoulders and went back to studying *The Wall Street Journal.* "Well, what am I supposed to think when I see her leaving his room at all hours of the night?"

"I'm sure there's a good explanation." My mom turned to me.

"Oh, there was an explanation all right," Dad said sarcastically. "But I'm not sure it was a good one."

"Chase, you weren't doing something you shouldn't have, were you?"

"No, Mom. Ellie's definitely not that kind of girl. Plus, I don't want to be that kind of guy. Really, there's nothing to worry about. I'm not doing anything."

"Good, but we will need to rethink this living arrangement." She gave my dad the look. "Joe?"

Dad sighed and looked up at me. "I shouldn't have joked about that, but I don't want you doing something you'll regret, and I definitely agree with your mother."

"It's no big deal," I said. "Nothing is going to happen."

At the sound of the girls coming downstairs, my mom said, "We'll talk about this later. Now, who wants pancakes?"

Ellie cast me a questioning look. Jessica, however, blurted out, "What the heck happened to your face? You look awful."

I spent the next few minutes retelling the fabricated story of my injury. Jessica seemed to wholeheartedly believe me, because her foot had been stepped on last year when Peanut spooked at a stray dog running around the corner of the barn.

Monday morning, on our drive to Hilhi, I finally got time alone to talk with Ellie. It was a relief to tell her what had happened. I considered censoring out Garrick's violence, but I didn't want to keep secrets from her.

Unfortunately, Randy, Ellie, and I still shared a table in Human Anatomy. It was awkward when we had to work as a group. Randy didn't hide the fact that he still liked Ellie. She was always nice, and I hoped she didn't become interested in him.

When he and I ended up alone in the locker room after school, he said, "So, I hear you and Ellie are like boyfriend-girlfriend now. Is that true?"

I paused before answering, wondering where he was going with this. "That's right."

"Isn't she living at your house?"

"Yeah."

"That's a little weird. I thought she was like a sister to you and Jessica."

I stuffed my backpack in my locker. "Maybe it's like that for Jessica, but not for me."

"Dude, you've got to admit it is weird—you dating someone who's living at your house."

Annoyed with his snooping into my business, I said, "Actually, Randy, it makes the dating quite convenient for me." I slammed my locker shut and walked toward the gym.

On the drive home from school that day, Ellie said, "Someone asked me to the winter formal dance."

Feeling like a bombshell had hit me, I nearly yelled, "What? Who asked you?"

"Ethan Carter."

"Ethan Carter?" I echoed. "How do you know him?" I asked, feeling instantly jealous that someone else had asked my girlfriend to the dance before I could. Ethan was a decent guy—nice, super smart. He was the type I imagined would be a rich, successful businessman someday.

"On several occasions I've conversed with him in the library after school and we've become friends," Ellie said.

I glanced back and forth between her and the road, while she stared at me.

"Well, are you going with him? What did you say?"

She smiled mischievously. "That depends."

"On what?" I asked in all seriousness.

"On you, silly. If my beau should fail to issue an invitation, I may be forced to accompany Ethan to the dance."

I breathed a sigh of relief. "Of course I'll take you. I want to take you to all of the dances, so consider yourself officially asked."

She leaned back and smiled again. "Thank you, kind sir. I shall look forward to it."

The next afternoon, the wrestling team left school early for a match against St. Helens. I hated the away matches, since Ellie couldn't come with me. Occasionally, I got a ride for her with my parents, but they weren't coming today, so Ellie took the bus home from school.

I wrestled a clean match and won. Then I put on sweats and pulled out my cell phone. Two new messages—both were from Jessica. I opened the first and read, "Call me b4 u go home." I opened the second message. "Never mind, go 2 Adam's." *What could that mean?* The wrestling team was leaving the gym, heading for the buses. I picked up my gym bag and started walking while I typed, "What is going on? Something wrong @ Adam's?" I hit "Send" and closed my phone before boarding the bus. It took Jessica over twenty minutes to reply. "Nothing's wrong. Will explain when u get here." I was irritated at my sister for being so vague. *If nothing is wrong, why do I need to go to Adam's?* But by then the bus was less than fifteen minutes from Hilhi. I could be at Adam's a few minutes after that. There'd better be a good explanation, or I'd be ticked that Jessica didn't just say it in her message.

When I pulled onto Adam's street, I saw my sister's car parked in the driveway. I was tired and hungry. Hopefully, this wouldn't take long. I wanted to go home and see Ellie, get some dinner, and hit the sack. After parking the truck, I jogged to the porch and rang the doorbell. I was about to walk in when Adam yanked the door open, grinning. "Hey, dude, are you here to see me, or your girlfriend?"

"What are you talking about?"

By then Jessica, followed closely by Ellie, pushed past Adam to stand in front of me on the porch.

"Jessica, Ellie, what's going on?" I asked.

"Shut the door, Adam. We need to talk to Chase for a minute—alone," Jessica said.

Adam glared at her but closed the door. Something had happened, and I didn't like the looks of it.

"Mom and Dad asked Uncle Steve and Aunt Marianne if Ellie could stay with them for the rest of the school—"

"What?" I interrupted. "How could they do that without talking to me? I can't believe it. This is ridiculous, Jess." Seething, I turned and paced back and forth on the porch.

"Chase," Ellie said softly, walking over to take my hand in hers. I wrapped my arms around her waist and buried my face in her hair. "It's all right. I won't be that far away, and it won't be forever."

I didn't say anything for a while, although I did relax my hold on her once I realized it was probably an uncomfortably tight embrace. "If something happens, it's far enough. What if I can't get here in time?" I whispered.

She leaned her head back and placed her hands on my cheeks, forcing me to look in her eyes. "We can't live our lives in fear of what may happen. We already tried that, remember? It didn't work. We've got to take what comes each day and make the best of it. Promise me you won't make a mountain out of a little old mole hill. Your parents talked to me this afternoon, and they feel they're doing what's best for you—for both of us. Don't be angry with them. They love you more than anything, and trust me, parents don't last forever." Her voice broke with emotion and she leaned her head against my chest.

Jessica sat on the bench by the front door. Every minute or so, the familiar buzz of her phone propelled her thumbs into a flurry of texting.

My stomach soon grumbled in complaint at the dinner delay.

"You must be hungry," Ellie said. "I wish I could make you something."

"I wish you could too," I whispered in her ear. "There's a part of me that wants to take you away from here and never come back."

"I know, but be patient. Remember, I'm only the touch of a button away. You can come see me anytime."

I forced myself to smile. "I guess you're right. Maybe it won't be so bad after all. Come show me where you're staying." I took her hand and opened the door.

"Marianne has me in their upstairs guest room. It's the last door on the left."

I walked into the room with Ellie, getting a good look around so I'd know where to come back to with the counter. "Do you need help with your stuff?" I asked.

"No. Jessica and I are almost done unpacking. But thank you for offering."

"Should I come back later tonight?"

"You look plumb tuckered out." Ellie brushed the hair off my forehead with her fingertips. "Go eat some supper and get to bed. I'll be fine. We'll talk at school tomorrow."

I nodded as Jessica walked into the room. "Thanks, Sis. I'll see you at home." I walked quickly out the door and down the hall, nearly running into my cousin as he left his room.

"Hey, Adam, take care of her for me." I slapped him on the shoulder.

"No problem, dude," he said with a big grin.

I turned to jab my finger in his chest. "But keep your hands off her."

He laughed and threw up his hands in a show of innocence. "Take it easy, Cousin. I will."

"Can you bring her to school in the morning?"

"Sure," he said.

I marched back to the truck and fired up the diesel. Part of me wanted to give my parents a piece of my mind, but another part of me considered what Ellie had said. I would be eighteen in a month, and done with high school in four and a half. Soon, no one would ever separate us again.

SEVEN
1863

I skulked into the house and went straight to my room, not wanting to talk to anyone. But after I showered and changed my clothes, my growling stomach forced me downstairs. When my dad came into the kitchen and launched into a lecture, I tried to cut him off, saying, "Dad, I already know. I talked with Jessica."

But he insisted on getting in the last word, so I held my tongue and followed Ellie's advice—to listen. Dad explained all his reasons for asking her to move out, and I mumbled back that I understood, all the while thinking to myself that he didn't understand and that I didn't agree with him one bit. After downing a mound of leftover spaghetti, I went straight to bed.

The next morning, I was more eager to get to school than I'd been in a long time. I showed up fifteen minutes early and stopped near the entrance of the parking lot, listening to the radio while I waited for Ellie. As soon as I saw Adam's car, I grabbed my backpack and pulled the keys out of the ignition. He parked next to me and let her out.

"Thanks, Adam," I said.

"You're welcome, dude. See you later, Ellie."

"Bye, Adam, Amanda. Thank you," she said as she closed the car door.

"How did you sleep last night?" I asked her.

"Quite well. It's a large, comfortable bed, and your aunt Marianne and uncle Steve are gracious hosts. And you, Chase?"

"Good." I held Ellie's hand as we walked across the parking lot in a light drizzle. Every day this week had been dark and gray, and I couldn't remember the last time we'd seen the sun. Thoughts of summer sunshine and warm temperatures left me wishing the sand would move a little faster through the hourglass.

"Did your parents say anything to you?" she asked.

"My dad gave me the whole lecture."

"And? What did you say?"

"I followed your advice and listened. I actually didn't say much, except that I understood."

Ellie smiled. "I'm sure this arrangement will work out fine."

The next two weeks flew by, and Hilhi's winter formal was only a few days away. Thursday evening my parents were in Tualatin, watching Jessica's swim meet. I had a rare evening at home alone and invited Ellie to study with me. After eating the stew she made us for dinner, I asked, "What do you want to do tonight?"

"Mary has been on my mind of late."

I remembered the kind black woman who had cared for Ellie's great-aunt, and then Ellie when she became ill. "What about her?"

"I often wonder what she thought of my disappearance. Did she know you took me?"

"I talked with her," I said. "She didn't want you to go anywhere at first. But when I told her I wanted to take you to a hospital, she finally agreed. I carried you out the door and behind the neighbor's hedge before I disappeared with you."

Ellie sighed. "I wish I could have bid her farewell. I know she must have worried over what became of me." She stared off into the distance.

Should I offer to give her what she wants? Archidus' warning replayed in my mind. Every time I had taken Ellie somewhere, it had been out of necessity. If I took her back in time to tell her aunt goodbye, I didn't know how he'd feel about that. But the sad, faraway look in Ellie's eyes tipped the scale. She'd left everything and everyone she knew to be with me. I could chance the wrath of Archidus to give her closure for that part of her life.

"I could take you home if you want." My stomach clenched as I said it. "Just as long as you promise me you won't change your mind and make me leave you in 1863."

Ellie's eyes brightened and she smiled at me. "You would do that?"

"I'd do anything to make you happy. To be honest, though, I am worried you might decide you want to stay."

She smiled and reached across the table to take my hand. "Perhaps you should reread the letter I wrote you. Nothing has changed for me. I have no intentions of leaving you or of ever living in 1863 again. I only wish to visit briefly, with you by my side."

I slid my chair back. "Okay, let's get ready and we'll go."

"I don't have anything to wear. All of my dresses are in Boston."

"I can fix that. Now that I've been in your bedroom, I can return us there. As long as Mary isn't in the room when we appear, you can get changed before we see anyone."

Ellie grinned.

I changed into my Erie Canal outfit, remembering to layer with thermals and Under Armour for warmth. I shoved my hat on my head and went back downstairs. Pulling the counter out of my pocket, I asked Ellie, "When would you like to visit?"

"When did I leave? I was so sick I don't even know what day it was."

"You left on December 22."

"For me to get well, I would have been gone at least a week. Should we go back on December 30?"

"Sounds good." I set the globe for Boston, Massachusetts, and the number dials for December 30, 1863. Smiling, I extended my hand to Ellie. She slipped her fingers between mine and I pressed Shuffle and then Go, careful to concentrate on appearing inside her bedroom in Boston.

We shuffled through the grasslands of Africa, where a pride of lions sunned themselves in the distance and zebras grazed on the savanna. Ellie and I enjoyed our brief safari before we shimmered to the next shuffle zone. The counter put us in the mountains of Peru. A chilly wind blew down the canyon. It was rugged, lonely looking country, and I wrapped my arms around Ellie, trying to shield her from the icy air. She started to shiver, and I could feel the wind slicing through all three of my layers.

Our next shuffle put us in the rangelands of Texas. Big longhorns grazed on the open plain in a haze of dust and flies. Walking across the parched grass, we waited to disappear. The next shuffle placed us in India, and the next on a tropical island in the South Pacific. Sadly, we appeared on the island's interior rather than a romantic beach.

When we finally appeared in Ellie's bedroom, we were relieved to find it empty. The bed linens had been changed and the room appeared neat and organized, as if awaiting Ellie's return. Thinking of Mary, I was now glad we had come back. I imagined it would be awful for her to never know what had happened. Ellie pulled a gray skirt and a white blouse from the wardrobe. Looking at me, she smiled and twirled her finger in a circle. "Turn around, please."

My face went red and I turned my back to her. While walking over to stare at the door, I listened intently. I thought I heard her shoes drop onto the floor, followed a moment later by the swish of fabric. Then she said, "I'm dressed."

I turned and watched as she used a few hairpins to transform her modern-day ponytail into a bun on top of her head. She picked up a broach from her dresser and fastened it to the high collar of her blouse. Then she gathered her jeans, sweatshirt, and Nike's off the wooden floor and hid them in the trunk at the foot of her bed. I started to smile as she closed the trunk and sat on the lid to pull on a pair of black boots. After she fastened the buttons on the boots, she stood to examine herself in the mirror. By that time I was smiling broadly, and on the brink of chuckling out loud.

Ellie turned to look at me. "Pray tell, whatever do you find so amusing?"

I shook my head. "You sure know how to make an amazing transformation."

She checked herself in the mirror again. "Do I look all right?"

"You look incredible." I walked over to her. "You're the prettiest girl I've ever seen."

I stood behind her and looked in the mirror. She gazed at our reflection and smiled. "I think we make a nice-looking couple."

"I've never noticed the couple part, since I'm always so busy watching you." I leaned down to kiss her cheek. "But I'm glad you think so."

She spun around and straightened my collar. "Well, as I've said before, you do make a handsome frontiersman."

At the creak of a door opening, we both froze. We relaxed once the sound of footsteps retreated down the hall and then the stairs.

"Let's try to get out the front door," I whispered, listening to the rattle of pans in the kitchen.

"What if Mary sees us?"

I led Ellie to the door and opened it quietly. "It is your house. Tell her you let yourself in. I bet she'll be so happy to see you she won't even notice." We tiptoed down the stairs. When we crossed the entryway to the front door we would be visible from the kitchen. I waited at the bottom of the stairs until I heard Mary poking around in the fireplace. Then I hurried out the door, pulling Ellie along behind me. It was a crisp, clear winter day. A dusting of fresh snow covered the walkway. I glanced at the hedge, thinking how nice it was to be here on the porch, instead of watching from over there.

Ellie glanced up at me. "Should I knock or walk in?"

"What did you usually do?"

"Walk in."

"Okay, then let's go in. It's cold out here." I reached in front of her to twist the knob.

"Mary?" Ellie called as we stepped inside. I closed the door behind us.

"Miss Ellie?" Mary ran from the kitchen, drying her hands on a towel. "Praise the Lord! Is that really you?"

Ellie crossed the entryway and wrapped her arms around the older woman.

Mary stepped back to hold Ellie at arm's length. "Look at you, all healthy and beautiful. Why it's a miracle, it is. How can this be? The doctor said there was no hope. What happened?"

Ellie turned to look at me, smiling. "Chase—although I believe you know him by his first name, Joseph—took me to a very good doctor."

Mary saw me and gasped, then threw her arms around my neck. "Thank you, Mister Joseph," she said between sobs. "Thank you for bringing my Ellie back alive. It's been so awful lonely 'round here."

When I wrapped my arms around Mary, she quickly pulled away and straightened her skirt. "You're welcome," I said. "Thank you for trusting me."

She wiped her eyes on the dish towel, then started for the kitchen. "You two come in here and I'll fix you something to eat."

Ellie and I exchanged glances. I put my hand on my stomach and rolled my eyes. I was stuffed from the stew and couldn't imagine eating again for hours.

"Mary, we ate before we came, but thank you," she called. "Are you hungry, though? I could help you make something."

"I was fixin' to have me a little tea and a sandwich."

"I can make your tea for you," Ellie offered.

I sat and watched Mary and Ellie bustling around the kitchen.

"Are you back for good?" Mary asked after she and Ellie joined me at the table.

Ellie looked at me. "No, we'll be leaving soon."

I shrugged. "We've got a couple of days."

"Are you sure?" Ellie looked surprised.

I smiled at her. "Yeah, we can spend a few days."

Looking from me back to Ellie, Mary said, "Mr. Griffith been asking after your whereabouts."

"And why should he care? I thought he was calling on Amanda Berkshire," Ellie said.

Mary stood to clear the table. "Far as I know, Miss Ellie, he is courtin' Miss Berkshire, but that sure don't keep him from pesterin' me 'bout you. Maybe if you and Mister Joseph go to the New Year's Eve ball, you can put the rumors to rest."

Ellie's brow furrowed. "And what rumors might there be?"

"That you died and I'm an ol' crazy who hid your body in the cellar. After the doc came by and you was gone, folks started talkin'. They's wantin' to know what happened to you and why I ain't fixin' to give you a proper burial if you've passed on to the next life. I've pert near had it with all the questions I ain't got no answers to."

"If that's what they're saying, the rumors must be put to rest at once." Ellie turned to look at me. "Would you care to accompany me to a ball?"

Something about the word "ball" sounded a little overwhelming. I'd barely stumbled through one waltz at the homecoming dance last fall. The thought of an 1800s ball freaked me out. But one look at Ellie's expression and there was no way I could refuse. Plus, I didn't want Mary to get a bad rap for what I'd done. "Sure, whatever you want," I mumbled.

"Oh, we'll have a grand time, but we must find you something to wear," Ellie said. "You're about the same size as my father, and there is a trunk full of his things in the attic. I'm certain we can alter one of his suits to fit you. I'll return directly." I wondered how the same event that made me feel like a death-row inmate had Ellie dashing upstairs like a kid on a treasure hunt.

With a wink, Mary said, "If you want to make yerself useful, Mister Joseph, there's a load of wood out back, just beggin' to see the sharp side of an ax."

I put my hat on and walked toward the door. "I'll get right on it." I wasn't big on the idea of attending balls and dancing, but handling an ax was definitely up my alley. I split and stacked wood until Ellie walked out with a shawl draped over her shoulders.

"Thank you, Chase."

I leaned on the ax. "You're welcome. What do you think Mary will do after you leave?"

"She already takes in laundry each week, but she asked about opening the house to escaped slaves who need a place to stay while they find work. I told her she can do what she thinks is best, but I thought it was a good idea."

I swung the ax again, sending a piece of wood flying toward Ellie. "Sorry," I said.

When it landed at her feet, she stooped to pick it up. A cold wind blew in from the harbor, rattling the brittle tree branches.

"Should we go in?" I asked.

"I suppose. It is chilly out here."

I loaded my arms with wood, then nodded to the piece she was holding. "I can take that and go add it to the stack." She balanced the wood on top of what I already held.

Ellie had spent the afternoon cleaning and altering one of her father's suits. After eating supper, I tried on the outfit. The tails of the black coat were cut long, coming down to the middle of my thigh. I ran my fingers over the smooth satin lapel. A burgundy vest buttoned in front, and a small black tie, which Ellie called a cravat, fastened around an uncomfortably high collar. After enduring her scrutiny during the fitting session, I finally got a nod of approval from both her and Mary.

"I do need to make a few more alterations to bring the suit up to fashion, but you look positively dashing," Ellie exclaimed.

I stuck my finger inside the collar and tugged. "I think you went a little heavy on the starch. This collar's as stiff as a board and feels like it's choking me."

"You'll get used to it," she said.

I loosened the cravat and undid the top button. "Used to choking to death? I doubt it."

"There are things you need to know before we go tomorrow," she said, sounding very serious.

"Like what?"

"A ball is a social event. Unlike the dances you're accustomed to, which are couple oriented, our dances are mostly done in formations of circles, squares, or lines. There are couples dances intermixed with the group dances, and couples should interact extensively with other couples. In fact, it is considered ill-mannered to dance with the same partner all evening. Everyone has a social obligation to mingle with others and make certain they are having an enjoyable time as well."

I raised my eyebrows. "Are you serious?"

"Yes, quite."

"You mean you're going to be dancing with other guys?"

"Yes, and you'll be expected to dance with the other ladies, so I need to teach you a few things. First, when you ask a lady to dance, you should say, 'May I have the *honor* of this dance'? You don't want to say, 'May I have the *pleasure* of this dance?' That phrase doesn't become a gentleman. Next, you must lead a lady lightly and gently. While you're dancing, you don't want to caper about, or sway your body to and fro. One must dance quietly, from the hips downward." Ellie danced lightly across the room, demonstrating as she talked. "Lastly, when a dance is completed, never abandon a lady on the dance floor. Offer her your arm and escort her back to her seat, or ask her to accompany you for some refreshment."

"Like that's going to happen," I muttered under my breath.

I must have had a dazed expression on my face, because Ellie stopped in front of me and asked, "Are you listening? This is quite a formal affair with strict rules of social behavior. Trust me, you'll want to be prepared."

"Ellie, I don't even know how to dance, except for the waltz, which I'm far from having mastered."

"Don't worry. I'll teach you the dancing part next. Let's practice the asking part first."

"What if I don't want to ask anyone else? Can't I just stand there and watch you?"

"If you did that, everyone would think you're an ill-bred gentleman without an ounce of common courtesy. Every fine fellow should do his part to ensure there are no wallflowers at a ball. And you, my darling," —Ellie touched my chest with her finger— "must do your part as well."

"Now, if for some reason you stop dancing during the middle of a song," she continued, "move off the dance floor before stopping, so the couple behind you doesn't take a fall by crashing into you. Let's work on the quadrille and the Virginia reel, the main group dances. If we have time after that, I'll show you more. For many of the dances, the dance master will call out the steps. If you listen and follow your partner, you'll be fine. The quadrille is done with four couples in a square formation with twelve feet open in the center. You stand there, and I'll be across from you, over here."

Ellie taught me the various dance steps and maneuvers until terms like "dos–à-dos," "left hand around," "forward and back," and "two hands around" spun through my head. This dance lesson, which I noticed she thoroughly enjoyed, tortured me for hours. After going left when I should have gone right during the Virginia reel, I almost knocked her off her feet. It had to have been the hundredth time I'd messed up. I shook my head and said, "Ellie, it's no good. I'll never pass for a gentleman."

Mary, who was sitting on a chair behind me, said, "Now Mr. Joseph, don't you go frettin' none. You got all the fixin's to make a fine gentleman. A little spit and polish is all you need. Keep practicin' and you'll see."

I slumped into the chair next to her. "It's going to take a lot more than practice."

Ellie took a deep breath and sat. "Perhaps we should retire for the night. We do have all day tomorrow."

EIGHT
All in One Night

They showed me to the guest room, and I snatched a quick good-night kiss from Ellie when Mary turned her back. With the time travel it had been an extra long day, and I looked forward to a full night of sleep. As soon as my head hit the pillow, I was out.

But Archidus had other plans for me, rudely interrupting my happy dreams. A disturbing vision began to play out in my mind. The barking of dogs filled the night air, and I saw the German family Garrick and I had helped, running toward a barbed-wire barricade. Ruth stumbled and her husband pulled her to her feet. Behind the dogs, beams of light bounced off the trees. As the dogs closed the distance, their ferocious barking grew louder. Ruth's husband reached the barricade first. He tried to push the wire aside to open a path for his wife and son. A moment later the dogs attacked the little family. Ruth's bloodcurdling scream was the last thing I heard before the coordinates of the counter flashed in my mind—Germany, November 12, 1938.

Shocked, I sat up and got dressed, trying to figure out the best course of action. I could think of no humane way to save the family from the dogs. I would need to go home and get a gun. I pulled out my counter and was about to press the Shuffle button when I remembered Ellie. I didn't like the thought of leaving her here, though if something were to happen to me, it would probably be best if she remained in 1863. Still, I couldn't leave without telling her I was going. I would never want her to wonder, even for a minute, if I'd intentionally abandoned her.

I opened her door and walked to her bedside. The pale moonlight coming through the window made it easy to find her in the darkness. I longed to linger and watch her sleep, but the urge to get to Germany and save Ruth's family consumed me. I settled for leaning over Ellie's bed and brushing her lips with a kiss. She stirred, stretching one arm above her head and yawning.

Suddenly, her eyes flew open. "What are you doing?" she asked.

"I've got to go for a minute. It's one of the other Keepers—she's in trouble at the German border in 1938. I didn't want to leave without telling you where I was going. Will you be okay without me for a few minutes?"

"Yes, but do make certain you come back for me. I couldn't bear the thought of being left here alone," Ellie said sleepily.

"I'll always come back for you."

During my shuffle time, I came up with a strategy for handling the situation in Germany. As soon as I reappeared in my house, I pulled out the Nazi trench coat and hat. Perhaps if I looked like one of them, they'd think twice before gunning me down. I checked the pocket for the handgun—still there. Not sure if I'd have time to reload, I put one of the Mexican vaqueros' six-shooters in the other pocket.

I ran out to the shop and dug through the tools, finally finding what I wanted—heavy-duty wire cutters. Thinking of where and when I wanted to appear, I set the coordinates, then pressed Shuffle and Go. My Nazi coat drew some nasty looks when I appeared on Main Street in a small Pennsylvania town in the 1950s. Other than that, I arrived in the German forest without incident at the location that would give me the best shot at the attack dogs. I checked both handguns, deciding to use the six-shooter first. I tucked the Luger pistol into my belt and waited. I heard the dogs barking in the distance, but the flashlights weren't yet visible as Ruth's family raced toward the border.

As they passed my hiding place, I called out, "Ruth!" Startled, she screamed and stopped running. Stepping from behind the tree, I handed her husband the tool. "Wire cutters, for the fence. Hurry!"

I watched the family's progress. With the wire cutters, they were well into the barricade when the dogs came into range. I took aim and pulled the trigger. My first shot missed, but the second one dropped a dog to the ground and left him whining in pain. The last dog continued racing toward its quarry. I fired two more times before hitting him.

I wiped the back of my hand across my sweaty brow and lowered my head in shame. The whimpers of the dying dogs were like a knife to my heart. But I couldn't justify using any of my precious ammunition to put them out of their misery until I knew Ruth had safely escaped Germany.

The family was halfway through the elaborate barricade when three German soldiers came into view. I couldn't stomach the idea of shooting them, like I had the dogs, so I picked up a heavy branch with my left hand. If non-lethal force failed, I still had the guns as backup.

I was working out the kinks in my plan when Garrick appeared directly in front of the Germans. Unarmed, he engaged them in a fistfight. I rushed into the fray. Two soldiers were exchanging blows with Garrick. In the random light of the fallen flashlights,

I saw the third soldier draw his gun. He yelled to his comrades in German while taking aim at Garrick. Instinctively, I raised my gun and fired at point-blank range. The German crumpled to the forest floor. I cast the empty six-shooter aside and swung the branch into the nearest soldier, disarming him. My second blow knocked him to his knees as a shot rang out behind me. Turning, I watched in horror as Garrick staggered backward, clutching at his stomach. He fell to the ground, a look of profound shock on his face. The other German soldier grinned, his smug expression illuminated by the glare of a fallen flashlight. I felt a surge of rage when he pointed his gun at Garrick's head. I dropped the branch and drew the Nazi handgun from my belt, then rapidly fired three times into his chest. The impact of the bullets threw him backwards.

A blow between my shoulder blades knocked me to the ground, leaving me gasping for air. I rolled onto my back. My attacker stood above me, holding the branch I'd dropped and shouting in German. Scrambling to the side, I narrowly avoided his next swing. My foot bumped one of the flashlights, sending the beam of light toward the ground at his feet and a pistol that now lay within his reach. He dived for it. Freaked out by what I'd seen happen with Garrick, I emptied my handgun into the last soldier. Then I slowly sat up. Blood and carnage surrounded me, and the silence of death hung in the air. Even the dogs had quit whining.

A groan from Garrick brought me out of my stupor. I returned the pistol to my pocket and crawled toward him.

"Harper, help me!" he gasped.

I grabbed a flashlight and touched his shoulder. "Where are you hit?" When I saw the blood flowing from abdomen, I said, "We need to get you to a doctor—a modern one."

"Where's Ruth?"

I raised the light to the narrow gap in the barbed-wire barricade. Ruth and her family were long gone. "She made it out," I said. I turned the light behind me, hoping there wasn't a Sniffer lurking in the woods. Garrick and I didn't have our swords, and he was in no shape to make a run for it.

He clenched his jaw, sucking air between his teeth. "I guess it's time for me to go home. Get my counter from my left pocket."

I turned back to my friend and pulled out his counter. "Where's home, Garrick?"

"Texas A&M in College Station, March 1968. That's northwest of Houston."

"What day in March?"

"Probably the eleventh."

I set his counter and handed it back as more dogs began barking in the distance. "Help me up," Garrick said.

With him nearly doubled over in pain, we disappeared. During our shuffle zones, it was all he could do to stay on his feet and not pass out. We finally appeared in a dark bedroom.

"Let me sit down for a minute," he whispered.

I lowered him onto the edge of the bed. "Should we call an ambulance?"

"It's not far to St. Joseph Hospital in Bryan. You can drive me. Turn on the lamp and get my keys and my wallet off the dresser."

I flipped on the lamp and found a set of keys next to a worn leather wallet. I grabbed them, sending a paper fluttering to the floor. As I picked it up, I read the letterhead and the first line. It looked like a draft summons for the US Army. I set it on the dresser. "Let's go."

"Harper, lose the Nazi coat, would you?"

"Oh yeah." I took off the coat and tossed it on his bed.

Garrick took one look at my frontier get-up and said, "You better keep going. There's a pair of Levi's in the top drawer that are too small for me, and the T-shirts are in the next drawer down."

"We don't have time—"

"Just change, would you?"

I pulled my shirt off. "What about you?"

"I don't have the strength. I'm sure you can come up with something if anyone asks."

After I'd put on Garrick's Levi's and a T-shirt, he pointed to a jacket on the bed. "You can wear my leather jacket. It has good pockets."

Not wanting to waste any more time, I threw on the jacket and stuffed my counter, Garrick's keys, and the wallet into the pockets. Blood had completely soaked his shirtfront, and my patience was running out. "Can we go now?"

"Help me up."

I half dragged Garrick through the two-room apartment to the door. We were on the second floor, and he groaned as we negotiated the stairs. From there it was a short walk to the parking lot. "Which car is it, Garrick?"

"The blue Camaro."

The third car down, parked directly under a streetlight, was a metallic-blue Camaro. "That one?" I said in disbelief at the sight of the mint-condition muscle car.

"My Christmas present to myself. A 1968 Camaro with all the bells and whistles."

"No way. What a sweet ride." I unlocked the passenger door. "Too bad you're going to get blood on the seat."

He rested his forehead against the roof of the car. "Good point, little brother. Go get me some towels and bring me a blanket. I'm getting cold."

"We don't have time for that."

"Get the towels, Harper," Garrick said loudly.

Knowing there was no use arguing with my stubborn friend, I ran back into the apartment and grabbed a handful of towels from the bathroom and a blanket off his bed. When I got back to the car, Garrick's head was still down. I spread the towels on the seat and wrapped the blanket around his shoulders. "You bought a car with white seats? Isn't that impractical, especially in our line of work?"

"Just get me in the car."

Nothing about the situation was funny, but I couldn't keep from chuckling.

It looked like the bullet had gone clear through, exiting from his back. The sight of fresh blood dripping onto the asphalt when he bent to climb into the car sobered me up. I ran to the driver's side and got in. After pushing in the clutch, I turned the key in the ignition. The steering felt heavy when I backed out, and it took me second to realize why. "No power steering, huh?"

Garrick sounded annoyed. "What are you talking about?"

"Oh, nothing." I shifted into first gear and let the clutch out. The car lurched forward and the engine died.

"Don't tell me you're one of those sissy boys who doesn't know how to handle a stick."

I started the engine and pumped the gas pedal. "I can drive a stick. I'm just not used to these ancient clutches."

He let his head fall back and closed his eyes. "By all means, take your time learning my clutch, little brother. It's not like I'm bleeding or anything."

I eased the clutch out, being a little more generous with the gas, and the Camaro zipped across the parking lot. "Where are we going?"

"Turn right and then take the first left at the stop sign. Keep going straight until you get downtown."

"What happened back there? It's not like you to show up for a fight unarmed. How did you miss seeing that guy pull a gun on you? That's the kind of thing I'd do, not you. You're a better fighter than that."

After another ragged breath, Garrick said, "I've got a lot on my mind right now."

"Like what?"

"Rose told me she's pregnant."

I felt my jaw drop. "How did that happen?"

"How, Harper? Me, how else?" I glanced back and forth between him and the road. He dropped his head into his hand. "After you left, I kept seeing her. On Christmas Eve there was an ice storm. The maple tree didn't hold up under the weight, and once the winds came, it split in half. One section of the tree fell onto the house, breaking the window in Rose's room. The crash woke me up and I ran in there in nothing but my trousers to see after her and Davy."

Garrick paused, shaking his head. "After I boarded up the window and took care of the broken glass, it was bitter cold in her room. Davy had slept through it all, and in the candlelight I could see Rose shivering. I pulled the blanket off her bed and wrapped it around her. I only meant to help her get warm and then go back upstairs." Garrick sighed. "But somehow . . . I knew Rose wasn't that kind of woman, and I should have know better, but . . ."

I looked over at him. "That's bad. What are you going to do now?"

He moaned, whether from physical or mental anguish, I didn't know. "It *was* bad. I should have shown more respect for her. I should have been the one to be strong, but I wasn't.

She looked so beautiful and I was so weak." In the light of the passing street lamps, I saw Garrick lean his head back and close his eyes.

We drove the rest of the way in silence. No wonder he had seemed so distracted and fought so poorly. I drove into the town of Bryan and found St. Joseph Hospital—a three-story brick building. It looked surprisingly small, but maybe that's what you got in 1968. I parked next to the entrance and helped Garrick out of the car. As soon as we stepped inside, I yelled to the receptionist, "We need help. My brother's been shot."

She sprang into action, calling for assistance before pushing a wheelchair toward him. Within minutes, two nurses whisked him through the large double doors.

"Wait," Garrick said. "Come 'ere, little brother." The nurse stopped, and I ran to see what he needed. He grunted in pain as he pulled his bloodstained counter from his pocket and handed it to me. "Take care of that."

"Sure thing, bro." I turned to the nurse. "Will you let me know when I can see him?"

"We need you to fill out the registration papers and then you can sit in the waiting room. Someone will come get you when he's ready for visitors."

The receptionist held out a clipboard with a carbon-copy form. "Y'all may not know all the information, but if you could fill out what you can I'd appreciate it."

"No problem," I mumbled, taking it from her.

Walking past her desk, I surveyed the ancient typewriter and the elaborate yet bulky phone system. I found the waiting room and looked at the first line of the form. It asked for the patient's last name, first name, and then middle initial. *Great,* I thought. *I can't even get the first line done.* I had never really thought about Garrick's last name. He was always just Garrick.

Remembering the wallet in my pocket, I pulled it out and found his driver's license. Eastman, Garrick A. *Good, one line done.* I copied the address from his license onto the form and found insurance information on a card in his wallet. I left the lines blank for "Description of the accident." I didn't want to risk saying something different than what Garrick might say. When I'd done all I could, I returned the form to the receptionist.

Around five o'clock in the morning, a nurse reported that my "brother" had been taken into surgery. Exhausted, I slumped back in the uncomfortable chair and dozed, but with two expectant fathers pacing the waiting room and talking about their wives who were in labor, quality sleep was hard to come by.

Hours later, the nurse finally took me up to Garrick's room. When I pulled a chair next to his bed, he opened his eyes. "How are you feeling?" I asked.

"I've seen better days," he said with a crooked grin. "Doc says I got lucky. It was a pretty clean shot, went straight through. They removed my spleen and repaired the damage to my intestines, but the bullet missed all the other major organs and my spine. It looks like I'll live."

I took a deep breath. "I'm glad to hear it." I had something on my mind and figured now was as good a time as any. "Do you think there was a Sniffer behind the attack on Ruth's family?"

"I didn't see one in the vision Archidus sent me, so I doubt it."

I sighed. "I'd hate to leave you alone while you're injured if a Sniffer might have followed us."

"I'll be fine. I haven't had one follow me home yet."

I nodded, hoping he was right.

Garrick tried to turn on his side, then winced and took a deep breath. "I've been doing some thinking. When I get out of here I'm going back to Rose, and I'm asking her to marry me."

"Will you tell her about the counter?"

"Maybe eventually. But the pregnancy is putting a strain on her, so I don't want to bring it up now."

"What about your age difference?"

"She's only two years older than I am."

"For now. Won't you stay the same, while she ages?"

Garrick scratched his chin. "Hmm. You've got a good point there. I hadn't thought about that, but I'll figure something out."

I used money from his wallet to buy breakfast and a newspaper. Garrick and I were busy reading the sports section when a slightly overweight older woman in her early fifties marched into the room and bent to give him a hug.

"Hello, Mother," he said. "How did you know I was here?"

"The hospital called me, but I should be asking why *you* didn't call me."

"Sorry. I didn't think about it with the surgery and all. I would have gotten around to it."

"I want to know where you were and what you were doing that you got shot, but I suppose that can wait until your company leaves. Who's this?" She smiled at me from across the room.

"This is my little bro—"

"I'm Chase Harper," I interrupted, "a friend of Garrick's." The doctors must have drugged him up pretty good or he wouldn't have started his typical introduction of me.

"It's nice to meet you, Chase. I hear you're the one who brought him in last night. The nurse thought you two were brothers. I wonder where she ever got that idea. Although, I suppose you do look a little alike." Garrick's mother glanced back and forth between us.

She fussed with his blanket. "Why haven't you shaved? You know I don't like beards."

He rolled his eyes, and I had to cough to cover my laugh.

"My razor broke," he mumbled.

"That's what a drug store is for," his mother said. "You have that sporty new car, so I know you have enough money for a razor blade. You should take better care of yourself if you don't want to be a bachelor forever. You know I wish you'd settle down. I'm not getting any younger, and I'd like to see my Garrick grandbabies before I'm too old to play with them."

He closed his eyes. "Mother, please. I don't want to hear lecture number forty-nine right now."

"Very well." She sat in the chair next to the bed. "I talked with the doctor, and at the earliest, you'll be released from the hospital in a week. After that, I think you should come home for a while. You know, there's a new kindergarten teacher at the elementary school in town. Her name is Mandy. She's around your age and pretty as can be. Hair as yellow as a wheat field and eyes as blue as the sky. I told her about you last week after our Sunday service and she's excited to meet you. I think you'd like her."

"No, I'll be fine. I wish you'd stop trying to find me a wife, especially right now. I've got other things to take care of and I can't come home. I'm sorry, Mother, but I'll have to meet her another time."

"Then I should stay with you for a while, until you're back on your feet. No doubt you'll need help doing your laundry, grocery shopping, and cooking meals."

I watched Garrick and could tell it was the cooking meals part that swayed him. What son can resist his mother's cooking?

"Okay, but only for a few days," he said finally. "Dad won't know what to do without you."

"Don't worry about your father—he'll be fine. Plus, your sister is planning to look in on him."

All day I had alternated between worrying about Garrick's situation with Rose and thinking about Ellie. I couldn't believe the mess Garrick had got himself into. Hadn't I told him to be careful? But there was nothing I could do about it; he would have to figure this one out on his own. Besides, I was anxious to get back to Ellie. It bothered me that I'd left her in 1863—a time that was now history. I knew it was all mental, but I preferred to leave her in 2012 rather than anywhere in the past.

I pulled my counter and the Camaro keys out of the pocket of the leather jacket and set it next to Garrick's bed. "I should probably get going. Your wallet and stuff are in the pocket. Thanks for letting me use your jacket. I'll leave your car at your apartment. When should I come visit again?"

"Two weeks or so. Hopefully I'll be healed up by then. Thanks, Harper, for everything."

"You're welcome. Take care of yourself. It was nice meeting you, Mrs. Eastman," I said, then left the room.

"Thank you," his mother called after me.

Anxious to get back to Ellie, I hurried through the hospital wing. I located Garrick's Camaro, which sparkled in the Texas sunshine, and retraced the route from the night before. I took the stairs two at a time, unlocked the door to Garrick's apartment, and slipped inside. What a mess! In the light of day, I could see old pizza boxes and Popsicle wrappers spread around the kitchen, as well as a trail of clothes leading from his bedroom to the bathroom.

I wondered which lecture he'd get when his mother saw this disaster. I changed my clothes and was about to leave when my conscience stopped me. The brotherly thing to do would be to clean up. I gathered all the trash and ran it to the dumpster, then piled all the dishes in the sink and put the dirty clothes in the hamper.

With the apartment looking halfway respectable, I pulled out my counter and carefully set the globe and date dials.

Since I had taken a detour to get the wire cutters, the Return button would take me back to my house instead of Boston. I didn't know what time I'd left Ellie, but I hoped it was after midnight. I set the date for December 31, 1863. Concentrating on the position of the moonlight I'd seen streaming into her room, I pressed Shuffle and Go. I worked my way through five nondescript shuffle zones before appearing in Ellie's bedroom.

Her eyes fluttered open as I stepped toward her. "That was quick," she said, smiling at me.

"Good, I like quick."

"Tell me what happened."

Once I began talking, weariness from the events of the past several hours caught up to me. I didn't make it past having to shoot the dogs before I sat on the edge of her bed and dropped the Nazi coat on the floor. I hesitated when I got to my triple homicide. With everything that had happened with Garrick, I hadn't yet internalized what I'd done. Although I worried Ellie would be repulsed by my actions, I didn't hold back. I confessed to killing the three soldiers and then told her I was sorry.

"Oh, Chase, I hate to think of you in so much danger," she replied. "It makes me anxious."

"Maybe I shouldn't be telling you all this. I don't want you worrying when there's nothing you can do about it."

"You should tell me. I'd much rather know everything and face it head on than worry about what I don't know or what you aren't saying. I'm certain my imagination would run away with itself and make everything seem much worse."

"I do need someone I can talk to, because right now I feel sick inside. I almost wish I wouldn't have pulled the trigger on those soldiers."

"Chase, don't say that. If you hadn't pulled the trigger, what would have happened?"

I thought for a moment. "Garrick would be dead. I might be dead. Ruth's family would have been captured. And the Nazis would have three counters."

"It's quite obvious you did the right thing," Ellie said.

"You make it sound so cut and dry, but it goes against my nature to kill like that."

"I suppose that kind nature of yours is what endears me to you. But I do hate to see you agonizing over something that circumstance forced upon you." She reached over to hold my hand, and I looked at her in the moonlight. "I'd rather love a fighter than risk losing the man I love."

I smiled back at her, then bent to grab the cursed Nazi coat. "I'd better let you get some sleep."

NINE
The Ball

The next morning after breakfast, Ellie announced she had business to attend to in town. I offered to go with her, but she said there was no need. Before Mary could suggest I make myself useful, I went to finish chopping her wood. Fortunately, I had split the majority of it the day before, because every swing of the ax sent pain shooting through my back where the Nazi had hit me. Slowly but surely, I worked my way through the remainder of the pile, and there were only a few logs left when Ellie returned home.

"I thought I heard you back here," she said, walking around the side of the house.

I leaned on the ax handle and watched her step lightly through the snow. "How's your morning going?"

She smiled. "Very well, thank you. I delivered my resignation letter to the school board and converted all my savings into gold and silver coins. It isn't much, but hopefully it will help you pay my hospital bills. Plus, I arranged a cab ride for us to the ball tonight."

I slowly raised the ax for another swing. "Sounds productive."

She watched me. "Are you hurt?"

"Not bad."

"What happened?"

"I got hit in the back last night. It'll be better in a few days."

She set her purse on the porch step. "Well, let me help you then."

"You don't have to."

She picked up a log. "Nonsense. I insist." Ellie had most of the wood stacked by the time I finished the splitting. It took me an embarrassingly long time to split the last few logs. Good thing Garrick wasn't here or I never would've heard the end of it. But then I smiled. Come to think of it, in his current condition he wouldn't even be keeping up with my snail's pace.

When the last of the wood was stacked, Ellie said, "Come in and I'll fix you something to eat. Then we can practice the dance steps."

"Do I have to?" I mumbled.

"Of course. We'll have a grand time." She slipped her arm through mine and propelled me toward the house.

I leaned the other way, toward the shed. "Gotta put the ax away."

"Well, hurry. I want plenty of time to practice before we need to get ready."

I took my time eating, but Ellie couldn't be fooled. "Why are you chewing so slowly?" she asked. "Does my cooking not suit you, or are you simply attempting to delay our practice?"

I smiled and shoveled in the next bite with gusto. "The cooking suits me fine. It's the dancing that's got my stomach in knots. I definitely admire how well you adjusted to modern life. I doubt I'll be able to blend in as well as you did."

"I'm certain you'll do better than you think."

I scraped the last of my meal onto my fork and into my mouth. "Okay, I'm ready. Let's do this!"

Once I decided to put a wholehearted effort into learning the dance steps and the culture, I actually enjoyed myself. After a couple of hours, Ellie announced it was time for her to get ready. She handed me the shirt, shoes, vest, and suit I was to wear, and I went into the guest room and laid the clothes on the bed. As I started to take off my shirt, I caught a whiff of myself and realized I needed a shower. Not wanting to bathe 1800s style, I pulled out my counter, set it for home, and pressed Shuffle and then Go.

I endured the five shuffle zones before appearing in my bedroom. Although I knew minimal time would pass while I was gone, I hurried. I tossed my Under Armour in the dirty-clothes basket, but I'd have to put on everything else for the return trip. I showered and shaved, brushed my teeth, combed my hair, put on deodorant, and sprayed on a little AXE. "Much better," I said to the mirror image of myself.

After pulling on my Erie Canal clothes, I scavenged through my closet. When I'd tried on Ellie's father's shoes, they were a little big. As it was, I had enough problems executing the dance steps without stumbling over my shoes. I found my black dress shoes, pulled out the counter, and pressed Shuffle and Return. Considering how far I could travel with the counter, and with such ease, I shouldn't have been bothered by the shuffle zones. Yet there were times, like this one, when it felt like an inconvenience.

Finally, I arrived back in the guest bedroom. I took off my clothes and carefully put on the fancy, three-piece dress suit. I left Ellie's father's shoes on the bed and put on my own. *Do people even notice shoes, anyway?* I thought. Hopefully they wouldn't look too closely at mine tonight. When I got to the cravat, I felt like a kindergartner tying my sneakers for the first time. After an unsuccessful attempt, I left it hanging loose and unbuttoned the collar. *May as well postpone the inevitable choking as long as possible.*

When I walked into the kitchen, Mary clapped her hands together and smiled. "My, oh my, would you look at that? You do clean up like a regular gentleman, Mr. Joseph."

Smiling, I pulled out a chair and sat at the table. "Thank you, Mary. Hopefully, I can dance like one, too."

She laughed. "Oh, you'll do right fine. Don't you go frettin' over it none."

A while later, Ellie rushed down the stairs wearing a dress that was full of ruffles and tied with a black sash. It had a wide hoop skirt, which must have been in style in 1863. Her hair was piled on her head in an intricate arrangement of braids and curls. As soon as she entered the kitchen, she said, "Oh, I forgot my black dress cape."

"You want me to get it?" Mary asked.

"Do you mind? It's on the bed."

"Not at all, Miss Ellie," Mary said, leaving the kitchen.

I stood up as Ellie approached me. "Wow! You look amazing."

She smiled and handed me two pairs of white gloves. "Thank you. These are for you."

"Why two?"

"One should always carry an extra pair in case the first one gets soiled from the refreshments or stained from touching the fabric of a dark dress. Put them in your suit pocket." She sniffed me. "Did you go shower?"

I spread my hands. "What kind of gentleman would I be if I took you on a date stinking like a dog?"

"Land sakes, you smell nice, and you look downright charming. I reckon all the girls will be setting their caps for you tonight."

Mary bustled through the kitchen, holding the black cape. "Here you are, Miss Ellie."

A knock sounded at the door. "That must be our cab." Ellie slipped the cape over her shoulders and walked toward the door.

I said good night to Mary, then followed Ellie out.

The cab was a lightweight carriage pulled by a single horse. The driver climbed onto a platform in the back and picked up the reins. I offered Ellie my hand, and she held it as she stepped into the carriage. Once we were seated, the driver snapped his whip and the horse trotted down the cobblestone street.

Ellie radiated excitement. "Chase, I'm so happy we decided to do this."

I, on the other hand, bounced my knee and took a deep breath, trying to calm my frayed nerves. "I'm afraid I'll make a fool of myself and embarrass you."

She wrapped her arm through mine and squeezed. "You won't. I'm sure we'll have a pleasant evening."

The ride to the hall in downtown Boston wasn't nearly long enough. I helped Ellie out of the cab and watched as she handed the driver a coin from her purse. He scowled at me before driving away.

"Did you see the look that guy gave me?" I whispered to her. "I'm guessing a proper gentleman would have paid the cab fare."

She slipped her arm through mine. "That is true, but it doesn't matter what the cab driver thinks." She nudged me as we entered the hall. "You'll want to put your gloves on now."

I fished a pair of white gloves out of my pocket and slid them on. They looked ridiculous to me, but a quick glance at the other gents revealed I wasn't alone in this foolishness. The ball opened with the grand march, which I danced with Ellie. I followed the guy in front of me, carefully imitating him. After the grand march, the music began for the second dance. Before Ellie and I were off the dance floor, a guy walked up to her and asked her to dance. I felt a little chagrined at having my girlfriend snatched out of my hands so quickly, but I'd expected it, so I relinquished my hold on her. As Ellie slipped her arm through his and walked away, she turned her head and mouthed, "Ask someone."

Instead, I hung back and observed. The orchestra seemed to alternate between couples dances and group dances. For the next three songs, I leaned against one of the pillars on the edge of the dance floor. Ellie never made it back to my side. Following each dance, her partner would begin to escort her in my direction. But each time another guy intercepted her, asking her to dance. I had to work at keeping my emotions in check when I saw her being passed from one guy to the next. That was their custom, I had to remind myself. Everyone at the ball was changing partners so fast it made my head spin. If you hadn't watched closely during the grand march, you'd never know which man had attended the ball with which woman.

I had my hands in my pockets and my posture was quickly deteriorating into a slouch when a woman with auburn hair and a spunky personality walked over to me.

"Good evening, sir. I don't believe we've met. I'm Jane Brody." She extended her hand.

I briefly held her hand and did an awkward little bow. "Hello, I'm Chase Harper."

"I don't believe that pillar is in any danger of collapsing tonight, Mr. Harper. Certainly it will hold should you wish to partake in the festivities."

I quickly pulled myself up straight. "Yeah, I suppose you're right."

She tapped her gloves against her open palm and asked, "You're not from around here, are you?"

"No, I'm from out west."

Glancing over Jane's shoulder I saw the dance had ended and that Ellie was again being escorted in my direction. I was hoping she'd finally make it back to me, when someone stopped her. This time I recognized the gentleman—Walt Griffith, Ellie's former beau and the man I'd seen pick her up from her Boston home during one of my reconnaissance missions last fall. I smiled gallantly and turned my full attention on Jane. "May I have the honor of this dance?" I asked, extending my hand as regally as I could.

She placed her hand in mine. "Why certainly. I thought you'd never ask."

I led her onto the dance floor, trying to figure out what dance I'd asked her to do with me. Based on what I'd learned this afternoon, it looked like a polka. I angled my way toward Ellie and Walt, intending to keep an eye on them. I got in position and began dancing my way around the ballroom. Unfortunately, the need to concentrate on where I put my feet kept me from watching Ellie as I'd intended. I did happen to make eye contact with her at one point, during which she flashed me an encouraging smile.

"Mr. Harper, I must admit, I've never been in the company of a finer-smelling gentleman."

Maybe I'd gone a little overboard by spraying on the AXE. I didn't know quite how to reply to her comment, except to say thanks.

"However do you avoid perspiring during such activity?" she wondered aloud.

"It takes a little more than the polka to make me sweat." While Jane laughed, I turned my head and rolled my eyes at my stupid comment. "Tell me about yourself, Jane. What do you like to do?" I asked, hoping to turn the topic of conversation away from me.

She smiled up at me. "My, but it is refreshing to hear a gentleman address me by my given name."

Not sure if Jane Brody meant that as a sarcastic remark or a genuine observation, I said, "I'm sorry, Miss Brody."

"I assure you, no apology is necessary, Mr. Harper." Jane proceeded to tell me about her involvement in the women's rights movement and the Abolitionist Society.

When the song ended, I remembered my manners and offered to escort her to the refreshment table. She accepted, slipping her hand through my arm. While we walked, I scanned the dance floor for Ellie. Luckily for me, she and Walt were headed in the same direction. She greeted Jane and said, "Walt, I'd like to introduce you to Mr. Chase Harper. Mr. Harper is visiting from out west. Mr. Harper, this is Mr. Walt Griffith. Mr. Griffith is studying to be a doctor and is in his final year of medical school."

When we shook hands, I might have squeezed his a little harder than necessary, but Walt made no attempt at hiding his disgust as he gave me a complete look-over. I'll admit I probably did some sizing up, too.

"What do you do out west, Mr. Harper?" he asked condescendingly.

"Horses. Barn building. Some farming."

Walt raised his eyebrows. "Interesting. How long will you be in Boston?"

"Not long. We'll be leaving in a day or so." While we'd been talking, Jane had left my side and joined another conversation. On the dance floor they completed a group dance, and the orchestra began playing a tempo I recognized. Of all the dances I'd learned so far, it was my favorite.

"We?" Walt said pointedly.

"Ellie and I" was my reply. Then I turned to her. "Hey, Ellie, it's the waltz. Do you wanna dance?"

Chuckling as if I'd made some private joke, she extended her gloved hand and curtsied. "Why certainly, Mr. Harper."

Walking past the scowling Walt, I led her onto the dance floor. "What's so funny?"

Smiling, she mimicked me. "Hey, Ellie, it's the waltz. Do you wanna dance?"

I grimaced and raised my fist to my forehead. "Oh yeah, I forgot the 'may I have the honor of this dance' part."

"That's quite all right, darling. I knew what you meant."

I couldn't resist holding her close. The flush of her cheeks left me fighting the urge to kiss her right then and there.

"Did Jane ask you to dance or did you ask her?" Ellie said.

I smiled. "I asked her, after she flirted with me, of course. Why?"

"She's only the boldest, most outspoken lady in all of Boston. I wouldn't have put it past her to be the one to ask you. She's forever the subject of gossip in every social circle. Jane's already twenty-four, you know. The speculation is she'll certainly be an old spinster."

"That's too bad. I thought she was pretty nice."

"Oh yes. But I expect Jane would do better in your society. She's far too liberal in her thinking for most of the men around here. I imagine she found your personality quite refreshing."

I slowed our pace and leaned toward Ellie, nearly kissing her ear as I whispered, "That's what all the girls say—I have a refreshing personality." I lingered there, savoring the feel of her in my arms.

Ellie pulled back. "Chase, people are looking. They're going to think you're an ill-bred scoundrel, acting like this."

"I don't care. Let them think whatever they want," I said, mesmerized by her beauty.

"Undoubtedly, they will next be thinking poorly of me for consorting with such a scoundrel."

"Sorry." I straightened my posture. "I hadn't thought of that."

She smiled. "You may not care about your reputation, but I should like to hang onto the shred of mine that is left intact."

"Why do you say that?"

"Word will eventually get around that I've left town with you. Surely you can imagine what people will say."

"Hmm," I mumbled, then finished out the dance in thoughtful silence.

Following the waltz, some other guy whisked Ellie away for the next dance. I did my social duty and found a few wallflowers to ask, successfully dancing the Virginia reel and the quadrille. One of the girls I asked was pretty uncoordinated, which made for a near disaster considering my amateur status. A few Union soldiers were in attendance, sporting medals of honor pinned to their neatly pressed blue uniforms. One moved with a distinct limp and wasn't dancing, so I walked over and introduced myself.

Richard Hancock had joined the army when the war first broke out. He had seen a bit of action and was discharged when a bullet wound in his knee failed to heal. I took the opportunity to do a little research for my history assignment and talked with him about life in the army and the conditions in the South compared to the North. He had a wealth of information and experiences, which he seemed eager to share. He acted older and more sober than a typical twenty-year-old. While we talked, a group of giggling ladies stared at me. One of them was Jane Brody, and the attention left me feeling self-conscious. Hopefully they weren't laughing at some stupid mistake I didn't even realize I'd made.

When Walt asked Ellie for a second dance, I figured that entitled me to a second as well. Without delay, I thanked Richard for his time and positioned myself to intercept her as she exited the dance floor. When the song ended, I walked over to them and said with all the gentlemanly flourish I could muster, "Miss Williams, may I please have the honor of accompanying you in the next dance?"

"Most certainly, Mr. Harper. Thank you, Mr. Griffith," she said, taking her leave of Walt before turning to me.

She slipped her gloved hand into mine, and I led her back onto the dance floor. The next dance was the gallop, the fastest paced of all the dances, and the one I'd had the most difficulty mastering. I wouldn't have dared ask anyone else to dance the gallop. But with a little coaching from Ellie, I successfully negotiated the dance floor. When the song came to an end, we were both winded.

Another guy approached Ellie to ask for the next dance, but she said, "I'm sorry, but I must refuse. I'm far too fatigued to dance again right now."

He didn't seem bothered by that and found someone else to ask. After he left, she said, "I'm thirsty. Should we get some refreshment?"

"Sounds good to me."

They rang in the New Year with a toast that it would be the year the war was won. I frowned, knowing they would be disappointed. As the last song ended, the guests began collecting their cloaks and hats.

"Why is everyone in such a hurry?" I asked Ellie. "I thought people would hang around and socialize a little."

She leaned her head toward me. "Being one of the last to leave implies you aren't accustomed to such activities and are trying to prolong the event."

"Oh, should we go then?"

"Yes." She put on her cloak and slid her hand through my arm.

A line of cabs waited along the street for their customers, and we were quickly on our way back to Ellie's house. During the cab ride, she pulled a coin out of her purse and handed it to me, smiling. "For the cab driver."

I laughed. "Thanks. You'll have me whipped into shape yet."

When we arrived, I helped her from the carriage and handed the driver the coin. "Thank you, sir."

We walked inside and found Mary asleep on the chair in the parlor. "She must have tried to wait up for us," Ellie whispered.

TEN
Confrontation

I kicked the snow off my boots and entered the kitchen with an armful of wood. I heard Ellie arguing with someone in the parlor and recognized the voice from the night before.

"Ellie, what's gotten into you?" Walt Griffith said. "I can't believe you'd make plans to run off with that drifter. You heard what he said last night. He doesn't have a home, a decent trade, or even a well-thought-out plan for his future. Barn building? That will never make him any money. And although it's a noble profession, the life of a farmer isn't an easy one. Spare me the agony of watching you break your back as a farmer's wife. You could do so much better for yourself. Has he even proposed marriage to you?"

"Not exactly. But he's very smart and incredibly kind," Ellie said. "You don't know him."

"I wouldn't want to. It's obvious he lacks social refinement, and the familiar way he speaks to and interacts with you is completely devoid of propriety. For your own sake, I must insist you reconsider my offer."

"And what of Amanda Berkshire? Are you not courting her?"

"She seems to have set her cap for me, but my feelings for her are shallow at best. I was only keeping company with her in hopes of making you envious. I had hoped you'd fear me lost and change your mind in regards to my proposal."

"Mr. Griffith! How dare you trifle with her heart like that? Now look who's the scoundrel."

"Ellie, forgive me, but I've never felt this way about anyone else. You'll be making a terrible mistake if you leave with that man."

"You'll not be changing my mind, Mr. Griffith, so I think you'd best be on your way."

"No, Ellie, I refuse to leave until I've convinced you of the folly of your decision. The fact that he's asked you to travel west with him, unwed and unchaperoned, is proof enough that he's no gentleman. You deserve better. I demand to speak with Mr. Harper at once. Where is he?"

Ellie raised her voice. "I don't think that's a good idea. Now, would you please take your leave?"

I decided this was as good a time as any to face the angry ex-boyfriend. As I walked into the parlor, Walt turned to face me and narrowed his eyes.

"Good morning, Mr. Harper."

"Good morning to you, Mr. Griffith," I said with a hint of sarcasm. "I believe the lady asked you to leave."

"May I have a word with you outside?"

"Sure," I replied.

He turned and opened the door, then stepped onto the porch. As I passed Ellie, she touched my arm. I glanced at her and she whispered, "Please be nice."

"Aren't I always?" I gave her a smile before I stepped outside and closed the door behind me. "What do you want to talk about?"

"Mr. Harper, I wish to plead to your good conscience, not to take Ellie gallivanting across the country unescorted. It simply isn't done. You'll make her the laughing stock of Boston and the topic of gossip in every ladies group for weeks to come, possibly years."

"She won't be unescorted," I said. "We've got a short train ride and then we'll be meeting my family. After that, Ellie will be with my mother and sister. I can assure you, my parents are diligent chaperones."

"May I inquire concerning your intentions regarding Miss Williams?"

"No you may not" is what I wanted to say. But thinking of Ellie's reputation, I put some thought into my response. "I intend on marrying Miss Williams when the time is right, and I promise you I'm a complete gentleman when it comes to the more intimate aspects of a relationship."

Griffith said nothing, so I continued. "Since Ellie made it clear she does not intend to marry you, I think what she does in the future is more my concern than yours. If you really care for her, perhaps you will do your part to quiet any gossip that arises." I paused a moment, but when he still didn't say anything, I extended my hand toward him. "Well, have a good day, Mr. Griffith. It's been nice talking to you, but I'd better get back inside."

He shook my hand, his eyes narrowing again. "I'll do what I can to quiet the gossipmongers, but I'd better not find out you lied to me, Mr. Harper." He walked back to his fancy carriage and rode away.

When I stepped through the door, Ellie was biting her lower lip and pacing the entryway.

"Nice guy," I said.

"What happened?"

"Nothing really. We just talked."

"There was no fighting?"

I wrapped my arms around her waist. "No, nothing like that. You would have been proud of me. I told him we're meeting my family and we'll have my mother and sister as chaperones for the journey. I think after what I said, he'll do what he can to stop any gossip concerning you."

"Oh, thank you, Chase."

"Anytime."

"So when did you want to leave?"

"Whenever you do, although I am starving."

Ellie smiled. "Perhaps I should demonstrate the proper way to scramble eggs in a cast-iron skillet."

"Sounds good." I chuckled at the memory of my cooking fiasco with Davy.

After eating a plate of perfectly scrambled eggs, I asked Mary what other jobs she needed done. She sent me out to shovel the walkways. I tipped my hat at two ladies from the Boston Abolitionist Society who stopped by to speak with Ellie and Mary.

That afternoon Ellie condensed her belongings into two bags, and we said goodbye to Mary. After adding my Nazi coat and dress shoes to one of the bags, I carried them out the door and headed toward the hedge I typically used to disappear. Ellie walked in the opposite direction.

"Darling, the train station is this way, remember?" she called to me.

Looking from her to the house, I saw that Mary stood on the porch, watching us. She waved goodbye, and I nodded back at her as I turned and followed Ellie. We walked for nearly ten minutes before locating a secluded location from which to disappear. Ellie slid her arm through mine. I held both bags in one hand while I set the counter coordinates. The air around us shimmered and we disappeared.

Once we arrived in my house, we changed our clothes, and I carried Ellie's bags to the truck. After three days in Boston, my clothes were filthy, so I threw them in the washing machine. Then I sat down at the kitchen table to tackle my homework. I had a math assignment and a report to write for History on the comparable conditions between the North and the South during the Civil War. Been there, done that. Thanks to Richard Hancock, my Union soldier buddy, I had all the information I needed. Ellie had the same assignment, so it would be an easy "A" for her. She joined me at the table a few minutes later with my mom's laptop and we were busy with our reports when my parents got home.

As my mom set a takeout box from a restaurant in the fridge, I asked, "How was the swim meet?"

"Great—Hilhi won. What have you two been up to this afternoon?"

My mom turned to pull a glass from the cupboard and I winked at Ellie. "Not much, just researching the Civil War era for a report for History." Ellie almost burst out laughing and started coughing instead.

"Sounds like a productive evening," my mom said.

"Hi, Chase, Ellie," Dad said, walking through the kitchen toward his office.

"Hey, Dad," I said.

It was late before Ellie and I finished our reports. I helped her save hers on a thumb drive and print it. After spending three days trying to conform to life in the 1860s, I was definitely impressed with how adeptly she had adjusted to the present day.

I drove her to Uncle Steve's and carried her bags to the door. After setting them on the bench, I wrapped my arms around her waist and bent my head to kiss her. "Good night, Ellie."

She broke the kiss to tell me good night. As I started to walk away, she reached out and grabbed my arm. "Chase, thank you for the trip. It meant a lot to me."

I smiled. "You're welcome. It was fun for me, too."

That night I lay awake for hours, haunted by the soldiers I'd killed that night in Germany. The memory of their faces, illuminated by the glare of the flashlights lying in the dirt, beat at my conscience with the force of a jackhammer. I saw no way around what I'd done, but that didn't save me from the disturbing flashbacks. Even in my dreams, the Nazis tormented me. They surrounded my house with their barking dogs. Beams of light bounced in the dark as I frantically searched for the Luger pistol.

"Chase, wake up." Jessica was shaking me.

I bolted upright. "What happened? Where are we?" The light from the hall streamed into my bedroom. Covered in sweat and breathing like I'd just finished a wrestling match, I stared up at my sister. My blankets were a tangled mess, and I shoved them away.

"You're in your room. Were you dreaming? You were yelling stuff about a gun."

I took a deep breath, rubbing the sleep out of my eyes. "What time is it?"

We both looked at the clock on my dresser—4:31 AM.

Jessica sat next to me. "Are you okay? I thought everything would get back to normal now that Ellie is home, but you still seem different to me—kind of distant."

When I didn't answer she said, "You can tell me, Chase. I'm your twin, remember? We share everything. No secrets, right?"

"Yeah, it's just that I've seen some things. Jess, I've done things—bad things. But it's a long, complicated story and I don't want to talk about it tonight. I'll be fine, I promise. Just give me a little time."

"I wish you'd tell me. If you change your mind and want to talk about it, you let me know, okay?"

I nodded.

She leaned over and gave me a hug. "Good night, Chase," she said, then walked out of my room.

I stayed on the edge of my bed, thinking about how my life had changed. Nothing would ever be the same, and I felt like I'd aged five years since finding the counter, instead of five months. What did my future hold? There were no guarantees anymore. Garrick could have died, and next time it might be me.

With the winter formal dance on Saturday, I had to pick up my tux, and Ellie needed to borrow one of Jessica's dresses. I wished I could take her shopping for her own dress, but I was on a strict budget until the medical bills were taken care of. I also wanted to go check on Garrick in 1968. Plus, there was homework—a project due in Shop and an English essay. My to-do list was more than full at the moment.

After wrestling practice, Ellie and I went to my house and she tried on dresses. Insisting I decide for her, she made me sit in the family room and look at each dress after she put it on.

"I like this one," I said on the third one, standing up to walk over to her. It was a dark pink color, with a knee-length skirt made of silky fabric. "Let me try it out," I said, bowing to her. "May I have the honor of this dance, Miss Williams?"

She giggled. "Why certainly, Mr. Harper." She took my hand and stepped into my embrace.

We waltzed a couple of circles around the family room before I stopped and said, "I think this dress will work."

"It's a little short for me."

Still holding her, I said, "I can see why you'd think that, but I sure like it."

"Oh, Chase." She playfully pushed me away. "I'm going to get changed."

I was chuckling to myself when my mom walked in from her shift at the hospital.

"What's so funny?" she asked me.

"Nothing, it's nothing."

"It's got to be something or you wouldn't be grinning from ear to ear. Tell me! After the day I've had, I could use a little humor in my stressful adult life."

"It's Ellie. She said something that struck me as funny, that's all. She's borrowing one of Jessica's dresses, and then I'm taking her back to Adam's house. I'll be home in a little bit." I picked up my keys from the kitchen counter.

"Hurry back. I'm going to start dinner."

After Ellie said hi to my mom, we drove to Adam's. I carried her backpack to her room, then closed the door behind me. Ellie turned, looking surprised. She already knew about Garrick and Rose, so I said, "Do you care if I go from here to check on Garrick?"

"No, that's fine."

I pulled out the counter. "I won't be long." I set the coordinates and thought of Garrick's room during the early morning hours when he would most likely be alone, then pressed Shuffle and Go. My counter had been kind to me lately—every shuffle zone was nonpopulated and relatively safe. Soon I appeared in the other Keeper's room, the gray light of early morning barely visible. He was home from the hospital and sleeping soundly. His room looked neat as a pin. I smiled. His mother must still be in town. An extra blanket lay folded at the bottom of the bed. I rolled it into a pillow and lay down on the floor to rest.

"Harper, when did you get back?" Garrick said, waking me up.

I climbed to my feet. "This morning at dawn. How you feeling, bro?"

"Great, but I'm itching to get out of here. I've been gone so many years, I don't even remember my real life, and to top it off, my girlfriend stopped by yesterday."

After a long pause, during which I changed into Garrick's old clothes, I said, "And how did that go?"

"I didn't know what to say to her. I think we argued before I left, but I can hardly remember now what it was about. She didn't bring it up, either—probably felt sorry for me. Frankly, I wasn't remotely interested in anything she had to say and I wanted to break it off with her, except I knew she'd want a reason. I couldn't very well say, 'I'm going to be a father; and by the way, the mother of my unborn child lives in 1818.' You can imagine how that conversation would have gone over. So I played it cool and got her out of the apartment by telling her I was tired, but she's bound to come back. Of course my mother spent the whole time doing her matchmaking. Now that you're back, maybe we can convince her to leave."

Garrick pulled a clean T-shirt over his head and sat back down. "I've been reading the Bible, and I've spent more time on my knees in the last week, pleading for the Lord's forgiveness, than the rest of my life put together. I can't change what I did in the past, but I can dedicate my future to making it right for Rose and our baby."

I nodded. "I'll do whatever I can to help you."

Garrick smiled. "Thanks." He finished dressing, and when he started to make his bed, I laughed. "Hey, quit laughing," he said. "You don't know my mother. I'll never hear the end of it if I leave this room without making my bed."

"I'll sit back and enjoy the show then. It's not often one gets to see you make a bed."

Garrick threw his pillow at my head, then grabbed his side and winced. "I'm not supposed to drive, so I want you to take me somewhere today."

I stood and set the pillow on his bed. "Sure thing."

With the help of my counter, I reappeared outside the front door. I knocked, and Garrick's mother invited me in and fed us fried eggs and bacon. He spent the whole meal persuading her to go home and check on his dad. Once he convinced her he wouldn't be alone, she relented. Mrs. Eastman packed her things and said goodbye to her son, making him promise to do everything the doctor ordered—no exceptions. When Garrick put his hand behind his back and crossed his fingers, I strained to keep a straight face.

"I promise," he said. "Goodbye, Mother."

"I love you, honey."

Garrick waved as she got in her car and drove away. As soon as she was out of sight, he pulled out the keys to his Camaro and tossed them to me. "Okay, let's go."

"Where?"

"I'll show you. Come on."

After driving for ten minutes, I asked again, "Garrick, where are we going?"

"We're almost there. Turn left at the next intersection and pull into the first driveway on the right."

I looked ahead at the driveway he pointed at. "A jewelry store? Why do you need to go to a jewelry store?"

"For Rose. If I'm going to ask her to marry me, I want to do it right. She deserves a nice ring."

"Won't a ring from here look a little out of place in 1817?"

"It's 1818 now," Garrick said. "I'll get something simple but nice. You'll see."

After an exhausting hour of shopping, he found the ring he wanted. Before I drove him home, we ate burgers and root beer floats at A&W, then filled his car with gas. Looking at the shockingly low price of thirty-four cents a gallon, I said, "Guess how much I paid per gallon to fill up my truck yesterday?"

"I don't know, maybe a dollar?"

"Try $4.29."

Garrick shook his head. "How does a man afford to drive with prices like that?"

"Yeah, tell me about it," I grumbled.

We drove home, and as soon as we were in the apartment, Garrick pulled out his Erie Canal clothes. "Are you coming, Harper?"

"You haven't started the spring digging, have you?"

He sat on the edge of his bed and pulled on his worn leather boots. "We probably won't start any regular digging for another month or two."

"I'll wait a week or so and then I'll come look for you in 1818."

Grinning, he said, "I'll look forward to it. If Rose is willing, I should be a married man by then."

I pointed at him and laughed. "You've got bullet holes in your shirt."

He shook his head. "Thanks, Harper. I hadn't noticed."

I changed my clothes while Garrick locked his apartment. He stuffed his antibiotics and the ring into his pocket and took out his counter. With a salute, he said, "Time to go back, little brother."

ELEVEN
Ambush

I pulled out my counter for the return trip. *Good luck, Garrick.*

After my shuffle zones, I reappeared in Ellie's room and found she had left. That struck me as odd, since she knew I wouldn't be gone long. I walked toward the door as someone on the other side jiggled the knob. Ellie had locked the door. *Strange.* I swung it open.

Adam came in and closed the door behind him. "Why did you lock it?"

"Where's Ellie?" I asked.

"She's downstairs. Weren't you listening? Amanda just yelled that someone was here for her."

"Uh, I was listening to my iPod."

"Dude, we need to talk," Adam said. "I don't want you to freak out or anything, but it's Randy. He came to see Ellie. Last fall, she left so fast they never talked about their breakup."

I tried to reach past Adam to open the door. "No matter where I am, I can't get away from the ex-boyfriends."

Adam blocked me, putting his hand on my chest. "Wait—let me finish. Maybe you and Ellie have always had a thing going, but from Randy's point of view, she was his girlfriend first. On top of that, he's saying you sucker-punched him at the Halloween dance. He thinks Ellie felt sorry for you when you got hurt that night and now you must be twisting it to your advantage. The way he sees it, you're controlling and manipulative."

"What?" I started pacing across Ellie's room.

My cousin paused before continuing. "Dude, you've got to admit it's not normal. You and Ellie are inseparable. Since she showed up last fall, you've completely blown off all your friends, including me. You act like you're obsessed with her."

"Yeah, well, I think the feeling's mutual."

"If that's the case, you've got nothing to worry about. Let him hear it from her and that'll be the end of it."

"Randy's hardheaded—he won't take no for an answer. Plus, Ellie's too nice. She'll tell him to leave, but she'll do it so sweetly he won't get the message. He'll think he's still got a chance with her."

"See? This is what I'm talking about! You're obsessed with her. You're freaking out and she's been down there for like five minutes. Dude, would you sit down and relax? They're just talking!"

"I'm not freaking out!"

"Yes, you are. Just sit."

I perched on the edge of the rocking chair, while Adam stood guard at the door. My knee bounced up and down as I watched the clock tick away the minutes. When my teeth started to ache, I relaxed my jaw. "Are you in on this with Randy?" I asked finally. "Did he send you up here to keep me out of his way?"

"No. I didn't know he was coming over. He told me all this in the weight room last week. Randy's been trying to talk with her for months. After Ellie left he asked Jessica for her number in Boston, but she wouldn't give it to him."

I stood and walked back to the door. "Okay, I'll let them talk, but I want to hear what he's saying. Come on, you've got to be curious."

Adam stared at me for a moment, then opened the door. "Okay, but stay out of it, or you'll only be proving he's right."

We walked into the hall and I heard talking, although the words were indistinguishable. Halfway down the stairs, yet still hidden from Randy and Ellie's view, I eavesdropped on their conversation.

"It's not like that at all," she said. "We— he's not what you think, Randy. You don't know all the facts. There's more to it than that."

"Well, I'm all ears. Why don't you enlighten me? Tell me the situation, so I can understand how he has you wrapped around his finger, doing everything he says. I swear he monopolizes your every waking second, Ellie. He never lets you hang out with other friends. You don't go anywhere without him. I don't know how you can stand it."

"Randy, I think you'd better leave. I've got to get going." Her tone of voice left no doubt that she was done.

"Ellie—"

She gasped. "Unhand me at once."

Gritting my teeth in frustration, I raised my hands and looked at Adam. He frowned and shook his head. "Go ahead."

We both rushed down the last few steps. Randy was squeezing Ellie's arm.

"Randy, I think she asked you to leave," I said, feeling a wave of déjà vu.

"Well, if it isn't the bossy boyfriend himself." He let go of her and turned to me.

She touched my arm. "Chase, are you well? What took so long?"

Realizing she assumed I'd been gone with the counter the whole time, I said, "I'm fine. I was talking to Adam."

Randy scowled. "You're a control freak, Harper. You know that? You're always hanging around. Give the girl a break, would you?"

I glared back at him. "You've got it all wrong, Randy. Unlike you, I follow orders, and I think she asked you to leave."

Adam stepped between us and looked at Randy. "Hey, let's go talk outside."

Before turning to leave, Randy raised a finger. "We'll finish this later, Harper."

They went outside and I turned to check on Ellie. "Sorry about that. He can be a real jerk. He didn't hurt you, did he?"

With a furrowed brow, she rubbed her arm. "I'm fine. I don't understand why he's so angry. We courted for a few weeks at most and I never made him any promises."

"Don't worry about it. I don't think guys are as gentlemanly today as they used to be. Sometimes you have to be really blunt or we just don't get it."

"Will you walk me upstairs before you leave?"

"Yes, ma'am, anything you say."

She smiled. "That's right. You're the one who follows orders."

"At least I try."

I kissed her good night by her bedroom door and left.

Adam passed me on my way out. "I think he's gone, dude. I told him I thought Ellie really liked you and he'd be better off letting it go. But you're right, he is hardheaded. He sure didn't want to take no for an answer."

"He's a jerk. Thanks for your help," I said.

"Sure thing. I like Ellie. She's good for you."

I smiled. "She is, isn't she?"

After discussing our plans for the winter formal, I left his house and crossed the quiet street to where I'd parked my truck. I didn't have a remote, and as I inserted the key in the door lock I heard someone approaching. I turned in time to see Randy rush me. Instinctively, I ducked to avoid his right hook. Catching me off guard, he body-slammed me into the side of the truck. His next blow landed on my jaw, and I tasted blood.

I got my act together and fired three punches into his stomach. But Ellie's words in Boston echoed through my mind. "Please be nice," she had said when I went outside to talk to Walt Griffith. It made her so happy I'd handled it diplomatically, and yet here I was, about to beat the snot out of the next guy.

Grunting in displeasure, I changed my strategy. Randy Jones may have been quicker and faster than me in the past, but he didn't stand a chance now. With everything that had happened lately, I surpassed him in strength, speed, agility, and experience. I endured two more of his wildly thrown punches before I twisted his arm behind his back and pinned him on the pavement. "What are you doing?" I asked.

"You freak," he yelled, struggling against my grip. "Let me go."

"Ellie's done with you. Promise you'll leave her alone."

When he didn't answer, I tugged on his arm, wondering if I'd have to dislocate it before he'd agree. I kept talking through my gritted teeth. "You could have your pick of the girls at Hilhi—you don't need to take mine. Ellie's not your girlfriend. I knew her long before she ever met you, so drop it, okay? It's over." I pulled his arm again, making him wince.

"Whatever," he said.

That would have to do, because right then a car turned onto the street. Within seconds the headlights would reach us and we'd be directly in its path. I jumped to my feet and stretched my hand out to Randy. He scowled at me as he stood, refusing a hand up. The glare of the headlights momentarily blinded me as I stepped back. The car pulled alongside us and slowed.

"Are you guys okay?" a man called out.

"Yeah, were fine," I said. "We're just leaving."

"All right, good night," the man said warily. He drove off slowly and stopped two driveways down.

I backed away from Randy, unsure if he would let the fight end there. When I reached the door to my truck, he skulked away. Turning the key, I sprang the lock and climbed in. A glance in the rearview mirror showed a smear of blood below my lip. After I turned around and drove down the street, I saw Randy getting in his Jeep. That psycho had driven his car around the corner to make it look like he'd left, and then he'd walked back to ambush me.

At home, I walked to the kitchen sink, filled my hands with cool water, and scrubbed the blood off my chin. "What happened now?" my mom asked as she pulled dinner out of the oven.

"What?"

She placed her hands on her hips and stared me down. "The blood on your face. You've got a split lip. I swear, Chase, this is worse than when you were a toddler. Sometimes it feels like you're an accident waiting to happen. Now, tell me the story."

Well, I thought with relief, *finally I can just tell the truth.* "Randy Jones, the ex-boyfriend. That's what happened."

"You got in a fight? Where?"

"On the street, in front of Adam's house."

"What was this fight about?"

I reached for a glass. "Ellie."

"You were fighting over a girl? That is so immature—like caveman behavior."

"I know, Mom, but I didn't start it, I swear. Randy's ticked that Ellie broke up with him, and he wouldn't let it go. Adam even talked to him and we thought it was all good. But he drove his car around the corner, then walked back and jumped me when I left."

My mom was shaking her head. "I can't believe it. Don't take this wrong, because I don't condone that sort of thing, but how did it end? Who won this fight?"

I smiled. "I did, Mom."

She shook her head again. "I don't know if that's good or bad. You didn't hurt him, did you? Am I going to get a call from his parents?"

"Don't worry, Mom. I went easy on him. And I don't think he'll be telling anyone, including his parents."

Worry lines creased her brow. "I don't want you fighting. You need to be solving your problems by talking."

With the counter in my pocket, I thought, *that's not going to happen anytime soon.*

TWELVE
Winter Formal

While I spent the morning working, I counted down the hours until I could meet Ellie. I did the barn chores for my mom and helped my dad in his shop. Then I showered and put on my tux. It must have been my lucky night, because I sweet-talked my dad into letting me borrow his new BMW.

When I got to Adam's place, I watched ESPN with him and Uncle Steve while Ellie got ready. She raised her eyebrows at the sight of my split lip, but didn't say anything until we were alone. In the car, she reached over and brushed her thumb across my mouth. "Did someone hit you?"

I smiled. "It's nothing, I promise. Just a scratch."

"Did you go somewhere last night?"

"No, I went straight home. Seriously, it's nothing to worry about." I didn't want to ruin her night by telling her about the Randy encounter. "Did you get your homework done?"

"Yes, and you?"

I chuckled, relieved she'd let me change the subject. "I'm still working on that."

Adam's date, Rachel, got along great with Ellie, and dinner flew by in a whirl of conversation. We got Adam's version of the Randy saga, as he filled Rachel in on the drama from the night before. But Adam didn't know about the fight, and I certainly didn't plan to bring it up.

We arrived at Hilhi to find the gym packed with students. A mass of snowflake cutouts dangled from the ceiling, and a large banner read, "A Winter Wonderland." Fake snow accented the perimeter of the large room, and winter silhouettes hung on the walls. Like the sparkle of snow in the sunlight, a dusting of glitter covered everything.

After snuggling Ellie during a romantic slow song—twenty-first-century style—I stepped back, squared my shoulders, and bowed. "Miss Williams, may I have the honor of waltzing with you this evening?"

She giggled as she took my hand and dropped into a deep curtsey. "Why certainly, Mr. Harper, I'd be delighted."

I led her to the edge of the dance floor and wrapped my arm around her waist. When we started to dance, I stepped closer. "You don't mind, do you?"

"Not at all," she whispered, leaning in to me. "There's a complete lack of propriety in nearly everyone's dancing. I should say we're rather tame in comparison."

Amused, I glanced across the dance floor. "I see what you mean. But I only care what you think, not anyone else."

"I'm quite content where I am, thank you."

We soon found ourselves in close proximity with Randy and his date. "We should say hello to Randy and Becca. We wouldn't want to seem rude or unsociable," Ellie said, starting to drag me in their direction.

I leaned back to slow her down. "We're not in Boston anymore, and I'm not sure that's such a good idea."

She continued to propel me forward. "Nonsense. Someone has to take the first step in developing a socially comfortable relationship." I gave up resisting and followed, hoping for the best.

"Hello, Randy. Hello, Becca," Ellie said. "I love your dress—it's simply stunning on you."

Becca had U.S. History with us and sat near Ellie. "Thank you," she said. "Same to you . . . you look so pretty. Hi, Chase. I heard you're having an awesome wrestling season. You're undefeated, aren't you?"

"If you don't count a couple of disqualifications at the beginning, I guess I am." I chanced a glance at Randy, who scowled back at me.

Becca held Randy's hand and smiled, clearly oblivious to his animosity. "Well, good luck at state."

I nodded. "Thanks, Becca."

"It's been enjoyable visiting with you, but I believe we're going to get some refreshments. Aren't we, Chase?" Ellie said.

Still annoyed by Randy's accusations the night before, I replied, "Sure. See you guys later," then followed Ellie toward the punch bowl.

When we were out of their hearing range, she said, "Becca was certainly pleasant. But Randy looked like he would have pounced on you if we had lingered any longer. I don't understand why he's so peevish."

"He's just jealous. I'm sure he's never had a girl actually break up with him before."

"You don't say?"

"Yeah, really. He's probably the most popular guy at the school."

"Well, I don't see what all the fuss is about. I found him to be self-centered and a bit too arrogant for my liking."

Suppressing my laughter, I handed Ellie a cup of punch. "I'll second that. If it's okay with you, I'm going to go work with Garrick pretty soon."

She smiled at me over her cup. "Certainly. But that reminds me, I want to give you the money I brought back from Boston. Perhaps it will help."

"I'm sure it will. As much as I like hanging with Garrick, I absolutely hate leaving you."

Ellie's smiled disappeared. "If it's any consolation, I don't fancy you leaving either. I fear you may not return, that something will happen and I'll never know what became of you."

"Nothing will happen to me." I took her empty cup, stacked it with mine, and tossed them in the trash can. "Let's dance again. It's almost over."

During the last song, I whispered, "How did I get lucky enough to be with the prettiest girl here?"

"How would you know I'm the prettiest girl, when you haven't looked at anyone else?"

"My point exactly. There isn't a soul in this gym worth taking my eyes off you for."

"Darling, you are such a flatterer."

"I'm only calling it as I see it."

The dance ended and I drove Ellie to Adam's house. Then I went home, checked in with my parents, and got ready for bed. But with thoughts of Ellie running rampant through my mind, I couldn't sleep.

My attention eventually turned to Garrick—the married man. Would he tell Rose about the counter? Surely she'd like the diamond ring. How couldn't she? Davy would be ecstatic to have Garrick for a father. They were good together.

Suddenly, I really wanted to see what 1818 would look like with Garrick married to Rose, and Davy trailing behind his new pa. Deciding not to wait any longer, I got up and dressed 1800s style. Maybe I was itching for an excuse to see Ellie again. It was hard to sort out my true motive, but one thing's for sure, I wouldn't leave without telling her I was going. Once dressed, I set the counter for today's date, glanced at the clock on my dresser, then envisioned Ellie's bedroom at the same time. After pressing Shuffle and Go, I disappeared.

I passed through five shuffle zones, then appeared in Ellie's room. I'd expected her to be sleeping, but the light was on. Turning, I scanned the room. The click of the bathroom door drew my attention. Ellie, wearing a lavender bath towel, stepped into the room, her damp hair covering her shoulders.

As she paused to close the door behind her, my jaw dropped and my eyes inadvertently scanned her from head to toe. She hadn't noticed me yet and I knew I should say something fast, but not a single word came out of my mouth. When I managed to clear my throat, she spun around and let out a startled scream.

I raised my finger to my lips. "Shh, Ellie. It's just me," I whispered, undoubtedly blushing as red as a tomato.

She clutched her towel to her chest. "Land sakes, Chase! Can't you knock first?"

"Not exactly."

A tap sounded on her door and we both jumped. "Ellie, I heard you scream. Are you okay?" Adam asked through the door.

Ellie looked from the door, to me, and then back at the door. I shrugged my shoulders, speechless. "I'm fine. I was startled . . . by a spider," she said.

"Should I come in and kill it for you."

"No!" Ellie said. "I took care of it with my shoe. But thank you. I'll see you in the morning."

"Okay. If you see another one, just holler and I'll get it for you."

"Thank you. Good night, Adam."

Ellie waited several seconds before turning to me, clutching her towel so tightly her knuckles had turned white. "Turn around. I can't talk to you like this. I've got to get dressed."

I faced the wall and shoved my hands in my pockets. "Look, I'm sorry." I heard her open and close the dresser drawers. *I'm an idiot,* I thought.

"Now, pray tell, what has you appearing in my bedroom at all hours of the night?"

I turned to look at her as she sat on the edge of the bed in flannel pajama pants and one of my old T-shirts. "I couldn't sleep, so I thought I'd go see Garrick. But I didn't want to leave without telling you. I'm sorry I scared you. I had no idea you'd be in the shower."

"You can't come popping into my room unannounced. Perchance, next time I don't have a towel on. Imagine how dreadfully embarrassing that would be."

I yanked my hat off my head and ran my fingers through my hair. "Yes, it would. I promise it won't happen again. I'll figure something else out."

She walked over to me. "Chase, I'm not angry with you."

I wrapped my arms around her waist, losing my train of thought as I breathed in the flowery smell of her shampoo. After a moment, she said, "I suppose I should allow you to be on your way."

I smiled. "I'll be back in a minute, so don't go getting in the shower again."

She stepped away. "I won't. Don't forget to come back, and be safe."

THIRTEEN
Married

I went through five exotic shuffle zones—Antarctica, the Australian Outback, the jungles of India, the Amazon rainforest, and St. Petersburg, Russia. I had set the counter for June 1, 1818, and imagined arriving at midnight, hoping to get some sleep before going to work. The room I'd always shared with Garrick materialized around me, and I walked through the darkness to my bed. As soon as I sat down, I realized it was occupied.

A deep voice yelled, "What in tarnation?"

I jumped up and backed toward the door. "Sorry—I must have the wrong room."

A boot flew past my head. "Get out, boy! Can't a man get a decent night's sleep 'round here?"

I threw up my arm in case he decided to pitch the other boot at me, then hurried out the door and slammed it.

I jogged down the stairs, glancing over my shoulder to see if the ornery geezer was chasing me. The next thing I knew, a shirtless Garrick slammed me against the wall, his forearm choking off my air supply.

"What're you doing in here?" he asked angrily.

I gasped. "Garrick, it's me—Chase."

He released me and stepped back. "Little brother, why didn't you say it was you?"

I coughed and rubbed my neck. "I just did. Why'd you try to kill me before you asked who I was?"

"I thought you were a burglar."

"Is everything all right, dear?" Rose stepped into the hall carrying a candle. Her other hand rested protectively on her large belly.

Garrick walked to her and wrapped his arm around her shoulders, pressing his lips to her forehead. "It was only my little brother. He got in late and tried not to wake us. But with Harry in his old room, it didn't work out like he planned."

"I'm sorry we gave your room away, Mr. Harper. When Garrick and I got married, it seemed a waste to let it go empty." Rose smiled up at her husband.

"It's no big deal," I replied. "I wasn't sure when I'd be back anyway."

"If you don't mind sharing with Davy for a couple of nights, we can put you in Mr. Edwards' room when he leaves on Friday."

"That's a great idea, Rose. Harper won't mind, will you?" Garrick reached out to slap my shoulder. "It sure is good to see you, little brother."

"You too." I glanced at Rose. "Congratulations."

"Thank you," they said in unison.

Garrick smiled at his wife. "You can go back to bed. I'll show Harper where to sleep."

"I am tired," she said. We watched the flickering light retreat down the hall.

"Come on, little brother. We moved Davy into his own room, but there are two beds in there so you should be comfortable enough."

"Sorry for waking you guys up."

"That's okay. Here we are," he said, opening the door to Davy's room.

Moonlight streamed through the open window and I easily found the empty bed.

I quickly slipped back into the Erie Canal routine. I enjoyed hanging out with Davy and declined Rose's offer to move into a room of my own. The spring rains left the ground moist, making the digging easier than it had been at the end of last summer, and all of us boys made significant progress on the canal.

Garrick amazed me. Never had I seen a happier man, yet I'd never seen him work so hard. He was always the first one up, building the cook fire for Rose, hauling water, and helping her fix breakfast. He regularly lingered over the kiss he gave her as he left for work, and I'd be stamping my foot and clearing my throat to get him out the door.

After a particularly exhausting day of stump removal, some of the guys asked Garrick to go to the tavern with them. He grinned. "Sorry, boys. No time for the tavern—I'm a married man now. I've got to get back to Rose."

"We haven't seen you for a game of cards ever since you got hitched," an old-timer said. "That woman's done got you hog-tied, boy. You best break loose while you still can."

"Jed, if this is what being hog-tied feels like," Garrick answered with a grin, "I'll take it and pray I never get loose. See you tomorrow, boys."

I had to jog every few steps to keep pace with Garrick. "So, no more late-night visits to the tavern, huh?"

"Nope. I'm going to be a father—well, I am a father, if Davy accepts me as such, and I'm aiming to be a good one. I don't figure a good father would be spending his time at the tavern when he could be playing with his kids, or taking care of their mother."

"Davy already thinks of you as his father. He calls you his Garrick Pa. You've got nothing to worry about there. That kid worships the ground you walk on."

"You think so? I worry someday he'll resent me, thinking I tried to take the place of his real pa."

"Wasn't Davy too little to even remember his father?"

"Maybe."

"I'll bet Davy has more memories with you than of his own father."

"You might be right."

We walked in silence for a time before I said, "Garrick, have you thought about what you're going to do in a few years, when Rose gets older and you haven't aged a day? She's going to notice eventually."

He smiled. "I have given it some thought. Maybe I'll come visit you. I don't want to go back to life at Texas A&M right now. It would be too complicated for me. I would have to go somewhere after 1968, though. No doubt it'll feel like torture having to leave Rose and Davy . . . and by then, the baby."

"Yeah, I think I know what you mean. It already feels like torture every time I leave Ellie. You still have my phone number in case you come see me, right?"

"Yeah, I've got it."

When we reached the boardinghouse, Garrick jumped into action, helping Rose prepare the evening meal. I played the part of the obedient little brother every time he barked an order. It was "Harper, go fetch Rose" this, or "Run get Rose" that. I admired his dedication, and their relationship got me contemplating mine.

Rose was a beautiful woman, with dark brown hair and the softest brown eyes I'd ever seen. She had a kind, gentle manner that reminded me of Ellie. I recalled Randy's and Adam's accusations that I was obsessive. I wasn't conscientiously being obsessive or overprotective—Ellie was simply my highest priority in life. Everything else paled in comparison to the urge I felt to protect her, and I began to wonder if our counters accentuated our natural protective instincts.

Once the chores were done, Garrick played with Davy until Rose said it was time for bed. Each night Garrick tucked him in with a bedtime story. Sometimes, Rose would sit in the room and do her mending. One night I paused outside the door, listening. Garrick's stories were his adventures with the counter, but told without revealing his identity. His far-fetched tales of a futuristic world full of cars and airplanes often had Davy and Rose laughing in delighted disbelief.

Payday came and I waited in line to collect my coins from the paymaster. Thoughts of Ellie had me counting the minutes until I could leave. I was so ready to see her again, and watching Garrick and Rose in love made my heart ache for Ellie all the more. I left my board money with Rose, although she tried to refuse, saying, "Chase, we're family now. You're welcome to stay anytime."

After saying goodbye to Davy and Garrick, I walked down the street. It was a busy summer's evening and I went a good mile before I was out of sight of another human being. I pulled out my counter and began my journey home. After the shuffle zones, I reappeared in Ellie's room. She had turned off the light and was lying in her bed, her damp hair fanned across the pillow.

She sighed. "You're back."

"Yup." Leaning over her, I placed my handful of coins in her palm. "Here's some money. Let's put this with yours and we'll go to the coin dealers next week and see how much we've got."

She touched the stubble on my chin. "Thank you for working so hard."

I kissed her, lingering over it the way I'd watched Garrick do with Rose and fighting the urge to climb into Ellie's bed.

Maybe she read my mind, because her hand landed on my chest and pushed. "You should leave now. It's late," she whispered.

That got me thinking clearly. This was probably the third lengthy good-night kiss I'd given her. Exhaling, I stood and pulled out my counter. "Good night, Ellie."

FOURTEEN
Presents

The next week, Ellie and I sold the antique coins and paid our bills. The money she had brought with her from Boston went a long way toward paying what we owed, and I was relieved to find I didn't need to rush back to 1818. Garrick would be disappointed, but I wasn't.

Digging dirt all day for two weeks had given me a lot of time to think. After my embarrassing appearance in Ellie's room, I needed a way to warn her I was coming. I couldn't use the regular phone because someone might overhear us and get suspicious. I didn't dare appear anywhere else in Adam's house for fear I'd run into someone on my way to Ellie's room. Two-way radios were out—the distance was too far. However, the solution had presented itself one blisteringly hot afternoon as Garrick and I struggled to remove the stump of an ancient oak tree. Texting—the perfect answer to my problem. It was quiet, reliable, and relatively confidential. I simply needed to buy Ellie a cell phone and show her how to use it.

The week before Valentine's Day, I went shopping. I wasn't sure a cell phone I'd purchased for my convenience was a good Valentine's gift, so I bought some See's chocolates. I ate enough of the them to make room for the phone in the center of the heart-shaped box. After wrapping the box in pink paper, I opened my phone and texted the number assigned to Ellie's. When she turned it on for the first time, she'd have a message waiting for her.

As Ellie and I drove home from school, I asked her if I could go see her that night for Valentine's Day.

She looked at me and smiled. "Valentine's Day isn't until next Tuesday."

"I know, but I can't wait. I've got something I want to give you."

"What about your parents? I thought they said no dating on the weekdays."

"They did, but I'm not talking about a date. I'm talking about popping in to see you before bed, say at 10:20?"

Her melodic laugh filled the truck. "What an odd time. Why not ten o'clock or half past ten?"

"Well, ten o'clock might be a little early and I don't want to wait until 10:30, but I can if you want me to."

"Chase, 10:20 is fine. I was teasing you. It struck me as funny—that's all."

With Ellie moved out, hanging out at home was downright boring. I finished my homework, did my barn chores, watched SportsCenter with my dad, and monitored the clock's progress toward 10:20 PM.

I faked a big yawn around ten o'clock. "I'm tired. I think I'll go to bed." Keeping up all pretenses of hitting the sack, I brushed my teeth before locking myself in my bedroom. A glance at the clock told me I needed to hustle. I pulled on a clean pair of jeans and my Hilhi Spartans sweatshirt. I tucked the pink box under my arm, and my room disappeared with the touch of a button.

My modern clothing drew curious stares during the shuffle zones, but other than that it was an uneventful trip. Like I'd mentioned to Ellie one day, the frontier clothes were definitely better for traveling. I appeared to find her waiting on the edge of her bed.

"Darling, you're late," she said.

"I am?" I glanced behind me at the clock. "Hmm . . . 10:21. Sorry about that. I'll concentrate a little harder next time."

She crossed the room and wrap her arms around my neck. "You know I am teasing you. The clock changed right after you appeared, and I simply could not resist."

"You've been doing that a lot lately."

Her eyebrows lifted. "Doing what?"

"Teasing me." I circled her waist with my free arm.

"It's so delightful to tease you, when you always believe me."

"Well, usually you're telling me the truth, but now I see I'm going to have to be careful. You're more of a troublemaker than I thought."

"No, I—" she started saying, but I smothered her words with a kiss.

When I pulled back, I found her speechless and smiled. "Happy Valentine's Day, Ellie. I have a present for you."

She took the pink box. "Why thank you. I'm making something for you, but it's not finished yet. I'll have it ready for your birthday next week."

"You don't have to do that. This present is as much for me as it is for you. Open it."

She sat on the rocking chair and tore away the paper. "What's this?" Obviously, she didn't recognize the famous See's logo.

"Chocolates?" She smiled as she opened the box, taking a deep breath as the sweet aroma filled the air, then pulled out the cell phone. "Chase, is this really a phone?"

I mirrored her smile. "Yeah, it is. That way when I want to come see you, I can knock, so to speak."

She turned the phone over in the palm of her hand. "How do I use it?"

I knelt next to her. "This button turns it on." We waited while the phone beeped to life. When the display lit up, it read, "2 new messages received."

"Push the button in the middle to read your messages," I said. She pushed the button and I watched her read the service message from the phone company. "Now, press this button to go to the next message."

"From you?"

"Yeah, it's from me."

She read my Happy Valentine's Day text message with a smile and said, "Thank you."

"If you want to reply to the message, press this button." I reached in and pressed the button for her. "Let's practice. You send me a message back."

Giving the phone a confused stare, she asked, "How do I do that?"

I reached over to help her again. "It's easiest if you slide the phone open, like this. Now you type in your message. See how it's arranged like a keyboard on the computer?"

"Oh, I see. Do I use my thumbs? That's what I see everyone doing at school."

"That's the easiest." I waited for her to compose a one-line reply.

"I'm done. Now what?"

I leaned closer and pointed. "Press this button to send it."

She pressed "Send," and a second later my phone's ringtone sounded in my pocket. I retrieved the phone and read, "Thank you happy valentines day chase." I slid out my phone keyboard, quickly typed a reply, and hit "Send."

"Oh," Ellie gasped as her phone vibrated in her hand.

"Do you remember how to bring the message up on your screen?"

She bit her lower lip as she pushed the sequence of buttons. "I think so."

I glanced over her shoulder to read my own message, "Ur welcome Ellie. Glad u like it. How bout we eat those chocolates now? And u look beautiful 2nite, as always."

"How did you do that so fast?"

"Practice, lots of practice. What about the chocolates?" I said while she intently studied the buttons on her phone.

Without looking up she answered me. "Oh, certainly, help yourself. I'm going to try again."

While she plunked out another reply, I took the box of chocolates and began searching out my favorites. A knock on Ellie's door interrupted our celebration. We both stopped what we were doing and stared at each other.

"Who is it?" she asked.

"Adam. Is Chase in there?"

I stood up and shook my head no, pulling the counter from my pocket.

"Don't go," Ellie mouthed silently, motioning me toward her closet. She pushed me inside, then closed the door.

"Why would you think that?" Ellie asked Adam through the door.

"Are you dressed?"

Ellie gasped. "Adam Harper! I most certainly am dressed. Why would you ask such a thing?"

"Because I'm coming in." I heard the click of a key sliding into the lock and the sound of the door opening. "Where is he?"

"Adam, get out this instant!" Ellie said.

"I heard you talking and I know I heard Chase's voice. Don't worry, I'm not going to tell. I just want to know how he got in here." My cousin sounded angry.

I held the closet door closed with one hand, my thumb hovering over the counter in the other.

"Adam, we were talking on the phone," Ellie said.

I smiled. *Brilliant.*

"That doesn't explain Chase's voice."

"Were you born in the nineteenth century or something?" she asked condescendingly. "Have you not heard of speaker phones?"

I gritted my teeth and fought back a laugh.

"I didn't think you had a phone," Adam said.

"I didn't, but I just got one. See?"

"Where's Chase now?"

"He was about to go to bed," Ellie said.

"Well, I'll give him a call then."

Shoot! I had seconds to turn my phone to silent mode before his call rang through. As I pushed buttons, I heard the familiar beep of Adam's phone on the other side of the door. I unlocked my phone, then pressed "Menu, Settings, Profiles, Silent." *Done!* I held my breath, worried at any second he would slide open the closet door and see me.

"He's not answering," Adam said.

"Like I said, he was about to go to bed. Maybe his phone is off now, or he's in the bathroom. If you leave a message, I'm certain he'll return your call."

"I guess you're right," he mumbled. "Hey, it's Adam. Call me back, dude. Bye."

"Now, do you mind? Because it's getting late," Ellie said. "Good night."

I heard the bedroom door close. Then Ellie opened the closet door and breathed a sigh of relief. After untangling myself from the clothes hanging around my head, I stepped out and whispered, "That was awesome. I should go call him back before he does something stupid."

"I suppose you should. Thank you for the phone and the chocolates."

I brushed her lips with kisses between saying, "Happy Valentine's Day . . . I'll see you tomorrow . . . Don't forget, you can text me anytime . . . Or call me, if you like that better . . . I'm number 2 on your speed dial . . . Number 1 is your voicemail . . . Push the "2" and hold it down to call me, okay? Good night, Ellie."

"Good night, darling," she whispered just before I touched the counter's button and disappeared.

After my shuffle zones, I expected to return at 10:20 PM— the time I'd left. But I returned at the precise time I'd left Ellie's room—10:55 PM. I was bewildered but didn't have time to ponder the mysteries of the counter.

I selected Adam's number on my phone and heard one ring before he answered, "Hey, where were you?"

"In my room. I'm going to bed. What's up?"

"It was the weirdest thing. I thought I heard Ellie talking to a guy in her room. It sounded like you at first, but—"

I laughed. "Bro, you're not getting paranoid on me, are you? I just finished talking to Ellie, and she was alone. She put me on speaker for some reason. I talked to her for over twenty minutes. I think I would have noticed if someone else was in the room."

"Yeah, I guess you're right. See you tomorrow, dude."

"Okay, 'bye."

My phone vibrated with an incoming message. It was from Ellie. "Are you home?" Short but sweet.

Flashing my thumbs over the keyboard, I responded. "Yes, I'm home. Talked w/ Adam. Everything's cool. It was weird. The counter didn't return me 2 the time I left my room. Returned me 2 the time I left u. Any ideas?"

Five minutes later my phone rang. "Hello."

"Chase, it's me." Ellie said. "It was taking too long to type everything I wanted to say, so I called. I hope that's all right."

"Of course. I love hearing your voice."

"I don't think a person can travel to the same time with the counter more than once. My grandfather always left our Sunday dinners in time to get himself to bed. I asked him why he didn't simply go back earlier so he could get more sleep. He said he had never been able to repeat a time he had traveled to with the counter."

"Hmm . . . interesting."

"When you came to see me, you traveled with the counter to the present. Therefore, I believe when you attempted to return, that period of time was blocked. The counter had you reappear at the next open time, which was the moment you left my room."

"That explains a lot."

"Is there anything else?" Ellie asked.

"No, I guess that's it. I'll see you tomorrow."

A week later, Jessica and I turned eighteen. Our parents wanted to celebrate our birthday by going out to dinner. We went to a nice restaurant in downtown Portland, but I would've rather spent the time with Ellie. Jessica and I got laptops for college. Secretly, it was a relief to officially be an adult. I had a gnawing worry that someday circumstances regarding either my girlfriend or my counter would create an unsolvable conflict. I hadn't decided what, if anything, I would tell my parents regarding my calling as a Keeper and Ellie's past if that happened. My dad made no effort to hide the fact that he hoped this fling would fade away once I left for college. It wasn't that he didn't like Ellie—he just didn't want me to get serious with any girl until I finished school. Little did he know, I had no intention of going anywhere without her. At some point I would have to sever the parental ties and follow my own compass.

Lost in thought, I hadn't noticed we were home. Jessica stuck her head back into the car. "Chase, you coming?"

I realized our parents were walking up the porch steps, while I was still buckled into the back of the BMW. "Yeah, I was just thinking." I grabbed my laptop box and followed Jessica into the house.

Mom had made our favorite dessert. We sang happy birthday to each other and blew out the candles together while my mom snapped pictures. I slammed down two pieces of cake before excusing myself.

"I'm going to bed. Thanks, Dad and Mom, for the new computer." I gave them each a hug.

My dad smiled. "You're welcome, Son. Happy birthday."

My mom didn't say anything at first, just gave me a long hug, then wiped a tear from her eye. "Where did the time go? I can't believe my twins are all grown up. I love you. Good night, honey."

"I love you too, Mom. Happy birthday, Sis."

Jessica hugged me quickly. "Happy birthday to you, too."

I jogged up the stairs. Ellie was waiting for me, or so I flattered myself. Of course she was too polite to call or text in an effort to hurry me along. I whipped out my phone and sent her a message. Several minutes later I got a reply.

"Yes, you may come over."

Chuckling at the reply time for so short a message, I responded, "On my way. C u soon." Her gallant efforts at mastering everything technological were endearing. After making sure my bedroom door was locked, I turned off the light, picked up the computer box, and shuffled away.

When I appeared in her room, Ellie was sitting cross-legged on her bed, typing on her phone. As if deep in concentration, she didn't look up when I first appeared. Finally, she glanced at me. "Oh, you're here already. I guess I don't need to send this."

"What did it say?" I approached to look over her shoulder.

"'All right, I'll see you then,'" I read aloud. "You're getting pretty good with that thing. It goes faster if you abbreviate some of the words. Like the word 'you' can be just the letter 'u,' and 'are' can be just an 'r.'"

She sighed. "Oh, I see. I'll try to remember that. Unfortunately, it takes me an insufferably long time to compose a message."

"It's only been a couple of days. You'll get faster. I got a laptop for my birthday. I thought I'd leave it here for you to use."

"That's not necessary. It's yours and it's new."

"I can use our old one, and I don't want you having to borrow Adam's all the time. It makes more sense for you to use this one. Don't argue with me, Ellie. I've already made up my mind." I smiled and kissed her cheek.

She smiled back at me. "My, aren't you a bossy one."

I unloaded the computer and plugged it into an outlet to charge the battery.

Ellie reached under her bed and pulled out a box. "Are you ready to open your present from me?"

"I hope you didn't go to too much trouble, because you didn't need to get me anything."

"It was no trouble at all and it's nothing big. I hope you don't mind that it's not wrapped."

"Not at all. It makes it easier for me to open."

Inside the box were two new shirts, handmade in the traditional 1800s style. Here was a present I could really use. Every time I went back with Garrick I was forced to wear the same stinking shirt, literally stinking with sweat, every day of the week.

"I know it isn't much and it's not practical for your everyday life, but I remember you didn't like washing your shirt only once a week. I thought you'd appreciate having a spare."

I swept her up in a big hug, lifting her feet off the floor. "Ellie, thank you. This is the best present. Now I feel like I need to go back and see Garrick just to show off my new shirts."

"I'm glad you like them."

"I hate to rush off, but I'd better. I wouldn't want my parents to check on me and find I'm gone. It's a real pain I can't go back to the same time I left."

"I know." Sliding her fingers through the hair on the back of my head, Ellie went up on her tiptoes and kissed me. Caught completely off guard, since I couldn't remember her ever initiating a kiss, I stood frozen in place. She brushed her lips across my cheek, and then next to my ear. "Happy birthday, Chase."

When she moved to step away from me, I snapped out of the daze she'd left me in. "Whoa, where are you going?"

"You said you had to leave."

"I did? I'm not in that big of a hurry. Not now, anyway." I pulled her back to me. I kissed her until my phone vibrated in my pocket and distracted me, which was probably good. I pulled away and looked to see who it was. Jessica. I slid open the phone and read, "Where r u? Dad is knocking on ur door, u idiot!"

"Crap, I've got to go. My dad's knocking on my bedroom door. 'Bye, Ellie. I'll see you tomorrow." I stepped away and pushed the Shuffle and Return buttons before she could respond.

The second I reappeared in my room, I yelled, "Sorry, Dad. I'm coming."

I ripped off my shirt, pulled my iPod off my dresser, shoved an earpiece in each ear, and kicked off my shoes. Opening the door, I spouted out a lame apology. "I didn't hear you. I was listening to my music."

My dad shook his head and yanked on the cord, emptying my ears. "Don't listen to your music that loud. You're going to go deaf if you're not careful. Uncle Steve called and wants us to go steelhead fishing—not this weekend but the next. Do you want to go?"

"Sure—" I started to say. "No wait, that's the state wrestling tournament, so I can't. But I could go any other weekend in March."

"That's not going to work. I'll tell him no," my dad said, then turned and walked down the stairs.

Jessica poked her head out of her room and I went to thank her. "What were you doing?" she asked. "It sounded like Dad was about to kick your door in."

"I was with Ellie. I owe you big time! Thanks for the text. If it happens again, text me, will you?"

"Chase! You sly little devil. How often are you sneaking off to Ellie's room?"

"Jess, it's not like that. She was giving me a birthday present."

My sister raised her eyebrows. "Whatever."

"It was nothing. I'm serious. But thanks, Jess."

I walked back down the hall to my room. My phone vibrated on my dresser. I smiled to see a text from Ellie. "Is everything all right? I hope I didn't cause u trouble."

My thumbs jumped across the keyboard. "Everything is fine. No big deal. My dad had a ? 4 me. I told Jess where I was. Sorry I 4got 2 take my present. I'll get it tmrw. Thx again. They r awesome shirts."

FIFTEEN
Disaster

The state wrestling tournament was held at the Memorial Coliseum in Portland and spanned two days. I expected I'd wrestle Travis DeMarco before the tournament ended. Our last meeting had been a disaster, with both of us getting disqualified. Travis had a reputation for playing dirty, and many of his opponents had found his fist buried in their guts when their backs were to the ref.

On Friday, I won my first-round and quarter-final matches. The way the brackets were organized, I would only meet Travis if we both made it to the championship round, scheduled for Saturday afternoon. The wrestling team spent all day at the Coliseum. Coach had wanted everyone there to support each other, even if we weren't wrestling. Other than a brief hello at school on Thursday, I hadn't seen Ellie in two days, and I was having withdrawals by Friday night.

When I came down for dinner, my dad took one look at me dressed to go out and scowled. "Where do you think you're going?"

"I'm going to a movie."

"With that girlfriend of yours?"

"Dad, you know her name."

"I don't think you should go anywhere tonight. You've got semifinals and hopefully the finals tomorrow. You need a good night's sleep. Do you really have to go to a movie tonight? Wait until tomorrow, after the tournament is over."

"Dad it's only 6:30. I'll be back by ten o'clock. If I stayed home I wouldn't go to bed any earlier than that anyway."

"Ten o'clock? You promise?"

"Yeah, I promise."

He picked up his fork to eat and by the expression on his face, I knew I'd won. "Okay, but be home on time."

"I will. Can I drive your car?" I said, since I was on a roll.

He took another bite, and without cracking a smile, he set the keys on the table. "Only if you drive safe and slow."

"Thanks, Dad." I slammed down a plate of food, guzzled a glass of water, and picked up his keys. "See ya later." I dashed out the door.

I thanked my lucky stars he had let me go out, because I had no desire to sneak around with the counter tonight. I wanted to relax, not watch the time and worry about Adam overhearing me, or my parents noticing my absence. Fifteen minutes later I knocked on the door.

Ellie opened it. "Hello, Chase."

Draping my arm over her shoulder, I pulled her next to me for the walk to the car. "Hey, beautiful."

"How was your wrestling today?"

"It was good—I won."

She smiled up at me. "I knew you would."

I laughed. "You did? I'm glad I didn't disappoint you."

"You never disappoint me," she said sweetly.

The movie ended far too quickly, and I now faced the miserable task of leaving Ellie at Adam's while I went home to appease my dad by going to bed early. As we left the theater with our arms wrapped around each other, I turned my phone on. No new messages. But a loud beep told me the battery was low. I held the car door open for Ellie before getting behind the wheel. No sooner had I left the parking lot than my phone rang.

I didn't recognize the number. "Hello."

"This is the AT&T operator. Will you accept a collect call from . . . Garrick?"

Shocked, I practically yelled, "Yes, yes, I'll accept the call."

"Thank you. Hold the line and I'll connect the call," the operator said.

"Harper," Garrick said, "you gotta help me! It's Rose. The babies won't come. She's dying. I need help. We need to get her to the hospital."

"Whoa, Garrick—where are you? Where's Rose?"

He took a deep breath and spoke slower. "We're at a pay phone, by a Chevron station on the corner of St. Clair and Burnside. In Portland, I think."

"You're here?"

"Of course I'm here. I need your help."

"Okay. I'm coming." Changing directions, I sped toward the freeway. "Tell me from the beginning what happened."

"Harper, we don't have time for that now. Hang up the phone. Get in the car and hurry. I've got to get her to a hospital before it's too late."

"Garrick, I am in the car. I'm on my cell phone. I'm driving right now. Give me thirty minutes and I'll be there. Why didn't you call 9-1-1?"

"What are you talking about? Just get here."

"I'm coming. Haven't you heard of calling 9-1-1 in an emergency?" My phone beeped again and I knew the battery would die any second.

"I have no idea what you're saying, Harper. Quit talkin' nonsense and hurry," Garrick yelled.

A faint scream sounded in the background and I strained to hear what was happening. "Garrick? What's going on? Are you there?" The line was silent for a moment as I waited intently for some word of what was happening.

"I'm hanging up. I've got to help Rose. Get here, now," he yelled, then hung up.

"Wait—" I lowered the phone from my ear, muttering to myself, "Gosh, you're bossy tonight."

The streetlights on the freeway flashed by in rapid succession. Weaving in between cars, I raced toward the Barnes Road exit. I didn't know where St. Clair Street was on Burnside, but I planned to start where Barnes Road turned into Burnside and follow it into Portland until I found Garrick and Rose.

Stunned by the phone call, I had almost forgotten about Ellie sitting next to me until she asked, "What's wrong, Chase?"

"I don't know, but something's going on with Rose and their baby. I can't believe he brought her here."

I looked between Ellie and the road. Her stunned expression mirrored my own feelings. "Oh my," she said.

One check of the speedometer and I took a deep breath, letting up on the gas pedal a bit. It wouldn't do Garrick any good if I got pulled over. I exited the freeway onto Barnes Road and soon passed Providence St. Vincent's Hospital. Depending on where I found Garrick, I expected to be coming back here with Rose. My phone continued to beep as I followed Burnside through the forested west hills of Portland.

When I neared the first stoplight in town, I tried to call the pay phone Garrick had called from. Without better directions, I'd be slowing down to check each street sign, and I had no idea how many Chevron stations there might be. Burnside

Road went for miles through downtown Portland, across the Burnside Bridge over the Willamette River, and then through east Portland. I called back the last number on my phone. It rang once before giving me the final beep and shutting down. Frustrated, I tried to turn it back on. Nothing. The battery was completely dead. Slamming the steering wheel in frustration, I threw down the phone.

"Dang it all! My phone's dead and I don't have a charger. Ellie, help me look for Garrick. He said he was by a pay phone on St. Clair Street, near a Chevron station. I'm guessing he's still dressed for the 1800s."

We searched for Chevron stations and pay phones and read every street sign as we started down Burnside. A moment later, from more than a block away I saw him—unmistakable in his white linen shirt, brown trousers, and boots, pacing back and forth on the sidewalk. The Chevron sign towered above him. I pulled up next to him and rolled down the window. "Garrick!"

"Harper, come quick. Help me get Rose."

I jammed the gearshift into park and turned on my hazard lights, as Garrick ran ahead. He crossed St. Clair Street and stopped near a large building. Leaning against the wall was a very pregnant and disheveled-looking Rose, her beautiful face streaked with sweat and fraught with pain. Garrick and I each wrapped an arm around her shoulders and carried her between us to the car.

When we helped her into the backseat, the blanket she had wrapped around her slipped off, revealing a large spot of bright red blood on her nightgown. This didn't look good. Rose was so weak she could barely hold her head up. Twice she mumbled, "Where are we? I don't understand."

"Hang on, Rose," Garrick said. "We're going to find a doctor. A really good one—one who can help you and the babies." He climbed in next to his wife and cradled her head against his chest. I turned the car around and raced back toward St. Vincent's Hospital.

"Is she having twins?" Ellie asked.

"Yes. The midwife said they're tangled up inside her and turned the wrong direction." He gazed down at Rose and when he spoke again his voice cracked with emotion. "Oh, Rose, this is all my fault. I'm so sorry."

Glancing in the rearview mirror, I saw Rose raise a shaky hand and place her finger over his lips. "Shh . . . Garrick, my dear . . . Nothing is your fault."

He shook his head.

"Promise me something," she breathed out weakly.

"Anything," he said.

She began to cry, and her voice quivered. "If I don't live, take care of Davy. Please."

"You have to live, Rose. I need you. Davy needs you."

"Promise me, Garrick, please. He has no one else and he loves you so. I have to know he'll be cared for." She begged him as only a mother could, and I felt a lump rise in my throat.

"I will," Garrick said. "Of course I'll take care of Davy. You know I love him like he was my own son."

Rose gasped. "Yes, I know you do, and I love you dearly. Thank you, Garrick. You gave me the best months of my life, and I was never happier than when I was with you." Her breathing became increasingly labored, and what sounded like it should have been a scream came out more of a whimper.

Garrick stroked her face. "Rose, please . . . don't leave me. Not now. I can't live without you."

I continued glancing between my rearview mirror and the wet pavement ahead as I sped through Portland's west hills. A moment later, the hum of the engine was all I could hear.

"Rose?" Garrick clutched her to his chest. "No, no, no, Rose—" He sobbed, laying his head against her silent face. I turned to glance at the tragedy playing out in the backseat of the car. His tone of voice shifted from grief to utter dismay, as he cried out, "No! This can't be happening to me."

Ellie gasped and I turned again to look over my shoulder. There in Garrick's arms was the crumbling form of Rose. As the Mexican vaqueros had done, she was disintegrating into dust before our eyes. Within seconds the distraught Garrick was left with nothing but her nightgown and a sprinkling of fine gray dust.

I stared behind me in horror. "Chase!" Ellie screamed, grabbing my arm. I spun my head around to see the headlights of a large truck coming directly toward us. I had veered into the oncoming lane of traffic. The horn on the truck blared out a warning as I slammed on the brakes and swerved back into my own lane. In my panic, I overcorrected. The car hydroplaned on the wet asphalt and spun off the road. After crashing through the underbrush, the BMW smacked to a stop against the trunk of a giant Douglas fir, and the air bags exploded in front of Ellie and me. Garrick, who wasn't wearing a seatbelt, flew forward over the middle console.

I leaned my head against the headrest, breathing deeply and hoping to slow the rush of adrenaline through my veins. "Ellie, are you okay?"

"Yes," she said, pushing the airbag out of her way.

"Garrick?" I could hear him climbing into the back seat.

"What have I done?" he said. "I made a mess of my own life, and now I've ended Rose's. Help me, Harper. Help me think of a way to fix this. If I'd only done what I knew was right in the first place, this wouldn't be happening. I should have known better. I did know better. This is all my fault. I've killed Rose. Harper, maybe if you went back and warned me, I would know to get her help sooner. Or you could come back Christmas Eve and stop me from staying in her room that night. Or what if I—"

When he suddenly stopped talking, I looked over my shoulder. "Garrick? Where did he go?"

Ellie turned and looked. The backseat was vacant except for Rose's nightgown, the blanket, and her dust. "I don't know," Ellie said, tears streaming down her cheeks.

I leaned over and buried my face in the soft curls next to her neck, fighting not to cry too. While she grieved for a woman she had never known, I rambled on about all of Rose's incredible qualities. When I mentioned cute little Davy, I coughed and swallowed hard. How would Garrick explain to a six-year-old boy that his mother was gone? A tear rolled down my cheek and I couldn't say any more.

We stayed that way for a while, consoling each other. Finally, Ellie slid her fingers down my arm and squeezed my hand. "It will work out. The Lord has a way of putting things to rights. But I don't understand why Garrick is so convinced it was his fault. Women sometimes die in childbirth. It's heartbreaking, yes, but not anything he should blame himself for."

I leaned my head against the deflated airbag. "Garrick's upset because he got her pregnant before they were married. He always regretted that. He wished he would have done things the right way and married her first."

"Oh, I see."

"I never want to disrespect you, Ellie. I have a responsibility to protect you physically, emotionally, and spiritually. Don't ever let me do what Garrick did before we're married," I muttered, not realizing at first that I'd spoken my thoughts.

Ellie touched my arm and I looked at her. "Is that a proposal?" she asked.

"Uh, not an official one. I can do better than that for a real proposal." I paused. "That was more like a declaration of intent."

"I see. In that case, I'll look forward to the real thing."

"I guess no one saw us crash," I said to change the subject. "The cops would have been here by now if someone had called them." The car had slid off the road and down an embankment, undoubtedly out of sight of anyone driving by. "Do you have your cell phone?"

"No, I'm sorry," Ellie said. "I didn't think to bring it."

"That's okay. I'm worried about Garrick. I don't think he used his counter to disappear. He was in the middle of talking to me. The only other explanation is Master Archidus. Remember when I disappeared last fall?"

"How could I ever forget that dreadful experience?"

"I'll bet Master Archidus wasn't too happy when Garrick brought Rose here."

"What should we do?" Ellie asked.

"Wait, I guess. How long did you wait for me?"

"Hours—it seemed like forever."

I pressed my fingers to my eyes. "My dad's gonna kill me. Not only am I out late when I promised I'd be home early, but to top it all off, I crashed his new car. And now I won't be calling him because my phone is dead." I sighed at my pitiful state of affairs. "Should we get out and survey the damage?"

"You could use the counter to go home."

I shook my head. "I'd rather take my dad's punishment than risk not being here when Garrick comes back."

"I'm so sorry, Chase. What a fix we've gotten ourselves into." Ellie shoved her door open against the underbrush.

I grabbed a flashlight from the glove box and turned it on. The way the car was tilted on the hillside, I was pushing against gravity to get my door open. Once I climbed out of the vehicle, the door slammed shut behind me. Blackberry bushes surrounded the car like a cocoon. Sharp thorns snagged my clothes as I made my way to Ellie's side of the car. The trunk of the tree had crunched the front bumper on the passenger side. Shattered pieces of the right headlight lay on the ground. Thankfully, it didn't look as if the main body of the car had suffered much damage. I panned the light across the car's side and groaned. It was too dark to tell for sure, but I'd bet the blackberry bushes had done a number on the paint job.

Ellie looked from me to the smashed front bumper and wrapped her arm around my waist. We stood staring at the car until it started to rain. "Let's get back in," I said. "There's nothing we can do until Garrick gets back. I won't leave this spot until I talk with him."

I opened the door for Ellie and helped her in. Still sickened by the tragic death of Rose and her babies, I walked to my side of the car and heaved the door open. The slam of it closing behind me sounded harsh above the quiet pitter-patter of rain on the windshield.

I stretched my hand toward Ellie with my palm up, and she slid her fingers between mine. I must have drifted to sleep a couple of times, but each time I stirred she gave my fingers a reassuring squeeze. Periodically, I turned the key in the ignition to check the clock and run the heater. The last time I checked, it was 2:11 AM. Ellie's eyes were closed, with her head resting against the window.

When a grunt sounded in the backseat, my eyes flew open and I turned to see Garrick sitting there. "What happened?"

He sighed. "I can't try to change anything. Master Archidus threatened me for taking Rose out of her time, then decided that allowing me to live with my own guilt would be worse than any punishment he could inflict. He should have killed me—it would have been easier."

Garrick fell silent and I thought about what that meant for his future. "So what now?" I asked.

"I'm under strict orders to leave everything as it is. I have to go back and convince everyone she died in childbirth in our bedroom. Then I have to go through the pretenses of a funeral so there isn't any suspicion."

After a lengthy pause, Garrick continued, "Before I brought her here, the midwives had tried everything. They said there was nothing more they could do to deliver the babies. They had given up all hope. I told them I wanted a moment alone with my wife and they stepped out of the room. When I tell them she passed away, they won't question me. The problem is, the womenfolk will want to dress her body and prepare it for burial." Garrick stopped talking as if to check his emotions at the mention of Rose's body. "I won't know what to tell them."

"I think I do," Ellie said. "Does she have any relatives in the area?"

"No. Her parents both passed. The only one left is her brother, who moved west to settle the Ohio valley."

"That's good," Ellie said. "If I went back as a relative I could claim to have dressed the body. We could say because of your anguish at seeing her and knowing you've lost your unborn babies, there will not be a public wake and the coffin will remain closed. You and Chase would need to find some way to weight it, but if the funeral is handled properly, no one will suspect a thing."

Garrick leaned toward Ellie. After straining to see them through the darkness, I gave up and flipped on the car's interior light. The pained expression on Garrick's face was hard to see. He nodded and asked, "Would you be willing to help?"

"Of course."

He stretched out his hand. "Thank you, Ellie. I'm Garrick, by the way. I don't think I've officially met you."

Ellie returned his handshake. "I've heard a lot about you, Garrick. I'm so sorry for your loss."

"Yeah, me too. What should I do now?"

"Tell us the exact date and time you left with Rose, and then you return with your counter and wait for us. If anyone except us asks to come into the room, tell them you want a few more minutes alone. If everything goes as planned—" Ellie glanced at me "—we should be knocking on your door about the same time you return."

"We'll be there, Garrick," I said. "We'll help you through this."

"On the night of August 22, Rose started labor. She was in labor all the next day and into the night. I lost track of time. It seemed like forever." Garrick's voice drifted off and I wondered if he was reliving the tragic ordeal. "Harper, set your counter for August 24, 1818, and arrive around midnight. The last thing I did was send the midwives, Mrs. Benson and Mrs. Gunderson, out to the kitchen so I could be alone with Rose. Watch through the back window and you'll know when to come in."

"August 24, 1818—I got it," I said.

"Do you need help with the car before I leave?" Garrick asked.

I shook my head. "No, I've got it covered. You go ahead. We need to change clothes and I have to deal with my dad before I can get away. But I promise we'll be there soon."

"Thanks, little brother." He squeezed my shoulder before slowly climbing out of the car and disappearing.

"He's so sad," Ellie said.

"Yeah. Come on, I'll take you home with the counter and then call my dad."

Following Garrick's lead I climbed out and walked around to Ellie's door. Once we were clear of the car, I set the counter for Ellie's bedroom and touched Shuffle, then Go.

Once we stood in her room, I slid my arms around her waist and softly kissed her good night. "I'll call you as soon as I'm free of my parents, and we'll go back to help Garrick."

"I hope your dad isn't too riled up." Ellie stepped away from me.

"I'll be fine." I took out the counter and concentrated on where I'd picked up Garrick and Rose, then pressed Go. A second later I appeared in the shadows across the street from the pay phone. I pulled two quarters out of my pocket, walked to the phone, and dialed my home number.

My mom's voice sounded anxious when she answered on the first ring. "Hello."

"Hi, Mom. It's Chase—"

"Oh, thank goodness. Are you all right? Where are you?"

"I'm fine, Mom, but I crashed Dad's car."

"Chase," my dad's voice cut in. "What's going on?"

"Dad, I'm sorry. I crashed the car. It's not totaled or anything, but it's stuck off the side of the road."

"Son, it's three o'clock in the morning. You should have called long before now." My dad's voice sounded as hard as steel. This was the tone of voice he reserved for when he was really mad. I would've rather had him yell at me.

"My phone died and there isn't a charger in your car that fits it. I know it's late and I'm sorry."

"Where are you now?"

"A pay phone on Burnside Road in Portland."

"What on earth are you doing in Portland?" my mom practically yelled.

"This was the closest pay phone I could find."

"Then where is my car?" Dad asked.

"It's in the west hills, off Burnside Road."

"Where's Ellie? Is she with you?"

"No, Dad. I already took her home."

"I'll come get you. Where exactly are you?"

"I'll just wait for you at the first stoplight as you come into Portland on Burnside."

"I hope there's a good explanation for what you've been doing tonight," he said, then hung up the phone.

"Chase, are you sure you're not hurt?" my mom asked.

"Yeah, Mom. I'm fine, really."

"Why were you in Portland?"

"I was helping a friend. I'm going to go wait for Dad, okay?"

"I'm glad you're not hurt, and I'll see you when you get home."

"'Bye, Mom." I hung up the phone and walked away. The rain had stopped, but a cold wind whistled through the quiet downtown streets as I shoved my hands in my pockets and followed the sidewalk. It didn't take long to walk the few blocks back to the first stoplight. I had been working on a viable excuse all night long, but nothing had come to mind. With the grief I felt for Garrick and Davy, my mind kept coming up blank.

I pulled up the collar on my jacket and hunched my shoulders against the wind. Finally, I heard a car engine and turned to see my dad park Jessica's car next to the sidewalk. I climbed in.

"I didn't see my car on the way here," he said.

"It's off the road."

"Let's hear it. What have you been doing all night? Here's your chance to convince me I shouldn't ground you from driving—indefinitely."

I let out a sigh. *Garrick's pregnant wife needed a ride to the hospital, but when she suddenly died in his arms on the way, I lost control,* I thought, but I said, "I got a call from a friend who needed my help."

My dad moved into interrogation mode. "What friend?"

"A guy I worked construction with. You wouldn't know him."

"You should have told him no. You gave me your word. Plus, how did he call you? Didn't you already tell me your phone was dead?"

I shook my head. No way could I have said no to my big brother from 1818, especially when he saved my life. "I got the call right before my phone died, and believe me, I couldn't say no. I was trying to help him when I got distracted and swerved to miss hitting a truck. Then we hydroplaned off the road. That's it. Trust me, Dad, I had the best of intentions, and I would have called sooner if I could."

"That's pretty lame considering you were missing for, let's see—five hours!"

"Dad, I wasn't doing anything wrong."

He ratcheted his voice up a notch. "Promising you'll be home by ten o'clock, not calling when you're late, causing your mother to worry, driving into Portland without permission, then crashing my BMW. Need I continue? It all sounds wrong to me. Plus I think you could have borrowed a phone if you would have tried. There are houses all along Burnside."

I leaned my elbow on the window and cupped my forehead with my hand. "I told you the truth. Do what you have to."

"All right then, no car privileges for the next month. You can take the bus, get a ride with Jessica, or use your bike."

I growled under my breath, then clamped my mouth shut as my dad stared straight ahead. When he didn't say more, I leaned my head back and closed my eyes.

"Where is the car?" Dad's voice brought me back to the present.

I sat up and studied the road. "Um . . . we're getting close, I think." I couldn't remember exactly where I'd crashed and realized I should have walked up to the road and marked the spot before I disappeared. "Slow down—I think it's after this curve in the road."

"I thought you had a better sense of direction. For just walking to the pay phone, you don't seem very sure about how to get back."

Catching a glimpse of some damaged brush off the side of the road, I said, "Whoa, stop here." As soon as the car stopped I jumped out and ran back to the spot I'd seen. There, nearly imperceptible in the dark, was my dad's black BMW. I pointed. "It's right here."

My dad was dialing on his cell phone as he followed me. "Hillsboro Towing, please," he said, walking to where I stood. He gave them directions to the car's location and hung up. "Well, Chase, should we go take a look?"

We followed the path the car had plowed through the blackberry bushes. Halfway to the car, with our feet slipping in the mud, my dad asked, "How did you climb out of here without getting muddy?"

"I must have got lucky."

When we reached the BMW, Dad said, "Get the flashlight for me, will you?"

I opened the passenger door and saw Rose's nightgown and the blanket lying in the backseat. "Here, Dad." I handed him the flashlight. As soon as he turned away, I wadded up the blanket and clothing and held it behind me. I backed toward a blackberry bush and shoved the bundle between the branches. As I waited for my dad to assess the damages, I picked a thorn out of my hand.

"What a mess," he said.

I felt sick to my stomach and wondered if I was coming down with something, or if the grief I felt for Garrick, combined with the guilt of ruining my dad's car, was to blame. "I'm sorry, Dad. I'm sorry for this whole thing."

"I'm sorry too. We'd better go watch for the tow truck."

An hour later, with the BMW winched out of the trees and loaded onto the truck, I watched as my dad paid the driver. When we got home his only comment was "We've got two hours to sleep before we need to leave for the wrestling tournament." He walked to his bedroom and I went upstairs.

I debated whether to get Ellie and go help Garrick now or after wrestling. I felt exhausted, and I imagined Ellie was asleep by now, so I set my alarm and climbed into bed.

SIXTEEN
State

On the way to the last day of the state wrestling tournament, my dad and I hardly spoke two words to each other. Just before we went our separate ways at the door to the Memorial Coliseum, I noticed he looked even worse than I felt. I regretted putting him though all the worry the night before, but I couldn't have abandoned Garrick.

As I left, Dad called out, "Good luck, Son."

I turned, offering him half a smile. "Thanks. I'll need it."

State was a double-elimination tournament. I hadn't lost yet, so my name was still in the winner's bracket. If I won the semifinal match that morning, I wouldn't wrestle again until the finals in the afternoon. If I lost, I'd move to the loser's bracket and would have to wrestle my way back for a chance at third at best. I didn't have the energy to fight my way through the loser's bracket and didn't want to settle for anything less than the win, but wrestling on two hours of sleep would be brutal.

I splashed cold water on my face before walking onto the mat for my match, then shook my head, trying to focus on my opponent. I'd never wrestled him before, so I had no idea what I was up against. The ref's whistle blew and we began.

My opponent bounced lightly on his feet, obviously pumped up, while I circled him, careful to expend a minimal amount of energy. My dad cheered from the stands and my coach yelled instructions from the sidelines. When my opponent lunged for my legs, I jumped to the side and grabbed his arms. We grappled with each other through the first period until the whistle blew and we separated.

Toward the end of the second period, my determination and super-human strength outweighed his bounteous energy and I pulled him off balance. Both of us fell to the mat, battling each other in a tangled mass of arms and legs. Inch by inch, I forced him onto his back and pinned his shoulders. The shrill blast of the ref's whistle signaled the end of the match. Breathing heavily, I rolled onto the mat and closed my eyes.

"Congratulations," the ref said, then pulled me to my feet and raised my arm.

My team cheered from the stands as my coach ran over and yelled, "Way to go, Chase!"

A halfhearted smile turned my lips as I accepted his handshake. "Thanks, Coach."

He pulled me into a one-armed embrace and slapped me on the back. "You look tired. Go rest up for the finals. If you win this next match, you've got a good chance at a scholarship. The OSU wrestling coach is here today, as well as a couple from the Washington schools. This is a big opportunity for you."

"Okay, Coach."

I found a quiet corner of a practice mat and stuffed my gym bag under my head for a pillow. After plugging my iPod in my ears, I closed my eyes and fell asleep.

Sometime later, Coach shoved his foot into my shoulder. "Chase, what the heck are you doing? They're starting the lineup. You're late—we've been looking everywhere for you."

I sat up and pulled out the earpieces. "Sorry, Coach. I fell asleep."

He scowled. "Well, get up quick. You don't even have time to warm up now."

I followed him at a jog across the coliseum and onto the mat. Each of the finalists in all the weight divisions faced off prior to the first finals match. I was the last wrestler to take my spot before the announcer began the introductions. I stood opposite the smug-looking Travis DeMarco. When I flashed him a smile after a jaw-popping yawn, he rolled his eyes. The announcer finished the introductions, and the lightweight finalists took to the mat. It would be twenty minutes or so before they got to my weight division, so I dropped my gym bag next to my coach and headed toward the restrooms.

My jog to the bathroom would have to be my warm-up. They were finishing the match for the weight division below mine as I weaved through the crowd to the mat. Coach was nearly having a coronary by the time I got there. I pulled out my head gear and shoved it on as I walked toward the center of the mat. My coach stuck to me like my own shadow, spouting last-minute directions.

"Remember, don't lose your cool. DeMarco might play dirty. You can't afford to let him get under your skin this time. Don't listen to his taunting. You keep your focus even if he tries to mess with your head. No warnings. You gotta wrestle clean today. And keep him away from your legs. You got it, Harper?"

I bent to tighten my shoelaces. "Yeah, Coach, I got it."

Glancing up, I saw my opponent glaring at me from the mat. The announcer called both of our names, and I stood to join Travis. At the cue from the referee, Travis and I shook hands and took our positions. Once the whistle blew, we circled each other. I shed the last of my grogginess, focusing on the task at hand.

Travis's intensity was almost comical. I had already decided two things. First, I would not be taunted into retaliation, and second, I would not allow him to pin me. After that, may the best man win. He glared and I smiled back. Then he charged me, locking my arms up with his before diving in for an ankle pick. He pulled me to the mat and scored two points on a takedown. Realizing I'd better get my act together, I twisted out of his grasp. We grappled with one another again. Travis dug his fist into my stomach when our backs were square to the refs, so I baited him. "Is that the best you've got? A cheap shot like that won't work on me today."

With two refs and the enormous crowd, Travis couldn't get away with much. Neither of us gave up or gained any more points in the first period. When the whistle sounded after two minutes, we separated and prepared for the second period.

Travis had won the coin toss and chose to start in the bottom position. Breathing heavily, we took our places and waited for the whistle. I expected him to attempt an escape by standing up once the period started. As it sounded, he grabbed my wrist and rotated his body to get a foot underneath him. Courtesy of the counter, I saw everything as if in slow motion. With lightning-fast reflexes, my free hand shot out and grasped his foot, yanking it out from under him before he could complete his escape.

As we continued to fight, neither of us made any headway at first. Grunting from exertion, I maneuvered one elbow behind Travis's knee and worked to free my other hand from his iron grip on my wrist. I ripped my hand free and hooked my other elbow behind his head. He called me a few choice names as I locked my hands together and folded him into the cradle hold. I slid one knee into his side and rocked him onto his back. Using one of my legs, I held his free leg on the mat. He struggled violently against my effort to pin his shoulders, arching his back and suspending my weight as well as his own on his feet and head. I focused on breaking his bridge. Using my weight and the strength in my legs, I forced him down, driving his shoulders deep into the blue mat. I pinned Travis DeMarco and won the 2012 Oregon state wrestling championship in the 195 division.

The ref counted and slapped the mat. The crowd erupted into a chorus of cheering. After the whistle blew and I let him up, I dodged his furious fists until the refs intervened. While one pulled Travis off the mat, the other ref raised my arm, acknowledging me as the champion. My teammates, my coach, and my dad rushed toward me. The OSU wrestling coach introduced himself and put in a plug for his school's program.

"Where were you, Dad? I didn't see you before the match," I said when he gave me a hug.

He laughed. "I was sleeping in the car. I almost didn't wake up in time."

"Yeah, I know what you mean. Me too."

"That was impressive. We've got to call your mom," he said excitedly.

Whew—finally I'd done something right. We stuck around for the presentation of the awards, but mentally I'd already checked out. While we waited, I texted Ellie. "How r u feeling? Did u get some sleep? I won state. Should we go back 2nite?"

As we drove home I got her reply. Unlike every other teen, Ellie wasn't accustomed to carrying her phone everywhere. I slid my phone open and read, "Congratulations, darling. I knew u would win. I am so happy for u. I slept well & feel fine. I am ready when u r. How did it go with ur dad?"

"Ha ha u have 2 much confidence in me. But I like it. Lol. I survived my dad. Grounded from driving 4 a month, but im alive. Maybe winning state will soften him. I'll try 2 renegotiate."

I smiled while I waited, accidentally letting out a chuckle as I imagined Ellie carefully plunking out her reply.

"What's so funny?" my dad asked.

"Oh, nothing. What did you think about DeMarco throwing a punch after the whistle?"

"In a weird way, I guess that was funny. You sure were quick to dodge his fists. Where did that come from?"

I smiled. *My counter.* "Probably the fencing lessons. Gotta dodge the blade, you know."

My answer seemed to satisfy my dad's curiosity and he nodded.

With the sleep we'd missed the night before, my parents didn't care that I went to bed early. I did notice my keys to the truck were missing from my dresser and the extra set wasn't hanging in the kitchen as usual. Apparently, my mom and dad were serious about my lack of driving privileges.

I changed into my Erie Canal clothing, then sent Ellie a text. "I can leave whenever ur ready. Can't wait 2 c u." I dropped my phone on the bed and stomped my feet into my Wellingtons.

"Chase?" my dad called as he knocked on my door.

I rolled my eyes. "Dang it," I muttered. I ripped off the boots and yelled, "Just a minute." I pulled off the pants and both of the new shirts Ellie had made, then kicked everything under the bed before opening the door in my boxers. "Yeah, Dad? What do you need?" I asked in my most polite voice.

"I wanted to congratulate you again and tell you how proud I am of your accomplishment. I know I wasn't happy about you wrestling last fall, but I see now I was mistaken. You've really got a talent for it, and I'm proud of you for sticking with what you knew you wanted to do. Your mom thinks I may have been a little severe on the grounding. If you can stay out of trouble, I may consider returning your driving privileges sooner rather than later. But I expect you to show me you're responsible enough to earn it."

"Okay, thanks, Dad. I'll try to do that." I hoped Master Archidus didn't have anything strange in mind for my immediate future.

"Good job today. Your mom and I are going to bed too." My dad turned to leave.

"Thanks for everything, Dad. I love you."

"Love you too."

I closed the door and relocked it as my phone vibrated on the bed. I slid it open and read the message. "I need to change clothes, then I'll be ready."

I hit "Reply" and typed, "Can I come over now?" I set the phone on my bed and got dressed again before sending the message. Then I sat, elbows propped on my knees, waiting for Ellie's reply. When the phone vibrated in my hand, I read, "Yes, see u soon."

I set the phone down but picked it back up again, deciding to take it with me as far as Ellie's room. If my dad came back before I left there, Jessica could text me. I set my counter and pressed Shuffle and Go.

SEVENTEEN
Deception

I went through five easy shuffle zones before appearing in Ellie's room. With her back turned to me, she tucked a strand of hair into the bun on top of her head. I smiled at the transformation. Again, I was looking at the Ellie I'd first fallen in love with. I watched as she finished her hair and smoothed down her long skirt.

When she finally turned and noticed me, she breathed in sharply. "Oh. How long have you been here?"

"Not long," I answered, mesmerized by her beauty.

"You were so quiet. I didn't hear you." She checked the locks on the doors to the bathroom and the hall, then picked up one of the small bags she'd brought with her from Boston. She flipped off the lights and slid her arm through mine. "I'm ready."

I pulled out my cell phone and tossed it on Ellie's bed before setting the counter to Rome, New York, August 24, 1818. I positioned the last dial to the beginning of the day, imagining the dead of night shortly past midnight, then pressed Shuffle and Go.

When we appeared in our first shuffle zone, I shoved the counter in my pocket and offered to carry her bag for her. "Why the bag?" I asked as I wrapped my hand around hers.

"What woman in her right mind would travel to visit her cousin toting nothing but the clothes on her back? I'll not be giving anyone reason for suspicion. And I allow the idea of having a change of clothes is appealing as well."

I chuckled, pulling aside the collar on my new shirt to show Ellie my layers. "I'm wearing my change of clothes."

"They look nice on you." She smiled and we disappeared.

As we materialized, the ground dropped away from beneath us and we sank into deep water. I swallowed a mouthful of salt water—we were in the ocean! Kicking my feet, I launched myself to the surface, sputtering and coughing. Ellie hadn't come up yet, and I tugged on her hand. The effort of pulling her up, combined with the swell of the sea, plunged my head underwater again. Salt stung my nose as I raised my head for another gulp of air.

Between coughing up mouthfuls of water, Ellie screamed, "Chase, help me!" Her free hand frantically grabbed onto my shirt, pulling us both beneath the surface of the ocean. She struggled so desperately that I yanked my hand out of hers and turned her back to me. Wrapping my arm around her head and neck, I kicked back to the surface. As soon as we reached air, the screaming started again. The fingernails of her right hand dug into my flesh, while her left hand reached behind her, grabbing a handful of my shirt and scratching the side of my neck.

"Hold still," I yelled, accidentally sucking in another mouthful of water. I shoved her bag in front of her. "Take this."

Ellie coughed. "I can't. I'm too scared."

She trembled next to me, and my anger at feeling like she was drowning me melted away. I coughed up more water, then said softly, "Trust me, Ellie. You hold the bag and I'll hold you."

Still gasping and coughing, she took the bag from me and clutched it to her chest. With my hand free, I grabbed my hat before it floated away and pushed it onto my forehead, kicking my feet to keep us above the surface.

The sea was a brilliant shade of blue, like nothing I'd ever seen before. I leaned forward and kissed Ellie's ear. "Shh—lay your head on my shoulder." She was still shaking, and I worried she would hyperventilate. "Ellie, relax. Take a deep breath. What's wrong?"

"Isn't it obvious?"

"You don't know how to swim, do you?"

Her voice quivered. "Of course not. Where are we?"

I chuckled, thinking the answer was pretty clear. "The ocean. Maybe the Caribbean or the Pacific. Look around— it's beautiful." I kissed her cheek, tasting the salt water. "Try floating. Relax your body and tilt your head back, then keep taking deep breaths."

"Beautiful? Downright treacherous is more like it."

A large swell lifted us, and the bright sun glistened off the water's surface. "Why are you shaking? Are you cold?"

"No, yes, I don't know," Ellie mumbled.

Her body felt as tight as a bowstring next to mine. "The water's not cold," I said. "I think you just need to relax. Trust me—I've got you. Nothing's going to happen." We rose to the crest of another swell and a school of dolphins came into view, their sleek gray bodies twisting through the air. "Ellie, look! See the dolphins jumping out of the water? Aren't they amazing?"

She glanced at them. "What? There are fish here? Those are big fish. I don't fancy big fish. What if they come near us?"

Watching the dolphins wasn't calming her nerves, so I touched my lips to her cheek, enticing her to turn her head. Completely absorbed in kissing her, I didn't notice the familiar shimmer. When we reappeared over dry land without our feet solidly beneath us, we tumbled to the ground in a soaking heap. I still cradled Ellie's head in the crook of my arm, and she landed on top of me with a startled gasp.

I loosened my hold on her. "Are you okay?" Dripping water, she rolled off me and knelt on her hands and knees. She stared at the dried grass between her fingers while I propped myself on my elbow and looked around. Enormous rolled bales of hay dotted the horizon, and the sun hovered above the skyline, casting the field in a fiery haze.

Ellie breathed deeply. "Never have I welcomed the sight of dry ground with such fervor."

"I didn't realize you don't know how to swim," I said.

"I can't believe Jessica does that. My eyes are stinging. My nose is burning. It was the most powerfully dreadful ordeal."

I sat up next to Ellie and checked on the counter, thankful it hadn't fallen out of my pocket in the ocean. "Jess doesn't swim in salt water. Maybe we should teach you sometime."

Suddenly remembering we were in the middle of a shuffle, I reached over and grabbed Ellie's wrist. She looked at me and put her other hand on her bag, not a moment too soon. We faded away from the hayfield and reappeared in the middle of a busy residential street. A horn honked behind us and I jumped to my feet, pulling her up with me. I wrapped my arm around her and led her to the side of the road. The teenager behind the wheel of the purple 1970s Pontiac stared at us as he drove by. There were enough kids riding their bikes and people working in their yards that I looked for a more private place to disappear.

It didn't take long before our clothes started attracting attention. Several people along the street stopped what they were doing to watch us. One house looked good—heavy foliage in the yard and no people around. I walked across the front lawn toward the gate to the backyard and glanced over my shoulder. The lady weeding her flower bed across the street stared back at me. I gave her a friendly wave before stepping behind the bushes.

We next appeared in a blast of Arctic air, and our drenched clothing accentuated the chill. I wrapped my arms around Ellie and pulled her next to me. "The counter has definitely not been kind to me tonight," I said. When I tried to tuck her head into my chest she leaned back, looking around.

"Why, Chase, this is Boston Harbor. What year is it?"

I pulled out the counter and looked at the dials.

"Well?" she asked again.

"It's December 18, 1863."

Her brow furrowed. "Right now I'm dying of pneumonia a mile from here."

I smiled. "Don't worry—I'll show up in three days to save you."

For the final time we disappeared, then reappeared behind Rose's boardinghouse. Candlelight filtered through the open window. I let go of Ellie and walked over to peer between the gap in the curtains. Rose struggled to give birth as the midwives huddled together, speaking in whispered tones. One of them left the room, and Garrick stormed in a moment later. He knelt beside the bed and buried his head in Rose's long dark hair, muttering something in her ear. Weakly, she lifted her hand and caressed the back of his neck.

He raised his head to look at the remaining midwife. "I'd like a moment alone with my wife."

She nodded. "Certainly, Mr. Eastman. We'll be in the kitchen if you need us."

I knew what would happen next, and a wave of sadness came over me. Ellie slid her arm through mine. Garrick stood and strode across the room to lock the door. He pulled Rose up next to him, wrapped her in a blanket, and flipped his counter open. They disappeared.

In the light of the full moon I turned to Ellie. Silent tears trickled from her beautiful eyes. I held her face in my hands and wiped my thumbs across her cheeks. "He'll be back any minute. We should go in."

She nodded once and followed me. I knocked before opening the kitchen door. "Garrick," I called, pretending not to know what was happening.

I held the door for Ellie. "Mrs. Benson, where's Garrick?"

We listened as the midwife explained the grave situation. There was nothing more they could do for Rose. It was in God's hands now.

"This is Rose's cousin, Ellie Williams. She came to help, but—" I didn't finish the sentence, considering the news they'd shared.

"It's a pleasure to meet you, dear. I'm Martha Benson and this is Betty Gunderson."

"It's nice to meet both of you, but it sounds like I should check on my cousin," Ellie said politely.

We watched her walk to the bedroom door and knock. "Garrick? Rose? It's Ellie," she called softly.

A disheveled-looking Garrick opened the door and let her in, briefly making eye contact with me before closing the door again.

The minutes ticked by slowly. Mrs. Gunderson had been eyeing me with a strange expression for quite some time before she must have worked up the courage to say anything.

"Mr. Harper, however did you and Miss Williams come to be soaking wet in the dry of summer?"

"We had a little trouble fording the river," I lied.

"How unusual for this time of year."

"Yes, it is. Carelessness on my part." I hoped Mrs. Gunderson would leave it at that.

She and Mrs. Benson and I sat across from each other in Rose's kitchen, and I knew that like me, the midwives were straining to hear what was happening in the next room. Occasionally, the low murmur of muffled voices escaped the closed door. When Ellie stepped out, her eyes were brimming with tears. She shook her head and walked toward me.

"She's gone. Rose and the babies are lost."

"I'm sorry," I mumbled, wrapping my arm around Ellie.

She wiped her eyes. "You should go sit with your brother. He's taking it hard and doesn't want to leave her side."

"Sure, I can do that." I walked into the bedroom and found Garrick sitting on the edge of the bed, cradling his head in his hands.

"Thanks, Harper," he said quietly. "Ellie said to stay put until the midwives leave. Then we need to climb out the window and fill some burlap sacks with dirt. We have to get them in here before dawn without anyone seeing us."

I sat shoulder to shoulder with my friend, silently mourning with him.

Soon, we heard the front door open and close, followed by Ellie cracking the bedroom door open to whisper, "Go ahead."

I pulled aside the curtain and jumped out the window. Thanks to Davy, I knew where the burlap sacks were. "Garrick, I'll get the sacks," I said. "You get the shovels."

He landed next to me on the dried grass and nodded. "Meet me by the garden."

The dark interior of the shed made it difficult to see, but I found the stash of sacks, piled in anticipation of the upcoming potato harvest. We filled three of them, and before long we were hauling them back to the house. "I'll get the last sack if you want to put the shovels away," I said.

"Thanks, little brother," Garrick said in a monotone.

Once the sacks were in the bedroom, Ellie laid out the next phase of the plan. "Chase, as soon as the town wakes up, you arrange for the casket. I'll talk with the preacher to schedule the funeral and burial. Garrick, you go to bed. I expect you're tuckered out after the last few days, and your eyes look as heavy as lead."

"What about Davy?" I asked.

Garrick pressed the heels of his hands into eyes. "I don't know if I can face him right now."

"Chase and I can care for him," Ellie offered. "You need to rest."

Garrick left the kitchen, walking like a zombie toward the rooms used by the boarders. I couldn't believe this had happened—couldn't believe Rose was really gone. It all felt like a bad dream.

The predawn light lit the eastern horizon as I slumped into one of the kitchen chairs. With her hands on her hips, Ellie surveyed the room. "What do we need to do to keep the boardinghouse running smoothly with Rose gone?"

"Breakfast, I guess. The guys will wake up and expect to find food."

"What do you think they'll want to eat?"

"Eggs and flapjacks are always a big hit," I answered.

"I'll look around in here for the flour. Do you want to find the eggs?"

"Sure. I know where the eggs are." I pulled my tired body out of the chair and got the egg basket from the cellar.

"Thank you," she said when I handed them to her. "Now, do you mind fetching wood for the fire and a pail of water?"

"Not at all."

After I started the fire, brought in water from the well, and set out plates and utensils, I watched Ellie. Within no time at all, she had the frying pan and the griddle full of scrambled eggs and flapjacks.

"Mornin', Mr. Harper. When did you get here?" a little voice said. Davy stood in the kitchen doorway, wearing his nightshirt and rubbing the sleep out of his eyes. "Who's that?" He pointed at Ellie.

"This is Ellie," I said. "She's your ma's cousin. I don't think you've met her before."

He walked across the room to stand next to her. "Hello. I'm Davy."

She smiled down at him. "It's certainly a pleasure to make your acquaintance, Master Davy."

He giggled and then asked, "Where's my ma?"

My jaw dropped and I stared at Ellie, who looked back at me with a furrowed brow.

"Where's my Garrick Pa?" the little boy asked next.

Ellie answered the second question. "Davy, your pa is sleeping right now. He had a very rough night."

"Where's my ma?" Davy asked again.

Ellie handed me the wooden spatula. "Perhaps you should take over the cooking while Davy and I take a walk outside."

"Mr. Harper doesn't know how to cook eggs," the boy explained.

"Is that so?" she said with a smile. "Certainly he can manage this morning, since they're nearly done. Davy, why don't you show me where your clothes are and we'll get you dressed before we go out this morning."

I turned to the pan and started stirring. "Remember to flip the flapjacks," Ellie said as Davy pulled her by the hand toward his room.

The men wandered into the kitchen. I set the eggs on the table and kept turning the pancakes. When one of the men asked about Rose, I passed along the sad news, warning them that Davy didn't know yet. The men ate in silence and left quickly. I cleaned up the breakfast mess and then went to find Ellie and Davy.

The two of them were sitting on the stump of an old tree, watching the chickens scratch in the dirt. I stopped behind Ellie and laid my hands on her shoulders.

"Davy, run get your hat and then you can show me where to find the preacher," she said.

"Yes, Miss Ellie." He hopped off the stump and walked toward the house.

She sniffled, then stood and wrapped her arms around my waist. "That was one of the hardest things I've ever had to tell someone."

"How did he take it?"

"He cried at first, but I told him about my mother and how I was able to cope without her. Children are so resilient. They are often much stronger than we give them credit for."

"Thank you for talking with him. I wouldn't have known what to say."

"I'm ready to go, Miss Ellie," Davy said when he returned. His eyes looked sad, but he held his head high.

Ellie wiped away her tears. "I'm ready too." She reached out her hand to him and they walked down the street.

The next three days were a whirlwind of activity. Ellie and I coordinated the funeral and gravesite arrangements. Garrick insisted on ordering the nicest marble headstone that money could buy. Samuel from the livery lent me a buckboard and I picked up the casket, then arranged the burlap sacks inside to simulate the weight of a pregnant Rose. Carefully, I nailed the lid closed. Garrick acted sullen and depressed, spending most of his time sleeping. One night we found him crying on Davy's shoulder when he should have been putting the boy to bed. The poor kid had trouble sleeping that night. He seemed to miss his ma the most at bedtime. Ellie and I found if we kept him busy during the day he was a happy little guy, doing all the normal things kids do. Little Davy acted like he was smitten with her and often clung to her apron as he followed her around.

Garrick and Rose's friends nodded in understanding when Ellie explained why there wouldn't be a wake and why the coffin had been nailed shut. Everyone agreed wholeheartedly that it was too painful for a man to see his wife like that.

An overcast sky attended us the morning we buried Rose, and the humid air felt oppressive as I stood gazing at the four-foot-high gravestone, which read: "Rose Adams Eastman, beloved wife and mother. Born September 16, 1791. Died August 24, 1818."

We listened as the preacher recited a prayer and spoke a few kind words about Rose. The townsfolk offered their sympathies, while Ellie and I stood quietly by. With a grief-stricken Garrick, the deception was complete. No one ever suspected we hadn't actually buried Rose that day.

EIGHTEEN
Shadow

The day after the funeral, Garrick went back to work at the canal. When I offered to stay and help Ellie with the chores, she insisted Garrick needed my help more. The dig site was now miles away from the boardinghouse, so Garrick and I discreetly used our counters to hop back and forth between work and home. Occasionally, we'd walk the distance so the other men would see us on the road and not become suspicious.

With time, instead of getting better, Garrick got worse. He sank so deep into despair over the loss of his wife that one would have thought he'd buried himself along with her. If it weren't for Ellie running the boardinghouse and caring for Davy, everything would have collapsed around Garrick. He tried to play with his son in the evenings and tried to tell him bedtime stories, but the man was a mere shadow of his former self. One day after work, old Jed invited him to the tavern, and Garrick accepted. I didn't say anything and went back to the boardinghouse.

Ellie frowned when I walked in the door alone. "Garrick didn't come home with you?"

"No, he went to the tavern." I could feel myself scowling, but I didn't have the energy to offer her a smile.

She had cooked a stew and baked rolls for supper that night. After the men ate, she and I sat together. Halfway through my meal, I took a deep breath and said, "Garrick is so frustrating."

"Everyone grieves in their own way."

"Yeah, but he needs to stop being so selfish and think of Davy."

Ellie glanced out the window to check on the little boy.

Suddenly, I realized she was feeling the brunt of my anger, which she definitely didn't deserve. "That's enough about Garrick," I said, managing a grin. "Tell me about your day."

She listed off all the things she'd done that day and explained which neighbor ladies had stopped by to chat and how well Davy was learning his ABCs. Ellie planned to teach him how to write his numbers next. I smiled to myself as I got a glimpse of what life could be like someday when I was married to her.

I helped her tuck Davy into bed, and then the two of us sat on the porch steps, watching the setting sun. I thought about Garrick, and I assumed Ellie was doing the same. When she yawned, I asked, "You're not working too hard, are you?"

She smiled. "I'm fine. A little tired is all."

"What should I do about Garrick?"

"He's a grown man. I'm certain he'll be fine."

"I guess you're right."

I stood and offered her my hand. She took it with a smile and I walked her to Rose's room, down the hall from the room I shared with Davy. Garrick had refused to sleep in Rose's room since her passing. Ellie placed her hand on my cheek and kissed me good night. Before she could open the door, I pulled her next to the wall, trapping her between my arms.

"I really appreciate all you're doing around here," I said. "I don't know what we'd do without you."

"You're welcome, Chase."

As I talked, I moved my mouth closer to hers. "You were amazing with the townspeople and the preacher. Garrick and I never could have pulled that off alone. No one suspected a thing."

Her eyes darted across my face and her tongue flicked out to wet her lips. "It helps that these folks are from the same generation as my grandfather," she said.

I covered her mouth with mine, pressing her body against the wall.

"Boy, you best leave that girl be, or so help me I'll take a belt to ya, same as if you were my own son."

Jerking my head up at the gruff voice, I glanced over my shoulder. Down the hall stood the old-timer who had the room Garrick and I used to share. The man scowled at me, and I didn't doubt for one second he'd follow through on the threat.

"You okay, missy?" he asked.

Ellie nodded and said, "Yes."

The geezer drilled me with his steely gaze until I stepped away from her. Then he disappeared around the corner.

"I guess I'd better let you get some sleep," I said, admiring her flushed face.

After she stepped into her room, I thought, *What a date*.

During breakfast the next morning, I realized we hadn't seen Garrick yet. I ate my biscuits and jam while I walked to his room. "Dang it," I muttered when I opened his door and found his bed empty. It didn't look like he'd come home last night.

Back in the kitchen, I found Ellie struggling to open a jar of strawberry preserves. I took the bottle and popped the lid off for her. "Garrick didn't come home last night. I'd better go look for him."

"You don't think he up and left, do you?" she asked.

I shook my head. "Nah, I don't think so. But it would sure be nice if we all had cell phones right now." I left the house and jogged down the street toward Tyke's Tavern. Halfway there, I ran into Mr. Van Duesen and his daughter Anna, bringing a load of produce into town. I nodded and tipped my hat, intent on continuing toward the tavern. But Mr. Van Duesen stopped the wagon to let Anna hop out.

"Mr. Harper," she called, following after me.

"Yeah, Anna?" I noticed her father had continued down the street with his wagon.

"Will you be attending the church social on Saturday?"

"I haven't heard much about it, actually."

"You're welcome to come with my family if you'd like. I noticed you being awful friendly with Rose's cousin at the funeral. Perhaps things didn't work out with the girl in Boston?"

Anxious to be on my way, I said, "I'm sorry, Anna. But the girl I was with at the funeral is the girl from Boston. If I go to the social, I'll be taking her with me."

Disappointment clouded Anna's expression. "Oh, I see."

"I need to get going before I'm late to work."

I ran the rest of the way to the tavern. There in the dirt, slumped against the side of the building, lay Garrick. I rushed to him, hoping he wasn't dead. After prying the empty whiskey bottle from his hand, I grabbed his wrist. Feeling a strong pulse, I realized he was just sleeping off all the stuff he'd drunk the night before.

I spun around at the sound of a gravelly voice behind me. "Came for yer brother, did ya?" Mr. Tyke, the barkeep, stood holding his beer belly and scratching his balding scalp.

"Yes, sir," I said, shaking Garrick.

Mr. Tyke walked closer. "Yer brother done got himself all roostered up last night. He ain't the only one who's looked for comfort at the bottom of a bottle. A man don't take kindly to losing his wife. 'Specially the way he lost her. It's a hard thing."

I nodded, then hooked my arm through Garrick's and dragged him to his feet.

"Time to go to work, little brother?" he slurred.

"Yeah, Garrick. It's time to go to work, but you might be too drunk to work a shovel."

He pushed me away and walked a crooked line toward the street. "Nonsense, Harper. I can work a shovel."

By the time we reached the boardinghouse he was awake, complaining about his pounding headache. He slammed down some breakfast and we disappeared with our counters. After appearing in the stand of trees near the dig site, we hustled to sign in with the paymaster.

When the workday ended, Garrick said, "I'll meet you at home. I'm going to grab a drink first."

"I don't think that's a good idea. What about Davy? He needs you—"

"Harper, you're starting to sound like my mother. I'm going to the tavern. That's final. Davy doesn't care about me. He'd rather Ellie tucked him into bed anyway."

"That's because you're ornery every night."

Garrick turned his back and waved me off.

I went home without him and enjoyed another evening with Ellie. Davy and I played soccer while she sewed him a new shirt. That night before I went to bed, I walked to the tavern and retrieved a drunken Garrick. He'd passed out next to his empty glass. Ellie frowned as I dragged him into the boardinghouse and down the hall to his room.

The next three weeks followed the same pattern. Garrick and I would dig the canal, go our separate ways—him to the tavern, me to the boardinghouse—and then I'd haul my drunken "brother" back home to bed. Ellie and I were so exhausted from the cooking, cleaning, and washing that we didn't make it to the church social. It would take too much effort to get cleaned up and ready to go.

After three weeks of dealing with a drunk, I'd had it. I understood Garrick was hurting. I knew he was grieving and experiencing guilt beyond what I could imagine, but I was fed up with his irresponsible actions. So, following a nice dinner with Ellie, I stood up and said, "I'm going to the tavern."

She gave me the strangest look and I realized what she must be thinking. "Not to drink—to get Garrick. He can't expect you to take care of Davy and the boardinghouse forever. It's time he man up and move on."

"Be careful, Chase," Ellie said just before I jammed my hat on my head and marched out the door.

I found Garrick drowning his sorrows in a bottle of whiskey. I stood next to him but he stared straight ahead, ignoring me. "Can I talk to you outside?" I asked.

He poured another glass. "If you have something to say, you can say it in here."

I glanced around the tavern. A few of the men were watching us, but most minded their own business. Placing my hands on the table, I leaned toward my friend. "It's time to come home. You're a father. You've got to think of Davy. He needs you. Rose is counting on you to take care of him, to love him. I know you're hurting, but you've—"

Garrick jumped to his feet, knocking his chair over. "You know nothing, Harper!" He shoved me toward the door so hard I nearly fell over the table. "Get out. I don't need you telling me what to do." At that point, every eye in the room zeroed in on us.

I pushed him back. "You're drunk. Enough is enough."

Anger blazed in Garrick's bloodshot eyes. He backed me toward the door, shoving me ahead of him. "Go home."

"Listen to me. You're not the only one who's lost somebody. Davy lost his mother, and at the rate you're drinking, he's going to lose his father, too." I pushed Garrick back again. "It's time you man up and take care of things. We can't stay here for—"

He punched me in the face, sending me toppling out the door. I did a backward somersault across the wooden planks of the tavern porch and hopped to my feet in time for his next punch. His fist slammed into my nose, and blood gushed down my face. I stumbled down the steps into the dusty street. With raised fists he followed me.

I touched my nose, hoping it wasn't broken. "Knock it off, Garrick."

When I tried to hit back, he batted away my fists like it was child's play. I ducked under his right hook, but immediately his left fist connected with my rib cage. His skill far surpassed mine, and the speed and strength from my counter gave me no advantage against another Keeper with the same gifts. He randomly alternated blows between my stomach and my face, leaving me guessing where the next punch would land. If I could have gotten my arms around him, I might've stood a chance at wrestling him onto the ground, but his fists kept me at bay. The tavern soon emptied, and a circle of cheering men surrounded us. My head was spinning and my bloodied nose throbbed.

Suddenly, Garrick's expression softened and he lowered his hands. At that moment, I punched him square in the jaw and his head rattled to the side. "You're a terrible boxer, Harper. I've got a lot of work to do with you. Guard your face better. Keep your hands up, like this, and move around. You're like a sitting duck. You're standing there like a punching bag. Be lighter on your feet and tuck your elbows in next to your body to protect your ribs."

I wiped the back of my hand across my face. It came away covered in blood, and I shoved him. "Shut up, Garrick!"

He looked back at the crowd of people and put his arm around me, "Come on, little brother. Let's go home." I jerked away, not wanting anything to do with him. We were nearly home before he got around to apologizing. "Look, I'm sorry, Harper. I don't know what got into me. I snapped. There's no excuse for my behavior. I was thinking about what you said, and you're right. I'm through with the tavern from here on out. I made a promise to Rose, and I'm going to keep it. Can you ever forgive me?"

I tipped my head back, pinching the bridge of my nose to slow the flow of blood trickling onto my new shirt. "Yeah, it's not like I haven't been beat up before."

Ellie and Davy sat waiting on the front porch. When we were close enough for Ellie to see the blood, she ran toward me. "Garrick, what happened to him?"

"Sorry, Ellie," he said. "It was my fault."

She handed me the dish towel from her apron pocket. "What do you mean? Did you drag him into one of your tavern brawls?"

I took the rag and held it to my nose. "He was the brawl."

Garrick dropped to one knee and opened his arms to Davy, who launched himself into his pa's embrace.

Ellie brought her hands to her hips and faced Garrick. "You hit him?"

He shrugged his shoulders and gave her a crooked grin.

"How could you? I can't believe you two—fighting like a couple of schoolboys!" With a huff she steered me toward the well.

"Do you want me to do that?" I offered when she began drawing up a bucket of water.

"No, you go lie down, and I'll bring you a cold compress. I'll need that shirt so I can wash it before the bloodstain sets in."

Her angry tone triggered a chuckle from me. I pulled my shirt over my head and set it next to her before walking to the house. With my hand on the back door, I glanced over my shoulder. Her eyes met mine and I winked. She turned away, probably because I'd caught her staring. I went inside and obediently lay down on my bed. Davy's delighted laughter drifted through the open window as Garrick wrestled with him.

Ellie came in holding a cold, wet towel. "Here you are." She sat next to me on the edge of the bed and frowned. "Why did he hit you?"

"I guess he was mad about Rose, and at me for telling him what to do. He needed an outlet for all that anger, and I was it."

"And that doesn't bother you? Why, the two of you came waltzing home like you're as thick as thieves."

"He apologized, and we're all good now."

Ellie shook her head, looking skeptical. "I'd best tend to that shirt before the blood dries." She walked out of the room while I held the cold towel against my nose.

After dinner the next evening, Garrick pulled me aside. "Harper, come out back. I want to show you something before it gets dark."

I looked behind me. The kitchen was clean, and Ellie was heating water for Davy's bath.

"Give me your hand," Garrick said once we stood near the woodpile. "Hold it out like this."

He extended his hand rigidly in front of him with his fingers separated. When I held my hand out, he pulled long strips of linen from his pocket and began wrapping my knuckles.

"What's this for?" I asked.

"Hand wraps, to protect your knuckles and wrists while we're sparring."

"We're sparring? My face is still sore from yesterday's beating."

Garrick finished my right hand and started wrapping my left. "Yes, we're sparring. What kind of big brother would I be if I didn't teach you how to hold your own in a fistfight? It was downright embarrassing last night in front of the tavern."

"I wasn't that bad," I said. "It's not like we were fighting very long."

"My point exactly. You were bleeding like a stuck pig within seconds. But give me a few days and I'll have you boxing like Joe Louis."

"Yeah, right."

He glanced down at my boots. "First, let's fix your stance. Put your feet shoulder width apart with your left foot out in front, and angle your toes on both feet to the right—between twelve and two o'clock. Keep your hips under your shoulders and your body centered over your feet."

I imitated his foot position. "Like this?"

"That's good. Now make a fist and raise your hands to cheek level with your palms inward. Slide your thumbs around so they rest on the knuckle of your middle finger." Garrick reached out to correct my thumb position. "During a fight, keep your elbows tight against your ribs to protect your body. The basic opening punch is the jab. It's done with the forward hand—that's your left. Extend your arm fully and rotate your fist so your thumb is facing the ground before you strike your target. Keep your elbow flexed a bit so you don't hyperextend it when you hit hard." He took up his boxing stance in front of me, demonstrating the punch. "Try that on me. Hit my shoulder."

"Are you sure?"

"Yeah, let's see it. Don't hit your hardest. Unless of course you're still mad at me for yesterday—then I probably deserve whatever you can dish out. But I'd rather work on your form tonight."

I practiced the jab, landing my knuckles squarely on his shoulder.

"Nice. Again. Step forward with your left foot, but keep your weight on the back foot." Following a few more jabs, Garrick said, "Now, let's add the straight right. In a fight, open with the jab and then give 'em a straight right. Shift your weight to the left foot and pivot your right foot forward as you deliver a jab with the right hand. After any punch, immediately go back to your beginning stance. Try that combo on me—jab then straight right."

While I completed my jab, straight-right combo, the back door to the boardinghouse banged open. Ellie's disapproving voice brought us to a standstill. "What in Sam Hill do you two think you're doing?"

Garrick and I lowered our arms and turned to face her. Hands on her hips, she scowled back at us.

"I'm teaching him how to fight," my friend said.

"Garrick, if you hit him again, so help me I'll . . . I'll . . . Why you'll be fixin' your own meals from here on out." She folded her arms over her chest.

"I'm being careful," he said.

"You better!" Ellie turned so quickly her skirt swirled around her ankles as she marched back through the door.

Garrick chuckled. "I guess your girlfriend doesn't want me messing up your face again."

"Guess not." I said, laughing with him.

He raised his fists. "Back to work. The next move I want to teach you is the uppercut. Take your stance, then drop your right shoulder and bend your right leg at the knee. Rotate your hips forward as you punch your right fist upward. For maximum power, keep your elbow bent at a right angle. The uppercut will usually force your opponent's head toward you. After a solid uppercut to the body, you can usually throw a second one into his face." Garrick finished demonstrating and turned his shoulder to me. "Now you try."

He endured a series of combos—jab, straight right, uppercut—before he called it a night. Rubbing his shoulder and his stomach, he said, "I guess we don't get to spar tonight because I plan on eating breakfast tomorrow. I tell you what, though. We need to make us a punching bag."

The next night, we filled a large burlap sack with sand and hung it from a tree. Every night after dinner, Garrick drilled me on the fundamentals of boxing. When I wasn't quick enough on my feet between the punching combos, he added jump rope to my nightly routine. Along with my work on the Erie Canal, the boxing practice left me utterly exhausted at the end of each day. Ellie eventually softened her opinion of the boxing, and she and Davy watched from the back steps.

NINETEEN
Return

As promised, Garrick stayed away from the tavern. He seemed to snap out of his depression and began acting almost normal, though I wondered if he would ever fully recover from losing his wife and their babies. Two weeks later, at the end of one of our boxing lessons, he announced that he and Davy had decided to sell the boardinghouse and move west to the Ohio Valley. "There's nothing here for us now," Garrick said. "I don't want to run a boardinghouse. I don't even know how to cook."

The prospect of an adventure clearly thrilled Davy. And although I had enjoyed being in 1818 with Ellie, the thought of a hot shower and an evening of ESPN sounded awesome. "That's a good idea, Garrick," I said.

Ellie stepped forward to unwrap my hands. "It's such a nice night. Would you care to take a stroll?"

"Sure." With Garrick caring for Davy in the evenings again, Ellie had more time to spend with me, and we were soon walking hand in hand down the dusty street.

"It has been strange, don't you think, being here like this?" she asked. "It's like living a second life."

"Yeah, it is strange. But I've been back here enough times I'm getting used to it. And this is definitely the longest date I've ever been on. What has it been, six . . . seven weeks or something?"

Ellie laughed. "It has been a long date. Are you ever tempted to stay here?"

"I was tempted when I thought I'd lost you. It was easier for me to be here than to be home. When I was here, I knew you hadn't been born yet. When I was home" —I shook my head at the painful memory— "all I was left with was the fact that your life had passed without me in it. Now, I'd only want to stay if you were here. Do you wish we lived somewhere else? Would you want to stay here?"

"Oh no," she said. "I'm rather enjoying living in the future. I fancy discovering new things, and I love reading about all the years I skipped. I've been given an amazing gift. My life feels as if it spans hundreds of years, instead of being limited to sixty or seventy like everyone else."

I nodded. "I'll definitely be ready to go home once Garrick sells the boardinghouse."

It was another two weeks before he completed the sale and bought a wagon and provisions. When Ellie packed up Rose's clothes for donation to the church, she found the diamond wedding ring wrapped in a lace handkerchief. Garrick took it from her hand and looked at it. Without saying a word, he folded the handkerchief around the ring and stuffed it in his pocket.

He planned to stay with Rose's brother in Cleveland through the winter and build a cabin for himself and Davy the next spring. The night before Garrick and Davy were to leave, Ellie and I said goodbye.

With tears in his eyes, the little boy hugged Ellie. "I love you, Miss Ellie. Will you come visit me in Ohio?"

"I love you too, Davy." She glanced in my direction before saying, "If I can, I'll come see you again someday. But for now, you help your pa, okay?"

"Yes, ma'am."

"Goodbye, Garrick," Ellie said, embracing him. "Good luck in Ohio."

"Thank you, Ellie, for everything. I wouldn't have survived the last two months without you. If you ever need my help, you let me know and I'll be there." Garrick nodded his head toward her as he turned to me. "Harper, you take care of this one. You won't find anyone better."

"I know. See you later, bro." I grabbed his hand and gave him a quick hug. I ruffled Davy's hair as I bent down and picked up Ellie's bag. "'Bye, Davy."

We walked out the door and down the street, then disappeared into the night. On the second shuffle, Ellie gripped my arm. "Each time I fear I'll sink into that dreadful ocean again."

"With all the shuffling I've done, that's only happened once. I doubt it will be a problem tonight."

When we eventually appeared in her bedroom, I smiled. "Safely home at last. And look, you're not even wet."

"Thank you," she said. "I do appreciate staying dry."

I set her bag on the bed and wrapped my arms around her waist. "You're welcome. But unfortunately I can't take the credit for that. I'm at the mercy of my counter, and he's been known to be mischievous at times."

"He? What, it's a person now?"

Giving my imagination free rein, I said, "Yeah, I think the sorcerer dude who made it hides out in there. He's got a wicked sense of humor, too."

Ellie lifted my hat off my head and held it behind my neck. I was absorbing every detail of her perfect face when she kissed me. I slid my hand behind her neck, hoping to keep her there as long as possible, and I wasn't disappointed. She so rarely initiated the kissing that when she tipped her head away from me, I couldn't resist asking, "What was that for?"

"Well—" Looking flustered, she tried to step out of my arms, but I simply tightened my grip.

"You know I love it when you kiss me, don't you?" I said.

"You do?"

"Of course I do. I'm just wondering what prompted that amazing kiss." I touched my lips to her forehead.

Again she attempted to wiggle out of my embrace. "You're not going to let me go until I answer, are you?"

"Nope. I've got all night, and after two months of digging the canal, I think I'm strong enough to hang onto you."

Ellie laughed lightly. "I'll warrant that's a known fact. All right, I'll tell you. I find it very appealing when you wear these clothes."

"And?"

"And I knew this was the last night I'd see you in them, so I thought to enjoy it. There, are you happy now?"

I kissed her one more time. "That wasn't so bad, was it? And yes, I am happy." Lifting my arms, I stepped away from her and retrieved my counter. "Ellie, thank you again for helping Garrick and for a very enjoyable date."

She smiled. "You're welcome. Good night."

I reappeared in my bedroom after five shuffle zones, then stripped off my dirty clothes and picked up the damp towel off the floor. My clothes smelled awful. After a month of no deodorant, *I* smelled awful. I didn't quite get what Ellie found attractive about the dirty, Erie Canal version of me, but I wasn't about to complain. I wrapped the towel around my waist and dashed down the hall to the bathroom. Daydreaming of my girlfriend, I guess I assumed it wasn't occupied. But as I reached for the doorknob, the door opened, flooding the hall with light.

"Oh my gosh!" Jessica screamed. "You scared me. What are you doing?"

"Taking a shower. What does it look like?"

"Come here," she said. Wide eyed, she pulled me by the arm into the bathroom. *"That's* what it looks like." She pointed at the mirror. "You've grown a beard, sprouted a suntan, and you need a haircut."

I rubbed my hand across my chin and took a closer look in the mirror. "Looks like I'm overdue for a shave. You can see why I need a shower." I loved toying with my sister, and tonight looked like a recipe for success.

She folded her arms across her chest. "I'm not leaving this bathroom until you tell me what you've been up to."

With a smirk, I stepped past her and turned on the water. "Close your eyes then."

"I'll tell Dad."

That brought me up short. "All right. I was back at the Erie Canal in 1818. My brother . . . I mean my friend, Garrick, needed my help with some stuff and I spent two months there."

"You should take me. I want to see what you're doing."

I shook my head. "That's not a good idea. I can't, actually. I would get in major trouble if I took you away from here."

"Oh. So, when did you leave?"

"After I said I was going to bed. But I came back a minute later. When I'm there, it's like time stands still here. And now my hot water is wasting. Do you mind?" I nodded toward the door.

Jessica shook her head as she left the bathroom. After I showered, I shaved and trimmed my hair to minimize my change in appearance.

After being away from technology, I didn't realize my cell phone was missing until I saw Jessica texting during breakfast. The last time I remembered having it was in Ellie's bedroom before we'd left.

I stood to clear my bowl. "I need to drive over to Adam's."

My dad nearly roared in protest. "I don't think so!"

"Oh, crap. I forgot I'm grounded."

"That's right. I said I might shorten it, but you're not getting off that easy."

"Sorry, I remember now. Jess, are you going anywhere today?"

"I can take you this afternoon," she said.

When Jessica finally took me to Ellie's, I knocked once on Adam's door and then walked in. "Hey, Aunt Marianne," I called as Jessica and I walked through their kitchen.

"Hi, Chase. Hi, Jessica. What are you doing today?" she said.

I let Jessica answer as I took the steps two at a time on my way to Ellie's room.

Adam stepped into the hall. "Hey, dude. What's up, man?"

"Not much. I came to see Ellie for a minute."

He smiled. "Congratulations! Ellie told us the good news."

"What good news?"

He looked back at me like I was a complete idiot. "Wrestling—state championship. You did win, didn't you?"

"Oh, that. Yeah, I did. Thanks, dude." I sighed, then stepped past him to knock on Ellie's door. I had wondered if she'd told

Adam I'd hinted at the "m" word—marriage. With me barely eighteen, my parents would flip if they knew I'd already decided whom I was marrying.

"Chase," Ellie said when she opened the door. "I didn't know you were coming over."

"Yeah, well—" I glanced at Adam, who stood in the hall watching us. "I thought I'd surprise you."

"Before we go downstairs," she said, "can you help me for a minute?"

"Sure." I followed her into her room and she shut the door behind me.

"Did you forget something?" she asked.

"Yeah, do you have my phone?"

She walked into the bathroom and came back a moment later. "I stuck it between the towels in the cupboard because it wouldn't stop vibrating last night. Your girlfriend must be missing you." Ellie frowned.

I slid open my phone and looked at the display—there were ten new messages, and they were all from Kim. I clenched my jaw. I hadn't gotten a text from her since Christmas vacation, and now this, on the one night Ellie had my phone.

"Ex-girlfriend," I corrected her. "You're my girlfriend. What the heck does Kim want with me anyway?"

"She's probably trying to win you back."

"Like that's going to happen." When I looked in Ellie's eyes, I saw a hint of concern. "You're not seriously worried about her, are you?"

She turned away and shrugged her shoulders. "Well . . . she's very pretty and so modern and smart."

"Ellie, come on. She's not that smart, and modern isn't all it's cracked up to be. She can't even ride a horse."

"Chase, when do girls around here need to ride horses? We come from such different backgrounds that I find myself worrying I won't always be right for you."

"That's ridiculous." I walked over and placed my hands on her shoulders, forcing her to look at me. "You are my type of girl, not Kim. As long as I live, I promise I won't change my mind. You have nothing to worry about."

Ellie dropped her gaze. "I'm sorry. I suppose I'm feeling melancholy after leaving Davy. He's such a sweet boy and I grew so fond of him."

"That's okay. We'll see them again. Next time I run into Garrick, I'll figure out where they settled and then I'll take you for a visit."

She smiled. "I'd like that."

"Ellie! Chase!" Adam's voice boomed. "It's dinnertime."

Aunt Marianne fed Jessica and me dinner along with her family. When Jessica said she had homework, I reluctantly told Ellie goodbye. *Come to think of it, I might have homework, too.* After the state wrestling tournament, the tragedy of Garrick losing Rose, and then weeks of living in 1818, I couldn't remember where I was with my classes.

Later that night, my phone vibrated in my pocket, reminding me of Kim's text messages. Sliding the phone open, I saw a message from Adam. He wanted to know if I would do track with him this year. I hit "Reply." "Sure I'm thinking javelin. Tell ur mom thx 4 dinner."

I started opening the messages from Kim. "Congratulations. I heard about ur state championship. That's awesome!" Next message: "Where r u?" Next message: "Did u get my text? Ur not ignoring me r u?" Next message: "Maybe ur already asleep. Party next Sat at my house. Can u come? Let me know. U haven't done anything w/ us in like 4ever!" Next message: "R u still sleeping? It's noon." Next message: "What's going on? R u mad @ me or something?" Next message: "Quit ignoring me. I can't believe u." Next message: "I thot we were still @ least friends. Why won't u answer me?" Next message: "Hello? Where r u?" Next message: "Grrr what r u doing?"

You've got to be kidding me. I can't believe it even crossed Ellie's mind that I'd be tempted to go back to this. Maybe I wouldn't answer Kim. I should keep her guessing until Monday. It would serve her right after all those annoying messages. My phone vibrated again—Kim. *Give me a break.* I slid open the phone and read, "Can u come to the party? Simple yes or no. Answer me pls." Obviously, she wouldn't stop harassing me until I replied. I typed, "Kim I'm busy. Date w/ Ellie. Can't make it 2 the party. Btw, lost my phone." Maybe that would get her off my back.

Seconds later my phone vibrated again. "Sorry abt ur phone. If u change ur mind, party is Sat after spring break @ 7 my house. Love 2 c u again I miss u. We shld hang out sometime." *Really?* I hit "Reply" again. "Not a good idea. U know I have a girlfriend. I've got homework. C u @ school." Thankfully my phone kept quiet after that, and I finished my assignments.

It didn't take long to realize that losing my car privileges was a real pain. I rode with Jessica to school and usually bummed a ride home with Adam. But he was sick on Friday, and I forgot to find another ride. I lost track of time weight lifting and found myself the last one in the gym. My dad didn't answer his phone, Jessica was swimming, and my mom's shift at the hospital didn't end until seven o'clock—an hour from then.

I went back into the locker room and checked all the bathroom stalls—empty. I pulled out my counter and set the date for today. Thinking of my bedroom, I pressed Shuffle and then Go. With ease, I appeared in my room. Gradually I relied more and more on the counter. Although I worried I'd get careless and be caught, the effortlessness of the travel was hard to resist.

After three weeks my dad's BMW was repaired and back in the garage. Sunday night he handed me both sets of truck keys. "Thanks for following the rules and staying out of trouble, but from here on out, slow down and be careful, will you? I don't want to lose you."

TWENTY
Illusion

The days grew longer, blossoms decorated the fruit trees, and grass sprouted after the dormant season. It would be months before the ground dried out, and I still tramped through the mud each day to feed the horses for my mom. Occasionally, a bright sunny day tantalized us Oregonians with the promise of summer, but it never seemed to last.

The track coach put me on two relays and had me running the 200-meter race, as well as throwing the javelin. My speed and strength surprised me at times and I had to be careful. I didn't want to attract too much attention. I already had colleges recruiting me for their wrestling teams, and it was a lot to process. What did I really want to do? If I put my mind to it, I could probably excel at whatever sport I chose. The counter gave me a definite advantage over everyone else, and I never had to worry about failing a drug test.

Archidus sent me a vision as I lay in bed one night contemplating my future. I saw myself standing in a darkened street on a steep hill. It was a residential area—townhouses smashed together with no yards, and narrow streets lined with cars. I heard a scream and followed the sound into an alley.

A pretty Chinese woman in a black pantsuit was fighting two rough-looking punks, covered in body piercings and tattoos. Thick silver chains hung from the belt loops of their pants. They had her purse and were pulling a computer bag from her shoulder. One of the guys drew a knife. They looked young, my age or early twenties.

The counter coordinates of San Francisco, California, April 20, 1993, flashed across my mind. Without seeing the woman's counter, I knew she was a Keeper.

I sat up, feeling the urgency to protect her. What to wear to 1993, the year before I was born? I threw on jeans and a T-shirt, then looked through the back of my closet at my arsenal of weapons. I had guns from the 1800s, the Luger pistol from Germany, the Mexican's knife, or my sword. I loaded the Luger pistol and stuffed it in my back pocket, then picked up the knife.

I set the counter coordinates and pressed Shuffle and Go. I appeared in a crowded airport terminal near the security checkpoint. "Crap," I mumbled.

I stuffed the knife under my T-shirt, but not before a businessman saw it. The suit and tie pushed his way up the line toward the security officer. I lowered my head and walked the other direction, looking for a bathroom.

"Hey, that kid's got a knife," the man yelled from behind me. I turned to see him frantically pointing me out to the officer. The security guy started running in my direction, calling for backup on his radio.

There was no way to discreetly escape this situation. I needed cover, fast. It wouldn't be long before I disappeared. I saw the men's bathroom down the hall, but two security guards were in front of it running in my direction, so I bolted into the women's bathroom. "Excuse me—sorry," I said, pushing my way past the ladies in line. "When you gotta go, you gotta go."

I stood among the rows of bathroom stalls, waiting for one to open up, while the women in line stared at me with shocked expressions. This would definitely be my most obvious disappearance yet.

"Security, step aside," an officer yelled from the hall.

From behind me, I heard the click of a door opening. I spun around and ran for the open stall. The old lady who stepped out screamed when she saw me. "It's okay, ma'am. Excuse me." I carefully moved past her.

"He's in there," I heard a chorus of women say.

"Come on, let's go," I muttered. I pulled the counter out of my pocket and got a look at the current date before I disappeared. No wonder everybody had freaked out. It was September 30, 2001, and running around the airport with a knife was bound to attract attention in the post 9/11 era.

The next four shuffle zones were relatively simple in comparison—a forest, a beach, a small town in the South, and the outskirts of a Revolutionary War battlefield. As the streets of San Francisco materialized, I heard a scream and ran for the narrow alley between the townhouses. Garrick appeared right in front of me and we nearly collided.

"Hey, how you doin'?" I asked as I slapped him on the back and kept running.

Garrick sprinted to catch up with me. "Where you been, little brother?"

We stopped short when we entered the alley. The Chinese woman had disarmed the young man with the knife and was holding off him and his friend with some fancy karate moves. The punks darted in again, trying to grab her, so Garrick and I rushed forward and took on her assailants. Following Garrick's lead, I practiced my boxing skills on the tattooed kid in front of me. After I used a combination of jabs followed by two uppercuts, my opponent staggered out of reach and ran from the alley, with his buddy hot on his heels.

Before we could congratulate ourselves on a successful rescue, the woman asked, "Who do you think you are?"

Surprised, I said, "I'm Chase Harper and this is Garrick."

She looked down her nose at us. "What are you doing?"

"Rescuing you. A thank you would be nice," Garrick said.

"I don't need help from some hillbilly."

"Well, pardon me," Garrick said loudly. "Next time Archidus wakes me from a good night's sleep after a hard day's labor, I'll remember you don't want my help and I'll keep on snoozing. Who are you, anyway? I want to make sure I know who doesn't want my help."

I put my hand on his shoulder, then turned to the woman. "Look, we're just doing our job. Those are some impressive moves you've got."

She folded her arms and looked at us, softening her expression a bit. "Thank you. If Archidus sent you, then who are you?"

"I'm the Protector, and this is Garrick the Guardian."

"Oh, I see. I think Master Archidus did mention something about you two."

"How long have you had your counter?" I asked.

She stooped to pick up her purse and laptop bag. "A few months."

"Which counter do you have?"

"Master Archidus called it Illusion. Look, I'm sorry for what I said. It's nice to meet you, but I've got a big presentation tomorrow with some developers and I need to get going."

"What do you do?" I asked as she started to leave the alley.

"I'm an architect." With that she turned the corner and left us alone.

"What a coldhearted woman," Garrick said.

I chuckled. "Oh, come on, brother, she wasn't that bad."

"Cold as ice, that one. But where have you been? I haven't seen you in years."

"What are you talking about? Three or four weeks ago I was with you in 1818, digging the canal."

"Huh? It's been over ten years for me and Davy. He turned seventeen last week."

"No way! You haven't changed a bit. You're not messing with me, are you? Davy's really seventeen?"

"He sure is. Archidus hasn't asked me to do anything in over ten years. You should bring Ellie and come see us. Davy must have asked about her at least a hundred times."

"I will. She'll be shocked. I know she'd love to see Davy again. She really missed him when we left you guys. Where do I find you?"

"End of January 1829, Cleveland, Ohio. When you get there, ask around and someone can give you directions to our cabin. We're on the south side of town. It'll be great to have you visit."

I smiled. "Okay, January 1829. I'll find you."

"See you soon." With that, Garrick disappeared, and I pulled out my counter for the return trip.

TWENTY-ONE
September Campaign

I walked into the lunchroom the next day and searched for Ellie. She was sitting with her friends, so I joined their table full of girls. "Hey, Ellie."

"Hello, Chase. How are you?"

I smiled back at her. "Great." Overwhelmed by female chatter, I focused on my lunch and shoveled a bite into my mouth.

She picked up her tray and moved next to me. "Lauren asked if we wanted to go to Kim's a week from Saturday. I think she called it an end-of-spring-break party. Everyone's invited, and most of our friends will be there. It sounds fun. What do you think?"

Lauren was on the cheerleading squad with Kim, but she'd become Ellie's best friend—next to Jessica, that is. Surprised at her suggestion, I said, "What do I think? I don't care. If you want to go to Kim's party, I'll take you. But I'm not going over there by myself, that's for sure." I stuffed another bite of food into my mouth.

"Oh, thank you." Ellie leaned forward to look down the table. "Lauren, we'll be there."

Lauren stood to clear her tray. "Awesome. I'll see you tomorrow, Ellie."

The first bell rang and the table emptied around us. With my mouth half full of food, I mumbled, "Guess who I ran into last night?"

Ellie slid closer. "Who?"

"Take a guess."

"Garrick?"

"Yup. And guess what he told me about Davy?"

With that I had her full attention. "Oh, do tell! How is he?"

"He's doing great, but he keeps asking about you." Slowly, I chewed another bite of food.

"And?"

I opened my milk and started gulping it down. "Guess how old he is now?"

"Chase, I'm growing impatient. We'll be late to class if you don't talk faster."

"Garrick said they're living in Cleveland, Ohio, and Davy turned seventeen last week."

"Seventeen? How did that happen so fast? You're not teasing me, are you?"

I picked up Ellie's empty tray. "I didn't believe him at first either. But for some reason, Archidus let ten years go by without asking a thing from him. Garrick wants us to come and visit them in Ohio during January 1829."

She followed me as I dumped the trays. "I can't believe he's already grown up. Seventeen. Why, that's almost our age."

"Yup. So, do you want to go with me?"

She slid her arm through mine as we walked out of the lunchroom. The second bell rang and we were both going to be late. "Of course. When?"

"How about Friday night?"

That night, another vision from Archidus interrupted my sleep. I saw myself standing on the edge of a town square in the chaos of war. In the smoke-filled sky, German airplanes lined up to attack the battered townspeople. Between the roar of the planes' engines and the exploding bombs, I heard injured people screaming and a child's frantic cry for his mother. Destruction filled the entire marketplace, and even in sleep I felt the shock of it.

A woman trapped beneath the rubble on the opposite side of the square drew my attention. I stared. Despite her bloody, soot-covered face, I knew her—Ruth, the German Keeper I had helped twice before.

Once I recognized her as the target of the vision, the counter coordinates of the location flashed before my mind. She was in Eastern Europe, with the pinpoint of light on the globe farther east than the last time I'd helped her. The date—September 10, 1939—seemed familiar.

Engulfed by a sense of dread, I jerked awake, turned on the light in my bedroom, and opened my backpack. I pulled out my binder and flipped it open to the World War II timeline assignment we'd done in History. There it was. Part of the September Campaign. The day more than seventy German bombers worked the skies above Warsaw, Poland, flying seventeen consecutive bombing raids on the city. The German Luftwaffe bombed hospitals, marketplaces, and schools, as well as military targets. The loss of civilian life was catastrophic.

Glimpsing my immediate future in this description of the past, I broke out in a cold sweat. I slammed my binder closed, then ran my fingers through my hair and paced the floor next to my bed. The last thing I wanted to do was race across a Warsaw marketplace during one of the bloodiest aerial bombardments of World War II to pull someone out of the wreckage. But no matter what I wanted to do, there would be no peace in my life until I did Archidus' bidding. I had already delayed leaving, and I felt a rising level of urgency. My body released a surge of adrenalin, my heart raced wildly, and sweat beaded across my forehead. I pulled my Erie Canal clothes out of the closet and changed—shorts and a Hilhi Wrestling T-shirt would look out of place in 1939. I loaded my Luger pistol and stuffed it in the waistband of the pants, leaving the shirttails hanging out to conceal it.

I picked up my counter and set the coordinates for Warsaw, Poland, September 10, 1939. Dreading this mission, I pressed Shuffle and Go. After four shuffle zones, a blast of heat from the Sahara put me in a full-out sweat before I appeared in Warsaw.

The deafening sounds and acrid smell assaulted my senses the instant the shimmering cleared. I took cover next to a building as airplane after airplane flew past, dropping bombs and shooting machine guns at anyone crazy enough to be out in the open. I hugged the wall with my back and searched the square for the pile of rubble I'd seen Ruth buried beneath in the vision. After I located her, I scanned the area for Garrick.

Three more planes passed. I couldn't wait for him any longer. I studied the sky, searching for a break in the Germans' formation. I needed enough time to run across the marketplace to Ruth before the gunfire caught me. Choosing the moment carefully, I raced toward her, jumping over building debris, downed trees, overturned carts, and the dead. I was still thirty feet from Ruth and the cover of the nearest standing building, when a double line of machine gunfire hit the ground and moved steadily in my direction. I couldn't outrun the bullets. At my present pace, they would overtake me in seconds.

At a dead run I pulled the counter from my pocket, depressed the small latch to open it, and pressed Go, all the while focusing intently on the open doorway of the bakery across the square. Rock chips from the spray of ammunition peppered my legs as I disappeared. The counter transported me to the doorway of the building so quickly that I was still running when I reappeared and slammed into a table. "Ouch! That's gonna leave a bruise." Rubbing the aching spot on my leg, I returned the counter to my pocket and hobbled back to the door.

At the next break in air traffic, I rushed to Ruth's side. "Let's get you out of here," I said as I hurried to free her from the rubble. Between glancing at the approaching planes, I pulled brick after brick off her battered body. One arm lay at an unnatural angle, and she moved her other arm toward her neck. The threatening double line of gunfire started in my direction again. I glanced at the approaching plane. We were sitting ducks out in the open. "I'll be right back," I said to Ruth.

I ran for the bakery, ducking through the doorway as bullets shattered the display window and sent bits of bread flying across the room. A bomb dropped behind the building, collapsing the back corner of the bakery. My hands flew to my head as the explosion rocked my eardrums.

I darted back to the pile of rubble. The moment I knelt next to Ruth, she begged me in her strong German accent, "Take this and go. It's too dangerous. My husband, my son—they are both dead. There is nothing for me now. Go!" Feebly, she lifted the gold chain over my head, leaving her counter dangling from my neck.

I continued to remove the bricks, still believing I could save her. "Ruth, hang on and I'll get you out. There's no reason for you to die too. Don't give up on me." I freed her upper body, but a heavy slab of concrete pinned her legs. *Where's Garrick? He should be here by now.*

The drilling of machine gunfire filtered through the ringing in my ears, and again I darted toward the cover of the bakery. My head jerked around at the sound of Ruth's scream. Bullets cut through her chest and continued drilling holes into the cobblestone street. Her body jolted at the impact and then lay still.

In a flash of anger, I pulled the Luger pistol from under my shirt and fired three shots at the swastika on the side of the retreating plane. "We'll get you for this, you good-for-nothing Nazis. You wait and see." I kicked one of the bricks at my feet, then ran back to her side. "Ruth? Ruth?"

"Go now, Keeper," she slurred, a trickle of blood escaping the corner of her mouth. I felt the sting of failure as I backed away, and for a moment time slowed, heightening my awareness of the tragedy. The gunfire from the next plane assaulted the street as if searching out my location. Another bomb dropped on the bakery, reducing it to a pile of bricks and mortar and throwing me to the ground. A plume of dust and debris shot into the air before raining down on me. I'd be joining Ruth in a matter of seconds if I didn't get out of here. Coughing, I tucked my nose under the collar of my shirt and climbed to my feet. With Ruth's counter dangling at my chest, I pulled mine out of my pocket and pressed Shuffle. I wandered through the five shuffle zones in a state of shock, eventually resetting the counter for home.

Glancing at my clock, I dropped my head into my hands and slumped onto the edge of my bed. Less than a minute had passed, but my life felt strangely altered. When I opened my eyes, Ruth's counter swung from my neck. Where had Garrick been? Was something wrong with him? I'd totally botched this mission. Ruth was dead, and now I had two counters to protect. Curious, I opened hers. It lit up in the palm of my hand, searching for a new Keeper. If Ruth were still alive, it would have remained dark.

I closed the lid, studying it, then pulled my counter out of my pocket and compared the two. They were nearly identical except for the detailed engraving on the top covers. Mine bore the image of a shield in the center. Ruth's had the outline of a pair of spectacles in the palm of a hand. I figured the symbols circling the pictures must have something to do with the names of the counters. Ruth's was Perception.

I tucked her counter under my shirt and returned mine to my pocket. With my boots off, I lay on my bed and wondered what to do. As a seer, surely Archidus knew Ruth had died. Wouldn't he have someone in mind to take the counter next? I couldn't think of anyone I would knowingly burden with the responsibility. Definitely not Ellie or Jessica—it would drive me crazy with worry to know the Sniffers were searching for them. I considered Adam. He was big and tough. He'd have a good chance at protecting himself. But then again, the counter wasn't mine to pass on.

When I awoke and looked at my clock, it was 6:59 AM. Yawning, I sat up. I still wore the dusty, bloodstained shirt from last night's ordeal, and Ruth's counter bumped against my chest. The responsibility of it, added to the weight of the gold, made it heavy around my neck. I pulled the shirt over my head and took off Ruth's counter, stowing it in my dresser drawer with my own. I hid my clothes in the back of the closet and wrapped a towel around my waist. Jessica had better be done with the shower. I needed to get to school early and talk with Ellie. Banging on the bathroom door, I said, "Jessica, you almost done?"

"No. Go use Mom's shower."

I stomped down the stairs and knocked on my parents' door. "Mom, can I use your shower?"

"Sure." When I walked past her she asked, "Is something wrong? Why are you in such a hurry this morning?"

"Nothing's wrong," I lied. "I've got to get to school early to finish an assignment I forgot about. Mom, you need to feed the horses for me this morning, okay?"

I had the shower turned on before she had a chance to answer. But I did hear my dad grumble, "Jen, you spoil that boy. He's got to learn responsibility. The world doesn't revolve around him. I'm afraid he's developing the entitlement mentality that plagues this generation. There's no appreciation. They think it's all about them."

I shook my head. What was he talking about? Of course I had appreciation.

Less than five minutes later, wrapped in a towel and dripping water from my hair, I darted upstairs. I dressed quickly and slipped Ruth's counter over my neck and mine into my pocket. After a bowl of cold cereal, I grabbed my keys and walked to the truck while I called Ellie.

"Hi, this is Chase. Can you be ready if I come pick you up for school right now?"

"I suppose so. What's going on?"

"I'll tell you in person. See you soon."

The diesel roared to life and I sped down the road. I knocked once before walking in my aunt and uncle's front door. Not seeing Ellie in the kitchen with everyone else, I yelled up the stairs, "Ellie, I'm here whenever you're ready."

"Hey, man, what's up?" I asked Adam as I stole a piece of toast off his plate, then jumped out of his reach.

He swatted at me. "Dude, make your own toast."

"Sorry, no time—I'm late. Hi, Aunt Marianne." I gave her a quick hug. I stuffed the rest of the toast in my mouth and licked the jam off my fingers. Hoping to hide my looming anxiety, I said, "When are we going steelhead fishing, Uncle Steve?"

He glanced at me over his newspaper. "Maybe a week from Saturday. I'll watch the weather and the water levels and let you know."

"Sounds great. I'll tell my dad."

Ellie walked in the kitchen. "Hi, Chase."

Like every other time I saw her, my eyes locked onto her like a high-powered magnet. She bent to drop her backpack. "I can take that for you," I said, then picked it up and slung it over my shoulder. Ellie's eyes twinkled as she smiled up at me. She made a peanut butter sandwich, grabbed a glass of milk, and we left. I opened her door and held her hand while she stepped into the truck. As soon as my door closed, she turned to me.

"What happened? You look as if you've seen a ghost."

I lowered my head onto the steering wheel. "Last night, I watched the woman I was trying to save die in front of me. Archidus sent me to help her and I messed up. She died, and it's all my fault."

Ellie touched my arm. "I'm so sorry. Where were you?"

I looked at her. "Remember the timeline assignment in History?"

She nodded. "Yes."

"Remember the Germans' September Campaign and the terror bombing in Warsaw, Poland?"

Her eyes widened in dismay. "You were there?"

The horror of the mangled corpses in the battered marketplace flashed before my eyes, and the drone of the airplanes rang in my ears. I shook my head at the memories. "Yeah, and it was bad—definitely the worst thing I've ever seen. Garrick and I have been in some tough spots before, but this was different. These were regular people, not soldiers. The women and the kids didn't stand a chance. The German planes just kept coming with their bombs and machine guns.

Ruth was buried alive in the rubble, but I didn't have enough time between the attacks to dig her out. They shot her right in front of me."

Exhaling, I put the key in the ignition and stared at the "wait to start" light. Ellie gently squeezed my arm and said, "I'm sorry. That sounds dreadful. I know you did everything you could, but I suppose when someone dies, hearing that doesn't make one feel better."

We were almost to the school when I noticed her studying me intently. "What?"

"Pray tell, what are you wearing?" she asked, pulling the collar of my shirt down to reveal the gold chain. She chuckled. "When did you start wearing a necklace?"

"Last night. Don't laugh at me, Ellie." But even my somber mood couldn't smother my smile at the expression on her face. I had worn a collared, button-up shirt over my T-shirt to try to hide Ruth's counter, but I hadn't fooled Ellie. She pulled on the chain and the counter dangled from her fingers.

"What made you decide to put it on a chain?"

Pulling my counter out of my pocket, I said, "I didn't."

She looked back and forth between the one hanging from my neck and the one in my hand, her eyes widening and her jaw going slack. "Land sakes! You have two of them?" She picked up mine and then reached for Ruth's counter. "What are you going to do with it?"

I intercepted Ellie's hand, gently moving it away. "Please don't touch this one." I couldn't risk her accidentally touching one of its buttons.

"Certainly," she said.

I let go of her hand and dropped Ruth's counter under my shirt.

Ellie held out my counter. "Do you want this back?"

I shrugged. "Ellie, something else is bothering me. Ever since I got the counter, Garrick and I have both been summoned whenever there's an emergency with another Keeper. But last night, Garrick never showed up. Rescuing that Keeper was definitely a two-man job. Garrick should have been there. It makes me wonder if something's wrong with him. I'm worried. He would never shun a fight for a good cause. Come to think of it, he probably wouldn't miss a good fight even if it was for a bad cause."

"What are you going to do?"

"Go look for him. Do you want to go with me after school, instead of waiting until Friday?"

"What about track practice?" she said.

I pulled the truck into Hilhi's parking lot. "I'll worry about that later. This is more important."

"Of course I'll accompany you."

"Thanks. After school I'll send you a text before I pick you up."

I grabbed our backpacks and walked around to open Ellie's door. She smiled, holding my hand to press the counter into it. "You'll need this." My fingers curled around the gold device. She touched the side of my face before kissing me. "It will be all right. You'll see."

I barely smiled as I pocketed my counter. "I hope so."

After school I rushed home, forgetting to tell anyone I might not be at track. I dressed for the 1800s and sent Ellie a text. "Can I come over now?" While I waited for her reply I compared the globe on my counter with the map of the United States in my History book. I practiced setting the counter for Cleveland, Ohio, January 25, 1829—the time and place Garrick had last referenced. My phone vibrated on the dresser. I grabbed the phone and read Ellie's message: "Just got off the bus. Wait a minute while I change."

I set the phone down and read what had happened in Ohio during the 1820s. They had constructed the upper part of the Erie Canal. With the completion of the canal and various roadways, the Ohio area was booming with settlers. My phone buzzed again as it vibrated across the dresser's surface into my keys. I slid it open and read, "I'm ready. See u soon." I took one last look at my bedroom, an ache filling the pit of my stomach. Shaking it off as nerves from the night before, I set the counter for today's date, Hillsboro, Oregon, and imagined Ellie's room. I pressed Shuffle and Go.

I moved through the five shuffle zones and appeared in her bedroom. With her back turned to me, she didn't see me right away. Her blue skirt touched the floor, and her white blouse puffed out at the sleeves. She set her phone on the dresser and turned. "Oh, you're here already. Do I need a coat?"

"I didn't think of that. You might want one since we're going back in January." She picked up a matching blue jacket and I grinned. "You look beautiful," I said.

"Why thank you. What about you? Won't you get cold?"

I looked down to set the counter. "Once we find Garrick, I can borrow one of his coats. I'll be fine." She put her arm through mine, giving it a squeeze.

Having never been to Ohio, I was at a complete loss as to what I should picture in my mind when I pressed Go. I hoped I'd placed the pinpoint of light in the correct position on the tiny globe. Upon appearing in our first shuffle zone, Ellie clutched my arm with both hands. We stood in a field of brilliant red clover, without a soul in sight. I looked at her panic-stricken expression. "What's the matter?"

She didn't loosen her grip. "Suppose we land in the water again?"

I laughed. "You're still worried about that?"

She lowered her gaze and nodded. I peeled one of her hands off my arm and placed it behind my neck. "Don't worry. I won't let anything happen to you." Smiling at her furrowed brow, I wrapped my hands around her waist and lowered my lips to hers.

We next appeared by the side of a building, in a bustling Midwestern town, in a time for which we were perfectly dressed. We still held each other as a stuffy-looking lady turned the corner and walked past, scowling at us. She turned up her nose and marched across the street, where she flagged down a man in a black suit to whisper in his ear.

"What's that all about?" I asked when she pointed at us.

Ellie giggled and let go of my neck. I, however, didn't loosen my hold on her tiny waist. When the man in the black suit marched across the street I raised my eyebrows. He looked like a preacher and not a happy one, either. Ellie shoved me away from her and hooked her arm through mine instead.

"Chase, no respectable girl would be hugging and kissing in the street. Right now that spinster is probably trying to figure out who my parents are." She pulled me along, farther away from the prying eyes of people passing on the street.

I stuck one hand in my pocket and glanced over my shoulder. That preacher looked like a hawk about to sink his talons into his prey—me. I chuckled. "I think he's working up a sermon."

"Young man, I'd like a word with you," he called.

I smiled at Ellie. "What did I tell you?" We would disappear any second, so I glanced back and yelled, "Sorry, sir. I'm a little busy right now." I broke into a run, pulling her behind me.

We rounded the corner of the general store and vanished. "Chase, that was powerfully rude, but funny nonetheless."

"You should have seen the look on that preacher's face. I'll bet he turns that town upside down looking for us." We laughed at his expense for the next three shuffles, finally appearing in a snow-covered forest.

Although chilly, the temperature wasn't bad for January. The overcast sky mirrored my mood, and the light of day would soon be gone, adding to the urgency I felt. All Garrick had said the last time I'd seen him was that he and Davy lived in a cabin south of town. But without knowing which direction Cleveland was, that information did me little good. I looked for some indication of which way we should go.

"I sort of hoped we'd appear in the town," I said.

Ellie pointed to a thin trail of smoke twisting through the gray sky. "Look. Perhaps we can ask someone for directions."

I nodded and led the way down a wooded hillside to a new log cabin. After I knocked, a man cracked the door and peered out.

"What're you folks doing out tonight? Storm's coming in. Where's your coat, son?"

"I'm fine, sir. We're looking for my brother, Garrick Eastman. Do you know where he lives or which direction we go for Cleveland?"

The man scratched his salt-and-pepper beard. "Well now, I'm new to these here parts, but Cleveland is thataway, across the Cuyahoga River." He pointed out the direction and kept talking. "The Red House Tavern is up the road, yonder. If your brother's lived here long, somebody there is bound to know where to find him."

"Thank you, sir. I appreciate your help." The man's gaze followed us as we left his house and walked up the road.

A flash of gray moving through the trees caught my attention, but when I turned my head I saw nothing. A chill shot down my spine, whether from the cold or something else, I didn't know. I looked behind me, wondering if someone else was on the road.

But there were only two sets of footprints as far as I could see.

"What's wrong?" Ellie asked.

I shook my head, trying to rid myself of the sensation we were being followed. "Nothing. It's nothing."

Before long a red house came into view. Raucous laughter and the voices of drunken men met us at the door. I paused with my hand on the doorknob, looking back at my girlfriend.

"Perhaps I'll wait out here," she said.

Although I hated to leave her alone, it would draw a lot of unwanted attention if I took her in the tavern with me. Based on my limited experience, I knew it wasn't the place for a well-dressed, respectable lady. I looked up and down the road, seeing no one. "Good idea, but if you need me, holler or scream or something."

She smiled. "I'll be fine. You go on ahead."

I nodded and stepped inside. A large fire crackled in the fireplace, and the warmth of the room was a relief after hiking through the snow in a linen shirt and cotton trousers. I stood in front of the hearth, warming my hands while I scanned the men at the tables—some drinking, some playing cards. Garrick wasn't one of them, which could be good or bad. Hopefully, he'd given up the drinking like he'd promised. On the other hand, I hoped his absence from the tavern wasn't a confirmation of my fear that something was wrong. I walked to the bartender. "Excuse me, sir. I'm looking for Garrick Eastman. Would you know where I might find him?"

The bartender paused to wipe his hands. "You ain't gonna find him in here. He ain't a drinkin' man. Only seen him come in once—mad as a hornet he was. Dragged his son out by the shirt collar for sneaking off to take a drink."

The door banged open, and I looked over my shoulder to see if Ellie needed me. Two middle-aged men with graying beards and heavy coats stomped the snow from their boots and walked toward the bar.

"Garrick's my brother," I said, turning back to the bartender. "This is my first time in Cleveland and I'm not sure where his cabin is."

"He lives at the south end of Erie Street on the edge of town. Stay on this here road, which is Columbus, and cross the Cuyahoga River on the new bridge. Turn onto Superior Lane, go through the public square, past the courthouse, and then watch for Erie Street on the right."

The two men stood at the bar listening, probably waiting to order a drink. "That your wife out there?" the one next to me asked.

I leaned closer. "What did you say?"

He gave me a knowing wink and a friendly elbow jab. "There's a mighty fine-looking woman standing out front claiming she's waitin' on her husband. Thought maybe that'd be you."

"Oh, yeah," I played along. "I'd better go." I turned to the bartender. "Thanks for the help."

I hurried out of the tavern and searched for Ellie as I stepped into the fast-fading light of evening. She stood next to the horses tied at the hitching post, warming her hands beneath the mane of a stocky chestnut. "Are you waiting for me, Mrs. Harper?" Smiling broadly, I hopped off the porch to stand next to Ellie.

She sighed. "Did those two men talk to you?"

"Yes, they did."

She looked down. "Land sakes, I'm sorry. It seemed like the easiest explanation to get them to leave off asking me questions."

If the lighting were better, I probably could have seen her blushing. She turned and started walking. I chuckled as I ran to catch up with her. "Hey, I don't care if you say you're my wife—at least I know you're thinking of me. But just don't let my dad hear it, or I'll be grounded for life."

Ellie stopped suddenly and propped her hands on her hips. "So now that you've had a good laugh, are we even going the right direction?"

I smiled. "Yeah, we cross the river, go through town, and turn right on Erie Street. Sorry about those guys. I shouldn't have left you alone so long."

She shrugged her shoulders. "They seemed nice enough, but they asked too many questions for my liking."

"If I remember right, one of them called you a mighty fine-looking woman."

That coaxed a smile out of her. "Well, that was kind."

"The bartender said Garrick's not a drinking man. The only time he's been in the tavern was to drag Davy out of there. I worried Garrick would turn into an alcoholic after Rose died."

"So did I. It's good that he has stayed away from the whiskey."

An old-fashioned covered bridge offered us a welcomed break from trudging through the snow. By the time Ellie and I walked past the courthouse in the public square, night had descended and big, fluffy snowflakes fell from the sky.

Ruth's counter felt cold and heavy against my chest. I wanted to get rid of it. Surely Archidus knew by now that I'd failed and Ruth was dead. Why hadn't he done something? He should have told me where to take it, or brought me back to his world—Algonia, he'd called it—so I could return it to him.

I squinted through the dim light to make out the street names. Several newer frame houses were intermixed with traditional log cabins. We found Erie Street and turned right. "Garrick said he was on the edge of town. I'm guessing he'll be one of the last houses."

We passed three log cabins and two white-washed frame homes before one caught my eye. This cabin was set farther back from the street than the rest. But what grabbed my attention was the neatly stacked woodpile along its side. The way the logs were stacked looked familiar. Smiling to myself, I said, "Ellie I think this is it."

"How do you know?"

"That woodpile has Garrick's name written all over it. I've never seen anybody make a neater stack." More than once I'd helped him chop wood for Rose, and if anybody knew his wood-stacking pattern it was me. Ellie and I stepped onto a shoveled walkway leading from the street to the cabin. I knocked and we waited. A moment later, a young man answered the door. He had dark hair and Rose's soft brown eyes.

"Can I help you?" he asked.

Ellie rushed into the beam of light. "Davy?"

"Miss Ellie! Mr. Harper! Come in." The young man turned and yelled into the cabin, "Pa, come look who's here!"

I stepped inside and walked toward the hearth, a shiver running down my spine from the snowflakes melting on my shoulders.

"Harper, welcome to Cleveland," Garrick said. His muscular frame and the familiar twinkle in his eyes eased my worry as he crossed the room. He hadn't shaved in a few days, but his light brown hair was still cut short.

"I'm glad to see you're okay," I said, returning his quick hug.

"Why wouldn't I be?"

I glanced at Davy and Ellie. They sat opposite each other at the kitchen table, talking. "Garrick, I need to ask you something," I said.

His brow furrowed. "Sure, follow me." We went into the back room and he closed the door behind us. "What is it?"

"Did you not get the message from Archidus about Ruth, in Warsaw?"

"No. The last I heard of her was at the German border when I got shot."

"Ruth's husband and son were killed in the air raids on Warsaw in September 1939, and she was trapped in the rubble of a collapsed building. Archidus sent me there, but I couldn't save her. She died right in front of me. Before she died she gave me this."

I pulled the counter from under my shirt and slipped the gold chain over my head. Garrick took the counter and looked it over. The eerie blue light lit his face when he clicked it open.

"This isn't yours," he said in amazement.

"Weren't you listening? No, of course it isn't." I pulled mine out of my pocket. "This one's mine. It's hard enough keeping track of one of these things. I sure as heck don't want two of them. What should I do?"

Garrick shook his head and handed Ruth's counter back to me. "I don't know. Keep it, I guess. Eventually, Archidus will tell you what to do."

I put my counter away and slid Ruth's gold chain over my head. "I hope it's sooner rather than later."

"Lord Arbon and his Sniffers would have a heyday if they knew what we have in this room right now," Garrick said.

"You're right about that."

He tossed me a blue flannel shirt. "You look cold. Put this on, and then let's go see Davy. It's been so long I want you to get to know him again." I pulled off my wet shirt and put on the dry one.

The four of us sat around the kitchen table and talked until the flame in the lamp began flickering, signaling the end of the oil. Garrick had spent the past ten years learning to farm, digging the Ohio and Erie Canal connecting Cleveland with Portsmouth, and raising pigs. When Garrick and Davy arrived in Cleveland in 1818, the town only had about 150 residents. Garrick estimated it now boasted nearly a thousand. He was proud of the town's new brick courthouse, which he'd helped build, and of the fact that his son worked as an apprentice at Doan's blacksmith shop.

All evening Davy studied me, and a hint of suspicion showed in his tone of voice when he said, "Mr. Harper, we've told you what we've been doing, but where have you and Ellie been these past ten years?"

Garrick abruptly stood up. "Well, we'd better hit the sack. Morning isn't far off. Davy, go bank the coals in the hearth. Harper, come help me."

We moved a bed into the main room for Ellie, and then the three of us men stared at the remaining bed. "Harper, you can have it," Garrick said.

"I can't take your bed. Plus you're older than me."

He laughed as he tossed a blanket on the floor and lay down. "You're our guest, so you're having the bed and that's final."

"We'll take turns then," I said. "I'll sleep in the bed tonight, but either you or Davy gets it tomorrow."

Garrick closed his eyes. "We'll talk about that tomorrow. Good night, Harper. Good night, Son."

Davy spread a blanket next to his pa, and I climbed into bed. The anxiety I'd arrived with hadn't completely disappeared at seeing my friend safe. Nothing felt resolved. If anything, I felt more anxious, waiting for what tomorrow would bring.

TWENTY-TWO
Perception's Keeper

I awoke the next morning and put my boots on. I tiptoed out of the bedroom, then paused at the sight of Ellie's beautiful face and her golden curls spread across the pillow. Her peaceful expression brought a smile to my face. Careful not to wake her, I stepped out the door and headed for the outhouse. At least six inches of fresh snow covered the ground, but only scattered clouds remained in the early morning sky.

When I trudged back to the cabin, I found Davy standing where I had been, looking at Ellie's sleeping form in the same admiring way. I closed the door and sat on a chair to brush the snow off my boots. All the while I kept my eyes on Davy, who moved past me to leave the cabin. Deciding the young man's stare at Ellie was probably nothing more than curiosity, I shoved away my jealousy.

She stretched her arms over her head, opening her eyes. "Hello, darling," she said sleepily.

I smiled. "Good morning. Did you sleep okay?"

She threw off the covers and sat up, fully dressed except for her boots. "Yes, but traveling without luggage is a bit of an inconvenience." After running her fingers through her hair, she wound it into a bun. Mesmerized, I watched her. Once she finished her hair, she slipped her feet into her boots and meticulously fastened each button. She stood, then straightened her skirt and tucked in her shirt. Next, she turned to make the bed.

"Would you care to stoke the fire while I make some breakfast?" She looked through Garrick's cupboards and pulled out flour and a mixing bowl. She stopped her work to smile at me, still sitting there staring at her. I jumped to my feet and started adding kindling to the banked coals. Blowing gently, I coaxed a flame out of yesterday's ashes. Davy pushed through the door carrying an armful of wood, stamped his feet, and dumped his load next to the fireplace.

Garrick stumbled out of the bedroom, still looking half asleep. He stepped into his boots and pulled on his coat and hat. "I'm gonna milk the cow," he muttered.

With Davy's help, Ellie found everything she needed and mixed up pancake batter. When Garrick walked in the door with fresh milk, we were ready to sit down to breakfast.

With a mouthful of pancakes, Garrick said, "Little brother, Davy's got to work today, but what do you say you and I go turkey huntin'?"

I looked at Ellie, worried about leaving her behind. "You go ahead, Chase. There's plenty to keep me busy around here. Apparently there's no butter, and Davy said no one's baked bread in ages."

Garrick ran his fingers through his hair. "I'm not too keen on churning butter, and Davy and I never really mastered the whole bread-making thing."

Ellie smiled. "That settles it then. I'll busy myself with bread baking and butter churning while you're gone."

Davy finished eating first. He threw on his coat and grabbed his hat and gloves. "See you tonight." He tipped his hat and winked at Ellie. "I can't wait to sink my teeth into some of that fresh bread."

I frowned. If I wasn't careful, Davy would be trying to win over my girlfriend.

An hour later, I kissed Ellie goodbye and followed Garrick out the door. "We'll be back soon."

"Be careful, Chase."

"You too, Ellie." I glanced over my shoulder, trying to shake off the unease lurking in the back of my mind. I didn't want to stay here long. Something felt wrong.

Carrying our guns, Garrick and I walked briskly through town, across the Cuyahoga River, and into the hills southwest of Lake Erie. When we heard the faint gobble-gobble of wild turkeys, Garrick set me up behind a clump of brush. He pulled a turkey call out of his pocket and laid out the plan. "I'll go a ways behind you and call them in. When you get a clear shot on one, take it. They should be coming right down that draw."

I grabbed his hand, looking at his turkey call. "Where did you get this?" It obviously wasn't something he would have found in 1829.

He grinned. "A few years back, I went home and picked up a couple of these from the huntin' store near Texas A&M. Couldn't have someone else taking the prize as best turkey caller in all of Ohio."

Laughing, I shoved him away from me. "You cheater. Get outta here."

His gobbling called in the flock, and I shot a big tom turkey. Garrick tried to call them back after the gunfire scared them away, but a storm moved in from across the lake. They must have sensed the change in the weather and taken shelter. The wind rattled the bare tree limbs as it whipped through the valley, and the temperature plummeted. We cleaned our turkey and then hiked back. The crack of a twig and a flutter of movement caught my attention at the edge of town. I turned, searching the trees and the road behind us, then tapped Garrick's shoulder. "I think I saw something. Could someone be following us?"

He spun around and searched the trees, then shook his head and smiled. "Nah, it's just the wind. Why are you so jumpy, Harper? I never took you for a scaredy-cat."

I adjusted the rifle on my shoulder and walked ahead of him. "Never mind."

Back at the cabin, we stopped at the cellar. Garrick loaded my hands with carrots and potatoes, then took only the part of the turkey we'd eat that night into the cabin, leaving the rest to the frigid temperatures. The aroma of fresh-baked bread greeted us when we stepped through the door.

Garrick took a deep breath. "Ellie, it smells like I died and went to heaven. This house was long overdue for a woman's touch."

She pushed a loose strand of hair behind her ear. "Hopefully it tastes as good as it smells."

He leaned his rifle against the wall. "It will. How about some of my famous turkey stew for dinner?"

She took the potatoes and carrots from me so I could shed my borrowed coat. "Sounds delicious."

Garrick cut the meat, while Ellie and I peeled the vegetables. "Harper made a great shot on this turkey today," he said with a smile.

"Congratulations—" she started to say, but the front door banged open and Davy burst into the kitchen, wearing an angry scowl.

"Son, what's wrong?" Garrick asked.

Davy glared at Ellie and me before answering him. "The gossipmongers have sure been busy. I heard an interesting tale at the blacksmith's shop today."

"What was that?" his pa asked in a level tone.

"Half the men in Cleveland are poking fun at your little brother for walking into town in the dead of winter—no coat, no horse, no weapon, no provisions—dragging his wife along with him." Davy spat out the word "wife" like it was a piece of rotten meat and then turned on me and Ellie. "Are you married? 'Cause you sure didn't act like you were last night." Without giving either of us a chance to answer, he launched into another tirade. "And if you aren't, why are you traveling alone, unchaperoned? Something isn't right here. I know I was only six the last time I saw you, but in over ten years, I'd wager neither of you has changed a lick. Why is it you never visited or posted a letter?"

Garrick stepped closer to Davy. "Son, don't go shootin' your mouth off. You—"

Davy spun around. "And you, Pa—everybody's starting to speculate on how you've aged so gracefully. How you could possibly have been old enough to marry my ma eleven years ago? In fact, some are saying you must have been scandalously young. But come to think of it, it appears to me you haven't aged a day since I met you as a child." Davy glared at each of us, as if daring someone to contradict him.

Ellie spoke first. "Davy, please forgive me. We aren't married, and I'm to blame for the confusion. When Chase was in the tavern inquiring after directions to your cabin, two men started questioning me. They were most likely harmless, but it made me nervous. Not wanting to appear alone, I told them I was waiting for my husband. I had no idea it would create an uncomfortable situation for you."

Davy nodded. "I can understand that, Ellie. It was a wise thing to say considering the situation Harper left you in." He cast a contemptuous glance in my direction. "Harper, how did you get here? Ships aren't running this time of year, and you didn't ride in on horseback. Regular folks don't walk from town to town in January, with no coat and no weapon. The wolves are aggressive in the winter, and you never know when you'll run into Indians. Not to mention any gentleman in his right mind wouldn't drag a lady along with him."

Ellie and I looked at Garrick, who said, "Son, go wash up for supper, and I'll answer all your questions while this stew cooks."

Davy stomped out of the room, then came back a few minutes later with his face and hands washed, wearing a clean shirt. Garrick put the stew over the fire and motioned for him to sit. He pulled a chair next to the table.

"Do you remember those bedtime stories I told you when you were a kid?" Garrick asked.

"Pa, what do bedtime stories have to do with anything?"

"You'll see. Do you remember them?"

"The stories about the Keepers?"

Garrick smiled. "Yeah. Well, they're true. I'm a Keeper and so is Harper, and Ellie's lucky or unlucky enough, depending on how you look at it, to be along for the ride." The only sound in the room was the crackle of the fire until Garrick stood up. "Okay then, let's set the table for supper."

Davy frowned. "Hang on, Pa. That's the most outlandish thing I've ever heard. You're not serious, are you?"

"Yes, he is serious," Ellie said. "My grandfather was a Keeper for nearly seventy years before he passed away. Chase found his counter buried in a cave in 2011, then met me in 1863 when he accidentally used the counter and returned to the approximate time my grandfather had buried it."

"Davy, the stories you heard as a kid were your pa's real-life experiences," I said.

Apparently stunned, he didn't say a word at first. Our dinner demanded attention, bubbling over the edge of the pot and sizzling as it hit the hot coals. Garrick moved the pan away from the heat and stirred the stew, then set out bowls and spoons.

Davy shook his head. "Harper . . . Ellie, that is the most confounded thing I've ever heard. I can't believe you're in on this." He looked at her. "So, you're telling me you came with Harper from the future using a gold counter? And that explains why you walked into town in the dead of winter?"

She smiled. "Yes. That's exactly what we did."

"What happened during the past ten years? When I was kid, everyone thought you two would be married within the year. Now it's years later and it's as if nothing has changed."

"Time travel is a funny thing," Ellie explained. She reached across the table and gave Davy's hand a reassuring squeeze. "For Chase and me, it was only two weeks ago that we were in New York with you and your pa. When Chase ran into Garrick on an assignment, your pa mentioned you were seventeen. We could have come back to any time during the past ten years. However, since Garrick invited us to this time and place, we decided it would be simpler to find you here. I'm sorry for disappointing you by not visiting sooner, but we thought it would be fun to see you grown up."

"Pa, what about you? Why aren't you aging like everybody else?"

"I was born in 1944 and left in 1968 when I was twenty-four years old. When I'm in any year prior to 1968, I'm out of my appointed time and I don't age."

"How long have you been living out of your time?"

Garrick scratched his head and then started ticking off numbers on his fingers. "Ten years with you, one with your ma, and about six before that, but I jumped around a lot back then, so it's hard to know for certain. But, all in all, about seventeen years."

"You and Harper aren't brothers, are you?" Davy asked.

Garrick smiled. "No, we're not biological brothers."

"You're not what?"

"We're not real brothers."

"Where are the counters?" Davy asked, looking between me and Garrick.

Both Garrick and I pulled our counters out of our pockets and set them on the table in front of Davy. He picked one up and studied the engraved designs. When he touched the clasp the counter snapped open, catching him off guard. "It's hard to see," he muttered.

He had opened my counter, so I reached out and touch it. The instant my fingers made contact with the gold surface, the eerie blue light lit up the globe and the dials. "What do these buttons do?" Davy asked.

Ellie smiled at him. "Nothing, if you or I touch them. But if Chase touched them the two of you would disappear."

An excited smile replaced the scowl on Davy's face. "Astonishing. Can you show me?"

"No, Davy, I can't." I said. "I'm forbidden to take anyone out of their time—except Ellie, that is."

He looked at his father. "In the bedtime stories you never used your name, or Harper's either. So who are you? I mean which of the Keepers are you?"

"I'm the Guardian," Garrick said with a grin.

"I'm the Protector," I said.

Ellie sliced the bread, while Garrick dished up bowls of turkey stew. Davy asked us question after question.

My mouth watered at the sight of Ellie's whole-wheat bread. Garrick and Davy ate nearly half a loaf each. The subject of Rose came up, and Garrick recalled the tragic details of her passing. Davy now knew of his gallant efforts to save her life.

When the fire burned low and the lamp again flickered with the last drops of oil, we finally went to bed. Garrick's shoulders sagged when I mentioned that Ellie and I would be leaving the next morning, but I reminded him it was far too dangerous to keep three counters under one roof.

As I slept, Archidus sent me a message. It was different from any of my previous visions. I saw myself handing Ruth's counter to Davy. That surprised me and I looked for Garrick, worried he would be angry. But when I turned, he stood beside me, smiling. He stepped forward and instructed Davy on the use of the counter. Then the two of them disappeared, leaving me standing alone in their Ohio cabin.

The vision then showed me Master Archidus' fortress. Davy stood before the Master in the same room I had. Archidus smiled and handed him the counter. The chain was gone and Davy confidently pocketed the gold device. They shook hands Algonian-style by clasping wrists. Davy glanced over his shoulder and smiled. But before I could see the person he looked at, I awoke.

I was on the floor next to Davy, staring at the blackness above me, while Garrick snored lightly on the bed. I thought about what I'd seen until he suddenly bolted upright. I turned, trying to see him through the darkness. Unable make anything out, I whispered, "You okay?"

"Yeah, little brother. I'm not sure if I should mention it or not, but I had a peculiar dream a moment ago."

"Me too. I think mine came from Archidus, though."

"What did you dream about?"

"Ruth's counter. How about you?"

"Ruth's counter," Garrick echoed.

I wanted him to say Davy's name first. "Did you see who I gave it to?"

"Yes, but I'm not sure if I should say. Maybe my own wishful thinking has clouded my vision. What did you see, Harper?"

I smiled at the hidden meaning in his words. "I think I'm supposed to give it to Davy. Are you okay with that?"

"That's what I saw, too. I'll worry about his safety, but I do that already. I'm glad we told him the truth last night. It's been a burden keeping the secret all these years. I've wanted to take him places, but that was never possible. But if he was a Keeper, just think of the possibilities. We could go anywhere together."

"It's a plan then," I said. "I'll give it to him first thing in the morning. It sure will be a relief to get rid of it." I closed my eyes, hoping for a few more hours of sleep.

Garrick sat on the edge of his bed. "This is going to be great, Harper," he said excitedly. "I think Davy will do a fine job as Perception's Keeper."

"Okay, good night, Garrick."

"The three of us could go places together. We should get jobs building the transcontinental railroad. Just think, we could see the whole country. Which side would you want to build? West going east or east going west? I think we should start in the east and work our way west."

"Garrick," I cut in, "can we talk about this in the morning? I'm trying to sleep here."

He let out a growl. "All right. 'Night, Harper."

When I heard Davy and Garrick moving around the room the next morning, I sat up. Still half asleep, I said, "Davy, I've got to talk to you about something."

"What is it?"

"A few days ago, Master Archidus sent me to help another Keeper, a woman named Ruth." I paused, rubbing the sleep out of my eyes. The term World War II would mean nothing to Davy, so I contemplated how to continue. "Um . . . there was a war going on at the time, and she was half buried in the rubble when I got there. As I tried to save her, she gave me her counter, but before I could free her she was shot."

Davy tossed his blanket on the bed. "What does this have to do with me? I don't need any more bedtime stories—I'm not a child."

"I know. That's why I have to tell you this. I've had her counter for the past two days, uncertain what to do with it. Last night Archidus, the Master Keeper, sent me a dream. In it I saw myself giving the counter to you. Your pa had the same dream I did. If you're willing to accept the counter and protect it and its secret with your life, I'm supposed to give it to you."

Davy narrowed his eyes and shifted his gaze between his pa and me. "You're not kidding me, are you?"

"No, Son, we wouldn't kid around about this," Garrick answered.

I pulled Ruth's gold counter from beneath the clothes piled next to my pillow. Dangling it by the chain, I offered it to Davy. "This is it. The counter's name is Perception. If you want it, it's yours."

A slow grin spread across his face. "Why not, huh? As long as my pa and my pretend uncle are Keepers, I might as well go the whole hog and engage in it myself." Davy reached forward and took the counter from my outstretched hand. The moment it left my possession, a weight lifted from my shoulders. I took a deep breath and exhaled.

Garrick stepped forward to hug Davy. "That's the spirit."

The last time I'd seen my friend look this happy was before he lost Rose. He pulled out his own counter and explained it to Davy. I half listened as I slipped my shirt on and rolled up my blankets.

Garrick chuckled. "Hand me that. I'll set the coordinates. Here, now press the button in the middle, followed by the one on the right, and let's go spy on your ma."

My head snapped around in time to see the grin on Garrick's face as they disappeared. "Huh." I smiled to myself, thinking of him finally seeing Rose again. I folded the flannel shirt I'd borrowed and set it on the bed. Davy and Garrick would be back soon, and Ellie and I could go home. It was time for a nice hot shower. I left the bedroom and walked into the kitchen.

To my surprise, Ellie's bed was made, and she was nowhere to be seen. I jerked opened the door, relieved to see fresh footprints in the drifted snow leading to the outhouse. I followed them until I met her on the path, hurrying back to the cabin with a blanket wrapped around her shoulders. "Good morning." My breath floated away in the frigid chill of early morning.

She smiled. "What are you so happy about?"

"I found out who to give Ruth's counter to last night."

"Who?"

"It's Davy. Master Archidus sent both Garrick and me a vision. I gave the counter to Davy this morning. Garrick's already off showing him how to use it. It's a relief to be free of that thing. I'll meet you inside in a minute." I turned to jog along the path to the outhouse.

On my way back I filled my arms with wood, planning to stoke up the fire, eat breakfast, and go home. My work here was done. Garrick and Davy could go anywhere together. They would no longer be tied down to the 1820s.

I stepped through the door and walked to the fireplace. Garrick was stirring the coals and adding kindling. He looked smugly pleased with himself, and it didn't take a college degree to figure out what he'd been up to. I added my armful of wood to the dwindling pile left from yesterday and looked for Ellie.

She had started fixing breakfast, and Davy was standing close to her. I knew I shouldn't feel jealous, but I did. He was showing her his counter, but he didn't need to have his chest touching her shoulder, or the side of his face so near hers as he admired the counter in her hand.

"Davy, how was your first time-travel experience?" I said, drawing his attention away from her.

He turned and glanced at Garrick. "It was great, except I had to sit around and wait for my pa."

I chuckled. "Oh yeah? What was your pa up to?"

"Nothing," Garrick said quickly. "It's none of your business."

"But you did see Rose, right? I sure hope you didn't run into your other self."

Garrick ignored me. "What's for breakfast? Should we cook oatmeal?"

Smiling, I walked toward Ellie, thankful that Davy had moved away from her. If he had the chance, I suspected he'd try to convince her he was the better man. I planned to keep that opportunity out of his reach.

TWENTY-THREE
Amateur

While I helped with breakfast, a vision of Raoul Devereux, Wisdom's Keeper, flashed before my eyes. I saw an upscale apartment building and watched myself type in a numbered code, then walk through the gated entrance. I moved down the corridor, entered the elevator, and selected the fifth floor. When the elevator door opened, I walked to the left and found apartment number 516. A nameplate below the brass numbers spelled out Devereux's name. The doorframe was splintered as if from a forced entry. I peered in. Massive mahogany bookshelves lined two walls of an ornately furnished room. I walked through the entryway and glanced at the expensive-looking book collection.

From a room down the hall, I heard a male voice yelling in French, followed by the sound of shattering glass. I ran to the door. Locked. A low grunt sounded from the other side. I stepped back and kicked the door in, leaving another doorframe in a splintered mess. A Sniffer was assaulting Wisdom's Keeper with a kitchen knife. Raoul bled from shallow cuts on his arms, but he was holding the Sniffer at bay with a metal lamp. Relief flooded his face as I entered the room.

The counter coordinates—May 25, 1991, Paris, France—burned into my memory before my mind returned to the present. I opened my eyes to find Ellie's hand on my arm.

"Chase, what's wrong? Are you unwell?"

I stood slumped over, my head lowered, with both hands resting on the table. I looked around to get my bearings. Settling my gaze on Ellie's concerned face, I stood up straight. Then I took her face in my hands and kissed her once. "I'm fine. But I've got an errand to run for Archidus."

Garrick went into the bedroom and started rummaging through his things.

Ellie squeezed my arm. "What happened? It looked like you passed out standing up."

I hooked my arms behind her waist and smiled. "I saw a vision of the French Keeper in some trouble. We've got to help him and then I'll be back. After that let's eat and we'll go home. We've got spring break next week."

She smiled at me and relaxed, but I hesitated to let her go. I looked over my shoulder and saw Davy staring back at me, almost glaring.

Garrick hustled into the kitchen with his sword strapped to his waist. He carried another one in his right hand and tossed it to me. "Little brother, catch. Stop hugging your girlfriend and let's get moving. I'm hungry." I snatched the sword out of the air with my left hand.

"I want to come too," Davy said.

"No," Garrick said. "You stay here with Ellie."

"Pa, come on. I'm old enough."

Garrick pulled out his counter and set the dials. "No! And that's final. Harper, you coming with me?"

I dropped my hand from Ellie's waist. "Sure." A gripping fear twisted my insides and my gaze locked onto hers.

"Be careful," she whispered, "and remember to come back for me."

"I will." I paused. "Uh—"

"Harper, let's go."

I turned to Garrick. "I'm coming. Wait a second."

What I wanted to say to Ellie, I'd never said before—other than to family. I figured she already knew, but the words had never crossed my lips. Certainly there were better circumstances for it, but I couldn't deny the gripping fear that tied my insides in knots. For some reason, I felt compelled to say it before I disappeared this time. I stepped closer to her and touched her cheek, then leaned forward and whispered, "Ellie, I love you. I always will. Don't ever forget that."

I backed away from her, never taking my eyes off her misty ones. Garrick's strong hand gripped my shoulder and the familiar shimmer surrounded me. I aimlessly followed him through the first two shuffle zones, pondering Ellie's sad expression as she'd watched me leave.

"Harper, that's a military sword. It's not forged with magic, so it won't kill the Sniffer. But it's the best I've got. Arbon must be getting desperate. That elf looked amateur at best. He fought with a kitchen knife, so I'm guessing he's not even powerful enough to transport a sword. If he runs, let's follow him. Hopefully he's as dumb as he looks. I'd sure like to get rid of him on the first try. Do you remember how to follow a Sniffer?"

Setting all thoughts of Ellie aside, I focused my attention on the upcoming engagement and strapped the sword to my waist. "Roll all the dials to zero and press Go."

"That's right."

A Sniffer's invisible shield could only be penetrated by a weapon forged with magic. It was unfortunate I hadn't taken my sword when I left my bedroom, but I'd never expected this. I probably should have gone back for the weapon, but I didn't.

We soon appeared on the quiet Paris street in front of Raoul's apartment building. I entered the code and heard the metal gate unlock. I swung it open and held it for Garrick, who walked past me into the building. He held the elevator door and pressed the "5" button. We rode the elevator in silence, anxiously watching the numbers tick by. When we stopped on the fourth floor, Garrick and I exchanged quick glances as the doors opened. The woman waiting to get on stared at our clothes and our swords. She let out a gasp, then muttered something in French as she walked away, her high heels snapping against the tile floor. The doors slid closed and the elevator continued to the fifth floor.

Garrick and I hurried down the hall to apartment 516. The door opened easily, and splinters of wood from the broken frame littered the floor. The sounds of a struggle led us to the bedroom. From the vision we knew the door was locked. "On three," Garrick whispered. "One, two, three." In unison, we kicked the door in.

We rushed through the doorway only to have Raoul thrown through the air toward us. He slammed into Garrick, nearly knocking him over. I rushed the Sniffer, drawing my sword as I ran. I'd caught him off guard, and if I'd had my own sword, it might have been a fatal blow. As it was, the blade merely glanced off his body shield. The look of shock on his face turned to glee. Except for parrying the kitchen knife, my sword was useless against the Sniffer. He attacked while I dodged the slashing knife. I needed to distract him long enough for Garrick to get his blade in the fight.

He detangled himself from Raoul and drew his sword. He lunged around me and his sword sliced through the empty space the Sniffer had occupied a split second before. The kitchen knife clattered onto the tile floor. "Confound it," Garrick growled, then pulled his counter from his pocket, rolled all the dials down to zero, and pressed Go.

I pulled out my counter and prepared to follow. With my thumb hovering over the button, I glanced up. Raoul stared back at me. "Are you okay?" I asked.

He waved me off. "I'm fine. Thank you, Keeper."

Nodding, I turned and followed a Sniffer for the first time. When I entered the space he had last occupied, I completed the step where he had reappeared. It felt like I'd missed a step down—as if I expected to be walking on a level surface when it actually dropped off. I lurched forward, my feet sinking into a foot of snow.

Garrick walked a few steps ahead of me, following the footprints of the Sniffer through the trees. Suddenly my friend's face paled. "Something's not right. I know where we are."

He started running and I raced through the snow after him. When I exited the trees, I saw what Garrick must have already known. We had reappeared in the woods behind his property. The Sniffer ran toward the cabin, his gray cloak trailing him in the breeze.

"Ellie," I muttered.

The sword banging against my leg was useless. I unbuckled it and let it drop behind me as I ran. I raced through the drifted snow, intent on overtaking the Sniffer before he reached the cabin. Garrick slowed down, fiddling with his counter, and disappeared. At a dead run I was gaining on the Sniffer, who kept looking over his shoulder to monitor my progress. At the moment he turned to look back at me, Garrick appeared in front of him. His sword was poised for action in his right hand, his counter still open in his left.

I grinned at the Sniffer and stopped running. After giving me a strange look, he turned in time to see Garrick drive the sword into his heart. An unnatural scream split the quiet of the snowy morning and my hands shot up to cover my ears. The Sniffer's body crumpled onto the snow-covered ground and disintegrated to ash.

Breathing a sigh of relief, I walked forward. Garrick leaned down and ran his sword through the snow, cleaning the blade. After drying it with the hem of the Sniffer's cloak, he slid it into the scabbard. "Congratulations, Garrick." I slapped him on the back. "Let's go eat."

Ellie's muffled scream floated on the breeze, followed by "Chase, leave!" Whatever else she said, I didn't hear it. My only thought was to get to her. Garrick ran behind me. A tall, thickly built Sniffer with blond hair and pointy elf ears yanked open the door to the cabin and dragged Davy down the porch steps.

Another Sniffer followed. He was shorter with long brown hair braided down his back. This one pulled a struggling Ellie out the door, his hand covering her mouth. She fought him every inch of the way. He yanked her next to the blond elf, who placed one hand on Ellie's arm and grinned. Garrick's son stood stoically next to them, not even resisting. All four disappeared before I took my next ragged breath of ice-cold air.

My eyes went wide. "Ellie! No!" Still at a dead run, I pulled my counter from my pocket, made sure the dials were still at zero, and barreled toward where the footprints disappeared in the snow.

Garrick yelled from behind me. "Harper, wait! It might be a trap."

I heard his warning but didn't slow my pace. I ran toward the packed snow in front of the cabin—the only remaining sign of

Ellie's struggle with the Sniffer. As I got closer I heard Garrick running behind me, saying, "Oh, what the—"

Before I could lower my thumb to press Go, everything went dark and I felt myself pulled through a black abyss. Suddenly I was dropped onto damp, leaf-covered ground. The silent darkness confirmed my suspicion—I hadn't followed Ellie and the Sniffers. *What went wrong?*

I heard a low grunt behind me as someone else fell onto ground.

"Harper, when are you ever going to listen to me?" Garrick said from the darkness.

"They've got Ellie and Davy. We've got to do something. Where are we?"

"Look around. Don't tell me you don't know where we are."

I could hear anger in his voice, and I wasn't sure if he was mad about Davy or mad at me for not listening to him. Whichever it was, I didn't care.

After the bright white snow of Ohio, my eyes were slow to adjust, but once they did, I knew. "We're in Witches Hollow, aren't we? Dang it! This is Archidus' fault."

"Don't be so quick to judge. I told you I thought it was a trap. They were practically begging us to follow them. Something wasn't right. Think about it—that Sniffer decoyed us away from the cabin. Then, after the other two had Ellie and Davy, he led us back."

We walked into the forest, looking for the path to Archidus' fortress. "Maybe you're right, but that doesn't change the fact that they have Ellie. If we could have followed them, we would've at least had a chance at saving them. Now we don't even know where they went."

"Save them with what? Your bare hands? Use your brain, Harper. We need a plan. They obviously had one."

"Shut up. I don't need a lecture." By the light of my counter I saw the faint path Quirus had taken when he led me to the fortress. "This way."

Garrick walked to my side. "You should be thanking Master Archidus. I'll bet he saved your life back there. Who knows where you would've ended up if he hadn't brought you here. You'd most likely be dead in some ditch right now and your counter would be on its way to Arbon. Where do you think that would leave your precious Ellie? I'll tell you—dead. The only reason they have her is to get to you."

"If you're so smart, Garrick, what are you doing here? Shouldn't you be sitting by the hearth in your cabin right now?"

He put his hand on my shoulder. "Take it easy, little brother. I wasn't about to let you go off and get yourself killed alone."

I jerked my shoulder away. "Humph."

We walked in silence for a while. I needed to apologize to Garrick for snapping at him, but I wasn't ready yet. "What was going on with Davy?" I said finally. "Didn't he realize they were Sniffers? It looked like he wasn't even resisting them."

"I noticed the same thing. I warned him about the Sniffers. He should have been long gone with his counter at the first sight of them."

"He probably tried some hero maneuver to save Ellie."

"I wonder if they recognized him as a Keeper. He had the counter for less than an hour," Garrick said.

"I don't know, but if they've got him they probably have his counter."

As dawn broke over the eastern horizon and we emerged from the forest, my heart was heavy. I'd never expected Ellie would be stolen away from me. I'd thought it more likely I'd be killed somewhere and never return to her. *What is she thinking?*

Is she afraid? Will they hurt her? What do I really know about Sniffers, anyway? I should've never brought Ellie with me. Or maybe I should've never left her alone. All this second-guessing was killing me.

Unlike my first trip to Algonia, the sky was clear and there was no mist to dampen our clothing. Yet despite the early morning hour, it was warm. The massive stone wall encircling Archidus' castle loomed ahead of us and I paused. "Which way is the door?"

Garrick looked left then right. "This way, I think."

The final seconds before Ellie disappeared ran through my mind. What I wouldn't give to have her back again—to change it all. It sickened me to think they were using her to get to me. Once they realized we hadn't followed them, would they kill her? What use would there be in keeping her alive? And where had they taken her? Which world? What time? The possibilities were endless.

I knew of only one person with the power to help me. When I had first met Master Archidus, he claimed to be a seer. He said he could see things—things in the past, the present, and the future. If anyone could tell me where they'd taken her, it would be him.

I followed Garrick until the enormous wooden door came into view. Above it hung a large blue flag featuring an eagle's head encircled by gold symbols, similar to the ones on my counter. Garrick raised his fist and said, "Here goes nothing." I watched our backs while he pounded on the door.

The slat over a peephole slid open. "State your business at the capital city of Cadré Unair," demanded the guard.

"Open the gate," Garrick said. "We need to see Master Archidus . . . please."

"Who are you to request an audience with the king?"

"We're Keepers. I'm Garrick the Guardian, and this is the Protector."

Only a sliver of the man's face showed through the small hole. He spoke with someone behind him before turning back to us. "You may enter." He slid the peephole cover closed.

We waited for the door to open. Instead, a heavy rope ladder fell on us.

"Ouch!" Garrick rubbed the top of his head and threw the rope off his shoulders. "Don't they ever open the doors around here?" He started to climb and I impatiently followed.

When I stepped onto the catwalk, three armed guards surrounded me. I stared down their razor-sharp blades. The sword at my throat felt like it would draw blood at the slightest movement. My eyes darted to Garrick. They had disarmed him and he now struggled against being locked in shackles.

"You have got to be kidding me," I muttered. "Tell me this isn't happening."

Garrick's only response was a low growl and a defiant shake of his shoulders before his arms were wrenched behind him. With his hands secured, the tips of the guards' swords prodded him down the walkway. Witnessing the result of Garrick's struggle, I knew it would be pointless to resist.

TWENTY-FOUR
Master Archidus

After we descended the narrow, winding staircase, the guards led us along the interior of the stone wall. Algonian villagers in the streets of the capital city gawked at us.

"Where are we going?" Garrick said. "We need to see Archidus. Does he know we're here? I guarantee you he'll want to see us."

When the guards ignored my friend, I said, "I don't think they're taking us to see Archidus."

Garrick kept looking toward the towering castle in the center of the fortress. "I don't think so either."

A trumpet sounded and I heard a commotion at the gate behind us. Our guards turned to watch. The locks clicked open and the gatekeepers removed the heavy beam securing the door. A string of men tugged on twenty-foot sections of thick rope to open the doors.

Attempting to find some humor in our awful predicament, I said, "Look, Garrick, they do open the door—for important people."

"I don't even want to hear about it." He looked humiliated at being shackled and marched along like a common criminal. He stared straight ahead, while I watched the gate. A large, black horse pranced through the doorway, followed by twenty armed and mounted soldiers. The leader turned in our direction and galloped forward, his horse's long, powerful strides devouring the distance. When the man reined his animal to a stop, the metal shoes threw up sparks as the horse's feet slid across the cobblestones.

I was so intent on watching the magnificent horse, I hadn't noticed our guards take a knee. The rider flipped off the hood of his blue cloak. "Release them," he ordered.

I smiled as I recognized Master Archidus sitting astride the prancing horse. His dark hair and neatly trimmed beard were streaked with gray. His clothes weren't fancy like I thought a king might wear, but he had a regal bearing and a commanding presence, and his soldiers clearly respected him. When the horse had slid to a stop, Garrick turned to look, and he smiled in satisfaction. It was short lived, however, because Archidus shot us a stern look.

"Follow me, Keepers."

He wheeled his horse and faced the castle. The guards released us from the shackles and stepped aside. Garrick walked to the soldier who'd taken his sword and yanked it back. The pace of the prancing horse forced Garrick and me to jog to keep up.

When Archidus reached the castle, a groom waited to take his horse and a butler to take his cloak. The king marched down a long corridor, a personal guard flanking him on each side. We ascended two flights of stairs lit with bluish orbs attached to sconces along the wall, then entered the same large room where I'd met with Archidus before. This time the fireplaces were empty. The only light in the large room came through the stained-glass windows lining one wall.

Archidus walked to the head of a large table and sat in a velvet-covered chair. He motioned to two empty chairs. "Sit."

I was dying to speak but held my tongue.

Once we took our places Archidus said, "I perceive you are hungry. I'll hear what you have to say while we eat."

At the click of his fingers, a guard opened the door and five servants walked into the room. The first set plates, silverware, and goblets before each of us and then lit the candles in the center of the table. The second servant presented a large platter of fruit, the next a platter of breads and rolls, and the next a platter of thick bacon strips and fried eggs. The last servant brought jugs of fruit juice.

I surveyed the incredible feast. Although famished, all I could think about was Ellie. The thought of putting even one bite in my mouth when that stinking Sniffer had his hands on her repulsed me. I sat staring at my empty plate, but Garrick loaded his and shoveled food into his mouth. I scowled at him across the table. How could he eat at a time like this?

"Protector Chase," Master Archidus said, "you disappointed me. You failed to heed the Guardian's warning. Had I not intervened, you would have found yourself in the Dragon's Lair amidst a squadron of Arbon's cavalry, fully armed and battle-ready. Your life would have been forfeited within seconds of your arrival. Although a most unfortunate incident occurred with the former Protector's granddaughter, you were a fool not to think of the counter's safety first and foremost." Archidus paused, the silence adding weight to his sharp reprimand.

Uncomfortable under his stern gaze, I shifted in my seat and glanced down.

"I do extend my condolences for your loss," he added.

My head snapped up, and I stared in open-mouthed shock as Master Archidus casually returned to his breakfast. "What are you saying? Have they killed her?" My voice cracked with emotion.

"Not yet, but it is only a matter of time. No one ever returns from where they are taking her."

I gasped. "What? No! There has to be something we can do."

Archidus lowered his fork. "On occasion one must sacrifice personal happiness for the good of a kingdom. Legard, Arbon's strongest ally and most loyal friend, is taking her into Shuyle—Arbon's kingdom. Once they are within the borders of Shuyle, there is nothing that can be done. You must forget her and go back to the old world. You will maintain strict diligence and use the utmost caution once you return. I doubt Legard will give up on you that easily. Do not allow yourself to be enticed by anything he may say concerning that girl. Regardless of what you do, they will never release her. She is dead to you now."

I clenched my jaw and stared at Archidus in defiance. "I don't think so."

"You don't understand our kingdoms, my young friend. There are only two ways one may reach Shuyle—an arduous three-day journey across the Borderlands, or transportation through Witches Hollow and the old world to the Dragon's Lair. The Borderlands are regularly patrolled by Arbon's soldiers and his dragons. One's timing would need to be impeccable to make the journey undetected."

"What about the transportation thing, through Witches Hollow? That doesn't sound too bad," I said hopefully.

"Your counter cannot take you there. You would need to be an elf or a sorcerer, skilled in the art of advanced magic, to make the journey. And you are neither."

Garrick finished his first plate of food and looked at Archidus. "What about my son, Davy? Why did they take him? Harper gave him Ruth's counter this morning. Does Arbon know Davy is a Keeper? Is that why they have him?"

"It is not clear to me whether Legard knew Davy was a Keeper. It may have been that Davy was taken as bait to lure you into their trap. However, Arbon will recognize him immediately, if Legard hasn't already done so. Davy's newly acquired gift of perception allowed him a moment's notice before the Sniffers appeared. I can only guess at why he chose not to disappear. But to his credit, he hid the counter before he was taken. Garrick the Guardian, you must return immediately and retrieve it for me. Once they realize Davy abandoned the counter, they will descend with a fury and scour the area. I expect you to collect it first. Once you have the counter in your possession, simply hold it next to yours and look at them. That will be my signal to pull you back to Witches Hollow."

"Any idea where he hid it?"

"I always know where my counters are. Open your mind and I will show you."

Archidus closed his eyes and laid his hand on Garrick's wrist. A moment later, Garrick opened his eyes, a knowing expression on his face. He stood to leave.

"May you return quickly," Archidus said in farewell.

I started to follow my friend, but the Master pointed at me. "Protector, sit."

At the door Garrick turned. His blue-gray eyes looked as hard as steel. "I am not abandoning Davy to the likes of Arbon. I made a promise to his mother that I intend to keep. When I get back I'm going after my son. Harper, you work out a plan while I'm gone." With that, Garrick spun and marched out of the room.

When the door closed, I squared my shoulders. "I'm with him. I won't abandon Ellie, either. I'd rather die trying to save her than go home alone."

Archidus looked annoyed. "You realize that is most likely what you will do—die trying to save her. You are a naive boy. What you contemplate is suicide."

I folded my arms. "I don't care. I've made up my mind."

The Master Keeper looked at me, and I could tell he was trying to stare me down. But this time I raised my chin and held his gaze. Finally, he spoke. "As much as I wish to forbid it, the choice is yours, but remember, there are other women. You would meet someone else."

I shook my head. I didn't want anyone else.

"If you are intent upon walking this path toward a most certain death, I cannot allow you to leave this room with your counter. It would be most unwise to carry one anywhere near Arbon's kingdom."

"Fine." I reached into my pocket, pulled out the gold counter, and slid it across the table toward Archidus.

He looked surprised that I'd given up the counter so easily. Obviously, he didn't understand that it meant nothing in comparison to what I felt for Ellie. He tucked the counter in the pocket of his jacket and stared at me for several seconds. Then he motioned to my empty plate. "I see there will be no changing your mind. If you're determined to go traipsing into Shuyle to fight off a squadron of armed cavalrymen to save this girl who's worth dying for, may I suggest you start with a full stomach. A famished man would be at a great disadvantage next to Arbon's well-fed brutes. And once you're on the road, food rations will be meager, and there will be little time for hunting game."

"I guess you're right." I reached forward and loaded my plate, though my stomach was still sickened by the loss of Ellie.

While I ate, Archidus watched me. "I would hate to lose you to Arbon when I am just beginning to like you. Might I ask how you propose to find this girl, when you don't even know your way out of Algonia?"

I waved my fork at the door. "Could you give me a map and some directions? I figured since you're a seer and all, you could see where they were taking her."

An amused smile crossed Archidus' face, and he tapped the side of his forehead with his finger. "Perhaps, but I see you and the Guardian traveling in a group, and I find myself contemplating what to do with these visions."

I thought for a moment, picturing the armed guards who had arrested Garrick and me. "Maybe you could help us round up some guys who want to wreck a little havoc in Arbon's neck of the woods."

"You should know this is not a quest I would order any of my men to take on," Archidus replied. "What you are proposing is madness. It would have to be on a voluntary basis only."

Between bites of fried egg, I said, "That's fine. How do we ask for volunteers?" I ate with more gusto now that we were getting somewhere.

Abruptly, Archidus stood. "Wait here. I'll spread the word of what you're proposing and we'll see if anyone responds."

I ate my fill and then paced the large room, wondering how long it would take him to spread the word. It wasn't like he could Tweet about our idea or update his status on Facebook and get nearly instantaneous responses.

The servants returned and cleared away the breakfast mess. After two hours, Garrick burst through the door. He was short of breath and dripping sweat from the exertion of running to and from Witches Hollow. Triumphantly, he set Davy's counter on Archidus' table and slumped into his chair.

"Any trouble?" I asked.

Garrick sighed. "Nah. It was easy."

"You might as well leave your counter on the table as well. If we go after Ellie and Davy, Archidus won't let us take them."

"Are you serious?" Garrick said, then fished his counter out of his pocket and slid it next to Davy's. "What's the plan? When can we leave?"

"Archidus is trying to gather a group of soldiers to accompany us. He said to wait here. He thinks this is a suicide mission." I stood in front of Garrick with my hands shoved deep in my pockets. "This might be the last thing we do. We may not see home again."

Garrick's serious expression was likely a mirror image of mine. "I can live with that—or die with it. What do I have to go home to anyway? I've already lost Rose, and now they have my son. My life's not worth much if I can't save Davy's. As long as he's alive I won't give up trying. I've seen the way you look at Ellie. If your feelings for her are anything like how I felt about Rose, I imagine you'll do the same."

A lump filled my throat and I swallowed. "I won't leave without her." I started pacing again.

"Harper, sit down and hold still," Garrick said. "You're wearing a trench in the floor. Before this is over, you'll need every ounce of energy you've got. Quit wasting it walking back and forth in front of me."

"Stop bossing me around." I sat down in the chair across from him. "What if we're too late? The Sniffers might kill them when they realize we didn't fall into their trap."

Garrick took a deep breath and leaned forward. "The way I see it, it doesn't make sense for them to kill Davy and Ellie right away. They obviously went to a lot of trouble to set up their trap, so I think they'll keep them alive and try to bait us again."

I rolled my head back in frustration. "I sure hope you're right. But I could see them killing Ellie just to spite me."

"Have a little faith, would you?"

The heavy door banged open and Archidus marched into the room, followed by his guards. The heels of his tall black boots clicked with each step. He placed both hands on the table and leaned forward. "I've nearly assembled your crew. It surprised me how many were willing to accompany you. And who. You will be pleased to know that Legard, the blond-haired Sniffer, waits at the Dragon's Lair in hopes you will fall into his trap. Fortunately, he does not seem to suspect you are here. Any moment now, the passageway he opened between our worlds will close. At that point he will know it is impossible for you to follow him with your counters.

"In his anger at you not following him, he momentarily faltered in guarding his mind. I've seen that he plans to deliver the boy and the girl to Arbon—alive. They face a three-day journey along the perimeter of the Borderlands before they can turn into the heartland of Shuyle. You may have a sliver of a chance at success if you can overtake them before they enter the Valley of Tierran—the gateway to Shuyle." Archidus smiled, almost as if what he'd said was a novel idea.

"That's great." Garrick stood up. "I can make a sliver of a chance work. When do we leave?"

Archidus motioned to the man waiting in the doorway. I'd met him at Witches Hollow on my first visit to Algonia. Although short of stature, he was Archidus' right-hand man. "Quirus will take you down to weaponry, where Theobald will outfit you for your journey," Archidus said. "Once all the members of your crew arrive, I will send for you."

Quirus led Garrick and me down the stairs. "It is a pleasure to see you both again, although I wish the circumstances were more favorable."

"Yeah," Garrick and I muttered in unison.

Quirus stopped at the end of a long hall and knocked on the door. An old man with a hunched back, a tuft of white hair, and a cheerful countenance invited us in. "Theobald," Quirus said, "I present you Protector Chase and Garrick the Guardian."

The old man stuck out his hand. "I'm Theobald, but then you knew that. 'Tis a pleasure to make your acquaintance. I can't believe I'm outfitting the Keepers for battle. The wife's never going to believe it when I tell her what I did today. She'll think me crazy, she will."

After we shook hands, Theobald continued to ramble until Garrick cut in. "All we need are weapons that kill Sniffers, and supplies to get us there."

"Oh yes, yes. Follow me, sirs," Theobald said. "We can most certainly do that."

He outfitted us with leather breeches and knee-high boots made from the softest leather I'd ever felt. Then he held out two khaki-colored leather shirts. "Now take off those white shirts," he directed. "You aren't goin' in there to surrender. These blend in with the terrain you'll be covering, and the weather's hot this time of year."

I walked a small circle around the room while I buttoned the sleeveless shirt. "These boots are really comfortable."

"Oh yes. Made by the elves they are, each boot crafted by magic to give the wearer the comfort he desires. In the heat, the boots cool the feet. In the cold, they emit warmth. Over rocky terrain, they cushion the soles and you'll feel as if you're walking on sand. I wish I had me a pair, but they are very rare and only used in special circumstances. Archidus ordered only the best for you two."

"Hmm," I said. "Thanks."

Theobald handed each of us a pack. "You'll find additional supplies and provisions in here." The old man looked at the body armor and chain mail hanging on the wall. "I hate to send you into battle without a good helmet and breastplate, but with the considerable distance you need to cover and the weight of it, it would do you more harm than good. Not to mention, that much metal is too heavy to transport through Witches Hollow, should that route be available to you."

"That's fine," Garrick said. "Armor won't do us any good if we can't catch them."

Theobald turned to a wall of silver and gold glittering in the sunlight. "Now for weapons. You'll need a good sword."

Garrick rested his hand on the hilt at his side. "I'm happy with the one I've got. It's killed a few Sniffers in its day."

Theobald looked over the hilt and scabbard as if with the trained eye of an expert. "May I see it?" he asked.

Garrick drew the sword and handed it to Theobald.

"Yes, Guardian, I recognize the workmanship. Crafted by the renowned sword smith Caverdale. His swords are very fine indeed."

Theobald nodded his head in approval and returned the sword, hilt first. Then he turned back to the wall and selected one. "For you, Protector, I think this would be an excellent choice. Forged by magic, it will penetrate whatever shields a Sniffer might employ." Bowing at the waist, Theobold presented the sword to me. Small emeralds adorned the intricate silver and gold hilt.

"Thank you." I raised the weapon, pleased with the comfort of the hand grip and the easy way the blade sliced through the air, like an extension of my arm. "This is nice."

"I am pleased it satisfies you. Now what else do you require? I have long bows, spears, javelins, battle axes—"

"I'll take a javelin," I said. A smile crossed my lips. Maybe I could make up for missing track practice by throwing a javelin on this expedition.

"The javelin was also forged with magic." Theobald motioned to the rows of weapons on the walls. "All of these are capable of killing a Sniffer," he said with pride. "And for you, Guardian?"

Garrick said, "I'll stick with my sword. I've got something else in mind."

I was admiring the balanced feel of the silver-tipped javelin, when a boy of about thirteen entered the room and cleared his throat. "Excuse me, sirs, Master Archidus summons you."

"We'll be right there." I turned to Theobald and shook his hand in the Algonian style. "Thank you."

The old man bowed and shook Garrick's hand. We turned to leave but looked back over our shoulders when Theobald said, "Keepers, whatever your quest, may you find success."

In the large room upstairs, we were met by seven burly soldiers, an old man, and a sullen-looking elf girl, all clothed and armed in the same manner as Garrick and me. Archidus stood in front of the small group, giving directions. I smiled as I recognized one of the soldiers from my first visit to the fortress—Marcus, the captain. He'd interrupted Master Archidus' interrogation of me to report the destruction of a village by Lord Arbon's army. His eyes met mine and he nodded in acknowledgement.

Archidus cleared his throat. "I'll not waste time with introductions, as you can find occasion for that on the journey, but I will tell you this. Legard and his cavalry have left the Dragon's Lair. They are traveling at a steady pace. But if he suspects he's being followed, he's fully equipped to make a run for it on horseback. You, my friends, will be on foot unless you commandeer horses from Arbon's cavalry. Wickliff" —Archidus paused to nod respectfully toward the old man, whom I now recognized as an elf from his fine features and the pointy ears barely visible through his long gray hair— "has agreed to transport you all through the Dragon's Lair. Since one cannot enter that portal directly from Witches Hollow, you must first stop in the old world."

Whispered excitement buzzed through the group. Wickliff nodded in return as many of the soldiers sent him appreciating glances. Archidus raised his hand for silence. "This will place you a half day's march behind Legard. Transporting a large group with this much metal will be a significant drain. To conserve Wickliff's strength, I will send you to the old world so he need bring you only through the portal to the Dragon's Lair. Garrick the Guardian will be first in command, with Captain Marcus Landseer as his second. Are there any questions?"

"May I suggest a location for our stop in the old world?" Garrick asked.

"Certainly. Open your mind and show me," Archidus said.

He and Garrick both closed their eyes.

"Intriguing," Archidus muttered. "That could create a troublesome ripple for us, but these are desperate times. I will allow you to do as you wish, Guardian. You may leave immediately. Once you arrive at Witches Hollow, I will start you on your journey."

Garrick exited the room, and the soldiers fell in behind him. Except for the elf girl, I was the last one to leave. She tried to follow me out.

"Azalit," Archidus nearly roared. "Sit down. You are not going anywhere."

"But Father, I can help and you know it! They may have need of a healer and I'm qualified. What if someone dies because you won't let me go? How would you feel then?"

She is Archidus' daughter? I paused in the doorway, curious as to how this would play out. "Azalit, my dear, it is much too dangerous for you to be that close to Arbon. Not to mention, you are far too young for a mission of this magnitude."

"But Father," she tried again.

"No! I will hear nothing more of it. Go back to your studies."

I took the final step out of the room, not realizing Azalit was right behind me until she pushed past me. She carried a pack, a long bow, and a quiver of arrows trimmed with silver-colored fletchings. She turned up her nose at me and then hurried down the corridor. I headed in the opposite direction and ran down the stairs, catching Garrick and our crew in the street in front of the castle.

We set out at a steady jog. Wickliff the elf, despite his age, kept pace with the younger soldiers ahead of him. He wore a pack on his back, but other than a long staff, he carried no weapons. Unlike the rest of us, he wore a billowy cloak that seemed to change colors with his surroundings. It had been gray when we left the castle, but once we entered the dense forest, the cloak took on a green hue. A large hood hung limply on the elf's shoulders. I imagined if he put it on, he would be a chameleon.

No one said a word as we ran through the forest to Witches Hollow. Bringing up the rear, I was the last to step over the tangle of exposed roots into the circle of trees.

After we stopped, Garrick said, "As you know, I'm Garrick the Guardian and this is the Protector, Harper."

I nodded and said hello. Like everyone else except Wickliff, I breathed heavily from the run.

"I appreciate your willingness to help us rescue my son and Harper's girl—" At that moment, in the middle of Garrick's speech, we all disappeared. The enveloping darkness and the pull on my neck no longer surprised me. We dropped in a heap onto the concrete floor of a darkened building. Rattling sounds interrupted the silence as the men got to their feet and felt around in the dark.

Multiple voices grumbled at once. "Where are we?"

"What's the meaning of this?"

"Hang on. I'll get the light," Garrick said.

He flipped the light switch, and I saw we were in a large shop. Workbenches lined the wall with guns laid out—all in various stages of cleaning or repair. Several gun safes stood in a row, and tools of all types hung from hooks. A 1920s car, with the hood open and parts pulled out, was parked next to where I'd landed. All the soldiers stood in open-mouthed stupor at the strange things they were seeing for the first time. They discussed the lights overhead, the building style, and the thing parked next to them.

"Garrick, where are we?" I whispered, following him to one of the workbenches.

He opened a drawer and pulled out a small key ring. A mischievous grin brightened his face when he turned toward the safes. "My dad's shop. He's a gun dealer and an avid collector as well."

"Is this what you showed Archidus?"

Garrick nodded. "Yup. Since we're so outnumbered, I thought we could even up our odds, little brother."

I chuckled as he opened the safe and shoved pistols into my hands. "Start passing these out," he said.

"Those guys won't even know what to do with a gun."

"We'll teach them, but for now make sure they know not to point it at anybody. Go."

I handed a pistol to each soldier, giving the briefest gun-safety lesson in the history of mankind. Garrick followed me, giving everyone an extra ammo clip. "For now put your gun in your pack and leave it there," he said. "I'll show y'all how to use it later. I'll catch the lights, then we're ready to go."

Wickliff laid his hand on the arm of the soldier next to him. "Form a circle. Each of you place your hand on the arm of the man to your right and don't break the link until I tell you."

While Garrick turned out the lights, I kept the spot next to me open for him. Once my hand clasped his forearm, he asked, "Is everyone ready?"

A chorus of deep voices grunted in agreement.

"Then we shall proceed," Wickliff said. The elf's voice was unlike any I'd heard before. It had a soothing, almost sing-song quality.

I had no idea what Wickliff did to transport us to the Dragon's Lair, though I heard him speak a few words in a strange language. But suddenly I felt a wave of motion sickness as the air stirred around us. As it grew lighter, I watched the elf. He opened his eyes and looked at the circle of soldiers. When all were present, he loosened his grip and slumped forward.

"You may break the circle."

TWENTY-FIVE
The Crew

Large boulders dotted the blackened ground, and everything within sight appeared charred. A rocky peak rose behind us. In every direction, horses' hoofs had churned the ground.

"Are there real dragons around here?" I whispered to the soldier on my left.

"The legends say they nest in the crags on the backside of that mountain, but no one knows for certain. They patrol the Borderlands, which isn't far from here. Truth is, few have ever come this close to Shuyle and made it back to tell about it."

Wickliff slumped onto the closest boulder, looking as if he'd aged years in the last few minutes. I walked over to him. "Sir, are you all right?"

The elf slowly nodded. "Yes. I am simply tired. Moving ten people that far takes a great deal out of one. But moving the weapons, or anything made of metal, drains one's energy even more." He removed his pack and pulled out a small flask. He took a generous swallow before replacing the cork.

We easily found the enemy's trail. Archidus had said they traveled with sixty horses, so it wouldn't be difficult to follow.

"Would you like a hand?" I asked Wickliff.

He took my outstretched hand. "Thank you." It seemed as if his knees would buckle under the weight on his back.

"Let me carry your pack." I reached to take it before he could refuse.

I slung it over my shoulders, on top of my pack, and the straps magically adjusted for the perfect fit. Wickliff moved easier after that.

"Thank you for bringing us here. I don't think we would have stood a chance at catching them if it weren't for you," I said.

"You are quite welcome. After the pain and anguish Arbon has caused my family, I would do anything to spare someone else the same fate."

"Would you mind if I asked what happened?"

"Not at all. Hundreds of years have passed since then, but the sting of it never fades," Wickliff said. "I fear it is the wound in my soul that will never heal. Have you previously been educated on the history of our world?"

"A little."

"Then I will tell you a little more. At the time our worlds were divided, seven counters were forged, each instilled with the magic of one of the seven sorcerers who crafted our world. I knew both the Protector and the Guardian. By holding their counters, you and Garrick inherit a portion of their strength and skill.

"At that time my wife and I had a lovely daughter named Courtenay. She was highly skilled in her use of magic and well respected among our kind. The counter Creation was entrusted to her care. For many years peace ruled the land. The seven Keepers were revered as the governing body of our world and composed the Keepers' Council.

"It was no secret that Arbon was sore at his brother Archidus for being selected as the Master Keeper. As the elder brother, Arbon felt the honor should have been his. After a time, he seemed to reconcile himself and all appeared well on the surface."

Wickliff paused and shook his head. "Little did we know of the great tempest brewing inside him. During this time, Arbon began seeing Courtenay. At her young age, she believed herself in love and expected they would marry. My wife never trusted Arbon. How I wish I'd heeded her warning and intervened.

"Legard, who is my sister's son and therefore Courtenay's cousin, was Arbon's best friend. On All Hallow's Eve, Legard enticed Courtenay to meet his friend in an obscure location. That day became a dreadful one in our world's history and my family's. Legard's betrayal allowed Arbon to take her life. When our daughter never returned, we searched for her. It took time to uncover the dark events of that day. No one, except Arbon himself and perhaps Legard, knows for certain what happened. It has tormented me, wondering how someone of her ability could allow Arbon to overpower her. Because he was her lover, I suspect she trusted him completely, and it proved to be her undoing. His conniving ways were nothing short of evil. He deceived everyone, and I don't doubt there was black magic at work that day. If it weren't for Archidus' exceptional sight, Arbon may have overpowered us all."

Stunned at the details of Wickliff's daughter's murder, I now understood why he would risk his life. Why he had exerted so much of himself to bring us through the Dragon's Lair. "I'm sorry about your daughter," I said.

"I thank you for your sympathy, young Keeper."

"Do you have any other children?"

"No, I'm afraid not. Females of our kind, both elves and sorcerers, are only able to bear young once during their lifetimes. I fear eventually the day will come when we are extinct."

"If that's so, how are Archidus and Arbon brothers?"

"Arbon's mother died when he was but a lad and his father remarried. Rumor had it, Arbon never took a liking to his new mother—despised her, in fact."

Garrick fell in line on the other side of Wickliff. "How are you feeling?" he asked.

With an optimistic-looking smile, the elf said, "Much stronger. I apologize for slowing your pace. I expect I'll be up to speed shortly."

"Let me know when that is. Until then, we'll continue to walk. Harper?" Garrick nodded at the extra pack on my back.

"I'm good."

Within the hour, Wickliff sent word that he was able to run. All afternoon we followed the broken soil, our footprints disappearing among the myriad of horse tracks. If Legard's cavalry moved at a trot, we needed to keep running even when they rested in order to catch them. The humid heat soon zapped my energy and I wanted to quit. Under normal circumstances I might have. But on this day, when I felt like stopping—when I thought my legs couldn't carry me another step—I replayed the nightmare of seeing Ellie yanked away by the Sniffer. I held the memory of her in front of me like a coveted prize, forcing myself to keep going when my body begged to stop. For the first time in my life I really wanted something. Wanted it bad enough to work for it, even die for it.

The scorched ground gradually gave way to scattered shrubs and brush. The trail broadened and became more distinct, resembling a crude dirt road. The hilly terrain and large rock formations prevented us from ever catching sight of the cavalry we followed. Before long, the dirt road wound its way into a forest. Next to us, a formidable mountain range separated Shuyle from the Borderlands.

We came to a river late in the afternoon. Weary soldiers dropped their packs along the bank and plunged their faces into the water. My mouth was parched and I gulped the cool liquid. After drinking my fill and topping off my water flask, I collapsed onto the grassy riverbank. A fine layer of dust clung to my sweat-drenched skin. Garrick sat down next to me and I opened my eyes. The soldiers pulled jerky out of their packs and chewed quietly. Garrick opened his pack and got out a piece, ripping off a chunk with his teeth.

"Not bad, Harper. You should try it."

I found my jerky and started eating. The soldier I'd recognized walked over and squatted in front of us. He nodded toward me. "Good to see you alive, Keeper. When I interrupted that night, it looked as if Master Archidus had a mind to send you to the gallows."

"He wasn't too happy with me at first," I said. "Who knows, he may still not be happy. It's Marcus, right?"

He offered his hand and I reached forward to shake it. In traditional Algonian style, he clasped my wrist instead of my hand. I wrapped my fingers around the metal-studded leather bracelet on his wrist and squeezed. Muscles rippled along his scarred forearm.

"Yes, sir. Captain Marcus Landseer, at your service."

I smiled. "Chase Harper, at your service."

Garrick leaned forward. "Marcus, may I ask what persuaded you to join an expedition like this?"

"I've been fighting this war since I was old enough to wield a sword. I've seen more death and suffering than any man should have to witness in a lifetime. But Arbon made me his personal enemy when his soldiers raided my parents' village last summer and stole my youngest sister, Brierly. They took four youth from the village that night. I expect they were used as slaves, or worse.

I don't imagine we'll get close enough to Arbon's stronghold for me to look for her. But if I can spare another girl the fate of my sister, that may be as close as I'll get to vengeance."

"It's an honor to have you," Garrick said as he shifted position. "Marcus, I want to find Legard before we stop for the night. I expect we'll need every advantage possible, so I'm hoping to spy on them for a day before we attempt a rescue."

"If we maintain our pace, we should catch them," Marcus replied. "This road runs parallel to the Shuylian mountains. 'Twill take them three days to journey from the Dragon's Lair to the valley of Tierran—the main entrance to Shuyle. Once they enter the valley, there are army outposts and small villages every few miles. Whatever we're going to do, it must be done before then."

I'd been torn between utter exhaustion and my desire to push on toward Ellie. But after Marcus's account of his sister's fate, the urge to find my girlfriend overpowered my body's need for rest. "Then we'd better keep moving," I said.

"Time to move out, boys," Garrick called.

Every soldier hopped to his feet and fell in line. We ran throughout the evening and into the dark of night. The nearly full moon rose over the mountains, casting its pale light across the road. I stared at the back of the soldier running in front of me, aware of little else except my own aching muscles. Suddenly, Wickliff whistled softly, bringing everyone to a halt, and motioned for us to follow him as he left the road and plunged into the forest. When Garrick and I caught up to him, he whispered, "A patrol is coming."

We passed the message along. "Take cover—a patrol's coming."

Six mounted soldiers trotted past our hiding place. They went a short distance before stopping to talk among themselves. Then they returned in the direction they'd come from.

"That's their rear guard," Marcus whispered. "They've most likely stopped for the night."

"Good," Garrick said. "Wickliff, take the rest of the men back a quarter of a mile and find a place to camp. Marcus and Harper, come with me. I want to see what we're up against."

Marcus placed his hand on Garrick's arm. "Leave the packs—it's easier to maneuver without them."

Garrick nodded and the three of us dropped our packs. Three soldiers retrieved them, and Wickliff led the remainder of our crew away.

Marcus took the lead. My heart thudded wildly as Garrick and I ran after him. Undoubtedly, the enemy's rear guard would return and patrol the very road we ran on. It wasn't a matter of if, but when.

Ahead of us, thin trails of smoke twisted into the sky, and the sounds of an encampment drifted through the night. Raucous laughter and bursts of angry yelling gave away the army's location. Marcus veered into the woods, and with painstaking caution we crawled on our bellies, moving from tree to tree as we worked our way closer to Legard's camp.

Crouching behind a bush, we watched them. Legard had picketed soldiers around the perimeter of the clearing. The smell of meat filled the sultry air. From the looks of it, a wild boar had been cut in quarters and now roasted over a bed of hot coals.

"Stay here," Garrick whispered. "I want to see something."

Before Marcus or I could respond, he disappeared into the night. I scanned the camp for Ellie but saw Davy first. His hands were tied, and a brown-haired Sniffer yanked him through the camp. Then, the blond Sniffer, who I now knew to be Legard, stepped into the open. He held Ellie by the back of her neck. Her hands were tied as well, but she wasn't about to be moved anywhere without a fight. Legard looked amused and roughly pushed her onto the ground, sending her crashing into Davy. I jumped to my feet. This close to Ellie, I could taste my fury. I wanted her back, and I didn't want their filthy hands on her. I gripped my sword hilt and stepped forward. I'd give Legard a taste of his own medicine.

Marcus grabbed me from behind, his bicep cutting off my air supply as his voice hissed in my ear. "Stand down, soldier. Do I make myself clear?"

Unable to breathe, I nodded quickly. He released his hold, and I moved back behind the bush, rubbing my throat.

One of the soldiers drew his dagger and whittled the end of a stick into a sharp point. He then sliced and skewered two chunks of meat, which he offered to the prisoners. Ellie shook her head, refusing to take the food. After Davy leaned over and said something to her, she accepted the meat.

With their long hair and scraggly beards, Arbon's soldiers were an ugly bunch, but I didn't doubt they would make formidable opponents. The men's broad backs and thick necks made them look as if they'd seen their share of battles. A plethora of weapons—axes, scimitars, swords, and bows—lay scattered around the camp.

When Ellie and Davy finished eating, Legard moved them toward the trees. Davy pleaded with her to cooperate, and I wished she would listen to him. But for Ellie, I suppose resisting was a matter of principle. Looking pleased with himself, Legard yanked her forward, agilely avoiding her attempt at kicking him. When he clenched her neck and she squirmed in pain, only Marcus's hand firmly on my shoulder held me in place.

"We'll need to separate the prisoners from the Sniffers," he whispered.

"Why's that?"

"If Legard can touch her, he can disappear with her, and if he can see her, he can transport to her location. This is no easy task we're facing."

As soon as Garrick returned, we retreated to the road. On the run back, we darted for cover as the jangle of tack warned us of another mounted patrol. We saw no sign of our camp until Wickliff whistled quietly, mimicking the sound of a night bird. Marcus raised his hand to stop us, saying, "This way."

We found the camp and dropped to the ground next to the sleeping soldiers. As soon as my head hit my pack, the soldier next to me leaned over and said, "Lad, you'll want to sleep on your sword."

"What?"

"Draw your sword and sleep with a hand on the hilt. You never know what might be afoot when you're asleep."

"Okay." I drew my sword and laid it next to me, the emerald-studded hilt resting under the palm of my hand.

"It's your girl we're after, isn't it?" the soldier asked.

"Yeah, her name's Ellie."

"I'm Segur and this is my big brother, Red." He nudged the soldier lying next to him.

Sounding half asleep, Red said, "Huh, that's me."

I smiled. "Nice name. Red is the name of my horse back home."

"Good name. Must be a good horse," he mumbled.

"My girl was killed in the attack on Radnor last winter," Segur said, "as well as our parents and little brothers. Red's wife and infant son also lived in Radnor. We were stationed near Cadré Unair when they attacked. Archidus dispatched the closest regiments, but it was too late for our families. We drove Arbon's army out of Algonia and back across the Borderlands, but by the time we reached Shuyle, we were out of provisions and exhausted. Our sorcerers couldn't hold off the dragons much longer, and we knew Arbon's reinforcements might circle around and cut us off, so we were forced to retreat. Except for one sister who is married, my brother and I are all that is left of our family. We lost everything to Arbon's bloodthirsty soldiers and I've taken a vow to avenge their deaths."

"Looks like you shouldn't have any problem doing that. There are plenty of Arbon's brutes to go around. Thanks for coming, Segur."

"'Tis my pleasure. I look forward to the morrow." He rolled over and soon took up the deep breathing of sleep.

I gazed at the multitude of low-hanging stars in the heavens. On this world, or dimension, or wherever it was I found myself, the stars looked huge. In the quiet darkness my thoughts returned to Ellie. At a half a mile away from me, she was so close and yet impossible to reach.

In the moment before I drifted to sleep, I thought of home. The first time I'd been summoned here, time continued to move forward without me. What would my parents think by now? What happened when they came home from work and found my truck, my keys, my cell phone, and my clothes lying around with no me in sight? What would everyone think when they realized Ellie had gone missing as well? No one, except possibly Jessica, would ever figure it out. Would she tell them about the counter? Would anyone even believe her if she did? Or would time move forward from where I'd left most recently, which was 1829, leaving my parents clueless about what was going on with me?

I tossed and turned that night, haunted again by the nightmare in which I'd lost Ellie. But when my eyes opened to the gray light of dawn, I realized there was no waking up from it this time. I was living my worst nightmare.

Garrick, Wickliff, and Marcus huddled together, talking. The other soldiers stirred in their beds. My stomach growled and I searched my pack—jerky or flat bread. I ripped off a chunk of the thick jerky with my teeth and chewed quietly. After I'd eaten it yesterday afternoon, I'd felt full for hours. Perhaps the elves made magic jerky as well as magic boots. Every inch of my body screamed at being asked to move, except my feet.

Before we broke camp, Garrick demonstrated how to load and fire a gun—without actually pulling the trigger, of course.

Segur raised his eyebrows. "I have me doubts as to whether this little thing will do any good."

"Trust me, Segur," I said. "It's a deadly weapon. The tricky part is aiming it in the right place."

Garrick finished his lecture with a warning. "Take your finger off the trigger when you're not firing. And whatever you do, don't point the barrel at each other. Also, guns are loud, so don't fire until I give the signal. Finally, keep your safety on when you're not shooting, and don't leave the guns behind for Arbon to find."

"Yes, sir," everyone said.

"Good. Let's stay out of sight today. Tonight we attack. Marcus, go ahead." Garrick stepped aside.

"Once they stop for the night, we'll take out their rear patrol," Marcus explained. "Then we split into groups of two and circle their camp. Last night they picketed six guards. I want each guard removed without a sound. Wickliff and Harper will go in to rescue the prisoners. Harper, once you free the prisoners, get them on horses and ride for the rendezvous. That location will be decided when we get closer. Everyone else, attack once Wickliff appears in camp. Harper, you need to realize that if Legard escapes Wickliff and can see you and the prisoners, it's a simple matter of thought for him to transport to your position and disappear with you."

I nodded and Marcus continued. "Once the attack commences, we need to make fast work of it. Surprise is our only advantage. We're outnumbered six to one and we're in enemy territory. We fight as long and as hard as we can, and then we retreat. Everyone needs to steal a horse before they leave. We can't expect to stay ahead of them on foot. It's a shame we don't have someone to release and scatter their horses, but we need every man fighting.

"When we rendezvous, if Wickliff has the strength to take us back, we'll ride for the Dragon's Lair. If not, we'll escape across the Borderlands. If anyone misses the rendezvous, or if we're overtaken on the trail, we scatter and work our way back to Algonia alone. Let's go show Arbon some Algonian defiance."

Every soldier raised his fist in approval.

As I slung my pack over my shoulder, Red offered me his hand. A few dried leaves stuck in his shoulder-length red hair. "Protector, good luck to you tonight."

We clasped wrists, and the strength of his grip cut off the blood supply to my hand. "Thanks, Red. Same to you. I'm glad you're here. We couldn't do this without you guys."

A cheery smile spread across his face. "A thank you isn't necessary. We're soldiers—this is what we do. Fighting Arbon is all I've got, so I figure I might as well make the most of it. It's about time Arbon was on the receiving end of his own strategy."

For someone who'd lost so much, Red had the brightest twinkle in his eye. Beneath the scruffy beard, the scars, and the weapons was probably a big teddy bear of a man. How different these men's lives were from mine. They'd been fighting since they were younger than me and had never known peace for long. What we were planning to do tonight turned my stomach, but for them it was just another day on the job. To survive this and get Ellie back, I would need to be more like them.

Every muscle threatened to rebel, and I wasn't the only one moving stiffly as we left camp that morning. Garrick started at a walk, but before long he had us jogging. Fresh dung piles littered the road once we passed the enemy's campsite.

My nerves were on edge and I sucked in a deep breath. If all went well I'd be with Ellie tonight. If it didn't go well . . . no, I couldn't think about that. Her life depended on the success of our plan. And my life? Would I walk away from this? It didn't matter. My course was set, and I would never give up. If we failed tonight, there would be no retreating across the Borderlands for me. I would enter the Valley of Tierran and follow Ellie into Shuyle if I had to.

The shortest soldier in our group interrupted my brooding thoughts. "Protector, I've not properly introduced myself. I'm Aiton."

He looked formidable, despite his height. Hands down, he boasted more scars than any of the other soldiers. A jagged pink line ran down the side of his face—a fresh scar. Both arms were covered with them and he ran with a limp.

I reached out and clasped wrists with him. "I'm Chase Harper. Thank you for coming."

He chuckled mischievously. "Aye, I wouldn't miss excitement like this for all the hot mead in Algonia. I've a debt to pay Lord Arbon of 999 soldiers, and I aim to start tonight."

I smiled. "Why 999?"

"Because, lad, that's how many of me friends and fellow soldiers were killed in front of me very eyes. I was stationed in Radnor with Captain Barculo when a covert regiment killed every man but me. I crawled into the jungle with an arrow broken off in me leg and a stream of blood soaking me breeches. Marcus found me the next day. Nearly dead I was. Still don't know how they did it. Must have worked some black magic to get past our guard, since no alarm was raised. We were surrounded in the dead of night and attacked in our beds.

That's where the 999 comes from—Barculo's thousand men, less the only survivor, me."

"I heard Marcus's report on Radnor's destruction," I said. "It sounded like your injuries were serious."

"They were, but those elves are good healers. This scar on my face will eventually disappear, if I ever put the tonic on it night and morning like the healer told me to do. Who has time for tonic twice a day? Look at me. I'm a soldier. I wear my battle scars with pride. I may well leave it as it is."

"The scars do make you look fierce."

He smiled. "That's what I think. Have you met Falon and Pellyn, the twins?" Aiton pointed to the two dark-haired soldiers running stride for stride in perfect unison.

"Not yet." Looking closely at them I saw the family resemblance, although I doubted they were identical twins. Each of them sported scars as well.

"Falon and Pellyn had two older brothers who were killed on the battlefield a few years ago. Those two have a reputation for being among the boldest and bravest soldiers. They fight as a team. To watch them, you'd swear they could read each other's minds. They'll be a great boon come fightin' time."

"That's good. We'll need them. Who's the guy talking to Wickliff?" I now knew everyone except him.

"That's Barhydt. Rumor has it he's part sorcerer. I've not fought alongside him before, but I hear tell he has some magical talents he can put to good use on the battlefield."

Barhydt and Wickliff tilted their heads skyward. "Seek cover! The dragons are coming," yelled Barhydt.

The soldiers fled the road and tucked themselves beneath the branches of the stoutest trees. I ran to where Garrick and Marcus stood with their backs pressed to the trunk of a towering oak. The low-hanging limbs dangled in front of our faces as we waited. I'd never seen a dragon, and curiosity had me wishing I could step out and take a peek. But the worried expression on every soldier's face made it obvious how foolish that would be.

We heard the dragons before we saw them. Their large wings swished and snapped through the humid air. Periodically, a low roar escaped their reptilian mouths in a burst of orange flame. As they flew directly overhead, I caught a glimpse. They were a dull, gray green color, with a lighter-colored stomach.

The massive creatures circled twice, hovering a moment over the area ahead of us. Were they curious about Legard's expedition? Suddenly, as if someone shooed them away, both dragons turned and flew off into the Borderlands, quickly becoming nothing more than two small specks in the distance.

"All clear," Barhydt said.

We moved back to the road and continued after Legard and the cavalry. When we crested a hill late in the afternoon, everyone in front of me came to an abrupt stop. I wasn't watching and ran into the back of Pellyn.

"Sorry," I mumbled as Aiton and Wickliff stopped directly behind me in a near collision.

"Back, back. Everybody get back, quick!" Marcus whispered.

We scrambled behind the trees and peered into the valley below. The road ahead went straight for almost a mile through an open grassland dotted with boulders. In the heat of the day the cavalry moved at a leisurely pace, traveling three abreast. Ellie and Davy rode in the middle of the group, flanked by Legard and the other Sniffer.

"They look okay," Garrick said to me.

"Yeah, but I hate seeing her with them."

He smiled. "Don't worry, little brother, we're going to change that tonight. I want Davy on a horse and riding out of there first thing. Don't let him hang around and fight—he's too young for that."

I nodded.

We waited at the crest of the hill for Legard and the cavalry to enter the trees on the other side of the valley. After the last horse disappeared, Garrick said, "What about the dragons? We're going to be in the open for a while."

Marcus turned. "Wickliff, Barhydt, do we have time to get across?"

"I don't sense them," Wickliff answered.

"Neither do I," Barhydt said.

"Okay, boys, let's hustle," Garrick ordered. We followed him at a run down the hill. I kept my eyes on the place where the road vanished into the forest. We were three-fourths of the way across the open valley when Barhydt raised his eyes to the sky and Wickliff yelled, "Faster!"

Great, the dragons are coming back. Gasping for air and pouring sweat in the blazing afternoon sun, I ran on. My pack, which had felt light when we started out, now weighed heavily on my aching shoulders. I didn't know what a dragon attack would look like, but I imagined it wouldn't be pretty. In the distance we saw two specks steadily growing larger as the creatures flapped their massive wings in our direction. If they had the vision of an eagle, we were dead.

With our chests heaving, the ten of us barreled into the woods and scattered, seeking cover next to the largest trees. Knowing my luck, the dragons would hear my heavy breathing and burn my tree down. As the ominous snapping of their wings sounded overhead, I leaned my head against the trunk and prayed they wouldn't see me.

Circling the valley, the dragons roared back and forth to each other. A blast of hot air fanned my face when one of them scorched the top of my tree. My legs cramped from standing still after running so hard, and I clenched my jaw to keep quiet. Even when I couldn't hear the beating of the creatures' wings, I didn't dare move until Wickliff gave the okay. What was probably only another few minutes felt like an eternity.

Finally, the elf stepped out from under a tree and announced it was safe to continue.

"Thank goodness," I muttered to myself. After walking a few steps, I stopped to stretch my cramped hamstrings.

Garrick slapped me on the back. "How you holding up, little brother?"

"I guess I don't need to worry about missing track practice."

He laughed. "Missing track practice is the least of your worries."

I smirked and shoved him. "Get outta here. I was being sarcastic."

"Let's move out," he called to the others.

I fell in at the back of the line next to Wickliff. Amazingly, the old elf appeared to be doing better than the rest of us. "Can I ask you something?" I said to him.

He smiled. "Indeed, my young Keeper."

"I normally live in the year 2012, but when I was pulled here I was in the year 1829 with my counter. When time is moving on this world, it seems like it is also moving there, but is it moving forward from 1829 or from 2012? Does that make any sense at all? I guess what I'm wondering is, will my parents know I'm gone?"

"My young friend, I do understand what you are asking. I've had little need to contemplate the mysteries of time since Courtenay was taken from me, but this much I can tell you. The time-travel capabilities of the counters apply only to your dimension of the earth. They were meant to work here as well, but for reasons unknown it has not been so. When Courtenay was killed, the remaining Keepers thought to reverse time and intervene on her behalf. Upon attempting it, they were unsuccessful. Their counters transported them to the location of the dreadful deed, but they were all locked in the present. Sniffers, as well as all elves and sorcerers who possess the necessary skills and are properly trained, can transport themselves through time and space on the old world, much as you do with your counter. Although we can jump through the time portals of your dimension with ease, time is unstoppable and unchangeable for us here.

"It is the year 2012 for us in Algonia as well, so the answer to your question is yes. Time is now moving forward in 2012." Wickliff looked at me solemnly. "Your parents will not see you there on this day, because you are here."

"I am so dead. My mom's gonna worry herself sick. And my dad will kill me for sure."

"As I was once a father, I am most certain your life won't end at your father's hand. He may be angry at first, but anger is usually a front to hide fear—the fear of losing you. When you return, have you considered transporting yourself with your counter back to the time you left, thereby extending mercy to your parents and salvation to yourself?"

"Will that work?" My excitement mounted as I worked it out in my mind. "Yes! It should work. It's not like I've been to that time with the counter before. There's no reason that shouldn't work. Thank you, Wickliff."

The old elf chuckled. "I'm pleased to have been of assistance to you."

TWENTY-SIX
Attack

The sun set, bringing a deep orange glow to the dirt road. We advanced with caution, knowing we trailed Legard's group by less than a half mile. When they camped early for the night, we expected their guard to patrol the roadway in our direction. At the sound of Wickliff's warning, we hid ourselves. Like the night before, the mounted guards trotted by.

Once the road cleared, we decided on a rendezvous point—a heavy stand of timber and brush a hundred yards off the road. It would be easy to get to on horseback after the attack, yet far enough away from Legard's camp that we could safely hide there for now. The heavy canopy of leaves above us blocked virtually all remaining traces of daylight.

I left the group to relieve myself before we attacked. As I fastened my breeches, I heard someone sneaking through the trees. They were on a course that would bring them next to the bush I stood behind, so I crouched down and waited.

I peered through the leafy branches, noticing the person wasn't very big. He wore a long, hooded cloak similar to Wickliff's, and I wondered if it was another Sniffer. I wrapped my fingers around my sword hilt.

Looking from side to side, he crept closer. When he stepped in front of where I hid, I jumped him. He was a lightweight, and I easily wrestled him to the ground. To stop his flailing fists from hitting me in the face, I grabbed both wrists and pinned him beneath me. As I drew my sword a female voice yelled, "Get off me!"

She shook her head and the hood slid off her face. I gasped. "It's you." Pinned beneath me with her face close to mine was Archidus' daughter, Azalit. I released her and scrambled away. "I wasn't expecting you to be sneaking into our camp." What was she doing here? This was no place for a teenage girl.

She brushed the dried leaves off her cloak. "You could have inquired before throwing me down." When she started to stand, I jumped to my feet and grabbed her arm. Her lip curled in disdain. "Remove your hand from me."

Getting angrier by the second, I squeezed harder. "No. And be quiet, would you? We're not far from where Arbon's soldiers are camped. I'll kill you myself if you mess up this rescue."

The orb on Wickliff's staff glowed a pale blue, and I pushed Azalit ahead of me into the circle of light. The soldiers, who were eating and sharpening their swords, paused to stare.

Releasing her, I said, "Look what I found lurking in the woods." I sat down next to my pack and ripped off a chunk of flat bread.

Marcus jumped to his feet. "How did you get here?"

Azalit raised her chin defiantly. "My father changed his mind and sent me, in case you need a healer."

"That's a lie. Your father would never send you here," Marcus replied. "And if he did, he would never send you alone. Speak the truth, Azalit. How did you get here?"

She squared her shoulders. "I took myself through Witches Hollow and the Dragon's Lair."

"You're not old enough to transport—"

"Of course I am," she interrupted. "I'm here, aren't I?"

Marcus stepped closer. "Yes, you are here. So, you can take your little self right back where you came from. Your father will have our hides if we allow you to stay."

He paced back and forth in the small space between where Garrick sat on a log and Azalit stood her ground. Every soldier watched in silence.

Wickliff cleared his throat. "At this late hour, far from the Dragon's Lair, would it not be more prudent to keep her with us?"

Marcus spun to face the old elf. "What are you saying? We reward this insolence by letting her stay?"

"Would we not find our heads on the gallows more quickly if we were to send her off by herself and she were to be captured, than if we kept her close enough to protect her?"

The captain seemed to think about that while Wickliff continued, "You said yourself we could use another pair of hands to release the horses once we attack."

Marcus shook his head. "Garrick, you're in charge."

"If she was my daughter I wouldn't want her here in the first place," Garrick said. "But considering she's already here, I don't think she should be running around in enemy territory by herself. Not to mention, we could use her help tonight."

"So you think she should come with us?" Marcus asked.

Garrick shrugged. "I expect this road will be crawling with soldiers by tomorrow. It will be difficult for anyone to return to the Dragon's Lair undetected, so I'm with Wickliff."

"Then it's decided." Marcus turned to face Azalit. "You may come. But in the future, you do what you're told—no exceptions. Do you understand?"

"Yes, sir," Azalit said, obviously pleased with herself.

Marcus stood in front of her and raised three fingers. "When Wickliff gives three owl calls, we attack, but you wait. Once you hear the sounds of battle, scatter their horses, but not a moment before. We'll need thirteen of them to escape, so make sure you leave at least that many tied or have them ready to go by the road. Whatever you do, don't engage the enemy. I want you to stay hidden. Understand?"

She smiled. "Yes, sir."

As we prepared to split up, Garrick and Marcus reviewed the plan for the last time. With so many contingencies, it was impossible to know what the night would bring. I loaded a fresh clip in my pistol and put an extra in my pocket, then paced across the dry ground. At this rate, the waiting would kill me before Arbon's soldiers even got a chance.

Garrick stepped in front of me, placing one hand on my shoulder and extending the other. "Good luck, little brother," he said, shaking my hand.

We held each other's gaze, and I hoped this wasn't goodbye. I swallowed the surge of emotion. "Thanks, Garrick. You take care of yourself."

Six soldiers drew back their bows as the rear guard came into view. "Ready. Release," Marcus said quietly. Six arrows flew through the moonlight, finding their targets. Marcus and the soldiers rushed forward and finished off the Shuylians, while Garrick, Wickliff, Azalit, and I caught hold of the horses' bridles. We led the animals closer to the camp and tied them to trees off the road.

Wickliff and I crept into position and watched the enemy campsite. I carried the javelin in one hand and the pistol in the other. In spite of the oppressive heat, Legard's group again had a large cooking fire. A log shifted and sent a shower of sparks into the night sky.

Ellie and Davy weren't tied up tonight, and I wondered if Legard assumed they were close enough to Shuyle that there would be no chance for them to escape. I struggled to stay awake myself as I watched the last of Arbon's soldiers drift off to sleep. When Davy offered his arm for Ellie to lay her head on, I felt a familiar surge of jealousy. Being forced to watch her sleep next to him kept me awake.

Except for the guards picketed around the perimeter, everyone seemed to be sleeping. The moon was well into its journey across the night sky before Wickliff gave the signal. Tapping me lightly on the shoulder, he hooted three times like an owl. Falon and Pellyn were to our left. Like panthers, they moved in to take out the guards closest to where Ellie and Davy slept. I tucked the pistol in my waistband and held onto Wickliff's arm. Anxiously, I rolled the javelin back and forth in the palm of my left hand.

In one skillful motion, Falon covered a guard's mouth and jerked his head back, slitting his throat. That was all I saw, because in the next second Wickliff transported me into their camp. I appeared, crouched in front of the beautiful, sleeping Ellie. Legard and the other Sniffer leapt to their feet. Wickliff stood to face them. Throwing their hands up, they began dueling. There were no traditional weapons involved in the magical duel, but they all visibly strained. The three of them had their arms raised as if they were pushing on each other from across the open space separating their bodies. Wickliff pointed his staff directly at Legard and stretched his other hand toward the brown-haired Sniffer. The air between them warped and crackled with energy.

Before anyone in Legard's company could raise a warning, Garrick and Marcus ran into the camp. In the fading firelight, I saw Garrick, with a pistol in each hand, take aim at the sleeping enemy. Marcus, who ran close on his heels, did the same, firing a gun for the first time in his life. A barrage of bullets shattered the silence. Falon and Pellyn, along with everyone else in our crew, converged on the enemy camp. In the first minute, almost half of Arbon's soldiers were shot dead in their bedrolls.

Over the gunfire, I yelled, "Ellie, Davy, let's go."

With my free hand, I pulled my startled girlfriend to her feet. She threw her arms around my neck. "You came for me! I thought I'd never see you again."

There was no time to enjoy the reunion. Arbon's remaining soldiers clamored to their feet. Marcus drew his sword, but Garrick reloaded his pistol and made quick work of every soldier who stood in his way. Marcus and the others in our crew seemed to forget about their pistols after the initial attack, falling into their old fighting habits. The sound of clashing swords rang through the clearing.

The four men who slept closest to Davy and Ellie scrambled to their feet. Drawing their swords, they ran toward me. With Ellie still hanging on my neck, I reached behind my back and drew the pistol out of my waistband. I took aim and emptied the clip into the soldiers running at me. The last one fell dead at my feet, his blood splattering the back of Ellie's skirt. She had glanced over my shoulder at the sound of my first shot, but quickly buried her head in my chest.

Davy stood behind Ellie and me, staring at the carnage. He looked surprised to see his pa fighting like a crazed warrior.

"Davy, go steal some horses," I yelled, sending him scurrying into the woods.

I pushed Ellie away. "Follow Davy and get us some horses. I'll be right behind you."

She stepped back, tears glistening in her green eyes.

"Go," I said. She turned and ran into the woods.

The duel between the elves continued, the whole space between them vibrating and humming. Wickliff looked like he was wavering, and I wondered if I should I help. The javelin I held had been forged by magic. It would kill a Sniffer if it penetrated the heart, and yet I had to get out of here before Legard overpowered Wickliff. Marcus's words echoed in my ears. As long as Legard could see us, he could easily overtake us with his magic.

Making my choice, I tossed the javelin into my right hand and threw it into the energy-charged space. Wickliff blocked my view of Legard, but I had a clear shot at the other Sniffer. The javelin sped through the air. As it entered the field of magic surrounding the elves it visibly slowed, allowing the Sniffer a moment to react. He leaned, but not far enough, and the javelin pierced his shoulder, knocking him to the ground.

In retaliation, he shot a blast of magical energy in my direction, and I experienced firsthand what was happening within their magical battle. The energy smacked into my chest, throwing me backward through the air more than twenty feet and knocking the wind out of me. All the while it felt as if a current of electricity ran rampant through my veins. I slammed into a clump of brush and came rolling to a stop at Ellie's feet.

"Chase," she screamed, kneeling down beside me.

The magic had every muscle in my body tied in knots. I sucked in a breath of air and managed to climb to my feet, nearly toppling Ellie in the process.

I scanned the campsite. Although several of Arbon's soldiers still gave battle, it appeared as if most were wounded. Some of them were on fire, screaming as they tried to put out the flames consuming their clothing. Some of our crew looked to be struggling with injuries as well. In the light of the fires that burned around the camp, I saw Pellyn fighting, with an arrow piercing his thigh, and Aiton bleeding from a shoulder wound. I didn't have time to notice anyone else because Barhydt, who had conjured up the flaming firebombs, abruptly stopped and stared at Wickliff, as if listening to an unspoken message. Throwing his last fireball, he yelled, "Retreat!"

At that, Garrick shouted, "Move out!"

Something was about to happen, and I didn't want my girlfriend here when it did. "Hurry, Ellie. We've got to get out of here."

With her arm around my waist she tried to run, but I could barely get my body to move. "Leave me."

She dragged me another step. "Never."

Everything felt heavy, like my blood had turned to lead in my veins. Leaning on her shoulder, I shuffled away from the camp. My free hand rested on the hilt of my sword, and I felt certain that at any moment I'd be fighting Legard to the death.

Appearing out of the darkness, Davy nearly ran into us on horseback. He was leading two horses behind the one he rode.

"Help me get Chase in the saddle," Ellie said.

Davy leapt down, dragged me to the horse, and shoved me into the saddle. I felt myself slumping forward, and he shook my arm, saying, "Hold on." He put my hands on the front of the saddle and then yelled at me. "Harper, pay attention! You best hang on." He shook me again.

"I got it," I mumbled, wrapping my hands around the front of the saddle.

Ellie and Davy pushed my feet into the stirrups before they each mounted a horse. Davy took my horse's reins and we trotted away. As we weaved through the woods back to the road, tree branches hit me in the face, threatening to knock me off the horse.

Garrick galloped up next to us. "Davy, are you hurt?"

"No, Pa, I'm fine. But Harper isn't."

"Let's get outta—" Garrick started to say, but four horses fleeing the flaming camp interrupted him. The lead horse slammed into the side of mine before jumping between Ellie's and Davy's horses to escape. I teetered in the saddle. My body throbbed with pain at each pulse of my heart, and I felt almost paralyzed. It was as if the Sniffer had separated my mind from the rest of me.

Azalit had obviously succeeded in releasing all the horses during the battle, and they milled around us nervously. Falon dragged his injured brother onto the road, where Azalit had more horses saddled and waiting, including the six from the enemy's rear guard. The screams of injured men echoed through the woods behind us.

Suddenly, Wickliff appeared in the road and crumpled to the ground. Barhydt jumped off his horse and ran to him. He dragged Wickliff toward Azalit, who ran a horse in their direction. They lifted Wickliff into the saddle. Within seconds, we all galloped toward the rendezvous point, scattering the remaining horses as we rode. Some of the animals galloped alongside us, riderless.

Davy still led my horse behind his, while Barhydt led Wickliff's horse and Falon led Pellyn's. Something must have happened to Red. He was nowhere in sight, and his brother Segur had grimly galloped away. I clutched the saddle and focused on staying upright. Ellie's horse ran next to mine. I couldn't do much, but I could watch her. Despite my agony, I was beyond happy to see her free.

We stopped at the rendezvous point to throw our packs behind our saddles. Garrick tossed mine to Davy, who tied it behind me before we galloped down the road. In the fog of my befuddled brain, I wondered where we would go from here. Wickliff didn't look strong enough to take himself through the Dragon's Lair, let alone anyone else.

TWENTY-SEVEN
Escape

Marcus fell back and spoke with Barhydt before returning to the lead next to Garrick. We galloped back to the open valley, then went cross-country into the Borderlands. When Marcus's horse stumbled and fell to its knees for a stride, we slowed to a trot. The horses were winded, and white lather covered their flanks.

Ellie put her horse next to mine, keeping constant vigil over me. Periodically, I'd slip into unconsciousness and wobble on top of my horse. More than once Ellie reached over to steady me. We pushed on through the remainder of the night. At first light, we halted near a crystal-clear river. After drinking, I collapsed on the grass, weak to the core. I watched Ellie and the others lead the horses to the river for water. She looked like she'd fared okay during the two-day ordeal. There was a tear in her skirt, and her clothes were smeared with dirt from sleeping on the ground. Her hair had come undone and hung loose over her shoulders, and the sun had left her face a rosy pink. When the horses finished drinking, she walked them over to a patch of grass.

Drawing my attention away from Ellie, Azalit retrieved her medicine bag and bustled around, surveying everyone's injuries. She removed the arrow from Pellyn's leg and pressed a brown powder into the wound. Next, she cleaned Aiton's shoulder and filled the deep gash with medicine. Falon, Garrick, and Marcus had minor cuts and bruises, but the three men waved Azalit away, refusing treatment. Segur had a broken arm—he said he'd gotten clubbed. Azalit mixed water from the river with dried red leaves from her medicine pouch. She set the bone, smeared his arm with the mixture, and wrapped strips of white linen tightly around the sticky red poultice from his wrist to his elbow. After fastening a sling around his neck, she said, "Drink this."

"What is it?" Segur grumbled.

"A potion that works with the poultice to seal the bone. You need to drink three doses—one each morning for three consecutive days. Here, take it."

Complaining all the while, Segur took the small vile from her outstretched hand and drank it. His eyes clamped shut at the taste. "Ugh, that's bitter. A man would think you're tryin' to poison him."

"I know, but you'll thank me in three days when your arm is as good as new."

Ellie sat next to me and pulled my head onto her lap, softly touching my face. Garrick smiled as he talked with his son, but Davy glared at me with open disdain. He definitely didn't look happy to see Ellie and me back together again.

I studied her face, wondering if there was something going on that I didn't know about. But I was tired, so very tired. She ran her fingers gently through my sweaty hair. The swirling breeze cooled my hot skin and I closed my eyes, thinking I could use a shower and a long night's sleep.

I heard someone approaching and opened my eyes. Wickliff sank to his haunches next to me, holding his flask. "Young Keeper, my deepest thanks. Your timely javelin throw was a great boon to me. It consumed an inordinate amount of energy to hold both Sniffers at bay. Preventing them from disappearing to go after you and the captives was a formidable task, and fortune smiled on us tonight. The unnamed Sniffer fled once he was injured, allowing me to concentrate my energies on Legard. I left him in a weakened condition, but how long he will stay that way, I cannot say. He is exceptionally skilled, and I expect he will return to full strength quickly. I only hope we are safely within the borders of Algonia when that day arrives."

I groaned in agony. "What's wrong with me?"

"Oh, dear me. I've forgotten my manners. Here, my fine friend, drink this." He popped the cork and held out the flask.

I propped myself up with my elbow and took it. "What is it?" I mumbled. Without waiting for an answer, I raised the flask to my mouth.

"Liquid energy. It will still take a day or so for you to return to your full strength, but this will speed along the process. Don't worry—you've not suffered any permanent harm from the Sniffer's blast."

"I'm not so sure about that." With my hand quivering, I took a swig of the dark liquid. The foul-tasting medicine burned its way down my throat. I shuddered. "Ugh." I pushed the flask back into the elf's outstretched hand while another shudder rippled through me at the aftertaste.

Wickliff chuckled. "Doesn't do much for the taste buds, but I guarantee it'll do wonders for the body." After pushing the cork into place, he returned the flask to his pack.

Ellie smiled sweetly. "Thank you, we're much obliged." The sound of her voice was music to my ears.

The old elf nodded toward her. "You're quite welcome, young lady."

Wickliff left to sit next to Barhydt as Garrick crouched next to Ellie and me. "Hey, little brother, how are you feeling?"

"Weak and tired. Everything hurts right now, but Wickliff says I'll be fine. I don't know what that Sniffer did to me, but I'm sure glad they can't do that in our world."

The liquid energy had gone to work on my system, and already my head felt clearer. I tried to sit up.

"I agree," Garrick said. "I don't think we would stand a chance against them if they had full use of their magic in our world."

"What happened to Red?" I asked.

Garrick shook his head. "He didn't make it. Everything happened so fast. He got surrounded and someone stabbed him in the back. Segur's a brave man. He'll not show it, but I think he's taking it pretty hard."

"That's sad. I liked Red. We owe these guys a lot. If it weren't for them we never would have made it this far."

Garrick smiled and stood. "You've got that right. I'm going to talk to Marcus and figure out how we're getting home."

As I climbed to my feet, I asked Ellie if she wanted something to eat.

"Shouldn't you be resting?" she said.

"Nah. I think that stuff Wickliff gave me is working. I'm actually feeling really hungry right now." I offered her my hand and pulled her up next to me. I hobbled to where my pack was tied onto the back of the saddle. "For breakfast today, the options are jerky and flat bread. Or flat bread and jerky. Which would you prefer, my lady?"

That coaxed a smile from her. "Let me think—such difficult choices. I suppose I'll have jerky and flat bread."

"Excellent decision." I removed two pieces of jerky and handed Ellie one. "It's tough, but the flavor is good." I tore a piece off and began chewing. "It must be magic jerky, because one piece fills you up."

With my mouth full of the chewy meat, I winked. Suddenly, she flung her arms around my neck. Smiling, I returned the hug and pulled her to the other side of my horse. "What's this for?" I whispered in her ear.

"I can't get over that you're really here. I was certain no good could come of being taken by those two. I had resigned myself to an insufferable fate followed by certain death. I suppose if it weren't for Davy's continual and almost annoying optimism, I surely would have given myself up to despairing within the first day. He always insisted help was coming. Never once did he waver."

"It's over now. Once we get across the Borderlands, we'll have Master Archidus send us home," I said in my most convincing tone. "In a couple of days this will be just a memory. We'll go back to school, and next weekend I'll take you to the spring-break party at Kim's house. Everything will be back to normal, you'll see." I hoped I was right.

Ellie looked up at me. "You think so?"

I grinned. "Sure."

"Thank you for coming for me, Chase."

"You're the one person I would never stop looking for. I'm like an echo—I'll always come back to you. My life means nothing without you. Promise me you won't forget that. I would rather die than fail you."

With a tear trickling down her cheek, she nodded. "I won't forget. I love you."

"I love you too." I wiped the tear off her cheek with my thumb, then lowered my lips to hers, kissing her with all the love and tenderness of someone who thought he had lost everything. I savored the moment—the taste of her kiss, the feel of her hands on my shoulders—vowing to never forget what it had felt like to almost lose her.

Garrick raised his voice. "Harper, quit kissing your girlfriend and listen up. We'll follow the river as long as we can. The trees there will give us cover once the dragon patrols start. Later this afternoon, if we're still in the clear, we'll hold up and catch a little sleep. For now, mount up—we're moving out!"

I held Ellie's horse as she got on, and then I handed her the reins. A smile touched her face as I stepped into the stirrup of my own saddle. Garrick, Marcus, and Davy galloped away, following the curve of the river. Azalit, Wickliff, Barhydt, Segur, and Aiton followed close on their heels. Falon helped Pellyn into the saddle. Ellie adjusted her reins and urged her horse into a gallop. I turned my horse in a tight circle to make sure we weren't being followed, before galloping toward the rising sun and Algonia.

Epilogue

Legard rested near the burning camp for hours. He'd had no idea his uncle was still such a formidable enemy. The old elf had held him in place while Archidus' soldiers wreaked havoc on Legard's cavalry. It was downright humiliating. The effort of trying to break Wickliff's hold left Legard weak and exhausted.

He thought of the other Sniffer. What a coward. He'd disappeared the moment his injury released him from Wickliff's grasp. If he had an ounce of fight in him, he could have at least destroyed some of Archidus' men. The only good thing he did was stun the Protector, although he could have killed him if he would have kept at it a little longer. Legard would kill that worthless Sniffer himself, if he ever caught him.

Once Legard had enough strength to walk, he and his least injured soldiers rounded up enough horses to continue into Shuyle. There would be no chasing the intruders with this rag-tag, wounded bunch of idiots. Legard needed to refuel his body before he could face Wickliff again and hope to survive. Once he retrieved the liquid energy he had stored at the castle, he would lay out his plan.

Legard had recognized the Guardian as the leader of the group. The trap had been laid for the Protector and the Guardian. Legard had hoped the new Sniffer, assigned to attack Wisdom's Keeper, would be successful in killing him. It had been a long shot, but Legard had been hopeful. The girl had the scent of the Protector all over her, so she clearly meant something to him.

Interestingly, the boy Legard had taken had turned out to be more than expected. Legard thought he was taking the Guardian's son, when in fact he'd taken a Keeper. It wasn't until the night of the attack that he recognized the scent of Perception. He found it the most difficult to follow, its scent so easily masked by the thoughts of its Keeper. The young man had done an impressive job of hiding the fact he was a Keeper. Legard never would have left the old world if he'd realized he was taking a Keeper without his counter. It pained him to realize there had been three Keepers within his grasp, and he had walked away with nothing.

As it stood, Archidus' soldiers had suffered only one casualty compared to the forty-nine Shuylians left dead at Legard's camp. Lord Arbon would be furious at this devastating turn of events. Fortunately, Legard's position was secure. Anyone else would face execution for a failure of this magnitude. But Legard and Arbon had been as close as brothers since they were boys. Legard had always been the muscle behind Arbon's rebellion. Without Legard, Lord Arbon would be nothing, and he knew it.

"They was all magic, they was," said one of the soldiers behind Legard.

"With magic comin' outta their hands, our men was droppin' like flies," said another. "We didn't stand a chance 'gainst all those sorcerer soldiers."

Annoyed at having his musings interrupted, Legard said, "Quit your whining. Other than the old elf, there was only one of them that was magical. They had guns, you idiots—weapons from the old world."

"What you talking 'bout, Legard? I know what I saw and it was magic. Loud magic."

"Silence," Legard yelled. This brainless chatter would drive him insane before they reached Shuyle.

What remained of their decimated squadron limped into the Valley of Tierran. At the first army outpost, Legard dismounted. As second in command, he demanded the utmost respect, and the captain of the outpost hustled to attention in front of him. "First, get me a fresh mount and some food, and then you can tend to the injuries of these men," Legard ordered.

"Yes, sir," the captain said.

With food in his system and a fresh horse, Legard galloped up the Valley of Tierran toward Lord Arbon's headquarters. As the last rays of the setting sun glinted off the rooftops in the capital city of Shuyle, Legard dismounted. He strode through the corridors of the castle toward his private quarters. Protocol dictated he report to Lord Arbon before all else, but he was desperate for a drink to reverse the effects of dueling Wickliff.

Legard unlocked the sealed door with magic and walked across the room. Staring at an obscure spot in an otherwise blank wall, he put his hand through the stones and pulled out a bottle filled with a thick brown liquid. He uncorked it and poured a generous portion down his throat, gagging at the foul taste.

Lord Arbon stepped into the open doorway and watched his friend. "Legard, my brother, what has happened?"

"Milord." Legard shook his head, then returned the bottle to the wall. "Archidus must have intervened. He prevented the Keepers from following us. The trap failed. Wickliff and a group of soldiers, including both Keepers, attacked us outside the Valley of Tierran. Their attack was ferocious, and they succeeded in releasing the captives. After a grueling duel with Wickliff, I was unable to follow and returned to replenish my energy. The old elf is in much the same state as I. He will not be strong enough to take them through the Dragon's Lair. Their only course to safety is across the Borderlands. I suggest we send out the dragons and muster our army. At this moment, three Keepers are making a run for Algonia."

"My friend, it will be done as you say."

About the Author

Kelly Nelson was raised in Orem, Utah, and now resides in Cornelius, Oregon, in the heart of the beautiful Pacific Northwest. She enjoys life on a ten-acre horse property with her husband, four children, and, of course, lots of horses. Kelly has a bachelor's degree from Brigham Young University. She worked as a certified public accountant for several years before opting to stay home and raise a family. As a young girl, she was an avid reader and had a passion for creative writing. Her travels to England, France, Egypt, Israel, West Indies, Mexico, and across the United States sparked her love of history, adventure, and exotic places, inspiring her to write *The Keeper's Calling* and *The Keeper's Quest.* Learn more about Kelly and the upcoming sequels at kellynelsonauthor.com, or follow her at facebook.com/TheKeepersSaga.

For a sneak peek at *The Keeper's Defiance,*

the next book in the The Keeper's Saga,

just turn the page.

ONE
Borderlands

Wickliff's sharp whistle pierced the air. "Dragons!" he shouted.

My head shot up. "Ellie, over here." I jumped to the ground, grabbed both horses' reins, and pulled the animals into a thick stand of willows. Ellie burrowed through the twisted branches ahead of me. Everyone in our group scattered, finding cover beneath the trees and brush lining the river's edge.

I sat on my heels next to Ellie and looked at the two horses next to us. Their eyes and ears drooped, and their lathered bodies quivered. We had ridden them hard most of the night and into the morning, and they'd been on the trail for days before we'd stolen them. I grimaced as I realized we were going to push them to their limits and beyond. There was no way around it.

My heart raced as the familiar snap of the dragons' wings grew louder. I knew Ellie and I were hidden from their view, but I wondered about our horses—all twelve of them. They were harder to hide. But the dragons passed by at a leisurely pace, and I repositioned myself to watch their retreat. They followed the river until they were nearly out of sight before angling north and fading into the horizon over the rolling plains.

I released a deep breath. *That wasn't so bad.* I looked at Ellie. "Are you all right?"

Her head was buried in her hands, her shoulders shaking. Convinced our horses weren't going anywhere unless we made them, I dropped the reins and wrapped my arms around Ellie. "It's okay. They're gone now."

She leaned into me and rested her head on my chest. Slowly I stood, pulling her up with me.

"I'm scared. I'm exhausted," she said. "And I don't see how we're going to get back home."

She choked back a sob, and I could tell she was making every effort to be brave. Seeing the fear in her eyes made my heart constrict. All I ever wanted was to keep her safe and make her happy. Right now, I was failing miserably.

"We'll get back home," I said more confidently than I felt. "We've just got to take it one day at a time."

Ellie wiped her eyes and squared her shoulders. "Yes. I mustn't let my fatigue get the best of me. Yesterday, I held out no hope of ever seeing you again. And yet here you are."

"Harper?" Garrick yelled.

I led both horses into the open, then held Ellie's stirrup for her while she stepped into the saddle. "Hang in there. Soon we'll be in Algonia. You'll be safe there. I promise."

She gave me a halfhearted smile. I mounted my horse and nudged it forward to follow the rest of the group. Ellie and I rode in silence, watching the sun climb in the clear blue sky.

"I thought dragons existed only in fairy tales," she said after a while.

"Yeah, they do. But we're in the fairytale world."

"What do you mean?"

"Wickliff explained it as an alternate dimension of Earth. Sometime during the Dark Ages or the Middle Ages—I don't know the exact date—a group of sorcerers split off from Earth and created a new world. They took everything magical with them and left the regular people on the old world, where we're from. All that remains of their magic on our world is folklore and fairy tales."

Ellie sighed. "Why did those Sniffers take us? I mean, I know they want the counters, but Davy didn't have his counter with him. And why take me?"

"They laid a trap for me. You were the bait."

"I'm sorry."

"Don't be. I shouldn't have left you alone."

We caught up to the main group, and I overheard Garrick say, "Those dragons didn't put a lot of effort into looking for us."

"I don't believe they were looking for us . . . yet," Wickliff replied.

"What do you mean?" Garrick asked.

"Considering the state in which I left Legard, and the condition of his cavalry, it may take them awhile to return to Lord Arbon. It will be Arbon who communicates our presence to the dragons. Believe me, Guardian, you will know when they are looking for you."

Marcus cleared his throat. "We follow the river until it turns south. I'm predicting we'll arrive by midafternoon. After that it's a hard ride over the Susack Plain before we reach the forests on the Algonian side of the Borderlands. We'll rest at the bend in the river until nightfall. With dragons around, it won't do to be out in the open during daylight."

The rest of us voiced our agreement and urged our horses into a trot to keep up with Marcus and Garrick.

With the sun directly overhead, Ellie shaded her eyes and turned to look at me. "How are you feeling?"

I grinned. "I'm doing a lot better. That nasty liquid energy of Wickliff's did the trick."

Her eyes twinkled as she smiled back at me. "I'm pleased it helped."

When the riders ahead of us moved their horses into a slow gallop, we followed suit. All of our mounts were nearly spent. The horse belonging to Segur, the largest of the men in our group, stumbled on the uneven terrain and went to its knees. It tried to regain its footing, but collapsed to the ground. Segur rolled clear of the sprawling horse and came to a stop in the grass. He staggered to his feet, favoring his broken arm. Ellie and I veered to the side to avoid trampling the downed horse and rider. I pulled my mount to a stop and turned to face Segur.

"Are you hurt?" I asked.

He waved his good arm and hobbled toward the horse. "I'm fine."

The animal's eyes rolled back, showing the white around the edges. Except for the rise and fall of its chest and an occasional moan, the horse lay still. I dismounted and walked to the animal's side. When Segur bent to untie his pack from the saddle, I reached in front of him. "I can do that."

The big man's lips turned up. "Thank you, lad. Me arm's not workin' too well yet."

I removed the pack and stood up. Garrick and Marcus rode back, their horses' flanks covered in white lather.

"We'll need to double up," Marcus said. "We've got to keep moving."

"Take my horse," I said to Segur. "I'll ride with Ellie." I carried his pack to where my exhausted horse stood, dripping sweat and barely able to hold his head up.

Marcus wheeled his horse around and galloped away. Garrick and most of the others followed. Davy paused, furrowing his eyebrows as he studied Ellie for a moment. I removed my pack and tied Segur's behind the saddle. He got on the horse and rode away. Ellie dismounted and walked slowly toward the suffering horse. With my pack fastened to her horse's saddle, I mounted and rode between her and the dying animal.

"Ellie, come on. There's nothing we can do for him."

Without saying a word, she turned and took my outstretched hand. I pulled her up and she seated herself behind me, with her arms around my waist.

Marcus slowed his horse to a walk, and when I slowed my mount, Ellie leaned her head against my back. Soon her body relaxed in sleep. When she started drifting to the side, I put my arm behind me and wrapped it around her back to keep her from falling. Once the horses caught their breath, Marcus again picked up the pace. I inwardly groaned at the thought of having to wake Ellie. Everyone else moved ahead of us, forcing me to speak or be left behind.

"Ellie, wake up. We've got to go faster."

She lifted her head and tightened her grip on me, so I let go of her and urged our reluctant horse into a gallop. The afternoon sun baked the grasslands in the distance. Yet where we rode near the river, everything appeared moist and green. A cool breeze wafted along the riverbank, and the towering trees provided relief from the blistering sun. If we weren't dead tired and running for our lives, it would have been a pleasant horseback ride.

"Dragons!" Wickliff yelled, with more intensity than before. A moment later the airborne reptiles' screams echoed across the plains.

My heart pounded as I steered the horse closer to the river. I swung my leg over the animal's neck and hopped off, then helped Ellie down. Pushing her ahead of me, I pulled our horse into the thick brush along the riverbank.

Hideous screams burst from the dragons' mouths as they followed the river toward us. Beads of sweat dripped down my forehead. I glanced back and forth between Ellie and the horse, wondering if everyone else was hidden.

Crouched on the ground, I held the horse's reins in one hand. The snap of the dragons' wings grew louder, and the smell of smoke drifted on the breeze. A deafening roar sounded as one of the enormous creatures spewed fire above us in a rush of hot air. The horse pulled backward, fighting to escape the fiery inferno raging overhead, and I toppled forward onto my hands and knees. The frantic animal dragged me across the ground as I struggled to hold on to the sweat-covered reins. When he stopped for a moment, I scrambled toward him. "Whoa there, boy. Shh."

I glanced up and gasped at the sight of a dragon's dull, gray-green scales through the leaves above me. The lush foliage sputtered and sparked as the fire fought to take hold, but the flames soon dwindled, leaving smoking branches.

The dragons heaved their next wall of fire into the trees above where I'd seen Wickliff and Marcus disappear. The squeal of a terrified horse mingled with a dragon's scream as it bombarded the treetops with flames. Suddenly, I heard the thundering of hooves—one of the horses had escaped. The dragons veered off the river and gave pursuit.

With the monsters preoccupied, Wickliff, Marcus, and Barhydt moved upriver, closer to Ellie and me. After calming my horse, I shifted positions to get a clear view. Wickliff's mount was missing, and from the sound of it the dragons were devouring the poor animal. Soon, they turned their bloody snouts toward the river and spread their wings. I retreated into the brush next to Ellie and tightened my hold on the reins. Both dragons focused their fire where Wickliff's horse had been hidden. Within seconds, smoky flames licked the sky. The dragons moved on, methodically searching the river ahead.

"Spread the word. Move out, but stay close to the trees," Marcus ordered.

I emerged from my hiding place and walked over to Segur's. "We move out, but stay close to the trees. Pass the word along."

Wickliff climbed onto the back of Azalit's horse. The elf girl's once proud and fearless expression was now one of humility and terror. I watched Ellie emerge from hiding, her face full of the same fear. Anxious to be moving, I mounted our horse and offered Ellie my hand. Once her arms encircled my waist, I urged the horse downriver.

Ellie shuddered as we passed the smoking trees. Flames engulfed the surrounding bushes, but I expected the fire would quickly burn itself out. Ellie and I searched the grassland for Wickliff's runaway horse. When we saw the animal's mangled carcass in the distance, Ellie hid her face against my back. Without some good luck, that would likely be the fate of us all.

An hour later, Wickliff raised the alarm again. "They're coming back."

We scrambled for cover. When a ball of flames erupted overhead, our horse again struggled to run free. Ellie lowered her head and clapped her hands over her ears, but I doubted anything could block out the dragons' haunting shrieks. With all their ruckus, at least they didn't hear the commotion my horse made. Once the danger passed, our horse stood quivering, whether from fatigue or fear, I didn't know.

We rode until late afternoon before Marcus called for a halt at a sharp bend in the river. It almost doubled back on itself before meandering south. Far to the east, the forested hills of Algonia were barely visible across the open plain. The dragons' fury had left singed treetops all along the river. In places, tendrils of smoke dissipated in the sky.

"Spread out and take cover," Marcus said. "We rest here until nightfall."

I scanned the tree line and saw a large stand of willows just past the bend in the river. I slid off the horse and walked closer. In the midst of the trees lay a level patch of ground. It looked well hidden and large enough for two people to lie down comfortably. I kicked a few stones out of the way and returned for Ellie. She slid off the horse into my outstretched arms and I whispered, "Let's get you into bed."

A smile flitted across her face. "Oh, you found a bed in there?"

I smiled back at her. "Not quite king-sized, but you'll be in the lap of luxury, my lady. I'll show you after I tie up our horse."

After watering the animal, I led him to a small cottonwood tree surrounded by larger trees, with a patch of grass at its base. I tied the sweat-soaked reins around the trunk and hoped the knot would hold up under a dragon fly-by. I untied my pack and slung it over my shoulder.

"This way." I took Ellie's hand and led her into the willows. "It's not a bed, but it's the best I could find."

"I don't care," she replied. "I'll take anyplace as long as I can lay my head down."

I pulled the thin blanket out of my pack and spread it on the ground. Once we sat down, I handed her the water flask. "You should drink a lot. You don't want to get dehydrated, and I don't know where our next water stop will be."

She took a drink and tried to hand the flask back, but I told her to finish it. "Do you want to see if we have anything to eat in our pack?" I asked as I climbed to my feet.

Before Ellie could answer, I slipped through the willows to the riverbank and stepped into the water. My boots from Cadré Unair were the ultimate in comfort and completely waterproof. I filled the flask, raising it to my lips several times in the process.

I wasn't the only one topping off his water supply before we left the protection of the river. Downriver, Marcus and Aiton stood knee-deep in the crystal-clear water.

I drank my fill and cleaned the sweat off my face and arms. From Marcus's description of the Borderlands, I hoped to be in Algonia by tomorrow night, although I didn't know if that necessarily meant we'd be safe. According to Segur, it would take another day or so to get from Algonia's border to the fortress. After that, it would be mere hours until Master Archidus could send us back through Witches Hollow.

I threaded my way through the willows to where Ellie had laid out a flat loaf of dark bread and two pieces of jerky. I sat across from her as she tore the loaf in half. Famished, I ripped off a chunk of bread with my teeth. The loaf was half gone before I thought to slow down and savor the meager meal. The bread was dense and filling, with a touch of sweetness to it. I was sick of jerky since I had eaten little else for the past three days.

I finished eating and rolled my nearly empty pack into a pillow. Then I lay down and felt myself begin to relax for the first time in days. The gurgling of the river behind me, and the canopy of curly willow leaves overhead, made for a deceptively serene setting. We were far from safe, but I had my girlfriend back and we were together.

When Ellie finished eating, I whispered, "Come here." I stretched my arm out, and she laid her head on my shoulder.

She brushed her fingertips over the stubble on my chin and smiled. "This place is beautiful, except for the constant dread I feel regarding those dragons."

I sighed. "Yeah, it is."

She shifted positions before the evenness of her breathing told me she was asleep. I settled my hand on the hilt of my sword and drifted off.

THE KEEPER'S SAGA: BOOK ONE
The Keeper's Calling

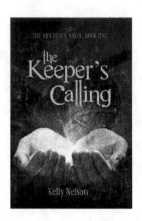

They come from two different worlds.
One fateful discovery will bring them together.
Neither of their lives will ever be the same.

Chase Harper's to-do list for senior year never included "fall in love" and "fight for your life," but things rarely go as planned. Tarnished gold and resembling a pocket watch, the counter he finds in a cave will forever change the course of his life, leading him to the beautiful Ellie Williams and unlocking a power beyond his wildest imagination.

In 1863, Ellie Williams completes school in Boston and returns to the Utah Territory only to discover that her grandfather and his counter, a treasured family heirloom, are missing. When Ellie is abducted and told she must produce the counter or die, an unexpected rescuer comes to her aid.